TRUTH BITES

THE HYBRID WOLF SERIES: BOOK THREE

CIARA DELAHUNT

DUBHLUNA
PUBLISHING

CHARACTERS

Eve O'Connor *(hybrid)*

CRESCENT PACK*
Luke Whelan – *surname pronounced 'wee-lan'*
Tom Whelan
Max Whelan
Helena Whelan (*human*)
Alice Whelan (*hybrid*)
Darren Donohoe
Paula Donohoe
Dylan
Joshua
Liz
Sorcha
Maggie
Áine

FAOLCHÚNNA PACK*
Ryan McKenna – *surname pronounced 'mac-ken-ah'*
Damien McKenna – *pronounced 'day-me-en'*
Rebecca McKenna
~~Nick McKenna~~
Mary McKenna
Fiona – *pronounced 'fee-own-a'*
Nadine

* *Werewolves unless otherwise indicated.*

OTHER

~~Kate~~

Craig

Béibhinn (*witch*) - *pronounced* 'bae-vee-n'

Cadhla (*witch*) - *pronounced* 'kai-luh'

Jonas (*vampire*)

Darius (*vampire*)

Larissa (*witch*) – *pronounced* 'la-ris-ah'

Gabriella/Gabi (*witch*)

Jeremy Walker (*werewolf*)

Lila Walker (*werewolf*)

Henry Edmonstone (*werewolf*)

Maya (*witch*)

Sarah (*sphinx*)

Lawrence (*vampire*)

Cassandra (*witch*)

Russell Stewart (*werewolf*)

Callum Stewart (*werewolf*)

BEFORE YOU READ

I write paranormal romance and as such, my books are aimed at adults. *The Hybrid Wolf Series* includes themes of an adult nature, and violent scenes typical of the paranormal romance and fantasy genres. This book contains certain subjects that some readers may be sensitive to.

Please stay safe and visit my website to check the content warnings for my books before reading:

www.ciaradelahunt.com/content-warnings

IRISH LESSON

Class is in session. By the end of this series, you're going to be fluent in Irish slang.

***Mam* is not a typo!** We don't say mom over here.

I know our names have too many vowels, but revert to this when you get stuck and enjoy the ride.

- **Boreen:** a narrow lane in the countryside
- **Cert:** certificate
- **Chips:** fries (we call chips 'crisps' here)
- **College/university:** interchangeable
- **Craic:** fun/entertaining
- **Faolchúnna:** wolves
- **Flash drive:** USB stick
- **"For fuck's sake!":** exclamation of frustration, similar to 'What the hell?'
- **Fresher:** student in their first year at college in Ireland *(approx. 18 years old)*
- **Garda:** police officer *(Bán Garda is a female police officer)*
- **Gardaí:** police plural
- **Garda station:** police station
- **In the nip:** in the nude
- **Keeping sketch:** view the area for approaching authority
- **Lie in:** to stay in bed later than usual in the morning
- **Lift:** elevator
- **Lose the plot:** lost their mind, to no longer be able to act normally or understand what is happening

- **Luas:** name of the tram service in Dublin
- **Mam:** mom/mother *(the Irish don't use mom)*
- **Path/footpath:** sidewalk
- **Piss:** to pee
- **Puke:** vomit
- **Punter:** your average paying customer
- **Runners:** trainers (shoes)
- **Snug:** a small room or area in a pub where only a few people can sit
- **Strop:** a bad mood
- **Tracksuit bottoms:** joggers
- **Twig:** to suddenly realise something
- **Wing mirror:** side-view mirror on a car
- **"You're taking the piss":** you're pushing it or you better be joking

It's highly possible I've missed something here. If you're ever confused, check my reader groups, or drop me a message on social media!

To the readers who found their soulmate while discovering their own strength, this book is for you.

Fear licked at my spine like the flames that tortured my mind. Fire, blood, death, and then a white-hot pain like nothing I'd ever felt before. I remembered every torturous second of it. From Luke's panicked voice behind Darius' steady instruction as they worked to pull the venom from my veins, to Larissa's magic binding me while she held me captive with a dagger to my throat. Right down to the image of my friend's face contorting in terror as the vampire attacked.

The wolf we failed to rescue.

The horrors I witnessed in that function room were carved into my mind, the nightmares playing on repeat each time I dared to close my eyes.

Exiled.

Luke explained briefly before we boarded the plane, right before he refused to give me an update on Craig. Exiled from our country, from his home, his family, the pack.

All because of me.

The bright lights of Heathrow Airport stung, and my body begged to shut down, but I couldn't retreat inwards. My mind was no sanctuary and burning retinas were the least of my problems. I thought I was going to die, lying paralysed in fear while they worked to save me. Panic constricted my throat, robbing my lungs of air every time I re-lived those memories.

"Eve?" Luke's familiar voice pulled me back to the present as if he were my tether to reality. "We have to get out of here."

I couldn't hold his gaze. The events of the last forty-eight hours had doused the warmth of his hazel eyes. An intangible space stretched between us, and it made me want to give in to the darkness all the more. Behind him, commuters and travellers gathered around the conveyor belts snatching up suitcases, probably worried about meeting some stupid meeting that didn't really matter.

Life mattered. Death mattered. *Living* mattered.

He cocked one eyebrow, his focus shifting to his outstretched hand that I hadn't even registered. "Are you okay? We can't stop here. It's not safe."

What he really meant was, did I need to go to the bathroom again to puke? Based on the judgemental looks from the flight attendant on our plane, and the amount of time I spent retching over the gross plane toilet, I don't think I did much for Irish drinking stereotypes on the trip over.

"I'm fine."

Luke shook his head, raking his hand through his hair with a heavy sigh. "You've been saying that since we took off, and we both know it's bullshit."

I flinched, tearing my gaze from the accusations swimming in his eyes.

Of course I wasn't fine. No one could be after what we had witnessed. Seeing people held captive and someone being used as a human blood bag was not something you just waltzed away from unscathed. The image haunted you.

The dark circles under his eyes, coupled with the way his shoulders sagged as he shifted between monitoring our surroundings and looking as lost as I felt, gave away just how much he was struggling under the weight we faced.

Exile.

I opened my mouth, ready to argue that he was just as un-fine as me, only to be interrupted by a garbled announcement ringing out over the PA system.

"Come on, we need to get moving." He pressed his hand against the small of my back, the duffle bag slung across his body. Darius had packed brushing my side as he urged me forwards.

A lump rose in my throat to match the tears stinging the corners of my eyes, but I shoved it down.

Despite his touch scorching the bare skin exposed by the crop top Jonas had supplied, he felt a million miles away as he guided me towards the exit.

In Dublin Airport he'd refused to let me go except for when I needed to puke my guts up. He'd held me as I switched between soaking his shirt with my tears and berating him for refusing to discuss vampire attacks in public. If I hadn't been so all over the place, watching Luke pass me off as a *Twilight* fanatic and joking with security might have been funny. Instead, a bloodlust that wasn't my own made me want to slit his throat. Vampire venom was no joke.

At least I was alive; I'd be fine. With Luke refusing to give any updates on Craig, I had no idea if my friend was going to survive.

The PA system shrieked with another announcement, and I cringed. The airport was bustling during London rush hour, the crowds bottlenecked at security making it difficult to scan our surroundings as all the different scents assaulted my senses. Between the thrum of hundreds of heartbeats and the distant roar of plane engines, this place was a nightmare for sensing a threat. We were exposed, and Luke was basically playing babysitter because I couldn't be trusted to function.

A woman with blue hair rushed past and for a moment I thought it was Kate, but I tore my gaze away. I'd been convinced one of the flight attendants on the plane over was my dead friend too, but Luke had been able to explain that one away as grief.

A shudder walked up the vertebrae of my spine as we moved

through the crowd, but when I looked over my shoulder, no one was watching us.

Something feels wrong.

I didn't realise my thoughts were so loud they pushed through our mind link until Luke glanced back at me, his brow furrowed with concern.

My emotions ping-ponged from one extreme to the other thanks to the remnants of vampire venom in my veins. One minute I was all too aware of his fingers brushing the small of my back, and the next the hairs on the back of my neck stood on end, and I couldn't shake the feeling we were being followed.

Luke made small talk with an airport security man who had been watching us with suspicion while I focused on walking in a straight line. I was on autopilot, but at the same time my mind was running beyond full capacity trying to figure out why everything felt wrong.

The crowd surging in on all sides made the airport like a furnace. I was in no fit state to argue when Jonas had grabbed a bunch of clothes from the lost and found of the Dark Night, Dublin's best paranormal hideout. While I appreciated the puffy bomber jacket he'd chosen given that it was winter, the stuffy arrivals area made me want to shred it with my claws.

My instincts were in overdrive as I searched the sea of faces around me. The edges of my vision blurred, and my stomach lurched. I swear I caught a flash of silver, but my heart thumping erratically in my chest did little to tell me if this was my gut warning of danger or if I was hallucinating.

I rolled my shoulders as a shudder worked its way down my spine. Something was wrong. Okay, a lot was wrong, but this was something more.

"Luke—" My teeth caught on my lower lip as a burly man in a suit shoved past me, his shoulder smacking into the side of my head.

"What the fuck?" I whirled on the offender, snatching hold of his forearm as my temper flared to life. Even sluggish, my reactions were faster than the average human. I found myself face to chest with a tall, broad-shouldered man, with bushy eyebrows and a moustache to match. His cheeks flushed with outrage as he looked between me and my biting grip on his arm.

"Watch where you're going, asshole," I hissed, swiping my hand across my mouth. My lips curled back in a feral grin as instinct took over, and the tips of my claws extended from my fingertips. The red stain on the back of my hand made some sickening hunger stir deep inside.

I didn't want to drain his veins like a vampire, but a different kind of blood lust was stirring. A homicidal one.

"You stupid little b—" His features twisted into an ugly scowl, the twitch of his hand enough to tell me that he'd hit a woman or two in his time. Unlucky for him, this bitch bites.

Before I could give in to the feral thoughts, Luke's arm clamped around my waist, and he spun me away. I scrunched my eyes up as the world tilted for a moment, opening them to find Luke had planted himself squarely between me and my prey. He didn't spare the offender a second glance. "Sorry, she's jetlagged."

The man scoffed, his "silly little woman" laugh making me run my tongue over my canines. I couldn't see him over Luke's broad frame, which was probably for the best because I wanted to acquaint his nose with my fist.

"Breathe." Luke ordered, his irises pulsating. I still had a sick feeling we were in danger, yet my stomach was somersaulting for another reason. "Can you sense that?"

The coldness to Luke's tone caught me off guard, but as a gust of wind rushed through the sliding door at the far end of the foyer, I caught the unmistakable scent of werewolf. One I didn't recognise. I didn't believe in coincidences anymore, and I highly doubted they were here to roll out the welcome mat.

Luke grabbed my hand, his phone already pressed to his ear as we stepped deeper into the bustling throng of people looking for a familiar face or their cab ride.

Unfamiliar faces stared past me from the nearby coffee shop, the welcome aroma of coffee beans and vanilla not enough to mask the hint of werewolf I could still scent.

"Where the fuck are you, Jer?" Luke's fingers tightened around mine as he scanned the crowd.

Adrenaline howled at my body to run—and to shift—but my magic reserves were weak. Vampire venom was toxic to werewolves. Even as a hybrid, the effects would take time to wear off. Darius warned Luke it could last over twenty-four hours. "Who?"

"Jeremy, my uncle on my mam's side." Luke nudged me in front, his grip on my hand unyielding as he towered over me. "He was supposed to meet us here. Dad contacted him just before we left."

I scanned the arrivals area for either the threat or a face familiar to Luke's, a lump forming in my throat as unease washed over me.

Luke kept me pulled tight against him, the dial tone of his phone ringing out with no answer. "We lived in London until I was almost two, and Jer pops over to visit whenever he can. He's a joker, but he'd never be late when it's important."

He couldn't hide the panic bleeding through into the last sentence. My heartbeat sped up with each unanswered ring. Our escape plan hadn't shown.

The call finally connected, and my shoulders slumped in relief.

"Jer! Where are you man?"

Rustling sounded down the line, but no response came.

Fear dug its icy claws into me, draining the air from my lungs. I focused on Luke's body pressed against mine, my tether to reality in this godsdamn maze, as he guided me to join the line filtering towards the nearest escalator.

"Luke..." I dug my nails into the back of his hand, the unease in my gut swelling as the werewolf's scent grew more distinct.

A snarl echoed down the line, followed by a roar that set my teeth on edge. Dread swamped my body like quicksand.

Luke froze, his wide eyes searching the crowd for a face I suspected wasn't to be found. "Jer?"

The glass doors of the terminal entrance slid open, and the air shifted, my nightmares becoming reality once more. My head whipped to the right to find a pair of silver-ringed irises fixed on us.

The line went dead.

Run.

CHAPTER 2

LUKE

Those movies where they race down an escalator on the run were a fucking lie. Or at least they weren't filmed during London rush hour. My heart thumped, pumping adrenaline through my body that I couldn't channel because I was trapped behind a line of suits on the slowest descent of my life as the escalator chugged along.

Eve was motionless, her white-knuckled fingers entwined with mine, a reminder of how fragile she was. Not in mind. No, she was smart and ferocious when she believed in herself. She was a kick-ass wolf who was really finding her fire. But life was fragile, *her* life was fragile.

And no way in hell was I risking losing her again. Not today, not ever.

What do we do? Her sweet voice broke my spiralling thoughts. Even in my head, fear laced her every word.

I don't think he knows we've spotted him, and we can't afford to make a scene. Keep calm. I'm going to get us out of here.

I could feel him watching us, silver eyes boring a hole in the back of my head. He was maybe twenty people behind, his presence causing the hairs on the back of my neck to spike. Too close. I would have loved nothing more than to pull some

Spiderman shit and leap down to the subway platform, but given our stalker, our arrival in London had already drawn too much attention.

Oh, and we'd just been wrongly accused of exposing our kind to the human world. Exile on punishment of death wasn't something I was willing to fuck with or have extended to the rest of Europe.

I hit dial again, this time doing what all good alphas in the making do when they've royally fucked up again: call their dad.

Eve's head whipped around, her brows furrowed at the sound of the call connecting. The way her expression softened as my dad's voice answered and her throat bobbed was like barbed wire coiling around my heart.

"Luke? What's wrong?" His assumption set that off that little voice in the back of my mind. I shoved it down. "Jer didn't show up at the airport."

The escalator stalled for a moment, taunting me. Adrenaline scorched my veins, basal instincts urging me to get Eve to safety.

Dad immediately switched into alpha mode. "Are you sure he's n—?"

"I don't really have time for an argument." The way Eve's eyes narrowed at my tone made me feel like an asshole. I tucked the phone between my ear and shoulder as we got ready to step off the escalator. "Jer wasn't there to pick us up. Something is wrong."

I stopped short of mentioning that someone had rolled a welcome mat that looked a hell of a lot like an executioner. Given the circumstances we left Ireland under, it wasn't surprising that a local pack in London would send someone to scope us out. I'd expected that, but the cloak and dagger vibes suggested they were sent to off us. Damien and Ryan, alpha of the Faolchúnna pack and his son, had too many connections. This was no coincidence.

Dad cursed under his breath, and a door slammed in the background, no doubt meaning he had left the kitchen to stay out of earshot of Max. My brother, who I couldn't hug and promise everything was okay. Fuck.

Despite my omission of details about the danger lurking behind us, it was evident from the concern in my voice that we were in trouble. Dad didn't need a mind connection to read me like a book.

We'll jump on the next one. Stay by my side. I'm not sure he knows if we've seen him, so keep talking like we haven't. I squeezed Eve's hand, more to reassure myself that she was safe beside me than anything else.

"He was on the phone to me an hour ago." The line crackled as Dad heaved a sigh, worry seeping into his tone. "Maybe he got the wrong terminal. Let me try him."

"Well, he wasn't at arrivals."

A gust of dead air hit us as we reached the platform. Bright adverts lining the dull tiled walls battled for attention, the fluorescent lighting above us flickering. If my nose didn't know better, I'd wonder if our assailant was a witch.

"This way, we'll just get the tube to the city." I moved the phone from my ear, keeping up pretences for our little stalker friend. The longer our connection stayed a secret, the more we could use it to our advantage.

I steered Eve away from the escalator and further down the platform. The weekend bag looped around my neck bounced with each step, threatening to send my phone crashing onto the ground.

Dad and Helena were talking on the other end of the line while she tried to get Jeremy on the phone, but most of my focus was on Eve and our surroundings. Our stalker's scent was easier to track once I'd locked onto it. I ignored the stench of the underground as we weaved through the crowd and put some distance between us.

The phone line hissed, dropping out for a moment. "Dad? My reception is going." I stopped mid-step as Eve jolted to a stop in front of me. The low growl rumbling in my chest died in my throat. A bony, wrinkled fist gripped her coat.

"What the fuck?" I zeroed in on the old woman with white hair to her waist, propped up on one of the metal seats. The thick winter coat she was wrapped in swamped her, knitting needles discarded on her lap atop a half-finished blanket. Her pale hands shook as she clung to Eve as if she were her lifeline.

Milky eyes met mine, their swirling depths making time stand still around us as her unseeing gaze slid from me to a stunned Eve who seemed rooted to the spot, all trace of colour having drained from her face.

"Marked." The woman rasped, her frail frame shuddering as if each breath she took was stolen time. She snatched Eve's hand, a hiss escaping her lips as Eve recoiled from her touch.

The taste of her magic hung in the air as her power swelled. This was not a normal witch. Her magic was like nothing I'd experienced before as it brushed against me like a tangible force.

"Marked one." She repeated, twisting Eve's wrist to force her palm to the dirty subway ceiling. The clouds in the depths of her eyes churned like rolling storm clouds. Yellowed fingernails traced Eve's life line, her tone growing sombre. "Such a burden to be destined for such a fate."

Magic surged in the air around us, the hairs on my arms standing on end as I tore Eve from the old crone's grip. "Get off her."

Eve stumbled back against me, flinching away from the woman's touch as if she had been burned.

The creases around the woman's eyes deepened, her expression twisting into one of unnerving amusement as she laughed, a withered cackle, and turned those unseeing eyes back on me. "And moon bound? So it truly comes to pass."

Despite the unmistakable power of the old lady, its presence was a gentle but lingering caress. It was ancient, more of a warning and promise than a threat. I didn't believe in fate, and I sure as hell wasn't going to start now.

Eve stared at her hand, her lower lip trembling as she flexed her fingers as if trying to understand what the woman had seen in the lines mapping her palm. "What do you mean?"

I was about to break every rule Dad taught me about respecting my elders when time slammed back into motion. The noise of an approaching tram squealing and the throng of commuters around us overwhelming my senses as reality kicked in.

Something about her words tugged at my memories, but I was too busy tracking the werewolf hunting us through the crowd.

Dad's voice buzzed from the phone speaker as the line reconnected. "Luke? Are you still there?"

We have to go now!

Behind us, the werewolf's scent grew tenfold, and I turned to find him frozen, only a handful of people behind us. I grabbed Eve by the waist and rushed towards the platform as a loud screech sounded from the pitch-black tunnel the tram tracks disappeared into.

"Yeah, still here." I snatched the phone just as it slipped from my shoulder, keeping a tight hold on Eve as we fought our way towards the platform edge. "We have a small problem."

Bright headlights split the darkness as the tram approached, brakes squealing. Over my shoulder, the werewolf advanced, but my gaze snagged on the now empty seat. How had she moved so fast?

"Luke? I don't know if you can hear me." Dad's voice blared from my phone speaker, battling with the roar of the engine as the tram slowed to a halt in front of us. "I can't reach Jeremy."

Another family member was in danger, and we were on the run. This shit storm just kept getting worse. I held on to the fact that he had said taken and not dead as we raced down the platform. "Where the fuck are we supposed to go?"

Eve stayed right by my side as commuters milled towards the

tram doors. Just as the warning noise sounded, we veered left and jumped into the carriage.

"I'm here." I panted, slipping my arm around Eve's shoulders and pulling her back against my chest. My heart hammered as the doors struggle to close around the rush hour commuters.

Luke...

Eve tugged my sleeve, and the air shifted. My head whipped to the right. A man in a long black coat stood at the far end of the carriage, staring right at us. His eyes flashed silver, and his lips curled back in a feral, hungry smile.

My dad was the calmest alpha around. I could count the number of times I'd seen him scared on one hand. But even with a sea separating us, his fear was palpable as he responded with just one order as the doors finally closed in front of us.

"Jeremy's been taken. London isn't safe. You need to leave. Now."

CHAPTER 3
EVE

I couldn't breathe.

The tram doors snapped shut, leaving us trapped in a tin can with the other werewolf as it rocketed along the tracks. A werewolf that was licking his lips and salivating, as if we were his next meal.

My heart beat erratically in my chest as if my ribs were caving in, starving my burning lungs of oxygen.

Luke's phone disconnected as we hurtled along the underground. We were alone. Our alpha couldn't help us. Alone and on the run in a strange city where we were most certainly not welcome.

The stranger stood at the opposite end of the carriage, watching. Waiting. He wrapped his hand around the metal pole and squeezed, a sinister grin tilting his lips that made me wonder if he was imagining it was my throat. A bead of sweat snaked its way down my spine.

Over here. Luke kept his gaze trained on the threat as he tucked me into his side and guided me over to an empty spot by the doors on our end. The carriage was cramped with clueless humans with their heads buried in their phone or a book as if nothing was wrong.

The weight of his arm around my waist offered little comfort. As his fingers dug into my hip, the image of his face contorted in fear as the vampire sank his fangs into my flesh flashed into my mind. This was something new. Luke was scared.

I'd heard what Tom had said on the phone. Who knew if Jeremy was even still alive? While he didn't say it was linked to us, death seemed to follow me. Perhaps it had a strange fascination with me, or maybe that creepy old woman hadn't been speaking in riddles.

I was living in a nightmare. The world was blurry but vivid at the same time in a way that made my temples throb. It felt surreal, except the threat staring us down was very much the real deal.

One minute it was the werewolf staring me down, the next I was back in the ballroom. The tram's roof morphed into panelled ceilings with gaudy chandeliers, flickering lights became a fire raging around us.

Eyes on me. Luke stepped in front of me, his voice in my mind cutting through the hallucination holding me hostage.

He took my hands in his as he blocked everything else from view, keeping himself planted between me and the wolf looking at us like we were a three-course meal. His gaze burned into me before I looked up to meet it.

"I need you to stay calm." The concern swirling in the hazel depths of Luke's eyes was a stark contrast to the cold, blood-thirsty stare of the werewolf hunting us.

"I am calm." I lied, my voice wavering as I fought to keep my emotions under control. *Push it down, keep breathing.* I wasn't cut out for this—fighting werewolves, vampire attacks, and near-death experiences. This wasn't my life. I wasn't made to survive in this world.

Luke ran his hands up and down my arms as if he could force some sense of composure into my body, lacing his fingers with mine and flipping my palms up to expose where my nails were beginning to become claws. "You sure about that?"

I wasn't sure if it was the venom or if I was just unequipped for the realities of the paranormal world, or maybe it was full-on PTSD. The image of the vampire tearing into my best friend's neck played out on repeat in my head, as if I was in my own personal hell, and this was my punishment.

Luke had once talked of how finding out about our kind could make the human brain fracture. That's how I felt, broken. As if there were some pieces of my soul shattered, never to be whole again.

"I can't handle this."

"You can do anything, but right now there's nothing to handle because that *man* can't do anything on a subway filled with people." Luke kept his voice low.

Our stalker knew we'd spotted him, so there was no point in keeping up the pretence.

I swayed slightly, the movement of the tram doing nothing to help the lingering effects of the vampire venom. "So what? We stay here and wait like sitting ducks?"

Luke's nostrils flared, and he released my hands to grab my waist again to hold me upright, the warmth of his palms against my skin going some way to keep me grounded in the present.

Hours ago, I thought you were dead. I waited by your bedside not knowing if you would ever wake up. We have been exiled. His brow furrowed, the haunted look washing over his face replaced by the alpha mask he'd perfected to rival his dad's. *One wrong move, and they can kill us without any recourse. I'm sure as hell not taking any chances with your life today.*

I opened my mouth to argue, but I snapped it shut as his irises flashed silver, and a low growl of warning rumbled in his chest. Who knew it was possible to be scared for your life and turned on at the same time? I wasn't quite sure what to do with that information. Vampire venom was one fucking hell of a trip.

His expression softened, at odds with his grip on my arms as he squeezed. "We need to stay on the tram until we're in the city, or else we won't stand a chance. Wait for my signal."

Before I could tell him I wasn't a mind-reader, Luke was in my head. Literally.

We can't jump out now. There's no way to lose a werewolf in the suburbs when we're not familiar with the area.

What's your plan? I asked, the barest hint of a smile tugging at the corner of my lips. Using the mind link always reminded me of that night where we ran under the stars in the pack lands together. A night that felt like a lifetime ago.

We stay on this damn thing as long as we can and then make a run for it. It's easy to lose someone in the middle of one of the busiest cities in the world.

I tried to focus on the present rather than the pain or the mounting worry surrounding Craig. I didn't know where we were going. London was just a place I saw on television to me. Sure, we'd planned a trip there for Kate's twenty-first birthday, but when I'd been researching things to do, 'How to Lose a Murderous Werewolf 101' wasn't on our agenda. That all too familiar sting of grief wormed in the pit of my stomach. Kate would never celebrate another birthday.

Trusting Luke's half-baked plan became increasingly more difficult when our stalker moved closer with each stop as commuters filtered on and off the carriage.

Every time the doors opened, my instincts roared at me to run.

I lost track of time, focusing on my breaths and holding my shit together as panic mounted. When the tram swung around a corner, a fresh wave of nausea hit. Above us, a speaker buzzed as the pre-recorded message announced that we should get off here to switch over to the tube.

This one. Luke's voice pulled me back to the present as the tram announced the next stop, a station name that meant nothing to me. I didn't care where we were. I needed to get off this damn thing.

He herded me towards the doors with a dark expression, his

gaze fixed on the werewolf quickly advancing on us as the crowd spilled out onto the platform.

We were in another tunnel that reminded me of Ninja Turtles on the TV and sewers, surrounded by tiled walls, and tracks that vanished into a gulf of darkness at either end. I wasn't claustrophobic, but being shoved along with the commuters striding towards their next destination while trapped underground with a murderous werewolf was an experience I didn't plan to repeat.

I wrinkled my nose as the stench of stale fumes and damp filled my senses, but my focus was on the stalker making a beeline for us.

Right. Luke took my hand, his fingers locked on mine as if I were his lifeline, and tugged me into the tunnel leading away from the platform. Like rats fleeing a drainpipe, we switched between a jog and speed walking to keep up as he shoved his way through the throng of people lingering on the stairs.

The signs and maps plastered on the walls were a blur. We reached a larger area of the underground with the same dull tiles, but this had elevators and escalators lined by advertisement boards with bright LEDs that had me squinting. Nowhere in Ireland had an underground, and I was disorientated as hell. Everything looked identical, with the same tiles and grimy floor. It was a maze I'd never be able to find my way out of.

Up here. Luke's lips were pursed in a thin line, his jaw set as he ushered me towards yet another flight of stairs with very little direction and no explanation. I followed his narrowed gaze to spot the werewolf stepping onto the first step.

I couldn't tell if he was one of Ryan's goons or a London wolf, and I wasn't planning on sticking around to find out. He had broad shoulders and strong cheekbones, the material of his leather coat straining against his oversized biceps. He flashed me a glimpse of his canines, as if enjoying the way my pupils no doubt dilated.

One minute, I was taking the steps two at a time to keep up

with Luke herding me from behind, and the next I was pitching forwards. I hadn't noticed the stairs had ended and was on course to smash my face into the grimy tiles, but my knee barely skimmed the ground before Luke spun and caught me under the arms.

"I've got you." Luke lifted me upright with one arm around my waist.

I cursed, my trainers squeaking as I found my balance. He pushed ahead, guiding me as weaved through the rows of people ahead of us. We stepped out into a brighter area that I could only describe as pure chaos as commuters criss-crossed the foyer in different directions. The werewolf hunting us had vanished into the sea of people swarming the station.

"How do I get through these?" I eyed the machines as Luke tugged me over to the turnstiles.

The crowd pressing in on us from all sides surged forwards. Luke towered over me, my back crushed against his chest as we slid into one of the queues.

He slid a black bank card into my hand as the person in front of us slipped through the turnstile, his grip on me tightening as the stalker werewolf's scent increased. "This one is on Darius."

I had no time to question him. A tall woman dressed to kill in the boardroom reached around Luke's hulking figure to tap my arm. He caught her hand, a low growl of warning rumbling in his chest.

"Scan the damn card!" She snapped, snatching her hand back and pointing a manicured finger at the scanner in front of the turnstile.

I did as I was told, and the doors slid open, the metal bars smacking into my thigh as I rushed through, closely followed by Luke. Some burly security guard several feet away yelled something, but we were lost in the crowd once more. No doubt our tram fair wouldn't max out an ancient vampire's bank account, but we were kind of in a hurry. Murderous werewolf on our tails and all that.

As we raced towards daylight, I caught a brief glimpse of silver eyes and that creepy long black coat in the crowd for a moment. Then he was gone.

Cold air scorched my lungs, along with a million scents and sounds as we stepped out into the city. My heightened senses in overdrive. The London skyline was a mix of old and new stretching up into the grey winter sky, the older buildings aged and weathered reminding me of those lining the streets of home. But Dublin didn't have glass skyscrapers piercing the clouds.

Luke and I locked eyes for a moment, his hand wrapped tightly around mine. With one look, he communicated a multitude of heavy emotions, but the overriding one was regret. Tears clogged my throat.

This isn't how I wanted our first trip to go.

A low growl of warning sounded behind us, shattering the moment. We didn't have time to stop and admire the view.

I spun to find the werewolf cresting the stairs to the underground, wearing that same sickening grin that spoke of a love of murder and pain. He wasn't avoiding eye contact or making any effort to stay down wind, he wanted us to know he was close. Some murderers liked to taunt their prey, they often got off on the fear.

Mission accomplished. I was scared and more than happy to run.

Luke led the charge down the sprawling streets of London, the stench of fumes and roaring engines mixed with the impatient blasting of car horns blaring around us. When people dashed through places in the movies, it always looked so damn easy. It's not. I rushed past bemused commuters, apologising as Luke whacked more than one person with the branded leather weekend bag slung over his shoulder.

We split up to dodge a fancy Mercedes parked illegally on double yellow lines and blocking most of the path, Luke pushing me ahead of him with a firm hand against my ass. Ever the gentleman.

I shrugged off the ridiculous puffy jacket, gladly dumping it in a bin as we ran past. I was overheating despite my breaths forming small vapour clouds in the winter air.

One minute Luke was right behind me, and the next the hairs on the back of my neck were spiking. I spun around. The werewolf's hands were wrapped around Luke's neck as he dragged him off the main street.

Dread-fuelled bile rose in my throat, and I cursed, skidding to a stop and racing around the corner onto a narrow side street just in time to see the two of them brawling. The werewolf charged towards the wall, and I shrieked as he smashed Luke into a tower of beer glass crates. His back hit the brick wall behind with a sickening crunch, glass shattering around their feet as the stack of crates smashed to the ground.

A waitress propped against a fire escape at the far end of the alleyway screamed, her unfinished cigarette smoking at her feet as she stared frozen in horror. Another crash sounded, and she bolted inside the building, slamming a steel door behind her.

A handful of people on the main street looked in our direction, but of course, no one stepped in. Two men brawling in the early hours of the morning could be excused as drunken antics following a night out, but I needed this to stop before their claws weren't mistaken as blades, or someone whipped out their phone and this went viral. We were supposed to lie low, not make headlines.

Blood stained Luke's T-shirt as the werewolf sliced open his shoulder, and the venom-heightened rage in me snapped as I launched into action.

Mildly conscious that I needed to keep my claws in check under so many eyes and no doubt a camera phone, I launched myself at the attacker's back. My stomach lurched as I latched onto him, distracting the werewolf enough for a dazed Luke to land a punch on the guy's face and splatter his coat with blood as he followed up with another. I hooked my arms under the werewolf's armpits, straining to keep his arms pinned back, saliva pooling in my mouth at the scent of his blood.

Luke winced as he shoved away from the wall, leaving a concave, cracked, Luke-shaped hole in his wake.

Eve, focus! Luke forced the werewolf back, raining down punches.

The man staggered, and I reached around, bile filling my mouth as I dug my finger into his eye-socket in a move I'd learned from films and not from training. He howled in agony, and I leaped off his back, rolling into a crouch in time for Luke to land a kick squarely to the attacker's chest, sending him sprawling out onto the main street where a crowd had gathered.

A crowd we needed to escape ASAP.

We took our chance, shoving past the teenagers peering down the alley, the jagged brickwork of the corner tearing at my T-shirt as we squeezed past and sprinted away from the carnage left in our wake.

Cars whizzed past as we shot across the road, angry beeps sounding behind us. Luke's bloody fingers were slick on my skin as he grabbed my arm, pulling me towards a taxi rank sign further down the road.

I expected the first driver to do a double take at Luke's bruised face, but he shrugged as Luke flashed a wad of cash that I probably had our vampire friends to thank for and waved us in. I dived onto the plush leather seats, adrenaline surging through my veins as the battered werewolf skidded out onto the road just in time to see Luke slam the door shut behind us.

"Where to?" The driver looked at Luke through the rearview mirror, clearing his throat and tugging at the collar of his polo shirt.

Luke was a mess. Blood streamed from his nose, and his jacket was shredded, the seam along his injured shoulder flapping open. He swiped the back of his forearm across his face, barely flinching as he answered.

"Larkhall Rise, Clapham." Luke slumped back in his seat as

the driver took off, those molten chocolate eyes of his fixed on me as he traced small circles on the back of my hand.

With the immediate danger disappearing in the rearview mirror, reality started to hit home. We were exiled. My new world had been turned on its head, and now I was no longer welcome in the new life I'd built. We were on the run, and too many supernaturals were out for our blood. I couldn't go home. Luke couldn't go back to his family.

It was all my fault.

CHAPTER 4

LUKE

The last time I'd seen Jeremy's place was before Alice disappeared. Not much had changed, yet there was something sinister in the way the winter clouds darkened, and misting rain pounded the pavement with our approach.

It was as if Mother Nature was trying to warn me this was a bad idea. Or maybe I'd seen one too many fucked up things, and I'd finally lost my mind. I was never one to believe in signs, and now I searched for them everywhere because I needed something to cling onto.

Hope.

I stared at the cracked screen of my phone, willing my dad's name to flash up. But it was dead, just like everyone who tried to help us. Eve's phone had fallen victim to the massacre ball, so we were on our own.

The driver caught my eye in the rearview mirror as I sniffed, dabbing my nose with the back of my hand only to add another layer to the crusting blood coating my cracked knuckles. Poor guy was scared shitless of me, but money talked.

Suburban London flashed past, three-story Victorian, yellow-bricked houses lining the roads we wound through. Jeremy was a doctor, and I'd always teased him about living on the posh side of

London when he acted anything but. A small smile tugged at my lips at memories of me and Alice running around their little garden, giving him grief for being a city wolf before I was old enough to shift.

I'd expected Eve to fuss about the blood in the taxi, but she spent the journey staring out the window as a storm rolled in and rain began to fall. Those raindrops carving their path down the fogged glass must have held the answers to whatever was on her mind, because she sure as hell wouldn't meet my eye. And this time, I didn't think the vampire venom was entirely to blame.

I couldn't look at her, and yet I couldn't tear my gaze away. Yellowing bruises marred her skin as her body fought to recover from being within death's clutches. They say trauma is invisible, but I could see the signs. The way she chewed her lip raw, the deep circles under her eyes. Each flinch in response to London road rage horn blasting right down to the way she twisted her hands in her lap.

The memories haunted me too.

Except my nightmare was the image of that vampire draining the life from her, and Larissa holding her hostage and the dagger slicing into her throat. The worry on Darius' face when he swore they would do their best to save her, but couldn't promise they would. The sight of Eve in a hospital bed, all colour drained from her beautiful face. The moment I heard her heart stop beating.

I swear, my heart stopped too. I'd never be able to repay them for saving her. I was forever indebted to both Jonas and his partner.

"Here will do." I cleared my throat and signalled to the driver. Nervous energy in my stomach writhed once more as we pulled up alongside the familiar house, identical to the rest of the terraced houses lining the street with manicured dainty front gardens, and posh cars parked on the street because the land was too valuable for driveways.

Eve cocked her head to one side as I handed the taxi driver an eyebrow-raising amount of cash. A tip for his silence and any damage I'd done to his seats. Not mine, of course. Darius had made sure we had everything we would need.

Rain-slick tyres squealed as the taxi pulled away, leaving us standing in front of an all too quiet two-story building that held so many good memories I feared were about to be tainted forever.

"Where are we?" Eve stood on the curb looking around at the picture-perfect streets.

I reached out, the black wrought-iron gate groaning in protest as I nudged it open. "Jeremy's house."

"Luke?"

I took a deep breath, raking a hand through my hair as I studied the house that had so many memories, knowing they could be destroyed by what we might find. "Yeah?"

She faced me, rain drops dotting her cheeks like the freckles I loved so much.

"Are you okay?" Such a simple but loaded question. She reached up, gently swiping her thumb across my jaw where a nasty gash was already healing. "I know, it's a stupid question."

I leaned into her touch, the pain grounding me in the present, and focused on the steady if fast-paced beat of her heart to calm my own. "It's not stupid. I don't think either of us are alright, but we will be."

The corners of her lips tilted up in the smallest of smiles as I clasped her hand. The increased warmth of her skin went some way to unwind the elephant-sized weight of fear sitting on my chest as I linked my fingers with hers.

"Ready?"

She simply nodded, squeezing my hand tightly as we turned to face Jeremy's house. Her silence only highlighted how empty the building seemed from outside. There were no cars parked out the front, not a single light was on. The logical side of my brain argued that they could just be out, maybe they got stuck in traffic, and that there were lots of perfectly reasonable explanations for Jer not showing at the airport. I so badly wanted that to be the case, but the icy fear taking hold howled that something was very, very wrong.

I hadn't realised I'd frozen in place until Eve's movement broke the spell, her sneakers squelching as she walked over to the living room window. She needed to rise onto her tiptoes to see in through the raised windows of the ground floor, her brow furrowing as she pushed damp hair out of her face to see.

The wind picked up, the last of the surviving autumn leaves dancing around my feet as I followed suit, moving to the window on the right. My bloodied reflection stared back at me as I took a deep breath before peering inside.

Besides a fresh lick of paint and a new suite of furniture, the room looked the same as I remembered. Old wooden floors that had been restored, a pristine bookcase taking up one wall lined with everything from medical journals to a few first edition books. Jeremy loved to learn. One of the few times I ever saw my uncle on the verge of tears was when his daughter Ellie was a toddler and had accidentally shredded a hard copy of his first article in a medical magazine.

"Looks like nobody's home." Disappointment rang clear in her voice as Eve re-joined my side.

My nose wasn't flagging anything unusual, but with the rain cleansing the streets, there was likely nothing left to find.

"No fresh scents either. The place looks normal." I frowned, studying the undisturbed living room before stepping back from the window. An open energy drink can sat on the coffee table beside a discarded PlayStation controller. Nothing was out of place, right down to a sock lying beside a half empty basket of washing on one couch. A typical family house, yet no sign of life. "Too normal."

Dread dragged like weights around my ankles as I started up the steps leading to the front door. "We need to get off the street. I'm not taking any chances in case we were followed."

I walked up to the front door, a brief smile ghosting my lips as I brushed my fingers over the bronze door knocker carved in the shape of a wolf. That was new.

The door creaked, the old wood groaning as the door opened a crack from my light touch. Eve and I locked eyes, the same sense of fear freezing us both in place. No one in the city left their door unlocked.

Stay behind me and watch your back.

Eve's pupils dilated until only small specks of blue remained, a tell that meant the vampire venom was surging again.

I eased the door open, my senses on high alert as the warm air inside hit. The house was silent. Like most werewolf homes, the interior walls had been soundproofed. No foreign scents caught my attention, only those of Jer, his wife Lila, and their two kids. All familiar, all missing.

The lock isn't broken. I nudged the dead bolt with my thumb, and it snapped back into place.

A rectangular dent gauged the door frame beside the strike plate where the bolt must have slammed into it. I told myself Jer's oldest, Aaron, was a teenager. Teens slammed doors all the time, I took one clean off the hinges when Dad grounded me.

Eve followed my gaze, her brow furrowing at the marks. She placed her hand on my shoulder, gently nudging me deeper into the hallway. *People slam doors all the time.*

In the human world, that was true. In our world, werewolves were being kidnapped and murdered, powerful witches schemed, and depraved ancient vampires tortured humans like they were prey. When danger is your shadow, nothing is a coincidence.

A floorboard squeaked as I shuffled along the hallway. The only mark on the pristine white living room door was a sticky handprint that smelled like energy drink, not blood. I kept my arm out to signal for Eve to stay behind me as I nudged it open with my foot, my shoulders slumping as it revealed the same normal sitting room I'd seen through the window.

I scanned the room, moving to examine the bookcase for some sign. I wasn't sure what I was looking for anymore, I'd expected them to either be home or, if they'd been attacked or taken, some sign of a struggle.

Jeremy is a doctor, right? Eve sifted through the notes littering my uncle's desk in the corner of the room.

Notebooks and scattered sheets of paper covered the table, but that was expected. If anything, a clean surface would have worried me more.

Yeah, he's a doctor and loves research.

She held up a notepad with several sequences of numbers scrawled across the top, some circled and others crossed out. *Not a mathematician then?*

They're not all numbers. I frowned, leaning over to examine the notes. The leaf of paper tore free from the notepad as she held it up. *There are letters too. Are they postcodes? I don't know how they work over here.*

Illegible scribbles thanks to Jer's doctor handwriting were scrawled between crude sketches of everything from the moon to what looked like a set of veins on the wrist. I picked up one of the texts lying open on the desk, leafing through the anatomy diagrams before pulling out the next one in the stack.

Eve's forehead creased as she studied the page for a long moment before dropping the notepad, picking up an old leather notebook instead. She thumbed through the first few pages before her gaze snagged on the cover of the book in my hand.

Why is he looking into werewolf origins? This looks more like a diary log than an encyclopaedia.

I tugged an old newspaper from under one of the many notebooks, knocking a pen onto the floor as I flicked through the yellowed pages of *The Times* to find a few reports underlined. Something about a body found in the Thames.

"What if he was looking into the disappearances for my dad?" I immediately cursed and switched back to speaking in her mind. This link would take some getting used to. *It wouldn't be the first time Dad didn't tell me what he was up to. What if Jer found something about the hybrids?*

For the first time since her brief dance with death, genuine hope sparked in those stunning blue eyes.

Come on. We'll grab the rest of these on the way out. Eve stuffed the first sheet of paper into her pocket, tugging me towards the hallway. *Whatever Jeremy found, we need to find them to get some answers.*

My gaze snagged on the picture frame hanging by the living room entrance. Jeremy stood on the beach with his wife, Lila, her head thrown back in laughter as she smiled up at him, her arms wrapped around their two kids. *Their oldest, Aaron is fourteen now. He turned for the first time. His sister Ellie was so jealous.*

Eve gave my hand a gentle squeeze, her lips curving in the smallest of smiles.

We crept further into the house, stepping through the open door leading to a large kitchen. I inhaled deeply, cursing under my breath when nothing strange caught my senses. What was worse? Finding or nothing, or that sick feeling something terrible was waiting around the next corner?

Eve drifted past me, running her fingers along the quartz countertops as she took in the room. The navy shaker cabinets were all closed, some plates stood stacked on the dish rack by the sink. Rain thrummed against the skylights, thick clouds robbing the extension of natural sunlight.

She paused by the back door, looking out at the overgrown jungle of wildflowers, cocking her head to one side.

What's that?

I frowned, walking over to the windows. *What?*

Not out there. Listen. She raised her hand, shaking her head as she scanned the room.

Raindrops bounced off the patio tiles outside, but no movement caught my attention. I frowned, hairs rising on my arms as I tried to follow her gaze. Her pupils had blown again. I couldn't tell if it was genuine adrenaline or if this could be another hallucination, and I hated not trusting her judgement.

There.

Something beeped, not outside but from the laundry room next to the back door. I paused outside, pressing my ear to the wood. The scent of fabric softener and manufactured pine drifted to me, along with scents of the family, but nothing unfamiliar.

I nodded to Eve and motioned for her to step back. We both held our breath as I eased the door open to reveal nothing but the latest washing machine and dryer combination and a set of freshly washed towels stacked to one side.

Eve shot me a nervous smile. *False alarm, sorry.*

My lips curved into a reassuring smile, the expression detached and alien as disappointment washed over me

I stepped out of the small laundry room, pacing over to the dining table where there was a half-finished cold cup of coffee. "I don't think they planned to leave."

"Would all of them have come to collect us from the airport?" Eve asked, moving from the kitchen into the hall once more. "Or would Jeremy have gone alone given the circumstances?"

There was no hesitation in my answer. "He'd never risk the kids, not knowing we were exiled. Dad would have warned him."

"How much did your dad tell Jeremy?"

"I've no idea, but Jeremy would never betray us." Her unspoken implication stung, but paled in comparison to the hurt in her eyes at the ice bite of my response. I wanted to snatch those words back and swallow them. "Sorry, I just... He wouldn't. He's family, he was there for Dad so much after my mam died. There's no way."

She studied me for a long moment before nodding and turning away as she climbed the staircase. "I believe you, but he has a family and kids to protect. We can't find him, and the way the line cut when you called him..."

"I know." I sighed, raking a hand through my damp hair as I followed her up the stairs. My nose was on high alert, but all I could sense was the scent of teenage boy as we passed the first bedroom. "There's no sign of a struggle, so they must have left by choice. I've no idea where they would go, but the only way they'd desert family is if the kids were in danger."

If there was a drop of blood in the house, my nose should have picked it up. But each step was weighted with the fear of what we would find.

We skipped the room that stank of teenage boy and one drenched in purple, stopping instead by the main bedroom. It felt a bit odd, as if I were infringing on an elder's privacy or something. It was empty, as expected, but there were a mix of shirts and sweaters scattered on top of the perfectly made bed.

"They were in a rush," I tiptoed around a fluffy cream rug that matched the ivory bed linen to spare it from my damp trainers.

Several drawers in the chest of drawers below a wall-mounted television were open, some half-empty as if they'd been scooped into a bag. Two lines marked the rug, the same distance apart as the two wheels of a suitcase.

"This is a good sign." Eve paused to look in the floor-length mirror hanging on the door to a large walk-in-wardrobe, wrinkling her nose at her reflection. "It means they're alive."

"Some of them, at least." I picked up an e-reader lying on the bedside locker, turning it over in my hand. "Did someone threaten them? Damien isn't smart enough to pull all the strings alone, Larissa definitely would have recruited others."

Eve poked her head out of the walk-in-wardrobe, her tone dripping with disdain. "Hybrid hate and power-hungry leaders aren't exactly a rarity."

My head snapped up as the distant noise of conversation came from outside, followed by the sound of the front gate swinging open.

Someone's coming.

CHAPTER 5
EVE

*F*uck.

The moment I met Luke's wide eyes, my ears zeroed in the voices coming from outside. I'd been too busy hiding in the doorway leading to the walk-in-wardrobe to hide my battle with another wave of nausea from him to notice anyone approaching.

Luke crossed the room in two strides. Before I had time to blink, his hands were on my waist pushing me backwards. Wooden floors gave way to plush carpet as he drove me back into the walk-in wardrobe, the tips of his claws digging into my sides.

My venom-addled brain wasn't processing things fast enough. A small gasp slipped from my lips as he spun me, clamping an arm around my middle as I was pulled tightly against his chest. The dull winter daylight vanished as he closed the door with inhuman speed, the bitter scent of metal on his palm as he covered my mouth and pulled us deeper into the room.

Some carnal recess of my mind hummed at how this would be really sexy if our lives weren't in immediate danger. Were vampires always this horny or was venom some kind of aphrodisiac? Because I needed off this trip if I was going to survive.

Darkness swamped us, my eyes adjusting to the absence of

light in time to notice the marks our damp trainers left on the carpet in our wake. I knocked a stack of clothes off the counter in the centre of the room to hide our footprints. I snatched a handful of leggings from the open drawers below it and scattered them as Luke continued to walk us backwards.

He mumbled some kind of praise over the mind link for smart thinking that I could barely register because my adrenaline was surging, the noise of blood pumping through my body filling my ears. My senses were heightened, but I had little to no control over them.

Despite the urgency of his movements, Luke was gentle but firm as he held me against him. His hand hid another sound as he stopped, my legs bumping into his. There was a whooshing sound as something slid open behind us before Luke stepped back once more, releasing my mouth to scoop me up behind my thighs briefly before setting me down.

The wardrobe door slid shut in front of me, leaving us trapped in a wooden box surrounded by doctor's scrubs that smelled like a hospital and dust mites making my nose twitch.

Below us, the bolt of the front door clicked open, and the voices grew louder. My hearing picked out two male voices and one female, all strangers.

Breathe. Luke's soothing voice sounded in my mind, the warmth of his hands as they dropped to my hips doing nothing to calm my heart which was doing its best to hammer its way through my ribcage. *I don't recognise any of the voices, do you?*

The voices grew louder, old floorboards creaking downstairs as they filed into the house. I shook my head, but there was no sense of relief. Just because it wasn't Damien, Ryan or batshit witch-bitch didn't mean we were safe.

A naïve part of me wondered if it was just a normal break-in until a loud bang sounded downstairs, followed by another crash, and the hairs on my arms rose as magic tinged the air. As if someone had thrown the coffee table across the living room.

Wolves, witches, who fucking knows what, and we were trapped in a godsdamned wardrobe.

I really hope the family are somewhere safe. And Jeremy.

Jer wouldn't disappear without a fight. He rested his chin on my shoulder, his hands grazing over my stomach as he slid his arms around me. The warmth of his breath on my neck sent a chill skittering down my spine. *I don't think it's a coincidence that visitors have shown up, they must have been tipped off. Lila would have taken the kids somewhere safe.*

Lila?

His wife. You'd love her.

I nodded, my response fizzling out in my throat because every time Luke mentioned someone in his life that I would love, I had to wonder if I'd cause their death before I got the chance to meet them.

Despite the soundproofed walls, we could hear enough loud banging coming from downstairs to know they were tearing the room below us apart, but I couldn't make out distinct words. My tongue was thick as I caught the faint scent of smoke as their noise moved towards the direction of the kitchen. They were destroying the house—a *home.*

"Looks like someone got the jump on us." A gruff voice carried upstairs as a step creaked under their weight.

"Aye, we know for sure the family was warned off. Whatever mole stole my fun is going to regret it when I get my hands on them." Another man spoke up, sniffing loudly. He sounded younger, his voice lacking the smoky rasp of his accomplice's. "Smells like wolf. You think it's the witch's doing or another pack?"

One wolf at least, can't figure out the others. Luke confirmed my suspicions, his body tense against mine as his fingers thrumming against my side.

"No shit. Either the family bolted, or they did the job elsewhere." The woman chimed in, her northern English accent thicker than the two men I'd picked out so far. "Just because those bastards crossed us doesn't mean we can't dig around. Information pays better than a hit these days."

Luke's chest vibrated, the building growl dying in his throat. No doubt he wanted to rip theirs out, and the venom-fuelled part of my brain really liked that.

They'd planned to kill Jeremy's family and for what? Helping us? My brain was spiralling so I focused on what I could.

How many packs are there over here?

Luke readjusted his hold on me as he rolled his shoulders, tension radiating from his body against mine. *Not everyone is in a pack, even in Ireland there are a few families that do their own thing. The UK is way bigger, Scotland and Wales do have multiple packs, and there are several packs throughout England. London has its own hierarchy, four families and then one kind of ruling pack.*

Does it work?

By the sounds of things, no. I'd heard rumours of unrest from Dad.

Before Luke could continue with my untimely history lesson, the older man spoke up once more. He was closer this time, his scent an odd floral mix that had a sour edge to it that wasn't wolf. "Alright, alright. I'll try find a clue about where they went, but the boss didn't give us much to go on. He was too busy losing his shit about them screwing up."

Either my nose was on the fritz, or he was human.

My chest loosened for the briefest moment before heavy footsteps began their ascent, a slow death march leading straight towards us.

"Use your fucking head, man. He's not looking for medical research or anatomy 101, look for anything on the origins or hybrids." The woman's tone grew icy, fading as she moved away from the stairs. "He said the witch mentioned something about a key."

Luke froze at the mention of hybrids, his grip on me tightening as if he thought I might slip from his grasp at the mere mention of the word. It wasn't a shock, though sickening worry made my stomach somersault as it was confirmed. What happened in Dublin was following us over here, and we were most certainly not welcome in London. It also meant it was our fault Luke's family was on the run or worse.

"Keep the pyro in check or else we'll have nothing to find," the same man hollered, the old floorboards groaning as if warning us of his location as he stepped onto the landing. "Relics and fucking myths, this is not what I signed up for."

My nose picked up a hint of magic that reminded me of Larissa. I glanced up at Luke to find his hard gaze fixed on the wardrobe door as if he could burn a hole through it and torch the man trashing his family's home. *Is there a witch downstairs?*

He nodded mutely, his jaw ticking as he tensed against me like a predator ready to pounce.

Shit, the notebooks. Luke's grip on me slackened in defeat. *We left all the research downstairs. What if they see?*

The stream of self-deprecating thoughts that followed caught me off guard. Failure, mistake, not being cut out to be alpha... Clearly I wasn't the only one that was adjusting to not projecting all my thoughts. I'd heard him voice some of these before, but the sheer venom in the way he thought about himself despite coming across as outwardly confident surprised me. He was so quick to call me out and protect me, did he think he wasn't worthy of the same?

"Someone has definitely been snooping around here." The human began humming to himself, a loud thump sounding from the bedroom as he rummaged around carelessly. "Things are all over the place."

He was going to find us. I had to stop him. My venom tainted senses craved blood, my magic howling at the feeling of sitting in wait like prey rather than the predator.

I slid the door open a fraction, Luke's hand shooting out to circle my wrist.

Don't you fucking dare.

It wasn't a request, it was a command that tugged on the

power in my core in the oddest way. I didn't have time to decipher any of it, because the sliver of room visible vanished as Luke shut the wardrobe once more just as the doorknob opposite leading to the bedroom twisted.

Against my instincts, I forced myself to take slow, shallow breaths as the human moved into the room. We could take him easily, but we had no idea what lurked downstairs.

The blood lust was stirring once more. My ribs felt as if they were caving in, saliva pooling in my mouth as the human's heartbeat maintained its steady rhythm while mine staccattoed.

Eve. Come back to me.

I'd inched forwards, straining against Luke's grip as the humming man moved closer. A confusing mix of panic that he would discover us danced with the feverish anticipation of sinking my teeth into his flesh, one very human fear mixed with the hunger of a creature that was unnatural to me.

The human paused on the other side of the door, my heightened hearing seeking out the pulse of his main arteries, fixating on the glorious sound of blood flowing just beneath the skin. So close.

"Amateurs, trashing a room to cover their tracks? Either someone was raiding the underwear drawer, or there's a safe in here somewhere. They never said we couldn't take any loot." The smirk was audible in his voice.

A loud crash came from beneath us, my body jerking against Luke's hold as what sounded like a mini explosion had the walls of the house shaking.

"Harriett!" He hollered, causing the mirrored wardrobe door to shudder and glass to crunch as he smashed his fist against it. "What the fuck was that?"

The scent of burning filled my nostrils, followed by a scream from downstairs and a loud crash that sounded like glass shattering.

"Get out! We need to get out now!" Gone was the confidence of the woman from before, her shrill screams piercing the air.

The man cursed, heavy footsteps thumping as he stomped away from us. Luke tugged the door open a crack just as the man's broad silhouette disappeared into the bedroom, the air around us already becoming hazy.

Move. Now.

I leaped out of the wardrobe, blood lust replaced with survival instinct as we sprinted across the clothes-laden floor into the bedroom. Something splintered downstairs followed by a surge of energy and the distinctive crackling of fire swelling to life. I flinched as a shrill beeping sound pierced the air, the fire alarm kicking in and deafening my sensitive ears.

Luke flung his arm out as we reached the bay window, stopping me short of running into view. The scent of smoke filtered through the old floorboards, wafting from the staircase into the room. Beneath us, three hooded figures spilled onto the street.

We can go out the back. I grabbed his sleeve, spinning towards the doorway.

Neither of us bothered to keep our footsteps light as a fire roared into life downstairs. My heart stuck in my throat as we ran onto the landing to find thick billows of smoke rising from the hallway, flames blazing a trail along the thin carpet at the base of the stairs. The acrid, suffocating scent of burning filling my nostrils.

Tendrils of smoke weren't the only thing robbing me of oxygen. Shadows of dancing fire billowing froze me to the spot. The sight of flames licking at the panelled walls and the intense heat radiating from the fire brought me back to Dublin, back to the ballroom where chandeliers collapsed and a vampire had his fangs embedded in my flesh.

"Eve!" Luke's voice blared both in my mind and right in my ear, my vision slowly piecing reality back into place to form an image of his face. He placed his hands on my cheeks, his nose brushing mine as those silver-ringed hazel eyes of his fixed on mine. "I need you to focus on me."

I'd thought I was, but my chest heaved, and the stale taste of smoke coated my tongue as his words overrode the fear holding them hostage.

"We need to get out of here now. I know you're scared, but I promise I have you."

I believed him, but the fear was all-consuming. The images of the ballroom flashing behind my eyelids were so real, the sensation of fangs slicing into my pale skin so raw they made acid rise in my throat as I forced another breath out.

He went to pull me into his arms, but I pushed back, shaking my head as if it would rid me of the flashbacks.

"I'm fine," I bit out, covering my mouth with my forearm as I to find the balance between forcing laboured breaths to calm my mind and not inhaling too much of the dirty air.

Luke caught my chin between his forefinger and thumb, forcing me to meet his gaze. I stuffed the feelings, the fear, and the fire blazing a trail up the stairs behind us to the back of my mind and focused on the small well of magic rebuilding inside me as I repeated myself once more, my voice steadier this time. "I'm okay, I promise."

He nodded, taking my hand and leading the way down the haze of smoke filling the landing towards one of the back bedrooms, not breaking his stride as he kicked the door open to reveal the little girl's room.

"The notebooks, Jeremy's research!" Tears pricked the corner of my eyes as I took in the purple walls knowing the fire would gut the room in minutes, robbing a child of all those memories. "Everything will be destroyed."

Luke was at the window, one leg on the bed as he kneeled the other on the windowsill. He glanced over my shoulder as a crash sounded, his throat bobbing. "Forget about them. We need to get out of here before this place comes crashing down or the fire brigade arrives."

I paused to snatch a unicorn teddy off the bed. It's probably not what Ellie would have chosen, but a girl was never too old for teddies.

Luke held out his arm, motioning for me to hurry. "We've got to go."

I stepped onto the bed, my fingers closing around his as he helped me onto the window ledge. Cold winds whipped through my hair, the winter air a contrasting bite to the furnace building inside. I stepped out onto the shingled roof carefully, using one hand to keep my balance as I stayed crouched.

Luke followed behind me, keeping a tight grip on my T-shirt as we snuck along the roof of the kitchen extension. I focused on keeping my footing as we neared the edge, inwardly thanking my werewolf side for keeping me balanced as I dropped onto the garden wall without falling despite my vision swimming. Luke landed behind me, his hand on my back urging me forwards as we sprinted along the brick wall towards the small laneway the houses backed onto. Only when we reached the end of the garden did I pause to look back.

The kitchen windows at the rear of the house were completely obscured by thick grey smoke, the curtain rail having collapsed, pierced only by hungry orange flames. The faintest hint of magic lingered in the air as if taunting. A fire engine sounded in the distance. The fire would run its natural course, but humans would ever find the cause.

I clutched the unicorn to my chest, a silent tear carving a path down my cheek. I didn't have the words as Luke scooped me into his arms, the burning building disappearing from view as he leaped off the wall and carried me into the night.

CHAPTER 6

LUKE

"Welcome to our home for the foreseeable." I gestured to the hotel in front of us, my nose wrinkling at how hollow the word 'home' sounded now.

Just off a bustling street stood a large building that spanned the length of the road, with a small fountain outside and elegant stonework with intricate detailing that exuded a rich history. It was originally a theatre, later becoming an extravagant hotel.

Our ride on the tube to the city had been filled with silent tears and awkward glances from onlookers. No one asked any questions though, one of the perks of a big city. I'd have loved to show Eve around the heart of London, but the sun was setting, and we'd had more than enough near-death experiences for one day.

I pulled Eve to one side, pressing my palm against a gold plaque marking a wrought-iron gate that seemed to lead to a boring storage area. A sharp zap of magic stung my skin as it connected with the metal. The pain was over in milliseconds like a static electric shock, and a grin tugged at the corner of my lips as the image of the hotel shimmered before our eyes like a mirage before morphing into an entirely different reality as the glamour lifted.

Eve gasped, her heel catching my foot as she took a step back. I chuckled, catching her by the elbow to steady her as what looked like hotel apartments attached to the building glitched before our eyes as the magic took hold.

The exterior morphed into that of a modern building, and the doorman vanished into thin air, all a part of the intricate glamour that let humans think it was a normal part of their world. No one questioned strange people entering a posh apartment complex, and much like the Dark Night club, any human who tried to enter would suddenly find themselves inclined to leave.

The glassy exterior of the hotel stretched far above the nearby buildings, the winter sunlight dancing off the surface like rainbows across a body of water. It was incredible, a complete contrast to the decorative ironwork and classical columns of the original hotel, yet also a beautiful compliment.

"Isn't it a bit much?" The bridge of Eve's nose scrunched, her surprise at our lavish accommodation going some way to lift her mood.

"This is what happens when bougie vampires plan your accommodation."

Her cheeks coloured the palest of pinks as she showed a hint of a smile and damn, my heart leaped at that tiny glimmer of the real Eve. She looked far too much like the pale half-dead version I'd watched Jonas work over for hours. I had to keep touching her to reassure myself that she was real. She was here. She was alive.

I guided her towards the revolving door marking the entrance, trying to ignore how strange it felt to walk on the lavish red carpet lining the steps. Carpet didn't belong outside, magical dirt repellent or not. It was way fancier than any place I'd ever stayed, and the weird looks I was getting for my crusty bloody nose told me that they were used to clientele that had suave suits like Jonas, not a scruffy werewolf.

The doorman of Château Minuit had cheekbones that could cut a diamond, his slender frame towering over me dressed head to toe in an expensive suit. Add the healthy quiff of dark hair that looked so fluffy even I was tempted to touch it, the guy belonged on a runway at London fashion week. Most vampires did.

I gave him a nod, and his lip curled back ever so slightly at the sight of my blood.

We stepped inside to find another two concierges guiding us towards an unnecessary elevator taking us to the reception, which was on the first floor. They had an entire floor just for a lobby. I kept my fingertips brushing the small of Eve's back, biting back a grin at the way she was staring at the sheer opulence of the hotel. It wasn't our kind of place, I'd rather hide out in a cottage in the middle of nowhere with her. Still, it was safe, and that was my priority.

The reception desk spanned the length of one wall, while the other side had a private book for dealing with VIP clients and a side entrance to a cosy bar with mood lighting. The walls were black and lined with red satin drapes that contrasted with the white marble floor. Everything was picture perfect, the staff as pristinely groomed as the building.

I paused, spinning Eve to face me before we reached the desk. Now that we were in a safe space because it was a matter of minutes before she would notice the distinct lack of hearts beating and weak thrum of magic.

"Before we left, Jonas did offer us a place to stay. I declined given the circumstances, but now we can't stay with Jer." I took her shaking hands in mine, watching closely for her reaction to what I'd say next. "Darius owns this hotel. It's completely safe, no werewolves will enter without permission—"

"You brought us to a Dracula hotel?" Eve hissed as the realisation hit, her pupils dilating and flashing silver as she watched the hotel staff glide back and forth with inhuman grace. Her fingers clutched mine, the hairs on the back of her hand rising.

I squeezed her hands. "No werewolves will enter because it's vampire territory."

"Yes, but…" She shot me a look that would cut any man, and I paused, her fear morphing into very valid anger aimed squarely on me. "That vampire was starved and tortured. He wasn't in his right mind. Even freshly turned vampires don't behave like that, none here would dare."

She ripped her hands free, but I caught her jaw in my palm and tilted her face up to meet mine. Accusations swam in her eyes but I held her fiery gaze. "You are safe here. I would kill anyone who laid a hand on you, vampire or otherwise."

Her mouth opened and then closed slowly, and I had to tap into my self-control as my focus snagged on her lips.

"Darius owns the hotel, they were warned to expect us. Everyone will be on their best behaviour."

"Okay." She nodded, inhaling and exhaling a slow, deliberate breath. "I don't like it, but I know not all vamps are like that. It's gonna take time."

We both knew time wasn't a luxury we had. But she had hugged Jonas before we left, her fear wasn't of all vampires—just strangers. It wasn't necessarily a bad thing given some vampires were sick bastards, like Lars. Her fear was understandable and the last thing I'd wanted to do was throw her in the deep end, but I also needed her safe, and this was the only haven we had available.

"It's ironic that the only way to stay safe during exile is hiding out with vampires when they're part of the reason we were exiled in the first place." Eve's top lip curled in disgust as she spoke of Lars, knowing full well every vampire nearby would hear. But it was purposeful, because when she lifted her chin to face them, not a hint of fear leaked into her voice. "I'm grateful Darius is such a strong ally of ours."

In every wolf, especially males, there is an inbuilt desire to protect your pack. This is heightened when you have feelings for someone, but fuck me was I unprepared for how hot it would be watching Eve exert her dominance on a bunch of vampires. The dull ache in my healing nose faded into the background as blood rushed elsewhere.

I chuckled, slipping my arm around her waist and guided us towards the VIP desk. "They're all well fed and fantastic hosts. We have nothing to worry about, for tonight at least."

She shot me a murderous glare, sidling closer to me. "I feel like a mouse staying in a cat's lair."

"You're not a mouse, you're a wolf. An apex predator," I reminded her, leaning in so my lips skimmed the shell of her ear.

I didn't miss the shiver she tried to hide with a roll of her shoulders as she bit her lip, the ghost of a smile slipping through.

There was a weird distance between us that I didn't like, but I could still see my Eve. The last forty-eight hours had been a disaster, but she was still here.

I pressed a kiss to her cheek before straightening as we reached the front reception. A woman with a tight blonde bob that accentuated her pale skin greeted us with a nod, tabbing the fancy headset strapped to ear. She held a hand up in apology until she was finished, politely signing off the call before turning to us with a smile that faltered for a millisecond at the sight of my bloody appearance.

"Welcome to Château Minuit. How can I help you?" The girl asked, in the same sing song voice I was convinced all receptionists had.

Eve tucked into my side, mumbling under her breath. "Minuit? I know he's a vamp, but Darius is a little too obsessed with the darkness."

"Midnight? Yeah. I guess between that and the Dark Night he does have a bit of a thing." I grinned at the connection my brain had never bothered making before. Darius and Jonas met in Paris over two hundred years ago, the timelines were blurry because they only spoke deeply of the past when we were all one too many drinks in. "Darius once told me that the moon gifted him Jonas, and so he owes his life to the night."

"Wow." She tilted her head, letting it rest against my arm. "I guess romance really isn't dead. Maybe he should give you some lessons."

The receptionist tapped her manicured nails against the shiny desk, coughing to get our attention. "Can I help you?" Irritation clipped her every word.

"Hi, we need a room for two please." I reined my amusement in, Eve's joke making the corners of my lips twitch.

The receptionist arched an eyebrow at my dishevelled appearance, but her smile didn't falter at the sight of my face—it grew hungry.

I ignored the way her eyes raked over my body, focusing instead on how Eve's nails bit into the back of my hand. So much for her nerves, she looked ready to stake a bitch. "Darius would have rung ahead."

His name alone got her attention, and the receptionist's spine straightened. "I have a suite on the top floor for a Mr. Whelan?"

"A suite?" Eve cut in before I could confirm.

I didn't miss the way her cheeks flushed, and it wasn't because of the raging winter winds that had chased us inside.

"Yes, adjoining rooms along with living quarters." The receptionist barely spared Eve a look, tossing the key card onto the desk. Her ruby-painted lips stretched into a feline smirk to reveal a hint of a fan as she fixed her hungry gaze on me once more. "I'm sure I can find a separate room for the hybrid if necessary."

I hissed in a sharp breath, levelling the woman with a scorching look of disgust. Darius did not run with vamps that pushed archaic views.

A low growl rumbled in my chest as I stood to my full height, towering over the ignorant vampire as I braced both hands on the desk. "Disrespect her again, I dare you."

The receptionist opened her mouth, her eyes widening as my fingertips made crescent-shaped dents in the marble desk.

"The suite is perfect, thank you." Eve cut in front of me, snatching the room card up. She reached out to tap the name tag clipped to the receptionist's dress, her claws extended in a silent warning. "Chloe. I'll be sure to let both Darius and Jonas know how welcoming you've been."

With that, she hooked her arm with mine and pulled me in the direction of the elevators. Her touch was the only thing stopping me from giving Chloe's bleach-blonde hair some blood-tinged highlights. As we stalked towards the elevator, Eve's heart rate sped up and I couldn't tell if it was anticipation or frustration.

Once we were alone, I'd have to tell her the truth, and then she'd regret not asking for her own room. I mean, who would want to share a bed with the guy who turned her world upside down in all the wrong ways? She'd lost so much since I'd come into her life. She'd given me my sister back, and I... I'd let her best friend die.

CHAPTER 7

EVE

My shoulders slumped, my snotty receptionist fuelled anger dissipating at the sound of the door clicking closed behind us, shutting the world outside off. For the first time since the horrors of the ball in Dublin, my lungs filled with air freely, my rib cage no longer feeling as if it might cave in. We were safe, for now.

Luke stood behind me, his presence as tangible as the silence stretching between us as I took in our room—our *suite*. There was a fireplace with a plush fur rug and a luxurious suede couch nestled in the cosy corner. Matte black walls contrasted with the pale ash chevron floorboards, the flickering candles on the silver chandelier hanging above a large bed casting a warm glow over the room. Speaking of the bed, it was a gothic version of the princess bed I'd imagined as a kid. Burgundy netting was tied to each of the four posts a contrast to the silk bedding that looked like a black cloud I wanted to sink into and never leave.

I moved further into the suite, buying myself time to find the confidence to voice the questions in my mind. Our teasing jokes in the middle of running for our lives, the way he'd held me as we watched his uncle's house burn, something had shifted. We needed to talk about what happened, but the words were lodged in my throat, the answers a pill I wasn't ready to swallow.

The bathroom was obnoxiously large, a bath that looked more like a Jacuzzi visible through the half-open door with black accented fixtures that contrasted the white marble tiles. To the right, a large window spanned the exterior wall of the room, with a door at one side that led onto a balcony. Sweeping crushed velvet curtains pooled on the floor, an obsidian waterfall framing a perfect view of the setting winter sun piercing broken clouds to cast a golden glow across the London skyline.

Opposite the bathroom, dim red lighting spilled through a second doorway. At first, I expected a lavish wardrobe that wouldn't have been out of place in a lavish room like this, but as I moved closer a narrow corridor came into view. Unless we were about to take an impromptu trip to Narnia, this was no wardrobe.

"It's the second bedroom for the suite, identical to this one," Luke answering the unspoken question my furrowed brow had raised.

I pulled the door open fully to find another at the end of the corridor. "Adjoined rooms?"

My heart sank. I stepped back into the main room, my urge to explore dying at his explanation. The small comfort his protective attitude with the receptionist had created was stripped away, replaced by the sting of rejection. After everything we'd been through, staying in separate rooms felt like a step backwards. It wasn't as if he'd chosen to leave with me, we'd been exiled. After everything we'd been through, staying apart felt like a rejection. As if he couldn't get away fast enough. Who could blame him?

"Well, because vampires are the main guests at Château Minuit, they often come here with..." Luke scratched the back of his neck, the corners of his lips twitching. "Friends."

"Friends?" I arched an eyebrow, walking back towards the window to study the skyline. It took a conscious effort to keep my voice calm, leaning into the comfort of jokes to plaster over the rejection I was feeling. "You mean snacks?"

"No," Luke's tone was firm, but edged with humour. "Darius would never allow that. Vampires can feed on other creatures, each other, or humans. It just makes sense to have easy access to their partner or friends."

My cheeks heated, so I kept my focus on the setting sun. I had a lot to say about that, and my brain was now wondering about vampire orgies and hoping the hotel had *very* thorough cleaners, but the nervous energy in the air between us was killing the mood.

Luke was keeping his distance, the reflection of his hazel eyes in the window tracking my every movement as he waited. His face was unreadable, a patchwork of healing bruises that gave nothing away. I needed answers.

We were exiled. I'd survived being bitten by a vampire, the same one that had attacked my human best friend. I'd no idea what happened after I lost consciousness in that ballroom. I didn't know what our exile meant for Tom and the Crescents. What happened to Larissa? What about the caged witch that had escaped? I had so many questions, but the one that scared me the most was top of the list.

"I need to know, Luke." I inhaled deeply, adrenaline spiking once more as my body's urge to protect me from more pain warred with my need for the truth. "Where's Craig? What happened after I passed out?"

The shadows in the room were palpable as my question hung in the air between us.

I wasn't ready, but I needed to know. Running for our lives had been a great distraction, but in the silence of the room only one image stood at the forefront of my mind.

Luke's jaw worked for a long time before he spoke. "You nearly died."

I turned, finally lifting my gaze to meet his. My response died on my tongue at the intensity in his silver-ringed irises.

"You nearly died." He repeated as he closed the distance between us in one step, his strained voice cracked on the last word. "Your heartbeat slowed to the point I thought you were gone. Darius and Jonas weren't sure if they could stop the venom, no one knows how these things work for hybrids."

My mouth opened and closed but no words came out. I'd felt it, my grip on life slipping as I'd faded in and out of consciousness while they tried to drain the venom. All I remembered was voices, death's icy tendrils taking hold, and Luke's tear-stained face staring in horror.

Luke's hands found my waist, the warmth and weight of his touch a tangible reminder that I was here. I was alive. He held me as if he needed that reassurance more than I did. "I thought I'd lost you."

"I'm here," I whispered, placing my hands over his as I remembered the crescent-shaped marks he'd left on mine from holding my hand so tightly while our friends worked to save my life.

He dipped his head, his eyes closing and his pain tangible as he brushed his lips across mine. My breathing hitched, the venom side-effects rearing into life once more at the simplest touch.

"When I the vampire attacked you, I saw red. He was dead in seconds, but I was too late. Vampire venom is lethal for werewolves, I needed to get you to the only person I knew who could stop it from reaching your heart. Jonas helped me bring you straight the Dark Night."

Disjointed memories that were mostly a blur flashed through my mind. Visceral agony as the venom entered my bloodstream, but the pain of watching my friend fall before my eyes was more painful. It was as if someone had chucked a bucket of cold water over me.

"You left Craig?" I recoiled, tears springing from the corner of my eyes at the thought of him abandoning my friend. The guilt followed, knowing I was responsible for dragging my human friend into this world.

Luke shook his head, the muscle of his jaw feathering. "I had no choice. We needed to get you treated immediately."

"Tell me you didn't." My voice was a barely audible cracked whisper, tears falling in earnest down my cheeks as my hands fell away from his.

"I—"

I slammed my palms against his chest and shoved him away with a force that surprised both of us, my voice rising. "Tell me you didn't leave my friend to die. You said he was alive!"

Craig's dead. He hadn't voiced my fear, but the guilt of his lie was written all over his face. My chest tightened, my lungs starved of air at the thought of the very venom coursing through my veins being the same weapon that stolen my friend's life.

"Dylan and Josh did everything they could." Luke caught my fists as I thumped his chest, his voice pleading as a heartbroken mix of fear and worry shone in his teary eyes. "I promise they tried. The venom takes hold too fast."

"You should have saved him!" I screamed, ignoring the crestfallen expression as I ripped myself from his grip. "What use is fucking magic and the paranormal if you can't save someone?"

He raised his hands in self-defence, but stood firm, refusing to back away from the flames of my fury. "We saved you."

"My life wasn't worth saving." My voice cracked, tears thickening in my throat so much I could barely get my words out. "I was the reason Larissa took him. Craig was an innocent in all of this, he deserved to live."

"There's nothing we could have done. The venom takes hold too quickly."

"It's all my fault. First Kate and now Craig. Everyone who cares about me dies." I fisted my hair, shaking my head as if it would change the past, as if I could erase it from time and memory, before advancing on Luke once more as grief broke into rage like a wave. "It's my fault he's dead."

"You are not to blame for Larissa and Damien's fucked up plans."

My venom and grief fuelled anger gave me enough strength to send Luke stumbling back is I slammed my palms into his chest. His eyes narrowed as his back hit the nearest bedpost, a low growl of warning rumbling. "You did nothing wrong."

"Craig didn't deserve this."

Luke fingers closed around my fist except this time his grip was unyielding. He held me against him, my protests in vain now that he had a full grip on me. He caught both wrists in one hand, them between us. His face was inches from mine, the intensity in his words piercing through my furious haze as placed his thumb under my chin and forced me to look at him. "My priority was you and saving your life. Hate me all you want, but I'd do it again faced with the same choice because you lived. You're alive and breathing and *that* is what matters most to me."

"You should have saved him over me."

"Don't ask me to regret the decision I made because I won't. I will never apologise for choosing you. It wasn't a choice." His voice was thick with emotion as he met my fiery gaze with his own, the silver surrounding his irises pulsing as if it were in sync with his heart.

I hiccoughed as another sob racked my body, pain and self-loathing warring in my mind and protesting his words. "It should have been me."

"Don't you dare say that." He caressed my jaw as his own tensed, his grip on my wrists loosening so he could pull my body flush against his. "Don't you ever fucking say that. Your life is important. *You* are important. I know this isn't what you wanted for Craig, but we will make it work."

My brow furrowed, grief robbing my lungs of oxygen and me of the ability to think. "Make what work? He's gone forever and it's because of me."

The words hung in the air between us, the image of Craig's lifeless body seared into the back of my eyelids.

Luke's frown mirrored my own until realisation dawned on

his face, his tone softening. "He's not dead, Eve, at least not in the normal sense."

I shook my head, uncaring as my snotty nose brushed against his hand at the movement. All sound seemed to leave the room, my ears ringing as if I'd dived head-first off a cliff at altitude and the world was spinning out of control.

My heart hammered at an erratic rhythm, my tongue thick in my mouth. Venom fuelled shock and adrenaline coursed through my veins, my thoughts racing in foggy circles. "I don't understand."

The edges of my vision darkened, and my body swayed, as if she shadows in the corner of the room were closing in. My ears were ringing, Luke's voice a distant muffled echo as if we were on opposite ends of a tunnel. Reality slipped from my grasp, a cloudy, hazy dream swimming in and out of focus before me.

"Craig isn't dead, he's a vampire."

The shadows took hold, darkness engulfing my world.

CHAPTER 8

As if I wasn't on the verge of heart failure from watching Eve dance on death's door with vampire venom, I got to relive that fear all over again when she collapsed in my arms. Her mouth hung open, her pupils dilating until all that remained were pools of black ringed by a sliver of blue before they rolled into the back of her head.

I caught her as she swayed, and her knees buckled as her body shut down from either shock, magic, venom.

"It's okay, I have you," I murmured, using all of my remaining self-restraint to refrain from yelling her name and shaking her awake. I focused on her steady heartbeat to stop myself from spiralling. She needed my protection. I had to keep my cool for Eve's sake, jolting her awake would do more harm than good. "You're safe here."

I wasn't sure if she could hear me, but I was more talking myself down off the proverbial ledge than trying to reassure Eve. She'd just found out her remaining human best friend was a vampire. Anyone would faint over that. She was unconscious, not dead. *Not dead.*

The logical part of my mind knew that from the rise and fall of her chest, and a deeper part of me could feel her, a tangible presence in my mind. But that didn't stop my fears from running wild down all the darkest avenues.

The moment I hoisted Eve into my arms and cradled her against my chest, her eyelids fluttered closed and a soft sigh slipped from her lips.

My stomach flipped in protest, my instincts howling that I needed to wake her. But that would be selfish. If her body had tapped out, it was because she had overdone it, she needed rest. Gallivanting across the sea and being chased by a murderous werewolf sent to off us, followed by escaping a house fire, was not what the doctor prescribed following a near-death experience. Never mind being faced with staying in a hotel run by the very creatures that turned your best friend and almost killed you recently. I'd put her through too much.

Her forehead didn't feel clammy when I pressed a gentle kiss to her temple, which went some way to ease my fears. I moved slowly, careful not to jolt her as I crossed the room and gentle lay her on the velvet couch, taking the faux fur blanket folded across the back and placing it over her legs.

As my hand brushed Eve's hip something snagged my wrist, that small stupidly painful stinging slice that only paper could cause. I frowned at the small sliver of white sticking out of her front Jean pocket, pinching it between my finger and thumb and tugging it free.

A folded piece of paper slipped from her pocket, its edges jagged and one corner torn. My heart leaped as I recognised the writing scrawled across the lined pages as I unfurled it. One of the pages from Jer's notebooks.

"You beautiful genius," I murmured, the healing cut on my jaw protesting as a grin stretched across my face.

I vaguely remembered her taking it, and as I studied the letters and numbers that made no sense, I couldn't help but lean into the budding shred of hope that bloomed at the gibberish in front of me. I had no idea what it meant, but it was something to go on. And fuck, did the universe owe us a win.

"What would I do without you?" I shook my head, tucking a stray strand of hair behind her ear, knowing full well the answer to my question was that I'd be lost. I was lost before I found her, and somehow she was helping me find parts of myself along the way. Now we had something to work with, a thread to pull on. "Rest for now, we'll figure this out in the morning."

She made a soft sound of protest at the broken contact when I pulled away that made my lips twitch, before clutching the soft fabric and pulling it tighter around her tiny frame. At the same time, she threw one leg over the blanket.

I stood there for a long time, just watching the rise and fall of her chest and the quiet snores she made as her body slowly released the mountain of stress she had been forced to endure. The sound of her breathing growing calmer went some way to unfurl what felt like thorns constricting my heart.

Images of bloodshed in the ballroom behind my eyelids chased any chance of rest away so I waited and watched Eve for what felt like hours. Darkness gradually cloaked the room as the sun greeted the moon and the city of London sprawling below us morphed into a different beast altogether.

I was fiddling with the light dimmer on the wall when a weird tapping came from the window. A raven hopped along the balcony floor, pecking the glass with its beak.

Eve barely stirred, her soft snores that had become a sort of calming metronome pausing briefly. I walked over to the glass door leading to the balcony, silently shooing the bird and broadening my shoulders to intimate the creature.

It hopped up on the balcony rail and turned to face me, its black eyes unblinking. The sense of calm that had settled in the suite morphed into something more sinister as I banged the window to scare it off. The raven's head swivelled to stare at me, the movement jagged and unnerving in the kind of way that reminded me of the horror movies I used to stay up late watching with Dylan and Josh. The bird solidified that feeling when it let out a shrill squawk, spreading its wings wide before torpedoing itself at the window.

"What the fuck?" I jumped back, watching in horror as the raven struck the glass right where my face had been.

The raven's body hit the window with so much force that a spiderweb of cracks formed where its sharp beak struck. Its claws screeched against the pane of glass as the bird slid down the door and dropped to the ground.

"Luke?" Eve's groggy voice pierced my shock, and I turned to find her sat up on the couch, rubbing her eyes twice as if she couldn't believe what she was seeing. "What's going on?"

I stared open-mouthed at the bird lying motionless on the ground, wiping my hand across my face. "I have no idea. The bird randomly took offence to my face?"

Neither of us laughed.

I turned the key in the door, wrinkling my nose at the creepy sight of raven blood streaking the glass and dripping from the base as it opened inwards. The dead bird's wings were stretched wide, those black eyes unseeing as it stared up at me. My brow furrowed, that all too familiar sense of dread knotting my shoulders as I noticed a ribbon tied around the raven's neck.

"Stay over there," I ordered without looking over my shoulder as the noise of Eve's footsteps padding on the wooden floor, along with the rustle of the blanket she was wrapped in. "I don't know what this is."

She scoffed, but her steps halted. "It's just a bird."

"It's a raven, and there's an unproven legend that extremely old vampires can either become on themselves or possess them as messengers." I swallowed the bile rising in my throat as I picked up the dead bird, turning it over in my hands to confirm my suspicion. Tied to its neck was a small black envelope that blended in with the raven's feathers. "Maybe it's not such a myth anymore."

Eve's face paled, her eyes widening as I turned to face her with the dead raven in hand and detached the envelope from its neck. "You said we were safe here."

"We are safe, in that they can't get in here. There's nothing stopping anyone sending a message, and this is definitely one hell of a message." I sighed, turning the envelope over in my hand.

There was no address, a tiny wax seal my only indication of who this was from. The seal was stamped with the London City pack's crest, the English flag centred at the coat of arms flanked by two blood thirsty wolves and the phases of the moon at the top forming a crown.

Eve moved closer, eyeing the raven and envelope with the same level of contempt. "What is it?"

"A note from the alpha of the London City wolf pack." I slipped a note from the envelope, my unease surging as I read the calligraphic message scrawled on the paper. "Dear Mister Whelan, Mr. Edmonstone requests a meeting with you at once. Please present yourself at the below address tomorrow, at one pm sharp. Regards, Henry Edmonstone, Alpha."

"I guess I don't exist then." Eve scuffed the edge of the plush rug beneath our bed with her foot, her eyebrows knitting together.

"I'd rather you didn't exist to them, that way you would be safe. But I'm not stupid enough to believe that." I crumpled the note up in my hand and tossed it with perfect precision into the empty fireplace, ashes scattering in its wake staying within the spelled bubble of the grate. "I won't be letting you out of my sight, and I most certainly won't be responding to a summons."

She cocked her head to one side, motioning to the dead bird flopping in my hand. "Is that wise? Their messenger was unnecessarily dramatic, and it feels a lot more like a threat than an invitation."

Before I could argue, a knock came from the door to the suite. My eyes narrowed as another brisk knock followed, and my body tensed. My senses didn't detect any signs of life outside the door, the only scents present Eve's and the general smell of vampire to be expected, but I wasn't taking any chances.

I reached behind me to slam the balcony door shut before approaching the main suite entrance, my shoulders set and my tired body ready to spring into action if needed. Flicking open the old-fashioned peephole revealed a tall, dark-haired, slight man dressed in the hotel uniform standing outside, holding what looked like a silver serving tray. Not a threat, but we hadn't ordered room service.

He jumped as I opened the door, confirming my theory that the rooms were soundproofed.

"Can I help you?" I planted my feet wide and stared the vampire down with one hand braced on the door frame while the other still cradled the dead raven's body.

The vampire's eyes widened, his pale lips popping open as he took in my bloodied appearance and the game in my hand. I wasn't one to make an entrance, but we were exiled and in danger, so leaving a lasting impression should work in our favour. Even if it was a slightly psychotic one.

"Good evening, Mr. Whelan." The vampire's throat bobbed as his gaze travelled over my face and dirty clothes that I hadn't bothered to clean, his eyebrows shooting up as the raven's head drooped to one side, broken bones from its snapped neck peeking through a mess of bloody feathers.

"Luke, please. Call me Luke," I corrected with a slow blink, licking my lips in a silent command for him to get to the point. As scary as I looked at that moment, I really wanted to get rid of the dead bird and get us both cleaned up. I'd had one too many surprises for the day. Eve hung back behind me, and I kept my foot jammed in the doorway, enough to keep the door open but my girl out of view.

"My name is Lawrence. Upon being informed of your arrival, Mister Montgomery assigned me as your personal assistant for the duration of your stay in London." Lawrence's shoulders stiffened, meeting my gaze with a cool one of his own as he smoothed any shock from his expression.

He definitely wasn't a newbie, which was good. Not that I'd expect anything else from Darius.

"Darius will send some clothes tomorrow, though he has supplied funds to procure anything you require." Lawrence whipped out a gold bank card from his pocket, pressing it into my hand without so much as hesitating at the sight of my blood crusted nails.

I wasn't surprised Darius had been informed of our arrival, or that he'd figured we had no way to contact him when I didn't give the heads up myself. I appreciated everything he did, but I wasn't sure I wanted him to dress me. If I was going to have to get in contact with other alphas, I didn't want to turn up in a three-piece suit with big dickhead energy.

"Great." As I took the card, I caught the distinct scent of metal and realised the trim was *actual* gold. "Is that it?"

"I do believe Mr. Montgomery requires your attention imminently." He lifted the domed lid to reveal not the dinner I'd expected but couldn't smell, but two shiny new mobile phones laid out like they were a meal. My stomach growled its disappointment.

"Can you send us up some food?" I asked, quickly clarifying before he decided to send up a platter full of Type O. "Pizza, something easy like that."

The vampire blinked slowly, his pale face humourless. "Excuse me, sir?"

"Food? We're starving and I presume Darius' credit extends to feeding guests, no? Even vamps like a burger now and then."

His eyes widened, and the molten depths of his irises flared as I addressed Darius so casually, his jaw feathering at what was probably deemed an offence. He nodded curtly. I needed them to know me and Darius were close. I trusted his staff, but they needed to remain tight-lipped about our presence here.

"Mister Montgomery requires your attention." Lawrence repeated, his fangs flashed into view as he spoke.

As if on cue, one of the phones buzzed, rattling on the silver platter as a number flashed up on screen. I recognised it immediately. Not Darius, my father. Not for the first time that day I wondered what exactly I'd done to piss off the universe.

My groan of frustration was cut short as something snapped behind us, and I spun to see the note I'd tossed in the fire burst into flames. Ashes flew from the grate all over the carpet despite the spell to hold them as the fire took hold, the logs in place igniting at a speed that defied human chemistry.

The vampire peering over my shoulder jumped back with a cry and pain shot from my fingertips. I dropped the raven on reflex as it too combusted, flames flaring into life and engulfing its lifeless body. Seconds later, the only traces of the bird remaining were black tendrils of smoke lingering in the air and a horrified Lawrence standing in front of me with one singed eyebrow and a thunderous expression that morphed into one of horror as the smoke formed a string of letters.

Two words.

Come alone.

CHAPTER 9
EVE

My best friend was a vampire. Craig. The same guy who had held my hair back on countless collect nights out while I puked my guts up. The one who pretended to be my boyfriend to ward off creepy guys. The friend who would turn up with his grandmother's cookies and a shitty rom com when I was having a rough day. *My* Craig was a *vampire*.

Despite the revelation, a sense of relief had settled over me to sooth some of the guilt since Luke's admission because Craig was alive. Well, not technically alive as in the living, but he wasn't dead in the sense I'd never see him again. Selfish or not, that's what mattered most to me.

"Is he okay?" I took a sip of the coffee Luke had helped us to when we'd snuck out the kitchen door of Château Minuit, the warm liquid lending me a small spark to battle the tiredness in my bones.

"You heard Darius, he's doing well." Luke gave my hand a squeeze, the shadows under his eyes a matching pair to mine as his head swivelled from left to right non-stop while he scanned the streets around us.

He'd been like this ever since we'd taken a fancy car with tinted windows from the hotel, getting dropped off at a random location to avoid being tracked. Whether he had a vice hold on my hand or hooked his fingers through the belt loop of my jeans, he maintained constant contact with me as if I might simply vanish before his eyes. I wasn't mad about it.

Luke had stayed up late on the phone bringing Tom up to speed and eventually Darius joined the line. I'd stayed awake long enough to grill him for updates on Craig. Once they confirmed he was doing well, the adrenaline rush from the raven incident faded, and my body called time on things. I'd drifted off into a restless sleep haunted by visions of vampires and flames.

At least my vampire venom fuelled side effects had passed, so I no longer wanted to jump Luke's bones at inappropriate moments. Instead, I felt like I'd gone on a week-long drinking session and was paying the price, it was the hangover from hell. Headaches, chills, nausea and next level anxiety. Losing the sickening urge to drain people of their blood was a small mercy.

I was relying on caffeine to get me through the morning, although judging by the rate the questions began to spill from my lips, I probably needed to dial it back a few espresso shots. "Does he know what happened? Will he still look the same? His gran! He'll need to tell her, he can't be kept away from family. Did it hurt? Was he scared?"

A myriad of expressions crossed Luke's face, the final one amusement. "The transition isn't painless, but he's past that part. Adjusting to his new life... that will take time."

"I don't know how he's going to come to terms with this. Craig's a lover, not a killer."

Thanks to the constant drizzle that had descended, we were able to hide under a nondescript black umbrella as Luke played navigator. I felt like a fugitive, I mean I *was* one, as we hurried down the streets of London City and tried to blend in with the crowd.

"Vampires don't have to kill to feed. Lars follows the old archaic ways, most modern vampires have at least a shred of morals."

I ducked left as Luke stopped paying attention to the umbrella he was carrying and almost took my eye out. "How do they feed then if they don't harm humans?"

"Witch blood works fine, along with a few others."

"I can't imagine a witch like Larissa offering to be lunch."

Luke chuckled, a rogue dimple showing on his cheek. "Despite lacking magic, humans actually work best and there are plenty of willing donors."

"Oh. *Oh.*" I thought back to the red-light corridor in our suite, my face heating. "So some humans like it?"

He winked, the playful smile lighting up his face throwing me off-kilter as he led us off the main street down a small laneway carved between two buildings. Before I could question the detour, he stole the breath from my lungs as he spun me so my back was pressed up against the brickwork. His hand slid down my arm to my wrist and pinned it above my head, shadows cast by the umbrella hiding us from onlookers as he closed the space between us so his body was flush against mine.

"Dirty, dirty mind." The husky gravel in his voice sent me spiralling as he leaned in to whisper. "There are many aspects of the paranormal world that humans find enticing, and for good reason. Not that I'd ever let anyone, vampire or not within an inch of your throat."

My lips parted in surprise and he took that opportunity to steal a kiss, robbing me of both oxygen my sanity.

"I'm more than happy to show you how good a werewolf bite can feel." He dragged his teeth over my exposed throat for emphasis, and my pulse thrummed in response, my free hand denting the paper cup of my coffee as I fought to regain a grasp of the English language.

Content with my inability to form a coherent sentence and the redness of my cheeks, Luke released me from his hold and stepped back.

"I meant blood bags from hospitals, though I like that's where your mind went first." He grinned and extended his hand to me, the gentlemanly gesture at odds with the dangerous glint in his eyes that held a promise of more. "Most vampires do prefer the vein and for those humans who enjoy the process, it can be mutually beneficial so long as they consent. Come on, we're going to be late."

I swatted his hand away with a scowl that had no bite behind it because all my mind could focus on was thoughts of him doing wicked things to me. He caught my hand, tugging me away from the wall and back into the centre of an alleyway that had bins stacked in one corner and shouldn't have felt half a sexy has it had when he'd pinned me.

Luke pressed his fingertips to the small of my back, guiding us back towards the bustling main street. I grumbled something about bossy wolves, readjusting my coat as if it would give me a sense of decorum back. I didn't need to catch my reflection in the next shop window to know that my face was on fire.

As I stepped back out into the pavement, a flash of copper across the busy road caught my eye. My boiling blood turned to ice.

"Eve?" He pulled up and stationed himself between me and whatever perceived threat I'd spotted. "What is it?"

A streak of red hair vanished behind the crawling traffic. I shook my head, blinking several times as if to summon what I'd seen, but when a black cab chugged forwards to move from view, there was no one there. Nothing but an expensive-looking glass jewellery window display. No redhead, no threat.

I sniffed the air, but all I could pick up was car fumes and the general cacophony of scents that belonged in a city.

Talk to me. Luke waved his hand in front of my face, his focus switching between me and the street swarming with tourists and locals like. *Is it the venom?*

"Nothing..." I exhaled slowly to centre myself, my surroundings zooming back into focus as a car horn blared. "I thought I saw Nadine, but it can't be her. I think I'm just imagining things. I didn't sleep well, we're both overtired, and it's been a crazy few days."

It couldn't be her. Nadine, the power-hungry redhead from the Faolchúnna pack who I'd caught Ryan cheating with, couldn't possibly have tracked us to London. Could she?

"That's an understatement." Luke's eyebrows drew together as he tipped my chin up to look at him, his hazel eyes searching mine. He broke contact only for a moment to glower at a stout man who went to shove past, making him think twice and give us a wide birth instead. "Promise you're okay? I don't think they could have found us this quickly."

"We don't even know if they'd follow us here. Surely getting your ex-girlfriend exiled from her home is enough?"

Luke snorted, but his laugh was charged with nerves. We both knew Ryan would stoop that low, following us to England would be aligned with his particular brand of psychotic. "I really wish it was. Please find another term for him, asshole would fit. The thought of him ever touching you or calling you *his* makes me want to turn into the alphahole you say I am."

The corners of my lips twitched at the possessive growl bleeding into his words. "Lead the way Mister Alphahole, we're gonna be late."

"Good thing it's just around the corner," he quipped, whipping out his phone to show off the time on the lock screen. "And we're fine thanks to my time keeping this morning."

I shoved my hair back from my face with a grimace, doing my best to ignore the sensation of my greasy roots. He'd robbed me of a proper shower after breakfast, and I still hadn't forgiven him for it. A quick rinse last night wasn't enough. I firmly believed standing under steaming water or trying out the Jacuzzi for hours would have done my venom hangover a world of good.

"I'm starting to have second thoughts about this."

"Contacting the girl's parents was your idea. And it's a good one, I just didn't expect Josh's mam to get an answer from them so soon." Luke shrugged, keeping a tight grip on my hand as we wove through the crowd while doing his best to whack anyone rude with the umbrella while keeping us covered.

Before passing out last night, I'd suggested contacting Gabriella's parents as an avenue of investigation. I hadn't expected them to be so eager to agree, but moving fast was a good thing. Especially after our ominous little raven visit.

"They were brought up to speed, right?" I took one last sip of my coffee before tossing the cold leftovers in a bin. "I don't want to have to be the bearer of bad news like 'Oh hey we think your daughter was kidnapped and possibly is being experimented on.' Breaking that news to you was one time too many."

He nodded, his thumb stroking my knuckles my tether to any sense of calm as we speed walked towards our destination. "They know everything we do about the kidnappings."

The rest of our walk was silent as I mulled over our breakfast appointment, struggling to keep up as one of his steps accounted for two of mine. The decision to ignore the morbid invitation was unanimous, Tom the most vocal in his orders to not engage. We needed answers and perhaps details surrounding Gabriella's abduction would help, especially when it came to why the Faolchúnna pack had targeted a witch.

"Almost there," Luke murmured, taking a quick glance at his rain blurred phone screen as we passed a sign for Covent Garden.

I stayed close to his side, damp beginning to seep through the canvas material of my sneakers as angry raindrops bounced off the pavement in front of us. We rounded one more corner, Luke stopping in front of a storefront build into a large building with age-dulled red bricks, the exterior woodwork painted black with an old-school sign rattling in the wind with the picture of a coffee cup. 'Stu's Brew' seemed as good a place to meet as any.

"Quick, it's about to come down." Luke opened the door, pressing his hand to my lower back to usher me inside.

A small bell dinging above the door announced our arrival. It was a modern spot with big light bulbs hanging from the ceiling that swayed each time the door opened to expose the sharp winter wind. Very hipster as Tom would say. Given the name I'd half expected the café to be run by witches, but the baristas rushing around the serving area all smelled human.

Luke followed me inside, shaking his hair out like a wet dog as he tied up the umbrella. My teasing insult died on my lips as that distinctive sense of magic crept over me. The way his head snapped up, his spine straightening to his full height as he rose to attention told me he sensed it too. Unlike Larissa's threatening brand of magic, this felt more like a gentle kiss of sunshine dancing in the air.

They must be here.

He inclined his head, then closed umbrella clenched in one hand like a baton as he took my hand with the other. I scanned the room for the source only to find a hooded figure sitting down the back of the café, their head down. Their face was completely hidden, a black baggy hoodie dwarfing their frame. The only giveaway besides the sense of magic was the untouched teaspoon stirring their cup of coffee.

This witch had come alone.

Luke's skin was alight, and a shudder of tension made him roll those muscular shoulders. His alpha senses were tingling.

That doesn't look like her parents. I pushed my thoughts to him, not missing how his hand tightened around mine.

Unease coiled in my stomach as we made our way towards the witch. Between the condensation coating the windows and the room divider partitioning off the serving counter obscuring them from view, they were impossible to see from outside. At the same time, their secluded spot had a clear view of anyone entering the premises. A smart choice. Calculated.

Luke refused to let go of me no matter how awkward it made navigating our way around tables as we moved towards the witch seated at the back of the busy café. Despite the conversations buzzing around us, all I could hear was the uneven breaths of the witch my senses had zeroed in on.

As we got closer, and I analysed the scent, the witch raised their head to confirm my suspicions.

I had no idea who had come to meet us, but it sure as hell wasn't Gabi's parents.

"Luke?" The witch lowered her hood to reveal a young woman that looked nothing like the picture of Gabriella that Josh had pulled up. No relative and definitely not the kidnapped girls' mother. Her gaze darted between us and the exit we were now blocking.

Luke widened his stance in response, his dripping wet hair and white-knuckled grip on the umbrella probably doing different things for me than the witch staring up at us. "Unless this is an impressive glamour, you're not Val—"

She held up her hand and rose to her feet, cutting him off mid-sentence. The door to the café blew open quickly only to slam shut as a gust of wind tore through the room. "I'm Maya, a friend of Gabi's. Sit please, we don't have much time."

Maya was only an inch or two shorter than Luke and couldn't have been older than seventeen unless she was masking her appearance with magic. While I'd learned that guessing a paranormal's age was often a futile game, especially when they had the ability to mask their age, the outfit consisting of cargo pants and a hoodie told me the witch's appearance wasn't glamoured.

Luke's jaw feathered, his eyes narrowing in suspicion and then annoyance as she kicked the chair opposite out from under the table, the legs screeching against the wet tile floor. "Where are her parents?"

"It was too dangerous for them to come." Maya's irritation at Luke refusing to take the seat faded as he shook her hand firmly, a smile of relief revealing the bronze glow at her cheeks. Box braids so long they brushed her waist swayed as she shook my hand next and gestured to the empty seat once more. "Eve, I presume? Please, take a seat. You're drawing attention to us."

There was a desperation to the witch's voice that told me she wasn't a threat despite her show of power. She radiated nervous energy, her focus lingering on the exit as if she was expecting a real threat to enter.

The barest hint of silver seeped into his irises at the order. Luke reluctantly took the seat, angling it so he could still see the exit at the same time while pulling one out for me.

"The Patel's send their apologies. Soon after your pack made contact, they received an anonymous order not to engage with you." Maya sat opposite us, her hands clasped on the table as she leaned in to speak. The teaspoon kept stirring continuously, as if it was a nervous tic similar to her knee bouncing under the table. "They were informed of the terms of your exile and instructed that it would a breach of protocol if they were to meet with you. It was less of a warning and more of a threat."

Luke's mouth hung open for a moment before closing and then opening once more as if the rage surging in his veins robbed him of words. The hand resting on my thigh flexed, the hint of claws appearing.

"I know. It's complete bullshit," Maya said, her shoulders shooting up as the bell chimed above the door, breathing a sigh of relief as a normal human entered.

"Since when do witches listen to a thing anyone else says?" Luke scoffed, rubbing his forehead with the heel of his hand in frustration. "Our exile only pertains to Ireland."

"I'm not your enemy. We can debate age-old rivalries all you want but that's not going to get us any answers." Her eyes narrowed into feline slits, the teaspoon clanging against the porcelain cup. "I came here on their behalf because Gabi is my friend, and I know what happened that night. No one would believe me until now, but you will."

"How can we trust you?" Luke countered, the cold edge to his tone catching me off guard.

"I'm not going to pop some truth serum to prove myself to you. I can show you a million photos of me and Gabi together before she was taken, but that would waste both of our time."

"I don't understand why they still wouldn't show. How could her parents care more about any threat than rescuing their daughter?"

"The threat is to one of your own. Late last night an anonymous message arrived claiming that it was in fact your pack's orchestrations and plotting that resulted in Gabi being taken. They claim to be able to rescue her if the Patels cooperate." Maya shook her head as Luke went to interrupt. "Gabi's parents know that's complete crap, but they fear what will happen to her if they are seen to get involved. So that's why I'm here."

"One of our own?" My blood ran cold as the witch pulled something from her pocket, slipping a small piece of paper across the table to us. Except it wasn't paper, it was a Polaroid of Jeremy.

I swallowed hard as I leaned in to look at the grainy photo, my heart sinking at the image captured. The Jeremy I'd seen smiling in framed pictures in his family home was on his knees, his wrists shackled and chained with his chest facing a wall to expose his back to us. His skin was marred with deep lacerations that looked like they were either caused by a whip or a dagger, open wounds no doubt doused in nightshade.

Maya shook her head. "This photo arrived along with the note. After reverse image searching and some digging on social media, I realised he was related to you and the rest fell into place."

"Who sent this?" Guilt clawed its way up my spine at the sight of Luke's uncle in pain because of us.

"We don't know. The Patels asked me to deliver the photo to you and not to interact, out of appreciation for your information on Gabi. But I've never been one to listen to my elders. I don't care about safety, it's a myth." She spread her hands on the table, a steely determination in her eyes and the set of her jaw. "If they took Gabi, there's nothing to stop them taking me next. I want her home."

"I know the feeling," Luke murmured, his fingers practically kneading my quads as he fought to keep control.

"That man in the photo, Jeremy, is Luke's uncle, and we

think he may have uncovered something that made them want him dead." I flicked open the only photo stored on the phone Darius had gifted me, placing it down over the Polaroid. "These are the only notes we could salvage, does it mean anything to you?"

Maya frowned, her eyebrows knitting together as she examined the photo and pinched the screen to zoom in on different areas of the page. "I'm beginning to regret studying the classics instead of archaeology. I don't understand the symbols, but I do know what some of the numbers mean."

"Addresses?" I gave Luke's had a squeeze as a spark hope rose from the ashes.

"No, they're library catalogue numbers. I worked in the university one over the summer. What do these have to do with Gabi? Books aren't going to help us rescue her."

Books. Not what I was expecting at all. Books felt all too ordinary a solution given our unique situation, but least it was an answer and not a setback for once.

I must have been thinking aloud because Luke shook his head, his tone grave. "Never underestimate the power of a book. Whatever Jeremy was researching led him to something important, possibly worth his life."

The witch nodded, fresh steam rising from her coffee mug as she circled her finger around the rim and teaspoon continued to rotate. "I still have university contacts in the library. I can find out what books he was looking for and where we can find them."

He sat forwards as if regathering himself, tearing his eyes away from the photo to meet Maya's steely determined gaze.

"Tell us everything you know."

CHAPTER 10

EVE

"One pepperoni pizza for the lady." A waiter with rosy cheeks placed a steaming pizza down in front of me, the smell of dough making my stomach grumble in anticipation. Vamp hotels had shit food. I get it, they're already dead but not all humans want to live on rabbit food.

I met Luke's gaze to find him grinning, more interested in my pizza induced glee than his own double cheese meat feast.

"What?"

"Nothing, it's just nice to see you smile." He shrugged, his foot brushing mine under the table.

My cheeks heated. "Well, it's been a while since we've had a chance to breathe freely."

We were in a tiny pizzeria not far from the hotel, a human establishment. It was a risk, but we'd kept our hoods up, and Lawrence had sorted us with a temporary glamour so no one would recognise us, allowing us to have our first date night in forever. When the waiter had called Luke my boyfriend, another broken part of me stitched back together.

There was Italian music playing in the background, each table covered in red-and-white chequered tablecloths, and the waiter bantered with the chef like they were family. I felt uncomfortable taking Darius' money. Luke had promised his dad would pay the vampire back no problem, but I didn't feel like he should have to cover my part. Not after everything. Knowing we were spending it on a small family-owned business and not a fancy clothes shop like Lawrence had encouraged, made me feel a little bit better about it.

I could only spend so long trapped in that hotel suite before my skin began to itch. We'd tried chilling in the hotel bar, but that hadn't worked. With all the vampires around having heightened hearing and one getting heavy with its very consensual prey in the back corner, any conversation died because it was too private for outside ears or I couldn't tune out the human's quiet sounds of pleasure.

Exiled, hiding in a pizza place wasn't very Bonnie and Clyde. Watching how my joy brightened Luke's features and those hazel eyes remained fixed on me, I was happy with whatever movie we were playing out.

"Do you remember the first time we got pizza together?" Luke was already halfway through his first slice.

I thought back to the night he'd found me in that police station, the sense of safety as I'd run into his arms. That night broke me, but somehow he held me together.

"Yeah, you asked me if I was the devil," I teased, choosing to focus on the sparks of light in the darkest of moments.

He rolled his eyes, a lump of burger meat slipping off his slice as he waved it about. "No, I asked if you liked pineapple on your pizza. That tongue of yours will land you in trouble someday."

I couldn't help but smile wider at the memory. Surrounded by so much loss and pain, that night he'd taken me in and brought me to meet his family. It had been the beginning of something new.

I stole a garlic dip off his plate, intent on making myself as undesirable to the vampires as possible, and dipped a pizza slice in before taking a bite. A little moan escaped my lips as my taste buds exploded. Oh, holy fuck.

"I missed this." My words were muffled by pizza dough and cheese as I took stuffing my face to a new level.

Absence really does make the heart grow fonder. A diet of salads and fancy foods had made me forget how good greasy food tasted. I was in heaven.

"If you keep making sounds like that, I'll have to show you what you're *really* missing." The huskiness in his voice caught me off guard, my mouth popping open mid-chew. His lips tilted in a smirk that promised dirty, not dinner table appropriate things. "Unless that's what you want, little pup?"

"I..." My eyes must have popped out of my head. I swallowed hard, coughing and reaching for my drink as the pizza lodged in my throat for a moment. No doubt my face was the colour of beetroot by the time I found my voice. "Should I be worried by how sexy you're finding me mauling a pizza?"

Luke hooked his foot around the back of my calf under the table, the wooden chair beneath me groaning as he pulled me closer. The hunger in his eyes made me gulp, grateful for the table between us because I feared he might take me then and there, in the middle of London with pizza smeared all over my face, and that just wasn't happening.

"I'm a little jealous that the last thing that made you choke isn't my cock."

"Luke!" I scolded, taking a gulp of my icy drink as blood rushed to my cheeks. I didn't need a mirror to know that my neck and face were a deep shade of pink, visibly squirming in my seat.

I was no prude, hell, I was Irish. I never thought I was one for dirty talk, but that man could say anything, and I'd happily drop to my knees. What was happening to me? I'd clearly lost my mind.

The pull between us was stronger, but maybe he was just like pizza. It had been a little while and cravings were normal, right?

Since my brush with death, there was this weird space between us, as if he felt he'd let me down. I felt the same way. I'd lost my new family and cost Luke his in the process, I'd been waiting for the rejection to come but it never did.

"What? Would you prefer if I kept it to myself?" Luke shrugged, casually munching on a chip loaded with garlic dip. He kept his leg locked around mine, his eyes darkening as he switched to the mind link. *Or should I just whisper dirty things in your mind instead? I could torture you all day, and no one would suspect a thing.*

Forget exile, this man would be the death of me.

I squeezed my thighs together and palmed my chest in an attempt to calm my heart that was urgently pumping blood to places I didn't need it. He enjoyed my squirming, and I silently cursed myself for choosing tights and a knitted dress from our Darius supplied closet. I was overheating, it was too hot. He was too hot. December may have been freezing in London, but Luke was a fire that seemed intent on engulfing me.

"Focus." I flicked a chip at him, sulking and trying to ignore the way my body was responding to his words. "We don't have time for games."

"I wouldn't call what I have planned for you a game," he mused, a wicked glint in his eyes as he licked his fingers clean.

I shook my head, pinching the bridge of my nose as I fought to keep myself under control. Thank fuck he hadn't pulled this shit when I was still dealing with the venom aftereffects or I'd have launched myself across the table and become an exhibitionist.

He wiggled his eyebrows as if reading my thoughts, and I scowled, digging my heel into his ankle. His damn leg didn't budge, intent on keeping contact between us.

"We need to figure out our next steps." I resumed munching my pizza, trying to make it as unsexy as possible. Though I didn't understand how a tomato sauce covered face was ever sexy in the first place. "Maya said that the night Gabi was taken, she went to meet up with a guy. I know she didn't have a description, and Gabi was being really shady about who it was, but it sounded so similar to what happened with Alice."

Luke stole his garlic dip back, already on his third slice of pizza when I was still on my first.

"Tell me more about the London alpha, after his freaky invitation and the Patels being threatened. I can't help but think he's involved."

"I never expected him to be an ally, but I didn't plan on him being deeply involved. I'd really hoped his appearance at the Dublin event was just because of his status. Maybe he's just a showy dickhead?" Luke sighed, stacking chips on top of a new pizza slice. "He's the overall leader of all the London packs, we needed his sway to back us contacting the other alphas. Without his backing, I'm not sure they'll believe us."

"Does he have any kids?"

"Two sons."

My brain was mulling away on something when my phone buzzed on the table.

There are tears of happiness, and then there are tears of pure joy. My heart had never been as full as when my best friend's name flashed up on that screen. Not only his name, but his face. Craig's very alive face.

"It's Craig!" I squealed, dropping the pizza slice in my hand and scrambling for a napkin.

Luke's hand shot out to catch my drink as I hit the glass, shaking his head with a laugh as water splashed all over his hand.

"Wait a second, you knew." I pointed my finger in accusation, but I couldn't wipe the grin off my face as I rushed to answer the call.

He didn't deny it, his smile only growing wider as I answered the call, and Craig popped into view on full screen.

My heart sang at the sight of him, tears stinging the corners of my eyes as I touched the screen where his cheek was. All of the fear and worry I'd harboured since seeing the vampire attack him bubbled to the surface, relief washing over me.

"What's up?" Craig's cheeks dimpling as his face lighting up.

The dam broke at the sound of his voice, tears springing from my eyes and rolling down my cheeks. He was alive. No amount of Luke, Darius, or Jonas reassuring me would assuage my fears until I saw it for myself.

"Hey." My voice came out squeaky, tears catching in my throat as I tried to take it all in.

Gone were the blue tips, his blonde hair now lighter and icy blonde in tone, complete with red tips. I couldn't tell if it was the transition or him getting his hands on box dye that caused the change, and I didn't care because he looked great. Better than great. Craig had always been pale, but the few freckles that once dotted his nose and cheeks seemed to have practically disappeared. His brown eyes were now a rich gold, the change noticeable despite the phone camera being able to pick up how breath-taking a vampire's eyes were.

Vampire.

"Hey?" Craig teased, his laughter a Band-Aid I didn't know I needed. "I die, and all I get is *hey*?"

"Only you would make a fucking joke about dying." I laughed despite the tears, my hand shaking as I balanced the phone against a salt shaker.

"Hey, if I have to suck people off for the rest of my life, I'm gonna make jokes."

"Craig!" My laughter descended into a giggle that vibrated in my chest. "That's not how it works."

He waved a dismissive hand. "Yeah, yeah. So Jonas keeps saying, but I have to drink blood, and I think I'd rather do it the kinky way or stick to blood bags. Except they kinda have a plastic taste that I'm not a fan of. If I must do it, I'm gonna make sure I enjoy the process."

Luke shook his head, muffling a laugh of his own. I glanced around the pizzeria to make sure we were alone. The only person out front was the waiter dancing around behind the counter to the radio, and if anyone did happen to hear they would just think we were unhinged.

They wouldn't be wrong.

"I'm so fucking happy you're okay." I chewed my lip, sniffing as I wiped my eyes with my sleeve. "I thought I'd lost you that night."

"I was awake before you were, kid. I'd thought I'd lost you too."

"I'm sorry you had to go through this, if it wasn't for me Larissa never would have taken you."

"Cut that out. I was snooping where I shouldn't when you had warned me not to. She probably knew I was digging through records and decided to kill two birds with one stone."

My nose scrunched in distaste at the images that analogy brought up.

"I know you told me about the wolf thing, but I didn't grasp the reality of your world until it was too late. I get it now. Don't fuck with the witches." Craig tapped the screen, his gold eyes narrowing. "It's not a life I'd have chosen, but it's really not so bad. I promise."

I nodded, fiddling with my sleeves. "Darius and Jonas, they're looking after you right? Teaching you the ropes?"

"Yep, apparently I'm pretty good at controlling the blood lust. The speed thing takes some getting used to, but at least I don't bruise like a peach anymore. Plus, the feeding thing isn't so bad. It sounds gross but once you turn, blood is like catnip."

"I know. My trip through the airport high on the venom effects was enlightening." I cringed at the memory, disgusted by the way I'd so desperately wanted to tear into someone's jugular and drink them dry.

"My skin looks incredible, and it's like I've got cool contacts in twenty-four seven. And the sex is amazing, apparently." He wiggled his eyebrows, just like his old self.

"Wait, why is your hair blonde?" Craig's eyebrows drew together, and he squinted, bringing the phone closer to his face.

I frowned and held up a strand of my brunette hair. Then I remembered the glamour.

"Oh, we had to use a glamour to leave the hotel tonight." I patted the seat next to me for Luke to come join me.

He was hovering off screen to give us some privacy, and I appreciated it, but I wanted him by my side. Despite my outburst in the hotel room when he broke the news, I knew he did everything he could to save Craig.

"A glamour?" Craig cocked his head to one side, the phone camera glitching as it fought to keep up with the speed of his hand movements. "Ooh, yeah! Jonas told me about the Fae stuff. Shit, there's just so much to learn."

"You'll get to grips with it." Luke scooted around the table to join my side.

"Lukey boy. Long time no see, you better be taking care of her."

"He is, all things considered." I laced my fingers with Luke's, pulling his hand onto my lap.

"Stop going all gooey eyed." Craig covered his eyes with his hand and laughed, his tone then growing sombre. "Tom and Alice explained about the exile when they visited."

I smiled at the thought of Luke's family looking after him, grateful to my pack. "It sucks. I wanted to come straight home to you."

"As much as I'd love to suffocate you with hugs, I'm not quite ready to risk biting my best friend's face off. I promise when all of this is over, we will have a sleepover and watch *Twilight* together with popcorn and make fun of the sparkly vampires. No boyfriends allowed so you can give me all the sordid details." Craig's impish features were so full of life and humour as he grinned. "Sorry Luke."

"There will be no sordid details," I interjected, jumping with a squeak as Luke's hand slid beneath my dress to squeeze the top of my thigh.

Luke winked, his hand settling in the most distracting position. "I promise there will be *plenty* to talk about."

"Good. If you have to be on the run, you might as well make the most of it." Craig saluted Luke, glancing behind him for a moment as if someone was talking. "I better go. Tom said he's heard from Lila, I'm not sure who that is. Even a vamp-charged brain can't keep up with all these names."

Beside me, Luke's shoulders sagged with relief.

The pizzeria door swung open, a draft of icy wind sweeping in to rob us of our short reprieve. Two men stood at the door, dressed in black suits with earpieces that made them look like they'd just stepped out of an action movie. Though the leather gloves made me think we might be living out the mafia dreams I never had instead. Through the sheet of rain pounding the pavement outside a sleek black car parked up with tinted windows, the headlights on and the engines running.

Werewolves.

I caught the scent of something that sent me hurtling back to that night in the Faolchúnna manor when I'd been hunted through the wolves. Nightshade.

"Eve?" Craig's voice blared from my phone speaker.

"We have to go." Luke jumped to his feet, positioning himself between me and the werewolves crashing our date.

The waiter looked up from his magazine with a bored expression, as if there was nothing that could walk through that he had never seen before. "Can I help you?"

"Luke Whelan?" One of the bodyguard wannabes spoke up, his thick cockney accent not quite fitting the bill.

I snatched my phone up off the table, moving to stand behind Luke. "We've gotta go, unwelcome company has arrived." I explained, grateful I no longer had to lie to my friend or hide the darker parts of my world from him. "I'll message you later, I'm so glad you're doing ok."

The wolves advanced, but we stood our ground. They didn't seem too pleased that I didn't end my call just because they'd rocked up. I was pissed. These assholes had cut my time with my friend short.

"I'll call soon. Darius and Tom want to speak to you later."

Luke's biceps strained against the sleeves of his shirt, a low growl of warning ripping from his throat.

I blew Craig a kiss, trying to commit his face on the screen to memory. Vampire Craig. "I'll try."

CHAPTER 11
LUKE

Helena often joked that I had an issue with authority, and she wasn't wrong. It took all of my restraint to maintain a calm exterior as we were escorted out of the car by two goons in suits. They forced us through an underground carpark full of fancy cars that I'd kill to take for a spin, and into a lift. I'd debated taking on the werewolves that cornered us and trashing the pizzeria, but once I'd caught a whiff of nightshade, I knew coming willingly was better than arriving weakened.

The London alpha worked in a shiny glass skyscraper that reminded me of Eve's shitty ex. The elevator stank of affluence, and not the earned by hard work kind. The type of wealth that passed through generations, gaudy and on display. With mirrored walls and a black chaise, complete with real gold finishes on the buttons marking each floor, every single thing about this building screamed that the alpha I was about to meet wasn't my kind of man.

We were supposed to try to raise support from other packs but after our morbid invitation and the timely threat to the Patels, it was clear someone in London didn't want us here. Henry Edmonstone was my prime suspect.

I'd heard rumours of his reputation, he was a buddy of

Damien's and lived up to his namesake. A player, cheater, wanker. Whatever you want to call it. And I did not appreciate being summoned.

Eve's arm was linked with mine, and she made a point of keeping one clawed hand clamped tightly around my wrist, as if she could feel my urge to burst from my skin. I could taste the tension in the air, and the alpha part of me wanted to strike a match to it. I wasn't sure if we'd all survive the ascent.

Counting floors as they rolled past at an agonisingly slow pace and fantasising about a sleek black Ferrari I'd ogled on the way in wasn't enough. So, I focused on keeping my breathing in sync with Eve's to keep myself from losing my shit entirely.

A grating ding announced our arrival at the penthouse, the doors sliding open to reveal a large foyer with three offices, natural sunlight casting prisms as it filtered through the glass exterior. A large nameplate marked the office front and centre as the alpha's, the other two assigned names I recognised as his sons as partners of the firm despite the fact they were both minors. Dream big, I guess.

"Alpha's 5 p.m. has arrived." One of the burley escorts announced, wrinkling his nose as he had to announce my name as if being exiled made us cockroaches. "Luke Whelan, exiled."

Eve stiffened at the snub.

On the last word, to punctuate the low blow, he shoved us out of the lift. I whirled on him, my upper lip curling back in a vicious growl of warning. He smirked back at me as the elevator doors sealed shut, and I was faced with a steel wall instead of my intended target. Denting it wouldn't do any good, my anger wasn't going anywhere.

Breathe. Eve's voice echoed in my mind, and I did my best to smooth my expression. I needed to channel my dad. Cool, calm, and collected. The inexplicable rage I felt when anyone laid a hand on my girlfriend was getting out of control.

The penthouse foyer was extravagant to say the least, with marble floors and an unnecessary water feature surrounded on all four sides by a stone border that doubled as a bench. Glass spanned the exterior, but the interior walls of each office had thick werewolf grade soundproofed walls. I couldn't hear any heartbeats besides the woman at the secretary desk situated outside the alpha's office, despite the shadow silhouette of a man moving behind the frosted glass of the door behind her.

I approached the secretary, taking my time to scan the foyer and mark any possible threats or escape routes. There were only two obvious exits, the elevator and a fire escape, though I highly doubted that the alpha didn't have his own secret way out.

His secretary barely spared Eve a glance as we stopped in front of her, instead looking me up and down as if appraising my worth. I guess my introduction and attire didn't pass the check, because she wrinkled her nose before pointing a dismissive finger towards the bench.

"Please take a seat, Mr. Edmonstone will be ready for you soon."

This wasn't a fucking doctor's appointment.

Another wolf entered the foyer, the way his expression turned to one of hungry lust as he scented Eve immediately raising my hackles. He disappeared into one of the son's offices, and I made a mental note to hand him his ass on a platter someday.

I leaned over the secretary's desk, drumming my fingers until she raised her head. "I believe it's rude to keep guests waiting. I don't believe I was introduced properly. I'm Luke Whelan, heir to the Crescent pack, and this is Eve O'Connor, my partner. We were personally invited by Henry himself."

"I don't see an invite." She sneered, flashing me a glimpse of her canines for my disrespect. No doubt she arranged the self-combusting invitation that lay in ashes back in our hotel suite.

"Fine." I turned on my heel, striding towards the alpha's office.

Since he had decided to abduct us to enforce this meeting, I was damned if I was gonna sit and wait like a good little boy. No, he had dictated enough. I wasn't playing by another pack's rules.

"Luke..." Eve hurried after me, clamping her hand around my arm. "What happened to calm?"

"The hybrid wasn't on the invite." The receptionist jumped to her feet, high heels clacking against the marble floor as she stepped out from behind her desk. As if she could stop us.

"Thought you didn't see an invite." My tone was flat as I shoved past, only using the minimum necessary force to get her out of my way rather than leaving a secretary-shaped dent in the wall. "She has a name, show some fucking respect and use it."

Silver bled into her green irises as she steadied herself before reaching under her desk, no doubt some sort of hidden panic button to summon security. "You can't do this."

I really don't like to be told what to do.

"If he didn't want Eve here, he shouldn't have forced our presence."

The elevator pinged and two men stepped out, stocky werewolves who had a bulge in their pocket that said they weren't happy to see me.

"She wasn't invited." The receptionist snarled, the two goons quickly moving to flank her.

They were too late, my hand closing around the door handle before they could intervene. I pulled Eve in front of me, flashing a wide grin over my shoulder at the three werewolves glaring daggers at us. "I got in the car without a scene, I even tolerated your snotty looks, but then you disrespected *both* of us. While I have complete trust in Eve to hold her own and would quite enjoy watching her maul you, I'm not leaving my girlfriend waiting outside. So, either she comes with me, or else this meeting doesn't happen at all. And your boss seems adamant that it must go ahead."

Eve grinned, the wolf part of me humming at the image my words conjured, but her laughter died as the door opened without any force, bringing us face to face with the London alpha. He looked more amused, than pissed at the scene we were causing.

She dropped back to my side as the door revealed a tall man, dressed head to toe in a flashy black suit complete with silver cufflinks that must have been spelled not to sting. Or maybe he liked a little zip to his handshakes.

"I thought I heard some commotion." Mr. Edmonstone stepped back and showed us into his office. "Please, do come in Luke. It's a pleasure to meet both of you."

Late twenties with short blonde hair and cold eyes, he was just as I remembered but older. I had been a teenager the last time we'd met properly, shortly before his father had passed away. Henry then became one of the youngest pack alphas in centuries. Now he had over a decade under his belt, and a confidence to match his arrogance.

I reached out to shake the alpha's hand, primed for a nasty sting off the silver which of course came. Sick bastard. I refused to flinch or show any sign of pain. "It's been a long time."

Don't touch the cufflinks.

Eve took his hand as he offered it, her fingers barely gracing his palm in a weak handshake that avoided the silver altogether. He looked between us, cocking his head to one side in question for a moment, as if trying to figure out how she knew, before directing us to the two seats in front of his ivory desk.

The marbled floors of the foyer extended into the office. Dark, walnut cabinets lined the walls, along with various family portraits and framed degree certificates. I counted two kids and a wife with a cold distant expression in the later photos. But that was all the information I could glean from the office. To get the answers I really wanted, I needed to hear it from the asshole's mouth.

"I suppose you're wondering why I summoned you here." The alpha leaned back in a large plush leather chair with his hands clasped. Based on the way his suit jacket stained across his pecs, it was one size too small, the top button holding on for dear life.

I bristled, dropping my hand to Eve's knee, my eyes

narrowing when his gaze dropped with it. "I did wonder how you knew we were in London."

"I have my sources. It's important that I keep tabs on any werewolves moving into my territory, welcome or otherwise." He waved his hand dismissively as if I would overlook his thinly veiled threat and roaming eye. "After that unfortunate scene in Dublin, I was informed of your exile. It made sense you would come to London given the family connections, though I did expect your father to join if you expected to seek sanctuary."

"I don't wish to join another pack." I leaned back in the chair and forced my shoulders to appear relaxed, despite the fact that every muscle in my body was ready to burst into action. The way he spoke to me, the alpha essence I could sense, it set me on edge. "My father is otherwise engaged at the moment, considering we just rescued my sister from the Faolchúnna pack."

"Ah yes." The alpha watched me carefully, intrigue sparkling in his eyes. "That incident."

I bit my tongue, trying to focus on the calm, collected demeanour my father always seemed to impose. There was a fine line between being an intimidating presence and losing my shit. My temper wouldn't do us any favours. Exiled wolf attacks another alpha was not a headline I wanted to bring to fruition.

"We did reach out for help from the other packs once we found out what the Faolchúnna pack were planning." I locked eyes with the alpha. "We never received any response. And when we didn't hear from my uncle, we were concerned. You don't happen to know where he's vanished to, do you?"

"Vanished? Impossible, I've received no such report."

I studied his reaction closely, but he didn't show a hint of surprise or worry. His mask remained perfectly in place, lacking the proper emotion and concern an alpha should display.

"Yes, he hasn't been since Monday. Nor has he attended his hospital shifts." I purposely didn't mention Jer's wife and kids. "Perhaps you need a new source."

"I'm sure he's fine." He stopped just short of rolling his eyes, his business-like tone when discussing someone's life grating on my already frayed nerves.

The word 'liar' was on the tip of my tongue. The calmness of his tone when speaking about the man he had bound and tortured was gasoline to the flames of my anger.

I must have been broadcasting my thoughts because Eve's hand found mine.

Don't. You'll endanger Gabi and her family.

Henry didn't try to fill the silence, rising to his feet and walking over to a drinks station by the window filled with everything from the finest whiskey to Fae wine and what looked like shot bottles of blood. The dark winter-dulled cityscape of London behind him was the perfect backdrop.

"Fancy a tipple?" He uncapped the whiskey decanter, offering a glass to me as if we were old friends talking and he wasn't yet another power-hungry leader with blood on his hands. "I've heard whiskey is your thing."

I shook my head, not missing the dig about my behaviour following Alice's disappearance. Eve following suit when he offered her the same.

Unperturbed, the alpha poured himself a generous amount. His gaze lingered on Eve, a feral smirk spreading across his face that made me want to rearrange it. "As for the other business you brought up, we have no evidence that the Faolchúnna pack as a whole is involved. From what I heard, that nasty kidnapping stuff was Nick's doing, and it's well known that Damien was losing control of his brother for some time. You killed him, did you not?"

Eve stiffened beside me, her jaw set. She could smell a rat from a mile away. Of course, the Faolchúnna alpha would blame the kidnappings on his dead brother. There was no low to which he wouldn't stoop.

"Yes, I took his head." I smiled at the memory, despite the gruesomeness and wishing it was either the Faolchúnna alpha or Ryan that I had ended instead. "Damien was injured, but not enough to stop playing games. From the information we have gathered, her has been working with both the Abhartach coven and Larissa to kidnap hybrids and other magical creatures."

"That is quite the accusation."

"Damien plans to use hybrids to breed new werewolves to strengthen the bloodlines again, with the intention of wiping out hybrids in the long run. Isn't that why you were there that night, Henry? Wife number two and a giant ass office not enough power for you?"

"My business in Dublin was purely business, Damien has always had a flare for entertainment. You're reading into things where there's nothing to find. What would Larissa or Lars have to gain from such an alliance?" The alpha re-joined us, perching on the edge of the desk opposite Eve. "What do you expect from me? This is all conjecture and speculation."

"My sister being held captive for years is not speculation."

The alpha shrugged. "As I said, you have no proof."

Eve all but growled, her knuckles white and nails digging into the pristine leather seats as she gripped the edges.

I leaned forwards, mirroring the alphas body language and keeping my shoulders squared and one eye on Eve. "My sister knows what she saw."

"Being held captive can addle the mind." Henry pressed his fingers together and stared off to the distance, as if deep in thought. "Perhaps she had to make up stories to keep herself going over the years. Word alone is not enough substance to such an allegation."

"I was the one who rescued her, I saw where she was being held. If you raided the Faolchúnna's lands you would find plenty of proof. Unless my entire pack's word means nothing to you?"

"You come to me with the word of an exile. You're not an alpha, Luke," he replied smugly, taking a long, victorious sip of his stupidly expensive whiskey.

"You have the word of my father too, but clearly you have little respect for us or the truth. The fact they didn't incite a war after we rescued Alice proves their guilt." I rose to my feet, and Eve shot up beside me. "Perhaps you're worried about what we would find."

"Acting rashly and making wild accusations is not the way of an alpha." He tutted, gesturing to his office and the sprawling city below as if he owned the place. "It's something I had to learn when dear Father croaked it. My sources say you have been behaving erratically since your arrival. Only being transported in unmarked cars and scrapping with another werewolf only hours after landing in England?"

It took all my restraint to school my expression. "Are you watching us, Henry? If so, you would know that wolf attacked first."

"You're an exile on foreign soil. You're well aware that without a pack, others can and will try to take their pound of flesh." The way his face lit up at that last word chilled my bones. "Digging where you shouldn't has already resulted in exile from Ireland. Haven't you lost enough?"

"Since when are you on the witch's payroll?" I snapped, leaning over the table towards him. "Selling out to the highest bidder. We've looked into it, I doubt the Scots or Welsh agreed to this."

My plan had been to talk him around, explain the truth, but from the moment he opened his mouth, the alpha wasn't interested. Handling this my father's way wouldn't work, I needed to be direct. Henry knew full well what they were up to, I could only hope that the other packs saw through his suave lies. If he wasn't on the witch's payroll, he was certainly on Damien and Ryan's. The only thing I wasn't sure of was the extent of his involvement. Was he just financial backing? A transport link? Or did this run deeper?

The alpha's jaw twitched. "I don't believe speaking to the other packs will do anything but incite panic. The few disappearances you have been looking in to have no links. This is the paranormal world, creatures die all the time."

"That's fine, I will contact them myself." I made sure to scrape the floors with the chair legs as I shoved it back and rose to my feet, holding my hand out to Eve. "I'd appreciate if you would tell your 'investigators' to keep their distance in future. Exiled or not, I can and will defend my own."

I turned to leave, guiding Eve in front when the alpha spoke up.

"I would like to speak to Ms. O'Connor before you both leave."

My temper grew wings and soared off a cliff, torpedoing into the fiery pits of hell, ready to erupt. I was seconds away from telling him where to shove his request when Eve caught my eye and shook her head, her voice entering mine.

I'll be fine. Let's see what he wants.

"Would it be alright if I speak with him, Luke? I'm sure Henry won't take long." She leaned up on her toes to press a pointed kiss to my cheek.

Instead of punching the alpha, I dropped my hand to the curve of her ass and crushed her body against mine. A low growl rattled in my chest as I pressed my lips to hers.

Her cheeks were flushed when I broke away, the kiss far too brief for my liking but enough to make a point. Not that she was mine, but an unspoken warning that I would not hesitate to rip him from limb if he touched a single hair on her head.

I held her hand to my lips, pressing a kiss to her knuckles before turning to the London alpha with a steely glare. "I'll be outside. You have five minutes."

With that, I stepped out of the office and slammed the door so hard the walls shook, and a single picture frame fell and smashed behind the receptionist's desk. I sat beside the water fountain, immune to its Zen, and fixed my gaze on the closed door as I counted.

Five minutes and I would put a wolf-shaped hole in that wall.

CHAPTER 12
EVE

Luke's kiss left its mark both on me and the atmosphere in the room long after he left. The alpha clearly didn't take kindly to the show of protection, but it did give me a confidence boost. Yeah, facing down an alpha we suspected had kidnapped and tortured Luke's uncle was scary, but I felt a hell of a lot safer knowing there was a literal guard dog waiting outside ready to rip his heart out for me. Before I'd entered this world, I'd have said that kind of thing was toxic. Maybe it was, maybe I'd seen too much. But it was exactly what I needed.

The alpha had pasted a predatory smile on his face when I turned to face him, still perched on the edge of his desk beside his fancy computer that he probably never used like he was some kind of finance bro. My gaze snagged on a flash drive sticking out of the hub beneath it, and I made a mental note. I moved back to my seat, making a point of keeping it half swivelled facing the door. I wasn't in the mood to play games anymore. Maya could call us any minute with the location of those books. I had better things to do with my time than sit here in silence. Hell, there was a Jacuzzi in our room. I'd had all kinds of plans before the alpha had interrupted our afternoon.

"Now that we're alone," he said, a red flag undercurrent to his words that set my instincts off.

I cleared my throat. "For five minutes, and I guarantee you it will be exactly that."

His upper lip curled at my tone, something he was probably unused to. He braced one hand on the tabletop as he leaned closer, whiskey sloshing in the glass of his hand as he waved the other about. "I have something to discuss with you."

"I'm not supposed to be here, unless my invitation got lost in the aviary?"

His eyes narrowed, zeroing in on their prey. While I often wished I was a true werewolf, being a hybrid did give me the backing to challenge wolves higher on the food chain outside of the full moon.

His hands were perfectly smooth, like he had never done a day's work in his life. His blonde hair was cut neatly, not a single blemish on his pale face. The bursting suit jacket was a testament to his ego, and if it weren't for his brown eyes, I might have thought him vampire. Everything about him screamed spoiled, self-indulged, and I found myself wondering if the packs actually approved of him being some kind of united leader or if it was just too late to stop him once he grew into his arrogance.

"Care to get to the point?"

I resisted the urge to smirk as blood coloured his cheeks, the first chink in his façade. His jaw tightened, fuelling my desire to push him until he tipped over the edge. However, as much as I'd enjoy watching Luke tear into him, we needed information.

"Yes, of course. What I want to talk to you about is your allegiances." Henry paused, as if waiting for another interruption.

I bit my tongue.

"You found out that you were a hybrid earlier this year, correct?"

If you need me, call my name, and I'll break his neck.

I nodded, trying to hide my smile as Luke's threat echoed in my mind. Everything about this alpha, the set of his jaw, the cocky tone to his voice, made my skin crawl. Call it a sixth sense.

"My allegiance is to the Crescents."

"That wasn't my question," he pressed, his eyes narrowing.

I shrugged, choosing my words carefully. "Yes, I found out earlier this year."

"You have gained incredible control over this time, and I have no doubt, that it is down to the excellent training and guidance you have received."

With each word, he studied my expression, and I made every effort to keep my face passive. Though I was far from stupid, I knew he was trying to insinuate that my control was thanks to Ryan. He didn't deserve credit for that, especially when he had tried to weaken both my self-belief and my powers. I was so much stronger without him.

"You know, with the right guidance, you could achieve great things. I'm sure I could pull some strings, even for a hybrid." The London alpha's tone poorly concealed his disdain for my kind. "I assume Luke has filled you in on the reputation of my pack and our extensive connections?"

I ground my teeth in an effort to keep my cool. "I've no interest in joining another pack. As I said before, I'm a Crescent and loyal to my pack."

He cocked his head, a taunting edge to his words. "From what I've been told, you first joined the Faolchúnna pack before beginning your involvement with Luke."

His statement was phrased more like a question, and I was more than happy to set his bullshit version straight.

"I never joined the Faolchúnna pack, I was held there under false pretences. Not quite kidnapped, but consent seems to be something that pack really struggles with." I painted a sickly-sweet smile on my face. "Much like Luke's sister, except I wasn't trapped underground in a room or kept drugged up. For the most part anyway."

"Indeed." He took a long sip of his drink and pursed his lips together, inching closer. "So, you claim you never joined the pack before Luke got involved?"

"No. I never joined their pack. As soon as I realised Ryan was a certifiable psychopath and what his pack was up to, I began working with Luke to free his sister." I held my hand up to silence the alpha before he could interrupt. The action caused his jaw to feather with displeasure and my wolf side to bask in the satisfaction of how much a woman speaking up bothered him. "Luke only ever offered advice on self-defence. Once he found out that the Faolchúnna pack were holding his sister captive, the Crescents got involved. As they had every right to."

"That's not what I was led to believe."

I bristled and ran my tongue across my teeth, choosing my words carefully. "Can I ask where you received this misinformation then? I would be more than happy to clear up a few things."

The alpha threw his head back and laughed, his eyes sparkling with excitement. He looked at me like I was some harmless little kitten who didn't know how to use her claws, and it really got my hackles up.

"Surely your boyfriend told you I don't answer to any other pack, I rule over the city. Ryan contacted me shortly after the Crescents took Alice back, by force."

"So force is warranted to hold someone captive against their will, but not to rescue a victim? Interesting, but not surprising." I earned another condescending chuckle that had my fingertips itching and my claws begging to come out.

"Perhaps. He told me about a hybrid he had trained, one the Crescents had turned against him."

I scoffed. "Ah yes, because a scorned man's recollection of a relationship's demise is to be trusted? Give me a break. What woman in their right mind would stick around once she found out they were running some screwed up breeding program for hybrids? Not shaming, but kidnapping and breeding are not on my kink list."

Curiosity sparked in his eyes, and I regretted letting my temper control my tongue.

"Of course not." The alpha purred, checking his watch before draining his whiskey glass and placing the empty glass on the table. A warning growl came from outside, apparently the soundproofing only went one way.

"I do believe I must let you go now, before Mr. Whelan decides to remove my door from its hinges. But I do hope you will consider my offer. Joining my pack could open so many doors for you."

I'd no doubt those doors would be slammed shut behind me. His offer was nothing but a poorly veiled trap.

I rolled my eyes but he took no notice, holding his hand out as he stepped into my personal space. I didn't take it, swivelling my chair so I could move away. He caught my elbow, spinning me to face him.

"Turning your back on an alpha can be viewed as an insult." He leaned in close, his whiskey breath doing little to hide the lingering stench of tobacco.

I recoiled from his touch, pressing a firm hand to his chest, and shoving.

He maintained his position between me and my exit, walking me backwards until the back of my knees hit the desk.

Eve? Something feels wrong. I'm coming in.

I sent back one command, keeping my focus on the alpha staring me down. *Wait.*

"Either you let me go, or you'll find out why you should fear hybrids," I warned, my throat vibrating with a growl. He had me pinned against the desk, but if I had to tolerate his body against mine, I'd make it worth my time.

"You have potential, girl. To have two alphas in the making falling over themselves for you... There's something special about you." A hint of silver flecked his irises as he slid his leg between mine, but the hunger in his eyes was all too familiar. Not the kind of desire for a woman, no. One blinded by power. "Don't forget where you are, Eve. You're exiled, the Crescents have no sway here."

"Do tell me what you think you should do then." I gritted my teeth as I reached one hand behind me and carefully felt around. "In all your wisdom."

"The Irish packs are some of the oldest in existence, they have many contacts and are well respected by the other werewolves worldwide." He eyed me up like I was a prime steak. "But they do not have the same connections as me and Luke could not possibly offer you the same level of protection. If you were to join my pack—"

"I'll just stop you right there because there's no point in dragging this on, and you have maybe half a minute before Luke kicks that door in." I raised my voice and looking at him dead in the eye as my fingers closed around the flash drive and slowly pulled it out. "I have no intention of joining your pack, or any other. I trust the Crescents. They're not going to sell me out."

He eyed me with an odd mix of disdain and amusement. "And I would?"

"Please tell me if I'm speaking out of turn." My words were laced with bitterness as I increased my pressure on his chest to keep distance between us. My temper flared as he spoke down about my pack, heating further at him insulting the man pacing outside ready to burn the place to the ground for me. "You'll never be half the man Luke is. Either you're a fool and your loyalties lie in the wrong place, or you're a power-hungry, twisted bastard, neither of which I want anything to do with.

"This is all so new to you, Eve. In time you will understand how things work." He shook his head, that predatory sneer back in place.

I slid the drive in my back pocket, exhaling a silent sigh of relief as he seemed too busy with his tirade to notice. Of course he wouldn't expect anything sneaky from a silly little woman.

"I don't need to be around for long to know that politics and lies go hand in hand, you're not as unlike humans as you think."

He reached out as if to coil a strand of my hair around his finger, but I slapped his hand away before he could touch me.

"You could do great things. Being exiled means you have no pack, but I could bend the rules for a hybrid if you asked nicely."

"I won't be asking, at all." No longer forced to tolerate his presence, this time my claws extended, and I shoved with all my strength. He took a step back, and that's all the space I needed to slam my elbow into his forearm connected to the hand holding a fistful of my jacket. In one smooth movement, I stepped out of reach as he released me on reflex, a malicious smile curving my lips as he grunted in pain.

"Not now, not ever."

Then the motherfucker laughed, an unnerving sound, drunk on power as if he thought he was untouchable.

I didn't grace him with a goodbye, striding towards the door knowing there was a werewolf itching to kill on my behalf waiting outside.

Luke was hovering so close to the door that I walked straight into him, bumping into his shoulder. I think I would have rebounded off him if he didn't spin and catch my arms, the entire scene witnessed by Henry's snotty receptionist. Worry was etched into every one of Luke's features.

"What did he want?" He all but growled as he set me on his feet, worry etched into the lines of his beautiful face.

Tension radiated from his body, but it dissipated from mine once in his arms.

I shook my head, pinching the bridge of my nose as I exhaled slowly. "A lot and nothing all at once. I'll tell you when we get back to—"

Luke pressed his lips to mine, silencing me with a kiss. I slid the flash drive from my pocket, keeping it hidden in my fist as I pressed it into his palm. His lips curved against mine, and he deepened the kiss before pulling away, lacing his fingers with mine and turning towards the exit.

"That's my girl."

CHAPTER 13

LUKE

I f you asked me how I'd spend a day and night cooped up with Eve in a fancy hotel, I'd have a long salacious list of things on the tip of my tongue. My answer would not be sleep. In fact, my list wouldn't allow for much sleep at all. Except Eve had passed out completely once she got off the phone with Craig after bringing him up to speed, as if the reassurance finally gave her body permission to relax. And as much as I needed some stress relief, my selfishness didn't extend to waking my girl when she was still recovering.

So, instead of getting any form of release, I'd spent hours switching between pouring over Jeremy's notes and staring at the ceiling until I, too, passed out cold.

But now we had a lead and were striding through the corridor of an impressive building with pointed arches and elaborate cravings that I could only describe as a goth's wet dream. Eve had almost broken her neck, too busy taking it all in, as we climbed the steps to the entrance.

While she'd caught up with Craig properly without interruption this time, I'd brought Dad and the pack up to speed. The only thing that took the edge off breaking the news to them about Jeremy being confirmed as held captive was that Dad had received word from Jer's wife, Lila. It was only a short call from a burner phone, but she promised both her and the kids were fine. She'd share her location once it was safe, but was able to confirm that Jeremy was researching into werewolf origins to understand the magic more and the connection to hybrid kidnappings.

On one hand, I hoped we were on the right track, on the other Larissa's cold voice reciting myths and talking about prophecies was one of the nightmares that haunted me in the dark hours of the night.

"Just this way." Our guide, a Cambridge student wearing so much cologne it made my nose twitch, placed a gentle hand on Eve's arm to guide us right. A hand he clearly didn't wish to retain given the way he looked at her.

"Thanks again for helping us, I know tours are generally banned," Eve said, the only one of us trying to make conversation.

The guide ran a hand through his glossy brown hair and winked with a laugh, the kind that told me he probably sent girls unsolicited dick pics. "It's all about who you know."

A low growl built in my throat, but I killed it before it became audible to the guy. Eve heard it, though, looking over her shoulder with a raised eyebrow in question.

Everything okay back there?

I nodded and waited until she turned around before tensing my back muscles and broadening my shoulders in a clear show of dominance as I fixed the guy with a scorching glare. He dropped all contact with my girlfriend immediately.

Eve glanced back just in time to catch me smirking and rolled her eyes. I wanted to make them roll for a different reason, but this would have to do for now. Ever since she was attacked, I had this overwhelming urge to be close to her. All we'd done since Dublin was kiss, and I didn't expect any more, I wanted to give her space to recover, but the need to *have* her was strong. It was a basal, carnal need that I couldn't explain to Eve even if I tried because it was just as crazy and possessive as it sounded.

"No talking as we pass through here." The guide's throat bobbed as made brief eye contact with me before staring resolutely at the door, studying the grain of the woodwork as if it was the most interesting thing in the world. "Once we go through the reading room, I'll pass you onto an archivist who can help you find what you need."

Smart man.

She glowered, and I laughed, quickly masking it with a cough as we stepped into a room of students shooting us dirty looks for interrupting. The room was a complete circle with three levels, all of which spanned by tall wooden bookshelves. There were several desks forming mini arcs and one large round desk in the middle, all were filled with students with their heads in books.

Eve was staring at ceilings again, but I followed her gaze to see the bookcases giving way to a decorated glass dome ceiling. Above us was a blanket of grey clouds visible through windowpanes lining the dome ceiling, raindrops decorating the glass exterior.

The admiration shining in her eyes thawed my heart just a little. We may not have been able to sightsee properly, but at least this was something.

I placed my hands on her hips, guiding her through the reading room so she wouldn't knock into anyone while getting to enjoy the view. She couldn't hide her disappointment as our guide led us through another door and the beautiful Belle-worthy library faded from view.

The corridor we stepped into was notably cooler, with whitewashed walls and what looked like original flagstone flooring. A woman leaned in the open doorway of an office, dressed more casually in trousers and a shirt rather than the usual librarian uniform. She was completely engrossed in a book, her glasses pitched forwards on her nose.

"Sarah?" Our guide approached her, doing that damn hair toss thing and walking with a swagger that made me want to turn his kneecaps to jelly.

"One second." She held up one finger, snapping the book

shut in irritation when our guide couldn't take a hint and invaded her personal space. She pushed her glasses back, her eyeliner and the shape of her frames giving her green eyes a cat-like appearance as they narrowed. "What is it, Jason?"

The guide had probably told us his name before but it was hard to hear when he made steam come out of my ears.

"The group looking to access the archives are here. You told me to bring them straight here?" Jason sniffed, grimacing as dust particles rose in the air from the book.

"Ah, of course! Friends of Maya's, yes?" The girl turned to face us with a beaming smile, her energy much warmer towards us than when she turned to Jason one last time. "You can go now."

Her icy tone made sense when I picked apart her scent. Sphinx. No wonder a murderous expression had flitted across her features when Jason interrupted her reading. It wasn't just eyeliner, the way she moved as she motioned for us to walk with her, her long nails and every hand gesture had a distinct feline touch to it.

"Come, Maya filled me in as much as she could. She was unusually secretive about some parts." Sarah's pupils shifting between cat eyes and pupils in a way that felt almost hypnotic. "Sorry about Jason, he's a creep."

"He seemed okay to me." Eve shrugged, all three of us falling into step together. "A bit shallow but that's not exactly rare."

"That's because you're pretty. Your boyfriend clearly did notice." Sarah wiggled her eyebrows, earning my trust based on her accurate assessment of the douchebag. "Wolves, right? Although you smell different."

"Hybrid." Eve admitted with a nervousness that made me want to shake sense into her and kill the monsters responsible for making her think she should be ashamed of who she was.

"Sphinx. Nice to meet another rarity." Sarah smiled warmly, leading us further along a corridor where the walls were now giving way to grey brickwork, the temperature dropping and the ground sloping as if we were moving lower underground.

Maya had better contacts than I'd expected. Sphinx weren't super common, and they were unmatched in their knowledge and passion for books.

At one point it felt as if we passed through an invisible curtain of magic, the hair rising on the back of my neck as it welcomed us. I presumed we were only welcome due to our sphinx friend and that curtain no doubt could become a guillotine if the wrong kind came snooping.

"Old school from here on, unfortunately." Sarah stopped in front of us motioning to the light track above us that stopped abruptly. She lifted a small lamp from a hidden alcove in the wall that I'd easily have stumbled straight past and tapped the base, whispering something in Latin that I couldn't understand. At her command, a violet flame flared into life. "Not far, I promise."

Though the descent didn't feel steep underfoot, I couldn't help but think it was some sort of illusion and that we were actually descending a spiral staircase into the depths of the library. The flame cast a purple hue on Eve's face as it danced, suspended in mid-air within the glass panes of the lantern. Her joy at the simplest of magic was contagious, a smile of my own lifting the corners of my lips.

"When it came to housing a paranormal library in the city, we thought it best for security purposes to keep it as close as possible to something the humans wouldn't destroy. If you liked the Maughan Library, you'll adore ours."

I lost track of what turns we took as Sarah gushed about their collection of books, completely disorientated by the time the ground beneath us levelled and the pathway widened into a cavern. Marking the end of the tunnel were two large wooden doors, the dark grain covered in carvings and gold detailing depicting everything from demons to high Fae basking in the dawn sunlight.

"Wow." Eve's back hit my chest as she stopped dead in her

tracks to take in the artwork. "That's incredible. I was starting to feel like I was taking a trip through the catacombs, but the walk was worth it."

Sarah grinned from ear to ear. "Incredible, isn't it? This is why I never take anyone down the escalator the first time, technology ruins the moment."

"The escalator?" I shook my head, Eve whining as she bent to rub her calves and distracting me entirely. "Seriously? I guess it would have ruined the view."

Sarah's nose wrinkled at my double entendre, moving forwards to trace her fingers across the masterpiece of the doors. "They were a gift from the High Fae of the Day Court a long time ago. Walking a bit is the least we can do to appreciate such art."

Both Eve and I nodded dutifully, no interest in finding out if that cat hand claws. I wasn't going to insult her library, sphinx responded well to an interest and respect for literature and artefacts, the last thing I wanted to do was offend her.

"If you think the doors are cool, just wait until you see inside. It's paradise." Her words oozed with excitement and possibly an unhealthy obsession with dusty paper as she pulled the doors open with a flourish.

No rubble fell loose from the ceiling of the tunnel as the hinges creaked, and the doors parted to reveal another library. It was similar to the human one, a half-moon red carpeted area filled with desks and small lamps except it was ten times bigger and breathtakingly beautiful. The details were incredible, the leg of every desk covered in tiny carvings.

Gold lamps on each desk illuminated stacks of books and notes, a set of inks and quills on each. The edge of the reading circle was lined with tall bookshelves reaching higher than any ladder could ever reach and several rows of shelves with walkways in between extended from the half-circle like the rays of the sun. Above us, rolling dark clouds covered the domed ceiling. Except, this one had no glass, the night sky and stars giving way to an endless stretch of darkness above.

"I don't think 'wow' covers this one." Eve pressed her palm to her chest, craning her neck as she rotated slowly to take it all in.

I nodded, my own well of words drying up as small owls flitting from one bookcase to the next, some with books in hand.

"Are they owls?" Eve's voice reached an octave I had never heard before, her eyes widening like saucers as she stared at the birds like they were kittens.

"It is truly magnificent." Sarah moved through the empty reading area, picking up mislaid books as she went. "But I must warn you, please do not pet the staff."

I snorted, choking as Eve pulled her elbow back sharply to catch me in the ribs.

"While select visitors are allowed in this area, do not stray into the book stacks. It's a maze, you'll never find your way out. Plus, some of the collection bites." The sphinx shifter shot us both a deadpan look that told me she wasn't joking, a shrill snarl rattling in the distance as if in agreement. She motioned to what looked like a reception desk stacked so high with tomes it was impossible to see if anyone sat there. "You won't know where to find anything, and I don't enjoy rounding up stragglers, so if you need anything, hit the chime at reception, and I'll come help."

At the snap of her fingers, sconces with the same ethereal flame sprang to life at the end of each bookcase flanking the arc of the reading area. Sarah led us down one of the bookshelf trails, trailing her fingers along the dusty shelves and smiling at a passing owl.

Eve stuck close to my side, her grip on my hand tightening to the point of pain.

"Eyes." Her nails bit into my palm as she veered away from one shelf. "The books have eyes."

I didn't believe her until I turned to find a book at eye level blinking back at me. The front faced outwards, what looked like a fully functional eye embedded in the cover swivelling to follow our path.

"Ah, yes. This one was only acquired last year, but it sure is a beauty." Sarah murmured, a leather eyelid folding over the eye as she stroked the book's spine. "It's one of a kind. It's believed the human sacrifice was the lover of the witch who bound the book. The idea was that their soul would be eternally bound to the book so their love could last for all eternity. When she passed the family decided to donate the heirloom."

Human. Sacrifice. Heirloom. I might have been born into the paranormal world but fuck me some parts would never sit right with me. Humans weren't the only ones with bloody, fucked up skeletons in their closets.

Sarah took a sharp turn to her left to stop in front of a plain door, unhooking a keyring with only three keys from her belt. The key morphed before our eyes as she fit it in the lock of a door, leading us into a smaller alcove off from the rows of bookshelves. It was a small room with one table in the middle lined with cushioned benches either side. A bookshelf stretched across one side, while the opposite wall was decorated with antique paintings. Beside the desk was a faux window spelled to show the night sky, like the dome outside.

"I could only find two of the three texts." She explained, setting the lamp down beside a stack of papers and two leather-bound books. An ink pot and quill had been supplied, along with a pen which looked so out of place in this place. "It appears the third has been mislaid, but I'm sure it will turn up."

"Can books be stolen?"

It was then I learned that there was such a thing as a stupid question. My words fell flat, the sphinx hissing as she snatched a rogue book that had been abandoned on one of the benches.

"I mean, the book we were looking for. Is there any possibility it might not be found?"

"The books are enchanted as a safety measure, they will self-combust if someone tries to bring them beyond the wards.

Especially ancient valuable texts such as these." The venom in her words was crystal clear.

Do not steal books. Got it.

Eve reached out to stroke the delicate binding of one of the books, marvelling at the details in the leather cover and silver lettering. "Wouldn't that destroy valuable information?"

"Sometimes knowledge is better lost than in the hands of those who would misuse it."

CHAPTER 14

EVE

The words on the page in front of me were either bewitched or moving or I'd been staring at the text for too long.

I sat back in my chair with a sigh and rubbed my eyes. Sure enough, the words settled back into place. I'd lost track of how long we'd been leafing through ancient books that coughed up plumes of dust every now and then when you opened a different part.

Luke sat perched on the window ledge with his arm balanced on his leg. The way his tilted head caught the starlight cast by the spelled night sky sparkling behind him, his chin resting on his hand as he scanned the book in his hand, made him look like a broody model in a magazine.

Luke caught my eye, his lips tilting into a smirk as he made a show of licking his thumb before flicking to the next page in his book. Where the leather cover of the book in front of me had different carvings etched into it and with real silver letters forming the title 'Liber Umbrarum', the one Luke held was decorated with bright jewels that danced in the light. In the centre there was a large moonstone, and the phases of the moon cycle were depicted in jewels along the spine.

The bookshelf to his left was stuffed full of more books in

varying condition depending on how many centuries or wars they'd had to survive. Thankfully, none of the books sharing the room with us had eyes or any other human features as far as I could tell. Between the magic spelled window and the sconces casting a low light throughout the room, it was as if we had stepped back on time. At least they stocked pens alongside the feathered quill and ink.

I leaned over to grab a pen, pausing as a low growl came from Luke's direction.

"Are you trying to distract me?"

A blush crept up my neck as I met his gaze. There was nothing fictional about the smouldering lust in his eyes. Ever since we had been left alone, tension had been building between us. It was so close to igniting, and I wanted to light the match.

"Me? Never," I replied innocently, knowing full well my position bent over the table had given him the perfect view of my cleavage thanks to the low-cut dress I'd chosen for that day.

He tugged his lip between his teeth, shaking his head. "You're a better liar than that."

I huffed, shuffling about the notes on the desk in front of me as if it might make the answer we were searching for magically appear. Luke lifted his arm above his head and stretched, the muscles of his chest and biceps tensing beneath the material of his T-shirt. He was being purposefully distracting, and it was working. I had read so many myths about everything from werewolves to nymphs, a hot werewolf showing off his physique was obviously going to win my attention.

He caught me looking again, and I pretended to be studying the antique paintings on the wall opposite. It didn't help my case that the main one depicted a woman being worshipped by several men, one of whom was on his knees between her legs.

"Stop looking at me like that."

"Like what?" I toyed with the top of the yellowed page, the edge of the paper almost crispy under my finger as I turned it and pretended to scan the next page.

Luke's voice dropped to a pitch that promised trouble. "Like you're having some kind of teacher student fantasy playing out in that dirty mind of yours."

"Sounds like you're projecting. I'm busy looking at fifty different drawings of the moon, and my head is ready to burst, no room for thoughts of you."

Really? Because you're always in mine.

I knew exactly what buttons to push. "You know, you were really rude earlier."

"I've no idea what you're talking about."

"This possessive thing is getting out of hand. You can't be rude to every man who speaks to me."

"Who?"

I rolled my eyes, flicking a crumpled piece of paper towards him. "Jason? The guide that brought us through the library."

"Hm. Don't remember him." Luke shrugged, grinning as if he had an invisible halo above his head.

"Convenient." I twirled the pen in my hand, crossing my legs so that the hem of my dress rode up and placed the lid of the pen between my teeth. "You don't see me losing my shit every time a woman falls at your feet, yet the moment a guy touches me you're all mister macho wolf."

I knew exactly what I was doing. His protective side was something I enjoyed whether I should or not. He was possessive, but not in a suffocating sense, in a way that lent me confidence to find my wings. And I wanted to fan the flames of his urge to protect me, I wanted to wind him up until he snapped. The entire time I was supposed to be looking for drawings or symbols that matched Jeremy's notes, I'd been imagining him taking me over the desk. I didn't have the venom to blame this time either, the need building inside was all me, and I needed release.

Luke snapped the book shut, his eyes darkening as he moved from the window across the small room. A small squeak slipped from my lips as he grabbed the narrow bench either side of me and twisted it to face him. Heat pooled between my legs, my heart thrumming with excitement.

"I may not be alpha yet, but that tongue of yours is getting out of hand." He hummed his disapproval, the muscles of his arms flexing as he leaned over me, his larger frame towering over mine.

I ran my tongue across my teeth, looking up at him from under my lashes like a siren begging to be rescued. I wanted to lure him overboard and drown in him.

"If I didn't know better, I'd think you were trying to distract me. Did that venom turn you into a little temptress?" He caught my chin between his finger and thumb. The pressure forced my head to tilt to the point my body had to arch towards him. I met the gaze of the man that looked like he wanted to devour my body, soul, and mind. And I wanted to let him.

"For the record." My breath hitched as he slid his hand down my throat, heat pooling in my core at the husky edge to his voice. "I don't enjoy women falling at me feet, nor do I ever want you to bow for me."

I swallowed hard, my breath coming in light pants. Not because he restricted my air flow. No, he kept the pressure either side of my windpipe like he knew *precisely* what he was doing. Like he knew exactly how to manhandle me, and I was trapped on this bench between his chiselled body and the desk, a damsel gloriously in distress.

He dropped his head to trail light kisses down the column of my throat in the wake of his hand as his fingers brushed lower. "However, I'd happily spend a lifetime on my knees for you."

My head emptied of words as he did just that, dropping to his knees in front of me with a wicked smirk that promised he planned to utterly destroy me.

I had seconds to wonder what he was going to do with sheer tights I'd worn to ward off the winter cold, but his claws extended. He grabbed a fistful of the material on each thigh and sliced straight through it. My gasp of surprise only seemed to spur him on, his tongue running over his lower lips as he tossed the ruined clothing aside as if it was a nuisance. His hands parting my knees were a silent command, my cheeks flushing as he hiked the skirt of my dress up.

"Luke!" I gasped, glancing at the open door leading back out to the main library. "Anyone could walk in."

"You started this." He placed his hands on my thighs, parting my legs to reveal lacy, black underwear that was already soaked, earning me a low growl of approval. "You shouldn't push a wolf if you're not willing to pay the consequences."

I scooted back on the bench as he ran his index finger down the seam of my underwear along the sensitive skin of my pubic bone, my voice rising an octave. "Someone will see. You said you don't like to share."

"I don't, and I won't be sharing. No one will see anything while my head is buried between your legs." He grabbed me by the waist, lifting me onto the desk so I was at the perfect height for him to torture me. His eyes were hooded with lust as he pulled me right to the edge with my knees hooked over my shoulders, my ass practically suspended in mid-air. "Like I said, your tongue is going to cause you problems."

"Luke..." My protests died on my tongue as he hooked my underwear to one side, his tongue carving a path down my centre.

The lace fell victim to his claws, the material sliding off and the coolness of the room hitting my bare pussy. But the cold was a short reprieve because his mouth was on me, my body bowing off the desk as his tongue found my clit and began dealing the punishment promised.

I clamped my hand over my mouth, trying to watch the doorway for anyone passing but his mouth was the most delicious distraction. He drew circles with his tongue around my clit, his thumbs digging into my inner thigh as he held me pinned at the mercy of his touch.

The sight of him on his knees for me, his head between my legs while he spread me on the library desk had my head spinning.

The hand not muffling the moans he elicited tangled in his short hair, a silent plea for more. He hummed his approval, the vibrations making me squirm in his grip and bite into my palm to avoid drawing attention. Though I was far less concerned about the door and more about the way his tongue flicked across my clit and then retreated, drawing a growl of frustration from me.

I dug the heels of my boots into his back in an attempt to force his tongue where I wanted it. The fucker laughed and pulled back, licking his lips with a purr of satisfaction. "Something the matter, Eve?"

"You know exactly what you're doing." I removed my hand from my mouth, hissing in frustration.

Luke drew his finger along the entrance of my pussy before pressing the pad of his thumb against my clit. He pinned me with the intensity of his gaze as he moved his thumb in slow, torturous circles. I cursed, the curve of my spine arching off the desk as he increased the pressure.

"Shhh, someone might hear you."

Before I could send a string of curse words his way, he dropped his mouth to my pussy and drew my clit into his mouth. My hips bucked in response, and a low moan slipped from my lips before I could cover my mouth again, shuddering under his touch as he slid one hand between my legs.

"Please." My voice was breathy as I spread my legs further, desperately grinding against his finger for friction as he teased my entrance.

Luke smirked up at me like the devil incarnate as he slid one finger inside my pussy, his breath hot against me as he leaned in to drag his tongue over my clit. "Good girl. See what behaving gets you?"

I didn't have it in me to glare, my eyes fluttering closed as he added another finger and curled them inside me. I was a grinding, panting, needy mess as I rode his hand. Ecstasy building steadily as pumped his fingers and continued his unrelenting torture with his tongue. The door didn't exist, it was just me and him as he grazed his teeth against the apex of my thighs, and I fell apart. My head hit the desk as I came, my eyes rolling into the back of my head and my hips bucking as pleasure washed over me.

Footsteps echoed in the distance, and I froze, but Luke didn't stop. His fingers stroked that sensitive spot inside, building the pressure inside me.

I panicked, trying to sit up only for Luke to press on that hidden spot at the top of my pelvis that increased the pressure on his fingers. I moaned, my hips moving against his mouth despite the footsteps moving closer.

"Luke..." His name was a soft moan, my pussy pulsing around his fingers.

He growled, as if annoyed at the interruption as he withdrew his hand. The sight of his stubble glistening with my cum as he looked up ignited something carnal in me.

The footsteps moved in a different direction, and my shoulders slumped in relief, my chest heaving as I propped myself up on my elbows. Luke leaned down, his lips hungry on mine as he stepped between my legs. "I'm not done with you."

He shoved the ancient book I'd been studying aside, grabbing me by the hips and flipping me over in one swift movement. My boots hit the ground, my hips trapped against the edge of the desk and my breast spilling out of the dress as he bent me over. The swell of his arousal pressed against my ass, a low moan of anticipation escaping me at the sound of him lowering his zipper.

He was going to ruin me.

I braced my hand on the desk, knocking the moonstone book Luke had tossed aside open in the process. He kneaded my ass with his hands, leaning down to nip between my shoulder blades and pepper kisses down my spine.

My body was alight under his touch, but my desire-hazed mind cleared as my gaze snagged on the page in front of me. "Wait."

Luke stopped immediately at my request.

"What's wrong?" He stepped back, gently helping me stand

up straight. When I spun to face him, his brow was etched with worry. Despite his belt hanging open and his jeans around his hips, all lust had been replaced with concern.

"It's one of the symbols." I tugged my dress down to cover myself up, almost tripping over the shredded material of my poor tights as I bent down. In the top corner of the page the book had fallen open on was one of the symbols I recognised from Jeremy's notes. I traced my finger over the sketch of a dagger with a moon carved into the handle, something written in a weird language underneath.

Luke frowned, scanning the page before flicking over to the next where there was a fancy Celtic knot design framing what looked like a poem.

Life-source of the undead,
The true heart of a hound,
Ancient magic spilled,
Bloodline and moon bound.
Trinity tied by the blade of magic intertwined,
Wielded by the blessed can history unbind.

"Moon bound? Fated?" I stared at the words inked on the page, my confusion only multiplying tenfold. "What the hell is this? There are more symbols on here that match Jeremy's research."

The sconces in the room flickered, shadows dancing on the walls as I reread the passage aloud. Luke's hands found my waist as we stood over the ancient text, once again left with more questions than answers and nothing to guide us.

Luke dropped his chin onto my shoulder, his chest against my back. "I have no idea, but I know a witch who might."

CHAPTER 15

LUKE

We stepped off the taxi in front one of the biggest night clubs in Europe, a line of people queueing the whole way around the corner. When I say *people*, the club was strictly supernaturals only. Vampires stood aloof, looking like super models—some probably were—pixies and Fae had glamoured themselves for the night to hide their ears but their penchant for colourful outfits walking the line of fashion gave them away. Witches, demons, shifters of all kinds stood in line tapping their feet impatiently. I scented some wolves, but I couldn't tell if it was just normal club goers or our every move being tracked again. We didn't risk a glamour for this, any hint of deception, and my contact wouldn't show.

"Ready?" I slipped my hand into Eve's and nodded towards the top of the line.

Eve nodded, staring at the line-up of paranormals and fidgeted with the hem of her skirt. I made a mental note to remember to thank Lawrence for the collection he'd picked up. The outfit Eve had chosen was a deep burgundy halter-top paired with a leather skirt and knee-high boots that I was going to enjoy peeling off her tonight. The entire outfit was destined to end up on the floor.

The club occupied a sizable old building in London, its exterior adorned with pale stonework and rows of elegant sash windows, much like the other historical structures lining the city streets. The windows were mysteriously blacked out, but glamoured to appear normal to humans. Once you crossed the threshold, what appeared to be three floors from the outside magically expanded to nine.

Neon lights lit up the pillars, casting a scarlet glow that complimented the rich purple carpet leading to the entrance. The queue stopped in front of two large sliding doors, stars and constellations swirling in the black glass. Two warlocks manned the entrance, standing with their legs shoulder-width apart and their hands clasped.

'Inferno' wasn't concealed by spells like the Dark Night. In London, the club was a known hot spot that was notoriously hard to get into, a place for the elites. Humans were turned away, unless accompanied by a paranormal creature. Those that were stupid enough to ignore the spells encouraging them to turn away and sneak in often never saw the light of day again.

Each time the door opened, dry ice wafted in spirals into the winter night as they motioned the next person through. No one pushed, no one shoved or started complaining about the wait. It was all very civilised, for now.

Dirty looks were thrown our way, along with few choice remarks, as I made a beeline for the main door and strode straight past a pair of nymphs that had been waiting at the top of the queue.

"Luke Whelan." I flashed a blank black card that flared into life at my touch. Like the doors, a spiralling image of cobalt and violet flames dancing appeared on the surface. For the first time in a while, my name actually held some sway.

Eve tensed against me, ready for the impending argument that should have come next, but it never did.

The bouncers waved us inside without argument.

The moment we stepped over the threshold, a deep bass beat

thumping rattled in my chest. We entered what almost seemed like a large warehouse, but the architecture was more like that of a castle. The ceiling was high above us, lasers piercing the mix thick black clouds and flames obscuring the roof from view room. There were nine levels playing on Dante's circles of hell, a wide balcony on each level overlooking the ground floor.

A spiral staircase marked each corner climbing the different levels, the back wall taken up by a large stage with dancers and two bars spanning the walls either side. The shelves were lit up, fully stocked with every drink known to man and then some. The dance floor was packed with a sea of people moving to the beat of the music, the DJ booth floating above the crowd on a cloud of shadows.

Eve's eyes framed by heavy kohl eyeliner widened as she took it all in, her cheeks flushing my favourite shade of pink as her gaze snagged on the second level. From our vantage point she could see a mixture of vampires, witches, warlocks, and no doubt some Fae on the balcony. Their cackles echoed, mixing with moans of pleasure if I strained my ears to hear. The music masked their debauchery, four-poster beds with drapes billowing in a magical breeze on the Lust level, the crimson lighting encouraging patrons to indulge in their deepest desires.

The only thing stopping me from dragging Eve to one of those beds or the nearest bathroom and hiking that dress up so her cheeks were flushed for a different reason was knowing that Cassandra would leave if we weren't on time.

"What kind of club is this?" Eve raised her voice over the music.

I wrapped an arm around her waist, my thumb stroking the exposed skin above the waistband of her skirt. "Welcome to Inferno. One of the biggest paranormal nightclubs in Europe."

"Is that some kind of vampy kink area?" She looked up at me, mischief dancing in her captivating eyes daring me to listen to the little devil on my shoulder.

I exhaled a long breath, using more self-control than I

thought I was capable of as I led us towards the bar instead of a bed. "The levels represent the nine circles of hell according to Dante's Inferno. Thanks to the aphrodisiac side effects of vampire venom, they're a big hit on level two."

"Lust?" Her pupils dilated, and I swallowed hard.

"I take it we're not meeting your contact there." The possessive edge to her voice did little to keep my desires in check.

"Nope. This is strictly a business contact so put the green-eyed monster away. Besides, I don't share," I added, leaning in to graze my teeth along the shell of her ear as we moved through the less packed crowd dancing on the edges near the bar. "You think I'd really fuck you while letting everyone watch? That would cost them their lives, or at the very least their eyeballs."

She bumped her hip into mine as we walk-danced through the writhing bodies, her cheeks dimpling with a grin. "I get it, Lukey doesn't share."

I growled, my fingertips kneading her hip and threatening to drop lower.

"Who owns this place? Darius?" She lifted a champagne flute off the tray of a waiter walking past with pink hair that glittered under the flashing lights.

I swiped the drink from her grasp and thrust it into the hands of a glassy eyed nymph lost to the beat of the music and took Eve's arm, guiding her towards the bar. "A partnership between a few witches, a vampire coven, and it's rumoured one of the Fae princes."

"Hey! My drink." She stared after the nymph who spun away before her attention snapped back to me. "I thought the different factions didn't work too well together?"

"First of all, don't drink anything unless you order it from the bar. The waiters on the floor are carrying Fae spirits and, while there's a time and a place to try the hard stuff, it's not tonight."

She frowned but nodded in agreement. The most she'd ever tried was one diluted shot at the Dark Night, this was not the kind of place to risk losing your inhibitions.

"Business and pleasure are two of the few reasons they make an exception. Inferno fills both needs. Paranormals need somewhere to go, everyone obeys the rules of the club for the most part. The owners get what they want."

"What they want?"

"Parts of Inferno cater to their darker... tastes. Last I heard, they lured a young vamp into their lair and toyed with him for hours. He was found crucified from the chandelier in the morning."

Eve paled, and for a moment I wondered if I had gone too far.

"Gross. How come they don't get in trouble for that?"

"No one notices, they make sure no trace is left. They prey on paranormals already in a dark place, those who won't be missed. Yes, it's against the laws to injure humans but we both know that so long as no one comes looking for them, many in this world don't care. Humans go missing all the time." I shrugged, a shiver rolling down my spine at the thoughts of what went on behind some of the walls here. "For the most part, it's just a club."

"So, who are we meeting tonight?"

"A witch, Cassandra. Though I doubt that's even her real name, she brings a whole new meaning to cloak and dagger."

"I know Maya is nice, but I'm not sure I want to bring another witch into this. There's no way Larissa is going to leave us alone if we keep digging into her plans."

"This one can be trusted, Dad helped her mother out a long time ago, and they were allies. She's done me a few favours over the years. She'll be meeting us soon, most likely on the top floor."

"Treachery?" Eve wrinkled her nose at the word 'favours', so I tapped it and smoothed them out for her. "Yeah, sure. Sounds real trustworthy."

"You'll like her, I promise." I rolled my eyes, pinning her between my arms against the bar so she was safely in my sight as I signalled to the bartender. I pointed to a bottle of glowing green liquid on the shelf. "Two shots please."

Eve tilted her head up to look at me, chocolate curls cascading over her shoulders in waves at the movement. The club lights made the blue of her eyes almost glow in the dark. It was when she did the smallest of things that she knocked the air clean out of my lungs.

"What?"

I shook my head to break her spell, tossing the bartender a note from my wallet full of Darius' cash without even looking. "Nothing, time for some Dutch courage."

Eve's eyes narrowed, her teeth snagging on her lip the way she did when nerves kicked in. "Maya was sweet, but most witches are scary as fuck. Cassandra more than anyone. She's a man eater." I handed Eve her shot and raised mine in toast, tiny bubbles rising in the green liquid. "Cheers."

We knocked the shot back at the same time, and I relished the burn of the liquid as it hit the back of my throat. Eve coughed, slamming her shot down on the bar with a grimace. "What the hell is that? Tequila on steroids?"

"A Lucky Charm." I grinned, brushing my thumb across her bottom lip to catch a drop.

It was a harmless drink that gave a tiny buzz, nothing that would endanger us.

She swirled her tongue across the bad of my thumb, her lips making a little popping sound as she sucked the last drop away. "Americans make leprechaun cereal, and paranormals make death in a bottle. Let's hope it works."

Work. You're here on work. My dick stood to alert as she looked up at me with a wicked smirk. Almost as evil as that damn tongue. She was my own personal brand of cocaine, and I wanted —no, I *needed* to have her. Our tryst in the library had barely taken the edge off, the need to hear her scream my name properly and beg for me was visceral.

"Sweetheart, if you wanted to get lucky all you had to do was ask." I dipped my head, stealing a kiss from her lips as my hands found her hips, relishing the little noise of surprise as her lips parted and let me deepen the kiss.

She wound her arms around my neck, pulling me closer. That was all the invitation I needed. I might not have time to fuck her, but we needed to keep our cover until Cassandra texted her location. I could think of plenty of ways to kill time until then and unravel that little minx in front of me.

I scooped her up by the ass with one hand, lifting her onto the bar stool to one side without breaking the kiss. Eve wound her legs around my waist, her skirt riding up as her thighs gripped mine, and I grinned against her lips. The music blared in the background, the bass beat drowning everything out as I gave myself permission to lose myself in her.

Her tongue explored my mouth, matching my hunger as her fingernails dug into the back of my neck. I spotted the DJ above the crowd drawing nearer as she tried to break the kiss, her chest heaving against mine.

Lips on mine. There are party drugs in the glitter.

I crushed my mouth against hers once more, her legs tightening at my command. Magic washed over the crowd in the DJ's wake, multicoloured glitter settling over the crowd as they cheered. As the supernatural ecstasy landed on their tongues, their eyes dilated and lost focus, wide grins on their faces as they swayed and moved to the music.

Eve nipped my lower lip, the heels of her boots digging into the back of my knee as she rolled her hips against mine. My hard cock strained against the seam of my jeans, driving me to distraction. This woman was going to be my undoing. It was risky, but my animal brain was loud, my wolf side desperate to claim her.

A low growl rumbled in my throat as I brushed my thumbs brushing across her hardened nipples under the thin fabric, one hand dropping lower. The way she spread her legs obediently as I dropped one hand to her thigh and toyed with the edge of her leather skirt made me question whether the meeting tonight even needed to go ahead.

My hand froze under her skirt as a masked redhead ascended

the spiral staircase, the scent of her godsdamned ex stopping me in my tracks. Eve frowned as I pulled away her cheeks rosy and her mascara smudged as she stared up at me.

"Stay here. Right fucking here where everyone can see you. Do not move."

Luke was halfway across the dance floor by the time my brain caught up. He'd ordered me to stay put, but the moment Ryan's scent reached me, my instincts screamed at me to run. I wasn't seeing things. Not only did we have the London pack sending suicidal bird invites and kidnapping us for meetings, but my past had also followed us overseas.

"What can I get you, miss?" A different bartender from the last appeared, his pointed ears and the faint scent of smoky air autumn leaves telling me which court the Fae descended from.

I shook my head, glancing back to find Luke had vanished completely. My heart hammered, blood pounding in my ears in sync with the heavy base beat. I scanned the room, each of the spiral staircases leading to the different floors were full of people but I couldn't make out Luke's familiar frame anywhere. He was gone, and I was alone in a sea of dancing bodies with the lady equivalent of blue balls.

My cheeks heated in both embarrassment and anger that my ex was still getting in the damn way. I fixed my skirt, playing with my empty shot glass as I studied the dance floor. Paranormal creatures of every kind danced to the rhythm of the music, cheering and jumping each time the base dropped. Horns, wings, claws, anything went here and based on the sounds coming from above, there were no limits to the acts being performed in this sanctum of sin. I searched their faces for the one I wanted, finding neither Luke nor the one I dreaded. Sitting alone at the bar was my own descent into hell, my foot tapping to the music becoming erratic as my knee bounced.

I gave in to the nerves and swivelled to face a barman with pointed ears. He wore no judgement on his face, only a wide smile and striking amber eyes.

"One vodka and coke please."

He nodded, moving with the grace of a swaying tree towards the far end of the bar. I watched the way his hips rocked to the music, wondering how his crisp white shirt was so clean when my own top stuck to me from the heat of the club. Maybe because he wasn't getting hot and heavy with a werewolf.

I wasn't sure what came over me before. Obviously, Luke was attractive and we had chemistry, but I didn't have the excuse of venom to blame for my horny teenager behaviour. Maybe there was something in the air vents making me lose my mind.

Cassandra is here. I don't have long with her. We're on the Treachery level, stick to the stairs and do not wander.

Relief unwound the knots of tension in my shoulders at the sound of Luke's voice, even if it was just in my head. I glanced up, barely able to see beyond the third level from where I sat. I still wasn't clear on how far the mind link between us worked, so I leaned into the idea that he must be close.

On my way. I smiled, something inside humming at the thought of being taken care of by Luke as I hopped off my bar stool and faced the dance floor. Granted, it was Darius' cash he'd slapped down on the bar, but it still made me feel warm and... Well, not fuzzy. Wet.

Treachery was six... or seven? I rummaged around in my bag for my phone. A quick google told me it was eighth. My heart sank. Eight levels. *Great. Couldn't she have chosen the damn Lust one knowing I was going to have to climb so many stairs?*

Leaving the bar felt unsafe, I was surrounded by paranormal creatures, most of which were high and would sooner fuck or kill me than rescue me if Ryan did show himself. We were both werewolves, why would they believe anything was off? I mean, I'd been dry humping Luke at the side of the dance floor. Who was to say I didn't just have an insatiable taste for wolf this evening?

The Fae returned with my drink, sliding the glass along the bar to me with a wink. "Don't worry about the bill, your boyfriend's tab covered it."

Every fiery ember of lust died in me as I turned, the sight of a familiar face down the other end of the bar freezing me in my tracks. Ryan stared back at me, his lips quirked in a smug smirk as he waved at me and raised his glass in cheers.

Fuck no.

Luke's command echoed in my mind, and a part of me wanted to obey it.

I needed to find him and the witch and get us the hell out of here. The fact that Luke had headed the wrong way in search of Ryan unnerved me, it was unlike him to miss when hunting someone. As if he'd been purposely misled. This had trap written all over. My instinct was to tell Luke. The moment he knew Ryan was near me, he'd come running, but I couldn't figure out if that was a trap or not. We needed the information from Cassandra.

I could hold my own.

Downing my drink for some much-needed courage and because I was sweating so much the lack of electrolytes was making me woozy, I jumped off my barstool and walked straight towards the nearest staircase. Despite my size, the sea of dancing bodies parted for me. Kate had taught me the whole 'shoulders back, tits out' thing. If you walked with purpose and confidence, people tended to move. I needed to fake it 'til I made it because I had no doubt if I showed any confusion or looked like a lost puppy climbing these stairs that it would be the wolf getting hurt in this bedtime story.

I glanced over my shoulder to see Ryan still at the bar, his icy stare tracking my path across the dance floor. His signature smirk stayed in place, as if egging me on to go give him a piece of my mind. As much as I'd have loved to rearrange his face, I had bigger fish to fry.

The wrought-iron handrail of the staircase was cool beneath my touch. I gripped it tightly, staring resolutely ahead as I started my ascent. I had no idea what kind of hell I was stepping into, but if I stuck to the stairs, I should be fine.

The distinctive smell of sweat and sex filled my nostrils as I ascended. A few patrons lingered on the steps locking lips. Hands dipped below waistbands and sighs of pleasure chased me as I climbed the stairs.

I caught the scent of blood, my stomach somersaulting as a blonde vampire fed on what smelled like a witch near the top. The strategic red lighting and shadows that seemed to move of their accord blurred the steps so much I had to focus not to fall, offering its patrons a sliver of privacy I'm not sure they cared for.

I crested the stairs onto the Lust level to find the vast balcony filled with standing tables, designed to encourage conversation. Benches that appeared innocent until closer inspection revealed restraints attached to the ends, lined the back wall. Several four-poster beds were scattered around the balcony, each adorned with gauzy curtains that swayed back and forth, revealing bodies in positions that I could barely fathom.

Thankfully, the spiral staircase to the next floor was a continuation, and I didn't have to traverse the sex-charged level any further or explore what lay beyond black doors leading away from the balcony. I had a feeling that if I dared enter, I would quickly be deemed a delicacy.

The next level was not what I expected. When I thought of gluttony, I thought of stacks of donuts, instead the balcony held several fountains. Each fountain pumped a liquid of different colours spanning the rainbow. My nose told me the red was blood, and the purple smelled like Fae wine I recognised from working at the Dark Night. Gold flashed under the lights of the club, revealing stacks of riches that seemed to be mostly surrounded by dragon shifters.

Other paranormals sat by the fountains, chatting and laughing as they refilled their glasses endlessly and smoked something that glittered. Their behaviour was more subdued than the previous floor. While I didn't feel the need to flee immediately, I wasn't enticed to join in.

My false sense of security was short-lived as the golden doors on the Gluttony level opened to reveal a line of waiters carrying out a large table on their shoulders. When they set it down to reveal all sorts of food complete with a human head, bile surged in my throat, and I hurried to the next level.

I didn't stop at the next balcony, keeping my gaze firmly fixed on the staircase. It took all my restraint not to take them two at a time so as not to draw suspicion to myself. The cool metal of the penknife tucked into the side of one of my knee-high boots was a small comfort. My feet were on fire from the climb in heels, but I pushed on. There was no way people climbed these stairs to get to the top level.

My suspicion was confirmed when a sliding door appeared from nowhere as I passed the next level, a group of drunk shifters stumbling out of it. Tempting, but risking getting trapped in a small box with strangers wasn't safe. Stairs burned like fuck, but I'd take the option to run over risking getting up close and personal with any paranormal frequenting these levels.

When I reached the fifth level, the spiral staircase stopped. I groaned, bracing myself as I turned to face scan the level I was trapped on for another way up. I'd heard the screams during my climb, but I was not prepared for the images I'd later want to burn from my memory. Anger apparently meant torture for the most part. Several stakes and different kind of restraints hung from the walls, everything from whips and genuine methods of torture like a fucking sword and something with too many spikes stood to one side.

A howl of agony came from the other side of the balcony, and

I looked across in time to see a witch using their fire powers like a blow torch on what smelled like some kind of Fae. It was hard to tell over the stench of burning flesh. I had no idea who consented to what or what the why was, and I really didn't care to find out. I needed off this fucking level.

Those magical elevators looked pretty damn tempting, but I'd no idea how to find them and feeling the walls up would only draw unwanted attention. I scanned the room, trying to unfocus my eyes as they passed over a bloodied body I wasn't sure still had a heartbeat. Who knew if they ever had one to begin with? The spiral staircase seemed to restart on the opposite stretch of the balcony. My heart sank, but I took a deep breath and strode across like I belonged there.

A glimpse of red hair beside the fire escape door caught my attention, and my anger ratcheted up to match the level we were on. They'd exiled us, what more did they want? Maybe I couldn't take Ryan on, but I could get a tiny bit of revenge on the redhead that had killed my best friend. The thought of avenging Kate had my temper climbing all nine levels of hell, ready to torch the bitch.

Nadine lurking in the shadows near a doorway that seemed to lead into an empty corridor rather than the club level. A predatory smile curved her lips, the personification of envy in a black fitted dress that clung to her waist and set her eyes off. Those dead eyes that only ever showed a spark of life when she was torturing me.

Maybe there was something in the air, or maybe I was too scared to cross the damn level and hoped the fire escape would let me skip one, but I found myself pivoting and heading straight for her.

Just as I was closing in, she slipped out the fire exit. I picked up my pace and wrenched the door open, stepping out into an empty concrete hallway that had none of the bells and whistles of the club interior. It did however have a staircase leading upwards. Luke said stick to the stairs, technically I wasn't disobeying.

The stairs led to a door, hopefully the floor I wanted. I pressed down on the handle, opening it to find myself in a deserted alleyway. The cold winter air caught in my throat, a fresh dusting of snow covering the walls and the bins lining the alley. Snow flurries whipped in the wind, catching in my hair. Unless one of the levels involved frostbite, the murky grey night sky above was real. It must have started while we were in the club. In the far distance, a cat screeched as if to confirm. Nadine's scent lingered in the air, but I wasn't about to go running through the streets of London while Luke was inside. If she didn't kill me, he would.

As much as I didn't want to face what was in store for me on the next level, I turned to head back inside.

Footsteps crunching the compacting snow sounded behind, Nadine emerging from the shadows with one hand on her waist and her hip jutting out like she was walking a runway.

"Eve, long time no see." Her high-pitched giggle pierced the night, malice gleaming in her eyes.

"Nadine." I nodded curtly, my hands balling into fists at my side. "I guess an alleyway is where I should have known to find you."

The muscle of her jaw twitching was the only slip in her perfectly painted mask, but I could see the anger. I knew how to get under her skin.

"What do you want?" I asked, sick of the niceties. "Ryan is waiting for me downstairs with a drink."

The flicker of irritation in her eyes was delightful.

"You don't have the upper hand, hybrid. So stupid, you ran right out here at the mere sight of him." She ran her tongue across her teeth, eyeing me like prey. Her canines glinted under the outdoor light above the door. "You and that boyfriend have been sticking your nose where it isn't welcome. It's time you were dealt with."

His scent was all over her in the same kind of way Luke had been all over me. Knowing her, she wanted to make me jealous.

All I felt was a tiny shred of pity and an insatiable thirst for revenge.

"This isn't the first time you've threatened my life, and I'm getting a little tired of it. How come you never have the balls to come for me outside of the full moon?"

Her smile brightened in the most unnerving way. "Oh darling, this isn't personal. You're just a means to an end."

At the click of her fingers, several figures emerged from the shadows to join her side. Four men and three women, four werewolves that smelled wrong and three hybrids. Were the hybrids here of their own accord? Or were they some of the girls the Faolchúnna pack had taken? Their eyes were empty silver pits devoid of emotion, their faces contorted with anger and a blood lust I'd associate more with vampires. Then men had broad shoulders and were built like a brick, thick corded muscle around their necks flexing as they eyed me with the same hunger as the hybrids. Their scent reminded me of a witch's or warlock's, and then something else I couldn't quite put my paw on. Their role was clearly the brawn, while the hybrids would no doubt savage me.

I didn't offer myself up on any of Inferno's levels, I certainly had no plans to be dinner tonight.

Instinct took over, and I sank my hips, pitting my feet shoulder width apart as a sketch plan formulated in my mind.

SOS. I'm outside of the club on the streets, exited some way between the Anger and Violence levels.

"There's no one here to save you now." Nadine's red-painted lips stretched as she smiled wider, the door creaking open to reveal a smug-looking Ryan.

Ryan and Nadine are here. Hybrids. Witches. Attack. Help.

I sent a string of words to Luke, hoping he'd read between the lines as I backed up until my heel snagged on a dirty bin bag. I kicked an empty can towards my ex, a low growl ripping from my throat as it missed my target and ricocheted off the door.

"I guess despite all those boxing sessions he never taught you how to aim." His grin was edged with malice, snowflakes settling in his pitch-black hair. Icy like his damn heart. "You've caused enough trouble, Eve. I can't let you get in the way of our plans, and the way you run around risking your life with no one to protect you isn't going to fly anymore."

"Ah yes, and your friends here are going to what exactly? Bring me to a fun little tea party? Because it looks like they plan on putting me in a coffin if there's anything left. Why don't you face me alone like a real man?"

My eyes darted between the two threats. The alleyway was flanked by two buildings impossible to scale. I'd gotten a lot stronger, but nine against one was more than I'd bargained for. I silently cursed whatever stupid magic had urged me confront Nadine. I wasn't ready to face Kate yet. Dying wasn't on my cards, I wouldn't allow it.

"You never knew how to shut up and come quietly." A scowl darkened Ryan's features, his lips thinning as he nodded to Nadine.

I was about to make a smart remark about his lack of ability to make me cum, but the insult never made it past my lips. Nadine raised her hand, a cackle of malicious glee bubbling from her lips as she pointed at me. "Get her."

Before I could give Luke any more information, the hybrids began to shift, and I swallowed hard as I found myself trapped between my unhinged ex and a pack of possessed paranormals ready to tear me limb from limb.

CHAPTER 17

LUKE

Every single level I passed was further confirmation that this was not my kind of club. But I didn't have time to worry about the screams, moans, or the cases where both were indistinguishable because my focus was fixed on one thing. Ryan. That bastard was here, Eve hadn't been seeing things before we met Maya in the café. It made sense. No doubt he'd paid Henry dearest a visit already to whispered poison in his ear, not that the London alpha needed more than a gentle nudge.

I needed to find him before he got to Eve. She could handle herself, but he could attack us freely over here. We were exiled, he could kill her or worse, take her from me like he had Alice. I would never ever let that man lay a fucking hand on anyone I considered family again.

As I stepped onto the Anger level, my fury multiplied tenfold. You could avoid the fairy dust, stick to normal liquor as much as you wanted, but when you dared explore the different levels, you gave an unspoken consent to explore that sin in its entirety. The magic didn't turn you into a kinky voyeur on the Lust level, but it certainly heightened your natural emotions to a level where consent became dubious in my opinion. I'd said as much when I'd ended up here years ago. Took one look at the second level and did a U-turn.

I was on level five and felt like I needed to scrub my skin raw to wash this place off me.

Ryan's scent grew stronger as I left the stairs and walked across to the balcony. My anger soared to boiling point as I peered down at the dance floor, the hairs on my arms rising with unease as I watched Eve sitting by the bar. The way she nervously tugged at her skirt, knowing that his presence made her withdraw made me want to trap him in this godforsaken place and rot here.

"Fancy seeing you here."

I whipped my head to the right to see Cassandra leaning against the balustrade post, her lips pursed in disapproval as she watched the next level down indulge in their desires. She never looked the same each time I saw her. Whether it was her eyes, hair, body type, she always changed something. Ever the chameleon like she was always running. A feeling I now understood all too well.

"You said you'd text." I dug my nails into the balcony post to ground as I forced myself drag my attention away from Eve.

This time Cassandra had gone for long, bright turquoise hair that bordered on being luminescent under the neon lights, and violet eyes to match her drink. She was dressed in a low-cut black dress that hugged her curves, the neckline daring men to take their life into their own hands. Her black lipstick contrasting with her pale skin added to the look of bombshell assassin that wasn't far off the truth.

"Nice to see you, too." Cassandra shrugged, tapping long black fingernails against a glass of something shimmering and purple, the rim dusted with crushed nightshade. "You didn't warn me there was heat on you, I had to make sure you were alone."

"You knew I was exiled. Wait, you're not the reason Ryan is here?"

"I'm going to pretend you didn't ask that." The witch

managed to walk the line between doll-like and murderous as her head tilted to one side, her tone clipped. "I would never work for them or with them. I'm not desperate for clients, and I don't break my rules, ever."

Cassandra was a Jill of all trades that happened under the cover of shadows.

That's why when Eve not so subtly asked if we had ever been a thing, I couldn't help but laugh. I chose life, my type was not a black widow spider.

"Sorry, I've been burning bridges left right and centre lately." I sighed, glitter that seemed to be getting everywhere falling onto my shoulders as I ran my hand through my hair. "Between what went down in Dublin and then Jeremy going missing, it's been a lot."

She pressed her finger to her lips in a clear but silent signal to watch my words. "Come on, this level is too...exposed."

I cast one last glance at Eve, my heart sinking at how lonely she looked toying with her shot glass. The idea of her being out of sight with Ryan around was beyond unsettling, but Cassandra wouldn't wait all night.

"Tell her to join us." The witch's voice was light and teasing, a twinkle in her eye as she smiled.

Her willingness to have a stranger join us was a huge show of faith. I'd always planned for Eve to be there, but I had been prepared that Cassandra might want to talk out of earshot. She wasn't big on trust.

Cassandra led the way up the wrought-iron staircase up two levels. The heels of her leather boots echoed as she crossed the floor of Violence, the sound swallowed by the bass beat of the music pulsing from invisible speakers. I flinched as the noise of a whip gliding through the air and connecting with flesh rang out as we crossed from one side of the balcony to the other where stairs continued on to the next level. I was only too eager to get out of this level of the club.

My guess was correct.

Treachery was where deals with the devil were made. Not the literal devil, but the broken souls of many who came here could give him a run for his money. Shrouded in shadows, this balcony less exposed and dotted with alcoves. Two large black doors offered access to more rooms within the level, but Cassandra led me to the nearest empty alcove.

I leaned over the balcony, cursing under my breath when the dance floor was too distant to spot Eve thanks to a mix of dry ice and shadows obscuring it from view. We were too close to the top level, privacy more of a concern for the elites.

Cassandra is here. I don't have long with her. We're on the Treachery level, stick to the stairs and do not wander. I cast my mind out, my body relaxing slightly as I felt my connection with Eve.

As we entered, the shadows parted to reveal a small table and cushioned benches either side. Once we were inside, the shadows obscured the balcony outside and the music along with any conversations of passers-by muted. Complete silence fell as the soundproofing magic kicked in.

Eve's voice in my head circumvented the magic. *On my way.*

"You didn't give me much to go on, but I have news on Jeremy." Cassandra reached into her handbag, her hand disappearing way further than physically possible before she withdrew a large manilla envelope. "Do you want the good news first or the bad?"

"Bad." I eyed the envelope as she tossed it down on the table, anticipation raising the hairs on the back of my neck.

"My kind of man." She opened the envelope, shaking out some documentation along with polaroids similar to the one Maya had given us. "You were right about Henry and the London pack, but it's worse than we expected. He's not a new addition to whatever scheming the Faolchúnna pack have cooked up. I have him linked to several kidnappings, some predating your sister. How is Alice, by the way?"

One of the polaroids showed Jeremy shackled, but this time

he was facing the camera directly. Tears streamed down his bloody face, the word 'Traitor' carved into his chest. Chunks of skin hung off his body, his healing powers clearly inhibited.

I shook my head, the steak I'd had for dinner making a reappearance as bile clogged my throat. "She... Uh. Alice is fine."

"Sorry." Cassandra winced apologetically, quickly turning the Polaroids upside down. "I wasn't going for shock factor, they're just proof if it comes to it."

"He's alive though, right?"

"Jeremy is alive. Someone on the inside tipped him off, and he stayed back to allow his family to escape." Her tone was so matter of fact that I wondered if the kind of life she led ever got to her. But then I caught the hint of emotion in her eyes when she mentioned his kids.

Images of him standing off with other wolves while Lila escaped with the kids was like a dagger to the heart. He'd do anything for his family.

"I believe that the timing may have been coincidental. I actually think they would have killed him if it weren't for your arrival and the fiasco in Dublin." She shuffled the Polaroids back into the envelope, her nails scraping against the table surface. "He's being tortured, obviously, but my contacts said he is being fed enough to keep him alive, and they don't intend on killing him. From what I can gather, he's leverage to keep you in line. Or more so your father, since you don't seem to be listening to their warnings."

"What would you have done?" I snapped, gripping the table edge so hard it started to bend. "We have to stop what they're doing to the hybrids and creatures they test on."

Cassandra placed her hand over mine, gently prying my fingers from the splintering wood. "I don't disagree. But your little show with Henry Edmonstone didn't go down well."

"I didn't mean to lose it. I planned to keep my cool, but with Eve, around and the way he was acting..."

"Luke. How long have I known you?" Cassandra chuckled, her tone softening.

I frowned, my brain struggling to do the math. I swear after twenty I stopped knowing my age without having to think first. "Since we were like ten?"

"Since *you* were ten." She grinned, patting my hand before sorting through the other documents from the envelope. "I've known you long enough to know that you have a temper, but you know how to handle yourself. So what's the common denominator with the changes?"

"Hells, you men really are the weaker species. Give me a call someday when you've figured it out." She rolled her eyes, pushing one sheet of paper covered in numbers that meant nothing to me across the table. "While I don't know where he is being held because they keep moving location, I have a source that confirmed that your girl's ex is heavily involved in coordinating of their transfer. I know you said Eve swiped a drive from the alpha's computer, but I'm no help with tech so Josh is probably still your best bet on cracking that. The other piece of good news is that I figured out some of Jeremy's notes."

I leaned closer, and Cassandra flicked her fingers to brighten the lighting.

"These aren't random letters, they're dates encoded using a cipher, and they all link back to different celestial events. All eclipses of some kind." She ran her finger down the page that I now realised was a list of dates tracking back hundreds of years. "The drawings weren't a complete win. I couldn't crack all of them, but a few were ogham."

"Ogham? I vaguely remember learning something about that in school."

"It's an early medieval alphabet used to write Irish, and I think it might be part of a spell." She flicked over to another page, pointing to a series of lines, and this time I really was lost. "It's highly unusual that a grimoire wouldn't be updated throughout the years and translated, I doubt there's a witch alive that could read this straight from the source."

I studied the weird line markings she'd transcribed from the photo of Jeremy's notes. "What does it say?"

"Life-source of the undead, the true heart of a hound, ancient magic spilled, bloodline and moon bound. Trinity tied by the blade of magic intertwined." Cassandra read the translation aloud, the exact same words we'd found in that ancient book.

She stopped before the last line as magic charged the air. It was unlike anything I'd ever felt, a tangible presence in the room with us. A cacophony of whispers and undecipherable chanting filled my ears, drowning out the silence in our room, so loud in my mind that I could barely focus as cobalt fire ignited all around the border of the page Cassandra had read the spell from.

Cassandra threw it down onto the table, her eyes wide as the page hovered suspended in the air. We both watched in horror as the flames rapidly engulfed the page, immune to the water the witch summoned to douse it. Except it didn't burn, instead the ink seemed to bleed from the page and pool onto the table. Once the flames converged at the centre, a hole ringed with ashes scorched through one small drawing she had etched on the paper. As quickly as they had appeared, the flames vanished, and the page fluttered harmlessly onto the table, becoming smudged with the molten ink.

"What the fuck have you gotten tied up in?" Cassandra looked from the ruined paper, to me, and then back again, as if trying to piece together some invisible jigsaw puzzle.

I'd never heard Cassandra sound scared or worried, or any kind of emotion that one should feel in dangerous situations. But the witch looked like she'd had a late-night visit from a banshee.

"We were able to trace two books Jeremy had been studying. One of them had that exact poem."

She shook her head, staring at the page as if it might grow teeth and attack, her tone grave. "It's not a fucking poem. This is old magic. Ancient, dangerous magic. I don't fuck with this shit and neither should you."

"I didn't ask for any of this, nor did Eve."

Her lips thinned, her expression grim. "I fear the fates may have given you no choice."

Eve's voice rang out in my mind, and my blood ran cold, my head emptying of all worries about magic at the fear in her voice.

SOS. I'm outside of the club on the streets, exited some way between the Anger and Violence levels.

Her fear was palpable, and I leaped to my feet without explanation, her panic rising as she sent a barrage of words.

Ryan and Nadine are here. Hybrids. Witches. Attack. Help.

CHAPTER 18

I had one plan: don't die.

The hybrids launched into the air, their corporeal forms shimmering as magic took hold and they shifted mid-attack on Nadine's command. I took my only chance, sprinting past them before they fully transformed into wolves. Pain shot through my arm as one of the hybrids jaws skimmed my shoulder, their teeth slicing into the flesh and grinding against my shoulder blade. I sprinted forwards with a hiss of pain, claws extending from my fingertips as I barrelled straight into my chosen target.

One of the warlocks tried to intervene, but I was faster. Nadine hit the ground first, our impact kicking up a dusting of snow. The icy cold sent a jolt of pain down my arm. I grabbed a fistful of her hair, my claws digging into her scalp, but I was hauled off her before I could land a proper blow.

Ryan pulled me away, throwing me straight into the arms of a warlock that looked like he could probably bench three of me. I slashed at his throat with my claws, narrowly missing as the warlock shoved me back and landed a well-aimed punch to my stomach. I groaned as his fist made contact, my knees buckling as the air rushed out of my lungs.

My shoulder was healing, but not as fast as I needed. He

lunged at me, and I aimed a kick at his chest as I fell backwards, my heel slicing through his shirt. He barely flinched as he followed me to the ground, trapping me against the freezing snow with thighs as thick as tree trunks on either side of my chest as he grappled to pin my arms too. I bucked and twisted in his grip, his fist glancing off my cheek as I reached into the top of my boot.

The paranormal world worked differently, but warlocks bled the same as humans.

I pulled the penknife free from my boot, flicking it open and sank the blade into his flesh in one swift movement. The knife edge struck with perfect precision, blood spurting as it slid deep into the narrow gap between his collarbones to slice through an artery. Shock widened his eyes as he pulled the knife free, blood pumping from the wound quickly soaking his shirt.

I was half human, and I would fucking fight like it.

Blood oozed from his mouth, dripping onto my face as I braced my feet against the ground, raising my hips to throw the stunned warlock off.

I scrambled to my feet and sprinted down the side street adjacent to the alley. I couldn't out-fight them, but I could run.

Nadine was hot on my heels. My heeled boots struggled to find purchase on the icy ground beneath the snow, and Nadine closed in, her fingers latching onto my forearm as she lunged for me. I spun with the knife raised, slashing the blade across her cheek.

I only had a split second to enjoy the way her pretty features contorted in rage before two paws slammed into my back, sending the knife flying from my hand and forcing me to the ground. Pain shot through my knees as they hit the black ice beneath the snow. The hybrid landed in front of me, its lips curled in a ferocious snarl as it eyed me up for dinner. This was it. Images of its jaws clamping around my neck sped through my mind before someone grabbed me by the hair. My head was wrenched back, forcing me to look up to see Ryan with a fistful of my hair wrapped around his hand and a sadistic grin lighting up.

"What have I told you about running?"

I didn't get the chance to answer, my balance falling off kilter as he shoved me forwards and forced my face into the ground. The shock of the cold compacted snow robbed me of air, my hotter temperature melting the ice just enough so it was like a puddle of slush, and I was drowning.

Stars danced in my vision, my heart hammering in my chest as it desperately tried to pump oxygen to my brain. I gasped for breath as Ryan yanked me up, the cold air stinging my throat. He glared down at me, his eyes a volatile mix of animosity and desire, the corners of his lips twitching at the sight of mascara-streaked tears streaming down my cheeks.

"You're making this difficult."

"Excuse me for not being a good little woman and coming quietly." I ground the words out, earning myself another mouthful of snow as he forced my face down.

I squirmed, coughing and spluttering as I struggled to draw breath. Snow filled my nostrils and my mouth, my lungs on fire as they strained to force air in. Panic set in, and Nadine's evil laughter in the background pierced through the ringing in my ears. Despite my efforts to keep my mouth closed, the pain of his knee digging between my shoulder blades made me give in to the urge to try to breathe. Melted, watery snow filled my mouth, and I gagged, my body convulsing as I choked.

Eve? Where are you?

Ryan kept me trapped with his knee, his fist digging into the back of my skull as he held me in place. If Luke found me dead, he'd no doubt end up being sentenced to death for the damage he would inflict in his rage if him blaming himself didn't kill him first. And what about Craig? Bound to live for an eternity in this new world and abandoned by me. And Kate, and how she'd lost her life all because of their pack's evil plans and an asshole thinking he had a right to me.

I couldn't give in.

Breathe. Fucking breathe for me baby.

Ryan's knuckles bruised my scalp as he held me there. I stopped struggling, my lungs screaming in protest as I went still. Black seeped into the edges of my vision, my heartbeat slowing and fear setting in. But my plan worked, and his grip loosened.

"Eve?" There was an edge of panic to his voice as he released the pressure on my head.

"Get the fuck off her!"

Luke. For a moment I thought I was hallucinating.

That was all I needed.

I braced my shaking, numb hands under my shoulders and threw all my energy behind the movement as I shoved my upper body up, my entire body shaking with the effort as I forced Ryan off. The moment there was air between him and my body, I flipped over onto my back, water pooling from my mouth as I coughed and spluttered. I gasped for air, greedily forcing it into my lungs as my vision cleared.

That's when I saw him, like some kind of guardian hellhound as he sprinted down the street towards us. His silver eyes burned with the promise of pain as he headed straight for my ex.

Ryan jumped to his feet, his mask of rage nothing on the thunderous fury that contorted Luke's features as he approached.

"I knew it." I croaked, a delirious smirk stretching across my face as I lay helpless in the snow. "You need me alive."

The weird warlock things advanced in the background, Nadine stalking towards me with venom in her eyes. Behind her, the pack of hybrids stepped forwards in unison, bloody spittle dripping from their jaws onto the white snow.

Ryan scoffed towered over me. "You think too highly of yourself."

A raspy laugh escaped me, and I winced, searing pain shooting through my ribs at the movement as I looked up at Ryan. "She doesn't know, does she?"

An orb of magic slammed into the back of my ex, sending

him to his knees just like he'd done to me. Nadine was next in the line of fire, magic sending a plume of snow into the air as she narrowly dodged the hit.

Luke raced to my side, framing my face in his hands while keeping his murderous gaze firmly fixed on Ryan. "Are you okay?"

I nodded, coughing up another mouthful of water and swiped the back of my hand over my mouth. "I'm good."

My body screamed in protest as I forced my limbs to move, and I swayed as I got to my feet. Luke steadied me, both of us faced with a wall of the remaining three warlocks flanked by hybrids stalking towards us. All of them had eyes completely engulfed by silver and blank stares.

Luke gave me a nod, and I shifted beside him, relishing in the fact I could call on my magic while Ryan dodged the blow of another spell. My paws hit the ground just in time as the hybrids charged. I leaped into the air, teeth and claws clashing as I collided with the nearest one mid-air. We crashed down into the snow, jaws snapping as we scrapped.

A shadowy figure ran across the shingle roof of the building next to Inferno, silent like a cat as they stalked closer to their targets.

I didn't seem to be their target, but I was certainly top of the list for the possessed hybrid warlock-hybrid army.

The wolves came for me and Luke while Nadine and Ryan retreated behind a dumpster. One hybrid caught a hold of my hind leg, its teeth hitting bone as it sank them deep. I yelped, kicking their muzzle with the free leg. My claws sliced across their jaw, the hybrids tongue hanging limply out the side of its mouth when I forced it off. They showed no sign of pain; in fact, they didn't show any emotion at all. Where Alice's friend had still held a shred of her true self, these hybrids seemed well and truly lost to whatever magic possessed them.

Duck.

Luke's order rang in my mind as I threw myself behind a stack of crates.

The witch I presumed was Cassandra, glimpses of her turquoise hair visible as she passed under a streetlight and sent a green and blue ball of fire flying into the dumpster. Sparks flew, the metal groaning and splintering as if it was made of wood.

Ryan and Nadine dived out of the way just in time. I took my chance to throw myself full force at the redhead that deserved an eternity in hell. Pain lanced through my body at the collision, but I grit my teeth and held on. My speed sent both of us tumbling onto the main street, a mass of limbs as her screeches echoed in the night.

I timed it perfectly, shifting back into my human form just as we rolled to a stop with Nadine on her back, trapped under the hybrid she despised so much.

This time I grabbed her hair, slamming Nadine's head back. It hit the ice with a satisfying crack. She hissed in pain and sank her claws into my wrist to force me to release her hair, a crazed look burning in her eyes. I kept her pinned, deciding to play dirty, and grabbed a handful of snow. I slammed my palm into her face, smearing the snow into her eyes and relishing the way she hissed in pain as the ice scratched her cornea.

We were back near to the entrance to the Inferno with an audience, just what I'd wanted. Witnesses all lined up in a queue to the club, our scuffle drawing unwanted attention.

I jumped to my feet, glancing behind me to find the hybrids paced back and forth at the edge of the side street, hiding in the shadows. They threw their heads back and howled in frustration to the moonless sky masked by thick snow clouds. Ryan stalked towards me, the knife I dropped, in his hand coated in blood.

Adrenaline coursed through my veins, but I ignored the pull of my magic, taking shallow breaths as I squared off to Nadine with my fists raised. Luke joined my side, the witch remaining hidden up on the roof. She'd killed her magic now we were out on the street. Exposing ourselves to humans had consequences, the exact reason I was in this mess in the first place. If they were going to exile me, I was going to use the same rules against them.

Nadine glared at us, fists clenched by her side. Her dress was singed, and I got a sick thrill out seeing the bruises on her wrists that were my handiwork.

Luke moved so half his body was in front of me, firmly placed between me and Ryan, along with the blood crazed hybrids and zombie warlocks. "Hiding behind numbers and your sidepiece now too?"

Ryan hovered a few paces behind Nadine, his face half cast in shadows as he barked an order. "Get the hybrids in check, we can't be seen."

Those bouncer warlocks from the club broke away from their post by the doorway, phones pressed to their ears as they marched towards us. Nadine gave me one seething glare and bolted into the distance with her bloodied warlocks in tow, the hybrids disappearing back down the side street after her. Ryan tossed the knife into a nearby dumpster, the metal pinging as it landed, and stuffed his hands in his trouser pockets as he retreated.

Luke's chest heaved, his breath forming vapours in the cold air against the winter sky. Once he was happy the coast was clear, he finally turned to face me. Silver moonlight swirled in his irises, his mouth set in a tense line as he took my bloodied appearance in.

"I said stick to the stairs and don't get lost." Luke closed the distance between us, buttons disappearing into the snow as he ripped his shirt off and wrapped it around me. His eyes swam with emotion, his hands stiff against my waist and tension bracketed his mouth. "I should never have left you at the bar."

I tried to smile but it was more of a grimace. "I was taking a shortcut."

His jaw feathered, the heat in his gaze at odds with the flurries of snow falling all around us. The silver showed no sign of retreating. A streetlight flickered above us, and my body swayed as I looked to thank our witch ally, only to find that she had vanished into the night. Before I could wobble again, Luke swept me into his arms.

My battered but healing body screeched in protest at the movement, and I groaned as he placed pressure on the shoulder wound, the adrenaline coursing through my veins begging me to shift so that I would heal faster. While most of our audience was paranormal, a human could walk around the corner at any minute. And we had created enough commotion to piss off the London alpha, and anyone else involved, ten times over without needing to break another rule and risk further exile tonight.

The warlock bouncers set off towards the side street we'd come from, but they would find nothing but the blood stains already being covered by pretty snowflakes as the weather turned and the wind picked up.

"I may not be alpha, but you sure as hell will listen to my orders in future."

"Whatever happened to equality? I had to improvise." I tried to ignore the countless sets of eyes on us. The cold night made goosebumps rise on my skin. Snow clouds rolled above us, blanketing the night sky.

He shook his head, his thumb brushing my cheek as he swept away my tears. "You call this improvising?"

"Badly." I let my head fall against his chest, my body sagging in his hold. The warmth of his arms felt like safety. He felt like home.

Luke cleared his throat as one of the warlocks turned our way, scowling. "And that's our cue to leave."

CHAPTER 19

The roots of tension refused to release their hold on my body, not even when we returned to the hotel. Lawrence was waiting for us by the staff entrance, warm light spilling out into the night from the open door where he took cover from the falling snow. He kept a healthy distance, his fangs extending a fraction and golden eyes dilating at the sight of both me and Eve covered in blood. He didn't dare say a word, taking the opposing silver in mine as a silent warning as I carried her over the threshold of Château Minuit and straight into a service elevator. Darius had sent a car for us the moment I called, especially when I threatened to hot-wire one if the driver didn't get there quick enough.

The vampire's concerned face disappeared as metal doors slid shut, and we were alone once more, two hearts beating in sync as the elevator carried us up the many floors. Eve stayed curled in my arms, her bloodstains barely visible on the bunched-up top she clutched to her shoulder. Her breathing was my tether to reality as I counted our ascent until we reached our floor.

I pressed my thumbprint to the scanner at the side of the door handle, and the lock clicked in confirmation, swinging open to reveal the empty hotel suite. Ryan and Nadine wouldn't be able to gain entry to the hotel, we were safe. I paused before entering, casting my senses out to triple check that we were alone.

"Home sweet home," I murmured, placing a kiss on her clammy forehead as I carried her inside.

She tried to mask her pain with a failed attempt at a smile that was more of a grimace.

Always trying to act tough, as if pain was something you should be ashamed of, when her vulnerabilities and heart were what made her one of the strongest women I knew. I was brought up to recognise and respect the power of women, Eve didn't need to hide any part of herself from me. She couldn't. She always saw straight through me, right into the darkest depths of my soul. Her soul sang to me in turn.

I glanced down to find her staring up at me with those captivating blue eyes of hers, glistening snowflakes beginning to thaw scattered through her hair like stars. Even injured, bloody, and exhausted, I felt like I was holding a Goddess in my arms.

"Keep that right there," I ordered, catching her wrist as she tried to stop putting pressure on the wound that was no longer gushing blood but definitely needed attention.

"I'm fine, the bleeding stopped in the car."

I knew it had, I could smell the difference, but it was a deep wound, and the muscle beneath was still knitting back together. So, I ignored her protests, heading straight for the bedside dresser where the items I'd requested were already set up thanks to our undead hosts. Eve might have werewolf healing powers, but I wasn't going to let her suffer for any longer than necessary. The sight of her in pain was like a vine barbed thorns constricting around my heart.

"Luke, I said I'm fine. I promise." She tossed the remains of her bloody, shredded top aside to prove her point, her half-arsed, weak wriggles in my arms doing little to convince me.

The deep laceration had closed, but the sight of the wound still raised and angry surrounded by deep purple bruising colouring her skin incited a carnal rage inside me. If Ryan ever laid a single hand on her again, I'd make sure he lost it. I had no taste for killing, but I had a thirst for revenge, and his name was top carved on my list.

I ground my teeth, my jaw twitching as I fought to keep my temper under control. "You're a bad liar."

She opened her mouth to argue, but her response died at the sight of whatever she saw in my face. I took the opportunity to capture her lips in a hungry kiss, a protective growl rumbling as my tongue explored her mouth. I didn't break the contact, tangling a hand in her hair and devouring her mouth until her breathing came in soft pants. My chest hummed with satisfaction at the sight of her rosy cheeks and the way chest flushed pink above the neckline of her top as I pulled away.

"I love arguing with you, and I'll happily debate how un-fine you are later. For now, please, let me take care of you."

This time she didn't argue, her expression softening and her body relaxing against mine. I could feel the tension leaving her muscles as she nodded with glassy eyes.

It was a simple request to some, but I knew her history. She was a fighter, a formidable fierce force of nature, but even a storm had to break.

Eve made a soft sound as I leaned down to kiss a falling teardrop away, allowing her to bury her face in my chest. She could hide from the world in my arms for an eternity.

Her skin was still cool to my touch, but beginning to warm thanks to the crackling fire in the corner of the room coupled with my body heat. I grabbed the two bottles off the dresser, one a metallic silver and the other orange, and carried her towards the bathroom. The lights flared to life on at the motion of us entering and the knots of tension in my shoulders loosened a touch at the sight of steam rising from the already full jacuzzi, covered in rose petals. I wasn't sure if Lawrence had added the petals for the calming effect or if the vamp had suddenly developed a sense of humour.

"Aw, you shouldn't have," Eve teased, wiping at her mascara-stained cheeks.

I rolled my eyes, placing the bottles down on the white marble countertop that matched the tiles covering both the walls and floor of the lavish bathroom, and carried her straight to the shower.

The bathroom of our fancy suite was like one large wet room, his and hers porcelain sinks on the counter lining one side with matte black bathroom fixtures and a large mirror. The outer wall opposite was taken up by the large inset Jacuzzi steps leading into it, right next to a spacious walk-in shower with two shower heads. The corners of my lips lifted at the memory of Eve's face lighting up, and her lecturing me about how amazing it was because she didn't have to deal with me hogging the water.

"Alright Mrs. Tough gal, do you think you sit down in here for a minute?"

Eve nodded, and I set her down on the built-in bench at the back of the shower. I kept my hands either side of her ribs as she swayed, only releasing her once she placed her palms on the bench, her fingers smearing the white tiling with blood as she steadied herself. She waited patiently, watching silently as I kneeled to peel my shirt off her shoulders.

Heat flared in tandem with my temper with every new mark on her perfect skin that came into view. Each cut brought up images of her face down and motionless in that snow. I'd felt her struggling through the link, felt the air leaving her lungs. I swallowed hard, pain lancing through my chest at the memory.

Eve's fingers closed around my forearm as I braced my hand against the bench to stand. Her touch was feather light as she reached up to cup my jaw. "You know you can't keep me trapped in here. There's a big bad world out there, and you can't hide me away forever."

"There are big bad *wolves* out there," I corrected her, gritting my teeth at the scent of her blood mixed with others. I nuzzled her hand, pressing my lips to her palm in a gentle kiss "I'll never trap you against your will, but forgive me if I like the idea of keeping you tucked up safely when I've had to watch you scrapping with danger one too many times."

My mind flickered back to visions of that level in Inferno, and I shuddered.

I should have never agreed to meet Cassandra there, but because of her line of work and desire to lay low, she only hung out in places were other paranormals wouldn't comment on her presence. If you're being a shady fuck, you were far less likely to admit seeing someone there. The logic was sound from her point of view, but it was a mistake on my part. Even without Bonnie and Clyde 2.0 turning up, we took a risk by going beyond the first few levels in Inferno.

Eve wore a similar expression, no doubt scarred by our trip to the club. "Danger seems to follow me."

"It seems to follow *us*, and I will happily take the brunt of the violence if it keeps you safe."

She relaxed under the spray of water while I rinsed off quickly, only leaving her alone when she'd regained some colour. I kept an ear out though, ready to jump in if needed while I tended to my own wounds. Eventually the soft sound of her humming became audible over the rush of water.

"Fuck." I hissed, flinching as a few drops of silver fell from the dropper I held suspended above a nasty cut just below my ribs. It was deep with jagged edges that had already started knitting back together. As soon as the unicorn blood touched the skin, a burning sensation spread through the area as the healing process accelerated. I inhaled deeply, my fingertips dipping into the water of the Jacuzzi as I gripped the sides of the ledge. No internal damage, thankfully those rabid wolves had terrible aim or else they might have caught a lung. I'd experienced a pneumothorax before. Yes, it healed, but it was an incredibly unpleasant experience I didn't fancy reliving.

The only thing stealing my breath was Eve when she emerged from the steam of the shower. Her wounds were healing well, and she showed no sign of pain as she moved. In fact, she was wearing nothing at all, having completely ignored the towel I'd left hanging by the screen door. Water droplets slid between her breasts, her body glistening under the dim lights as she moved, and I remained frozen in place.

"You're making a mess, Luke." Her voice was low and a seductive smile curved her lips. She knew exactly what she was doing as my name rolled off her tongue.

I glanced down at the silver pooling on the tile of the Jacuzzi border, unicorn blood dripping everywhere as I simply stared at the vixen stalking towards me. Her hips swayed as she walked past me and with each step she took, ripples forming on the water surface as she descended into the clear water that displayed every inch of her body. I told myself to take it slow, she was healing, she needed rest. But then she turned to face me, her hand extended and a silent request blazing in her siren eyes.

Who was I to deny the woman who held my heart?

CHAPTER 20

EVE

I needed him.

It was a longing that surpassed desire, as if the ember burning inside me needed him like I needed oxygen to breathe. I knew lust, this wasn't her doing. It was something deeper. Something basal that pumped through my veins and made my mind spin, emptying of all thoughts but *him*. There had always been attraction between us, but I could never fully describe the feeling that had taken hold of me as if it had always been there, growing, building, waiting for this moment.

Waiting for him.

When I met Luke's silver-eyed gaze, I knew he felt it too.

It was in the set of his jaw as he stood and dropped his towel, in each tauntingly slow step he took descending the steps into the water. Something deep inside me purred in delight knowing that body of an alpha, all of him, was mine.

He flicked a switch in the wall, and I expected the lights to dim, but instead what looked like a normal tile wall at the back of the Jacuzzi smoothly slide to one side to reveal an extension of the glass window of the suite. A dusting of snow coated the balcony rails framing the London skyline. The night sky had cleared, the silhouette of the crescent moon peeking through the clouds to bask the city in its glow.

The heat in Luke's gaze was loaded with promises as he took my hand, his movements slow and controlled as he brushed his thumb along my jawline. I leaned into his touch, my breath hitching as he tipped my chin up, and I was forced to face the fire in his eyes, a burning intensity that I wanted to drown in for an eternity.

"Beautiful, but nothing compared to you."

I had no words as he leaned in to claim my mouth with a kiss. At the touch of his lips something was unleashed. His control snapped, and he crushed his mouth to mine, dragging his nails up my back to tangle his hand in my hair while the other dropped to the curve of my waist and pulled me flush against him. I slid my hands over his chiselled chest, wrapping my arms around his neck as he deepened the kiss.

He grazed his teeth against my lower lip as his hands dropped to my ass, lifting me in one easy movement. I didn't need a second invitation to wrap my legs around his waist. A low growl of approval that sent blood rushing to my core rumbled in his chest as the movement caused his hard erection to brush against me.

Water sloshed around us as he waded through the rose petals and carried us deeper into the Jacuzzi. His lips never once left mine as he kissed me with an insatiable hunger, as if he wanted to devour me body, mind, and soul.

He trailed light kisses along my jaw, his hand fisting my hair and tugging my head to one side so he could continue down my neck. His teeth grazed the column of my throat, making my heartbeat thrum and my thighs clamp around his waist.

"Tell me baby, do you know what a werewolf bite feels like?"

No, but I sure as hell wanted to find out. My head emptied of all thoughts as he ran his tongue along my throat before nipping, my head falling back in invitation. He hadn't even touched me properly, and I was soaked between my thighs, the press of his hard dick against the curve of my ass a constant tease.

Water rose around my waist, stopping at the swell of my breasts as Luke lowered us into the Jacuzzi. I unravelled my legs from around his waist, kneeling over him as my shins met the seat beneath us. He made a low noise of frustration, his hand on my ass brushing against my clit as he moved to grip my thigh and force my legs to spread wider. My breath hitched as his length pressed against my soaked pussy.

"Use your words, Eve." He smirked and nipped my collarbone in warning.

I shuddered, and it only seemed to drive him wilder, the points of his canines pressing against my neck in one final request.

"Show me." My voice was breathy as I rolled my hips against his, desperate for friction. "Please."

His grip on my hair tightening was my only warning before his teeth pierced my skin with a growl, the sound a possessive claim I'd never heard before as he sank his teeth in deeper.

The sharp sting of his bite only lasted for a moment before heat spread from the site, a wave of pure bliss chasing through my veins. His was nothing like the vampire bite, devoid of pain and setting my body alight with pleasure. Delicious ecstasy rushed over me, radiating through every inch of my body. I was burning up inside, and I wanted to bask in the fire of his touch. I wanted to burn for him.

"Oh, God." A loud moan escaped me, my eyes rolling into the back of my head as the sensation overwhelmed me.

He slid his teeth deeper, pulling my hair so that my back arched and exposed my throat to him. His claws extended as he gripped my ass, his cock throbbing between my legs.

Just when I thought I might black out from the sensation of his bite, his hand slid up my stomach to cup my breasts. He withdrew his canines from my neck at the exact same time as he pinched my nipple between his finger, causing my hips to buck against his.

"God isn't here right now, but I promise by the end of tonight the only name you'll be moaning for the rest of eternity will be mine." He pinched again, swirling his tongue over the mark from his teeth. His lips curved in a wicked smirk against my neck as he drew another moan from me.

My cheeks flushed at his dirty words despite the fact I was naked an exposed on his lap, facing the London skyline as he bared me to the world. At the same, he made me feel like I was a show he would kill any other man for witnessing.

His grip on my hair pinned me in place at his mercy as he nipped and sucked the bite marks until I was a panting, needy mess grinding against him. He kept my body wound tight, dropping his hand between my legs to brush his fingers against my clit, his touch irritatingly light. My pussy clenched, my body writhing with pent up frustration. I didn't know it was possible to crave the feeling of him inside me so badly, my need for him driving me wild.

He denied me the friction I wanted, his finger moving in slow circles around the bundle of nerves until I thought I might snap.

"Please, Luke, I need you."

He ran his thumb over my clit, releasing my nipple from his teasing to grin up at me like a devil before switching to give my other breast some attention. His words sent vibrations through me as he dragged a finger down my slick core. "I do love when you beg."

The cityscape behind Luke blurred as he slid two fingers inside me, curling them towards him to hit the perfect spot. My breath hitched, my body straining against his grip as he fucked me with his hand. There was no easing in as he added another finger, and I moaned at the delightful feeling of him stretching me, my knees sliding on the tiles of the Jacuzzi seat and my legs spreading wider in invitation. I didn't want him to be gentle, I wanted him to destroy me.

He released his grip on my hair to drag his claws down my back, and my head fell forwards with a soft moan, my breath hitching as he added another finger. "Good girl."

My inner wolf preened at his praise. I rocked back and forth, my breath coming in sharp pants, and nipped at his earlobe with a growl. The warm water of the Jacuzzi splashed around my waist as I rode his fingers, raking my nails across his shoulders as I leaned up to kiss him. Pressure built in my core, and I slid my hand down his chest and stomach, my fingers tracing over the taut muscles there before closing around the base of his hard cock. The feral wolf inside of me hummed in delight at his need for me.

He nipped at my lower lip, muffling my moans as he picked up the pace and drove his fingers deeper to stroke the fire building inside of me. His groan of pleasure as I swirled my thumb over the sensitive head with each pump of my hand only sent me hurtling over the edge. He broke our kiss as if he wanted to hear me, leaning in to drag his tongue across the sensitive bite marks and pressing down on my clit in one final command.

I broke for him, pleasure washed over my body in waves as I rode out the orgasm, his pace refusing to slow as he forced the pressure to build. It was his name that fell from my lips a second time. He scrapped his teeth against my neck, fingering my pussy until my legs were shaking.

My waist sank deeper under the water as he withdrew his fingers, and I wrapped my arms around his neck, my breath coming in short pants.

Luke's eyes were hooded desire as he looked up at me, reaching up to brush a damp strand of hair behind my ear. With the London city lights shining in the distance behind him, the moon reflecting in his silver eyes as he looked up at me, he was all my fantasies brought to life and more.

"I've been meaning to say this to you for too long, and I'm not risking another day going by without you knowing the truth." He dropped his hands to my waist, his thumbs stroking the curve of my hip as he stared up at me with adoration I couldn't fathom deserving. "I love you."

My eyes widened at his confession. His heart hammered against his chest, the beat perfectly in sync with my own. I thought I'd known love, but my feelings for Luke surpassed anything I'd ever felt before. He was my friend, my lover, his soul the twin to complete mine.

"I love you, too."

The moon shone in his eyes as he nuzzled my cheek, a smile curving his lips as they brushed mine. I cupped his face in my hands, my eyes fluttering closed as I lost myself in his kiss.

Luke had taught me what real love was. He was my protector but also encouraged me to grow. We complimented each other's strengths and balanced one another, holding space where needed. He saw right through me, never shying away from the darkest part of me, and what I saw as broken shards, he viewed the makings of a masterpiece. He'd taught me how to love myself, which in turn allowed me to love him without restraint. I was irrevocably and eternally his.

His grip on my hips tightened as he lifted me, the head of his arousal pressing against my entrance. My moans were lost in our kiss as he slowly lowered me onto his hard length. It was the most glorious form of torture, my back arching as my body tried to accommodate him. He never once broke eye contact, his gaze scorching as his cock stretched my pussy inch by inch. He kept me pinned, forcing me to take every part of him as he guided me down onto his cock until my ass hit his thighs, my inner muscles contracting around him.

Only then did he unleash himself on me.

His hands gripped my ass as he lifted me, sliding me along his full length before dropping me down once more. I cried out, my head falling back as he hit the deepest parts of me. My nails bit into the back of his neck as he lifted his hips to meet mine as they rolled, my chest heaving as he picked up the pace.

The feeling of him fucking me raw ignited the carnal part of me, my nails biting into his neck as he slammed into me. A low growl rumbled in his chest, making my pussy clench as he only deepened his strokes. He slid one hand up the curve of my back, a shiver climbing up my spine in the wake of the feel of his claws between my shoulder blades. His fingers closed around the back of my neck, tilting my head to one side to expose my throat before tracing the two bite marks on my neck with his tongue.

My cheeks were flushed in the reflection in the window and rose petals scattered around us. The two puncture marks were visible on my neck as my body arched, shaking with each thrust as Luke impaled me on his cock. He drew his teeth over my throat, his head tilting to show a flash of silver and mischief in his eyes as they met mine the reflection in silent question.

"Yours, I'm yours."

With that, he sank his teeth into my neck and at the same time drove his cock deep inside. My cries of pleasure echoed in the bathroom, my body trembling against his as ecstasy took hold. The water splashing around us and rose petals swirling as he fucked me like I was his last dying breath. Colours bloomed in my vision, the city lights sparkling like the stars below. Something built besides the pleasure inside me, the hair on my arms rising as the surrounding air became charged.

He slid one hand between my legs, finding my clit and stroking in tandem with his thrusts, stoking the fire he'd ignited in me. The carnal growl as he sank his teeth deeper set me alight. I was high on pleasure, but I needed more. I needed him—all of him—because he had all of me. I was utterly lost in him.

He nudged my legs farther apart with his knee, the angle driving him deeper inside me. I came apart, the sensation of his bite making me feel like I was free-falling as he slammed into me. I screamed for Luke, his name tumbling from my mouth like a prayer as I broke, over and over again like the waves of pleasure washing over me.

Luke's pace was unrelenting, claiming me with each slam of his hips against mine. I was left at his mercy as he fucked me like I was his last dying breath. My vision blurred at the edges as the lights flickered overhead. His dirty thoughts filtered into mind over the mind link, and I saw myself through his eyes as I came for him. I could feel the thrill that ran through him at the sight of me coming apart for him as he claimed me.

Another surge of pleasure built, my pussy tightening around him as I moaned his name. The lights went out, cloaking the room in darkness before moonlight spread across the room and basked us in her glow. Luke buried himself in me with a roar as he came, water splashing as power surged around us and the bottle of unicorn blood sliding off the edge of the jacuzzi and smashing onto the ground.

It was just me and him, his heart was mine as we fell apart and came back together. My eyelids fluttered closed and warmth spread inside me, his claws digging into my side. He fucked me until we'd both rode our orgasms out, stealing my breath away until my legs shook. I collapsed in his arms, my body spent and little aftershocks of pleasure making my hips twitch.

He withdrew his teeth from my neck with a growl, holding me tightly against him as if the city outside might snatch me away. I sighed softly as he flicked his tongue over the bite marks, tracing slow circles on my back.

Luke's eyes widened as I opened mine, the moon's glow behind him lighting up the room as if he was some kind of God.

"Eve…"

I looked up at my reflection in the window beside the night sky, London city sprawling below us. Silver eyes stared back at me.

I didn't need him to explain, I could *feel* it. That inexplicable bond between us, an invisible string binding us that was always more than just the normal mind link. Our hearts beat as one.

"Mates." Luke's expression was one of awe as he reached up to touch my face, captivated by the silver of my eyes. "You're my mate."

CHAPTER 21

EVE

"A witch, vampire, and werewolf do what with a dagger? It sounds like the beginning of a bad joke." Luke shook his head, his tousled hair and dark purple under eyes giving away how little we had slept. There had been a lot of bonding and not nearly enough time to talk about what had happened. I think he was giving me space to process. "Why can't witches just write what they mean? At the very least there should be ingredients."

Maya rolled her eyes, pushing her braids back out of her face as she leaned closer to read the spell we'd transcribed. "Magic isn't like baking, you can't just throw down ingredients and hope for the best."

"So the words matter then? This exact phrasing is the spell?" I rubbed my temples as pain radiated behind my eyes from trying to crack this for days now.

"Yes and no. Witches have grimoires that contain all sorts of notes, spells, potions, and even family histories or details of important events. You name it, and it's probably in there somewhere." Maya explained, her brow furrowing as she reread the text once more. "They used to be handed down from one generation to the next, but between humans raging wars, paranormals doing the same, and the intermarriages between families, the majority have been lost or destroyed over the years. They're a big hit on the black market too."

Luke sighed, drowning his sorrows in curry as he stuffed another forkful of chicken and rice into his mouth. "I knew we should have stolen the book."

Luckily the Thai restaurant we'd holed up in was quiet at this hour and no one seemed to be listening in on our conversations. After following Ryan and Nadine around London City all day, we needed to recharge. My misguided belief that Dublin was big was well and truly put to bed after wandering around for hours, having to dive on the underground and grab taxis just to keep up. Dublin may have been a city, but much like Ireland, it was tiny in comparison to the rest of the world. A pang of homesickness squeezed my chest. Ireland was imperfect, but it was home, and I loved it.

"Did you see that ceiling and how far those book stacks stretched into the darkness? For all we know they've godsdamned dragons guarding them." I moved my fork around my plate, my stomach growling. Despite the delicious smell of the mountain of food laid out in front of us, my appetite was dead in the water.

"How can they have dragons with the owls flapping about? A dragon would have a field day."

I shrugged. "Maybe they only let it out when someone is trying to steal books. There's no way they don't have protection beyond the wards."

"I think I could have managed it." Luke grinned, bumping his hip into mine as he scooted closer on his chair.

Butterflies bloomed in my stomach at his smile. I felt like a schoolgirl; this whole mate thing was weird in the best way. The darker part of my mind wondered if it was real, but then Luke would do something, and I could *feel* him as if his heart and soul were entwined with mine.

"You could have tried, but whether it was a dragon or one of those creepy ass books with eyes that came for you, you'd have been on your own." I laughed, chewing my lower lip as I fought back a grin of my own.

"Nice to know you have my back."

"I'm not a gambling woman, wolf versus dragon are not odds I wanna take. It would be your own fault for stealing anyway, that sphinx was very clear about the rules, and I think we broke enough of them."

"I disagree, we didn't break enough," Luke countered, mischief glinted in his hazel eyes.

"I don't think we need the book, and I'd rather neither of you decided to take on a dragon. This thing doesn't sound like any spell I've heard of. It reminds me more of a prophecy than a spell." Maya cleared her throat, interrupting our back and forth. "Did you take any photos of the book?"

I nodded, slipping my phone from my pocket. "Yeah, we took the page with the symbols along with a few others."

When I flicked through them, the only photos on my phone were of the hotel, Luke scoffing pizza, and Jeremy's notes.

Luke noticed my frown, his own brow furrowing. "What's wrong?"

"Did we take them on yours?" I asked, motioning to his phone on the table.

"I don't think so." He picked up his phone to check, confusion creasing his brow as he turned the screen to face us. His most recent photo was of me sleeping that morning, the rest were from before we'd visited the library. "I do think I took one, but it's gone."

Anxiety crawled along the back of my neck as I scrolled, drawing my shoulders up. Nothing. No photos from the library at all. "They're not there, I even checked the trash. We took pictures of the book, the spell, and even the symbols I'd spotted first. All of them have vanished, there's no way I'd delete them."

"Sounds like they had more than just physical wards, or maybe it was the books themselves," Maya mused, slumping back against the plush cushions of the couch lining the wall on her side of the table with a sigh.

"Wait, magic can fuck with electronics like phones?"

"Of course, otherwise humans would have found out about the paranormal world. Everything is energy, and magic is the master manipulator." There was a sense of awe in her tone despite the ominous connotations. "Describe the book to me."

I turned to Luke, trying to tamp the blush colouring my cheeks as I rolled back to that moment in the library. "We found the spell in the book you were looking at, right?"

"Yeah, it was in my one. There was no title on my books, they just looked really fancy."

Of course that was the extent of his description.

My lips thinned, and I gave Maya that look that silently said *'men.'*

"I'm gonna need a bit more to go on than that. Markings, age, were there pages missing?" The corners of the young witch's lips twitched in amusement.

"Both of the books were huge, like those giant textbooks from university. They were hardback and bound in what looked like leather, the lighting was poor in there so not to damage the books, but the one we found the spell in was a kind of slate grey, maybe faded black." I cast my mind back, visualising the book while trying to block out the not so relevant parts of our little study session. "There were jewels all over the book. I'm not sure if they were real or not, but most looked like sapphires or rubies, something like that. Then there was a large moonstone in the centre of the front cover, and smaller moonstones carved into different shapes depicting the phases of the moon cycle along the spine of the book."

"Handwritten?"

"With drawings too, sketches of the moon, some of the sun and then diagrams I can't really remember. I recognised one symbol, it was in Jeremy's notes, and I'm pretty sure I learned about it in history classes too." Words failed me as I tried to describe the damn symbol, so I typed a quick search into google, showing them the symbol and thanking the wonders of modern of technology. "This thing."

Maya tilted her head to one side, pointing with a prawn cracker in hand. "Triquetra."

I shrugged. "Sure? That caught my attention, and when we turned to the next page, we found the spell. It was framed by a really intricate drawing of wolves, the moon, and a dagger."

Luke pulled the page we'd scrawled the spell onto closer. "Some bits were coloured red, maybe they were blood?"

"Could be. The spell was definitely handwritten, the text was all squiggly with fancy lettering."

The witched nodded, as if considering her options before finally speaking up. "Okay, I know I'm only a baby witch, but my grandmother is a grimoire fanatic. She taught me all about them, and I've seen the only one left from our family that she's salvaged. That doesn't sound like a grimoire."

"What else could it be?"

"Predating paper, during the earlier years of witchcraft, information was passed down through word of mouth." Maya explained, the shift in her energy palpable. Tension bracketed her mouth as she eyed the spell with a nervousness that walked the line of respect and fear. "Everything from traditions, spells, how to make certain potions and elixirs, and history."

Her nerves were infectious, an insidious sense that something was very wrong pooling in my gut.

"Once written language became a thing, those with the knowledge and means began to document things. One of my special interests is the ancient art forms of magic. I know we couldn't find that last book but based on where it was categorised in our archives, it was a book of curses."

I swallowed, my mouth going dry. "What's the difference between a spell and a curse?"

"A spell has a finite lifecycle. Even things like wards have to be reinforced. You can't 'spell' a person forever, but you can curse them."

"Like the curse on werewolves." Luke's expression was grave, his hand gripping my leg under the table to stop it from bouncing. "I don't think the moon and sun are a coincidence."

"This is…" Maya stared at the curse scrawled in pen because I couldn't work the damn quill, exhaling slowly as if she could lift the weight of that knowledge off her shoulders. "I don't know for sure because the origin story of wolves and vampires has never been confirmed publicly by the Royals, but the amount of blood shed over all this makes me think it might be real."

"Didn't Larissa say she wanted to lift the curse to bind creatures to herself?" My heart skipped a beat, fluttering like a trapped bird in my chest.

Luke's brow creased. "That's not the kind of curse you can lift, both of the witches involved are long dead."

"I don't know, but nothing good comes of messing with ancient magic like this. It's called a curse for a reason." The hairs on Maya's arms stood on end as she pushed the paper across the table towards us, as if even being in the proximity of such a thing. "There's no such thing as good or bad magic, only who wields it."

"Whatever that witch has planned, it's nothing good."

Something jingled beside us, and my ears zeroed in on Maya's tote bag. Something rattled against the contents, causing the various badges she had attached on the outside to jiggle. Luke tensed beside me, on high alert as his focus moved to the restaurant doorway.

"They're on the move again." Maya reached into her bag, sliding out a battered booklet containing a map of London and a crystal attached to a metal chain that vibrated in her palm.

The fistful of hair I'd ripped from Nadine's scalp came in handy. You know the way they always say to get as much of your murderer's DNA under your fingernails as possible? Well, that bitch had tried to murder me one too many times, and this time I made it count. Thanks to my little violence trophy and Maya's powers, we had been able to track Nadine's movements all day, and we finally had a lead. A small spark of hope in the darkness.

"Are you sure about this?" I asked, shifting in my seat.

Maya unfolded the map of London for the fiftieth time that day, nudging a bowl of steaming rice out of the way. "I'm sure. I know it's harder to trust when they're not on the streets, but I promise this works."

Luke snatched up the basket of prawn crackers before she could move that out of his reach.

She was right. Each time we'd pinpointed their location it had been correct. I was sceptical at first, but each time we followed them around both by car and on foot, Maya's magical tracking proved itself correct. We'd tracked them to a fancy hotel not too far from Edmonstone's office, reaffirming our suspicions that they were partners in their sordid business. Maya's tracking had been accurate right down to their lunch date in a lavish restaurant. I'd felt like a weirdo watching from across the park, but Maya couldn't risk getting close to them and she needed to be within a certain range to glamour us. She was an incredible witch, but she was young and still learning.

I worked with Luke to rearrange the table and weight down the worn corners of the maps with glasses and a knife, spreading the paper flat to reveal the many streets of London. The gold chain of the pendulum jiggled as Maya held it over the map, the flame of the small candlelight on the table bending towards the purple crystal as if drawn to the power.

We didn't bother trying to hide what we were doing, the only other people in the restaurant this late on a Tuesday night a teenage couple in the corner who clearly didn't want their date to end. Young love. Cute. While we were tracking down power-hungry werewolves that were trafficking and murdering paranormal creatures.

Life was weird.

Maya let the pointed crystal fall until the chain went taught, the amethyst twisting and the hexagonal faceted sides shimmering as they caught the light. She pinched a strand Nadine's red hair between her fingers, along with the chain a few inches from the end and closed her eyes. The pendulum started rocking from side to side, suspended in the air above the map, before rotating in an arc. The circle of rotation got smaller as Maya murmured what sounded like Latin under her breath.

I met Luke's eyes as the candle flickered in an imaginary wind, seeming to extinguish completely before flaring back into life. Just like the lights had in the library.

The pendulum came to a dead stop over a location not far from us, hovering over the square outline right next to the alpha's office building. The same place the crystal had revisited several times over the last few days and each time we checked for the past two hours.

"I know Henry liked his cars, but either he's got one hell of an extended carpark or the crystal has met its quota for today." I frowned as the crystal seemed to vibrate in defiance.

"It's not wrong." Maya made a point of trying to sway the crystal, beginning the rotations again only to end up with the same outcome as the crystal guided her to hang over the same spot. She tugged a handful of smaller crystals from a small velvet pouch, warming them in her hand before letting them scatter on the map. The tiny arrows engraved on the crystals all pointed to the same location.

I pulled it up on google maps, only finding an inconspicuous three story building next to the high rise that housed Henry's office. "It looks like apartments or something."

Luke sighed, rubbing his forehead. "Maybe they're using underground tunnels? Or they're fucking in a car parked outside?"

"As much as I really don't want to see that, there's only one way to find out. They've done nothing but eat and hide in their hotel all day, this has to mean something. Maybe they'll be meeting with the alpha."

Maya was the only one of us that didn't get to her feet, her expression pensive as she drummed purple-painted nails that matched the crystal against the map.

"I know you want to come, but it's not safe," I said softly, reaching out to squeeze her hand.

She returned the gesture limply, puffing a frustrated sigh. "Not safe for a witch, but you two wolves get to run head-first into madness."

Luke shrugged his jacket on, not that he needed any layers. He ran hot on a good day, never mind when we were tracking missing hybrids.

"I know you want to rescue Gabi, but please hear me when I say risking your life isn't worth it." Luke turned to Maya, pity and an intimate understanding shining in his hazel eyes. "I did a lot of really stupid, reckless things when searching for Alice the first year. She was lucky she had a brother to come back to in the end, and none of it got me any closer to finding her."

Maya's lips thinned, her face a mask of steely determination. "You're not that much older than me. I'm eighteen in a month."

She didn't say it, but I could hear the way her voice cracked at the thought of hitting that milestone without her friend. I swallowed the lump rising in my throat knowing I'd face the same thing, except one of my best friends was gone forever. Gabi still had a chance, and we had every intention of bringing her home.

"Maya, if I could guarantee your safety I would one hundred percent want you by our side. But I can't, and I refuse to let those bastards take another life. Imagine how guilty Gabi's parents would feel for involving you?" That air of confidence Luke always seemed to have seeped through. "It's not safe for us, and I would really prefer Eve sat this one out too, but she'd just find a way to sneak out anyway so I might as well have her within my sights."

She cracked a smile at that, and I stuck out my tongue at him, but didn't argue. Because he was right.

I shrugged on my black thermal jacket, lightweight but warm. The fancy coats the vampire assistant kept supplying didn't work when I was skulking around alleyways. The snow may have turned to slush over the past few days, but the London temperatures hadn't thawed in the slightest.

"You'll call me later?" Maya slumped back into the comfy couch lining the wall of the restaurant, dropping the pendulum onto the map in reluctant acceptance.

"I promise."

The young witch had tears in her eyes as I leaned in to give her a hug, squeezing her extra tight as I whispered in her ear. "You're an incredibly talented witch. I'm not risking your life either, not when your future is so bright."

I couldn't promise that I'd rescue Gabi that night or even find her at all. But I could promise her a call. I just hoped we had good news for once.

CHAPTER 22

LUKE

Our breath lingered as vapour in the cold night air, the noise of rain running down gutters and the distant sound of horns our only company answer neared the street Maya's pendulum had marked on the map.

The closer we got, the tighter the knotted mass of worry and fear wound in my stomach, apprehension dragging a shudder down my spine. I had no idea what we would find. A testing facility for the wolf packs, depraved experiments Lars probably funded just for kicks? With Larissa as the mastermind orchestrating their plans, there was no telling what horrors this place could hold.

I could have done without the added guilt of leaving Maya behind. The witch was wickedly smart and had helped us so much, but I didn't want her caught up in this. We had no true proof that Gabi was still alive, and I wasn't going to risk her life on a chance.

Not that I was willing to risk Eve's either, but no matter how much my protective side longed to keep my mate safe, she was my partner in crime. I didn't just want her by my side, it was a *need*. It felt surreal even thinking that word. The way our mind link worked had raised my suspicions a few times, but I never believed I'd be gifted a mate.

How was I worthy of her?

Fated mates were a gift from the universe, and I just couldn't wrap my head around the idea of her truly being mine in that way.

I forced myself to focus on the present, and my role as navigator, checking the map on my phone.

Next left.

She nodded, her head tilting to one side as she monitored the wind direction. Sticking to the shadows cast by the many skyscrapers piercing the London skyline wasn't the issue; we had to approach downwind if we had any hope of sneaking up undetected. We had no idea if they were inside the building or below ground, so we weren't taking any chances.

A silent notification flashed up on my phone.

CASS

Source confirmed that Jeremy is being held near the office, not inside the premises. Couldn't get more details than that. Sorry.

I'd messaged Cassandra to corroborate Maya's findings. Not because I didn't trust her magic, but because we had no idea what Nadine and Ryan were up to. Lingering right next to where the alpha worked for so long had to mean something, and we weren't risking our necks just to catch them scheming.

The screen flickered as another message came through, my brain reading the warning as if she was in my head.

CASS

Don't do anything stupid.

I showed Eve the message. *Cassandra said Jeremy is here.*

Her eyes widened, the blue of her irises popping under the moonlight. *Let's hope Gabi is too.*

The stakes had just doubled, and I was more than ready to start disrupting their fucking plans.

Both of us were on high alert, constantly scanning our surroundings. We were both dressed head to toe in black workout gear, ready to bolt if needed.

I gripped her elbow, pulling gently to slow her down as we took the next right. We turned the final corner and stepped out onto the street that housed a bunch of skyscrapers full of offices and fancy penthouse suites. A few older buildings were dotted between the glass buildings, as the city's history refused to let go completely no matter how hard businessmen wanted to take over.

Over there. Eve pointed to a small side street between Henry's office and the building the pendulum had highlighted, figures moving in the shadows. The office's glass exterior was dark, the only illumination exterior security lights. Not a single window in the building showed any sign of light or activity.

I nodded, signalling for us to continue. Our feet were light as we approached, keeping to the opposite side of the street. An unmarked van sat between the buildings, its headlights off but the low rumble of the engine audible from our position. We crouched down behind a parked car opposite, peering out over the hood. Inside the black van were two men, one of which was the main honcho that had brought us to meet with the alpha. I never forgot a face I wanted to punch.

The scent of multiple werewolves and at least one vampire carried on the wind to me, none of them Ryan or Nadine's.

The pendulum must have meant they were inside. Can you smell Jeremy?

I tried casting my senses out, but his scent wasn't there. Could they mask the scents? Who knew what magic they had working along this operation. There was no way that van was delivering office supplies.

No sign of him.

There was a grunt and a flurry of movement around the back of the van before the sound of doors slamming shut rang out, followed by a rev of the engine. I started forwards, my legs moving on autopilot. The van's headlights flashed on, blinding me as they accelerated onto the street.

Eve grabbed me, her nails biting into my wrist as she yanked me back down beside her. *Where are you going?*

What if Jer is in there?

Tyres squealed and the van sped away. Terror that our one chance to find my uncle might be disappearing into the distance consumed me.

She shook her head, her hand sliding down my arm to lace her fingers with mine. *You'd have recognised his scent.*

I nodded, clinging on to that logic and rolling my shoulders as if I could shrug off the tension there. The moon wasn't in its full phase, but my wolf side was still very much awake. Knowing my uncle was being held in chains nearby didn't help. I'd spent the day wanting to snap any man, woman, or otherwise who had looked Eve's way for longer than a second, saying I was on edge would be a gross understatement. I was tiptoeing on a crumbling cliff edge.

Two shadowed figures jogged around the front of the townhouse, jumping over the railing cordoning off the basement level and disappearing from view. Whatever was happening, it wasn't in the London alpha's building, which was good news for us.

Let's go.

I crouched low to the ground as I prowled around the front of the car before bolting across the empty road. Eve was right behind me, both of us speeding back under the cover of darkness.

I peered around the corner to find the side street empty. This side of the building was windowless, and the office foyer was empty, the barriers lowered in front of the carpark entrance marking the end of the alley. My nose caught a whiff of blood, and a small pool of blood wound between the cobblestones.

Witch's blood.

Eve was pacing up and down the front of the house when I returned. *How the hell do we get in there?*

The townhouse looked like the Georgian buildings back home in Dublin, the windows of the basement floor submerged below ground level. From the listing of buttons on the buzzer by the door, much of the older buildings within the city, this one had been converted into apartments. The railing cordoning the drop off had one gate, but it was shut with an added padlock to boot. Cat burglary wasn't really my thing, but we needed to get some concrete proof if we were to convince other packs to stand with us against the Faolchúnna pack and their allies.

I wrapped my fingers around two of spikes on the railing and leaned forwards, peering down the steep stairs. They led to a narrow servant door almost hidden beneath the steps leading to the main door. The two sash windows either side were completely boarded up and blacked out. Even from a distance I could sense the wards.

Bastards have this place completely locked down.

I looked up to find an empty street, cursing under my breath and racing around the corner to find Eve hovering down the bottom of the side street. My eyes adjusted as I moved away from the streetlight to see that she was standing on a set of black metal steps almost completely shrouded in shadows. A fire escape nestled right between the carpark and old building.

It could easily be mistaken for a back gate from a distance, just a few steps and a rail, but as I climbed the steps to join Eve, I realised it wound the whole way up the back of the building.

Bingo. Looks like the witch isn't the only one good at finding things.

She grinned in response, possibly the most adorable looking little assassin I could have imagined.

I hesitated for a moment, doing mental gymnastics to figure out what was safer. Neither was ideal, but I opted to go first. Given we were planning to break in, our threat was most likely on the inside. We'd hear someone coming from below well before they got close enough.

Do not let go unless there's danger. I took her hand, grabbing a fistful of my T-shirt at my hip and pressing the material into her hand. *Don't touch anything but the railing. Stick to the mind link.*

I pressed a chaste kiss to her lips as she wrapped her fingers around my shirt before we started our ascent.

My guess about apartments was quickly proven right by the time we hit the second floor. The first window not obscured by blinds or curtains revealed middle aged man cooking in his kitchen while a younger boy watched football on a tv. Even without the window open a crack, I knew they were human.

I don't know what I expected, maybe cells like where Alice was kept. What the hell are they up to so close to humans?

Eve brushed her knuckles against the curve of my spine in silent agreement. We climbed the whole way up all four levels, ducking under window frames, to find nothing out of the ordinary. Just seemingly normal humans going about their daily lives unaware. I hadn't imagined the blood on the street below or the sinister feeling lodged in my bones. Maya's magic was right, they had to be here somewhere.

I was about to give in and call it a day when we got back to ground floor until I noticed the fire escape went down one more level. The basement. Cliché, but isn't that where all murderous lunatics hide their victims?

Eve kept right behind me as we descended. The steps led to a narrow alley, almost invisible between the overhang of the fire escape and an even larger building backing onto the townhouse.

I inched forwards, every fibre of muscle in my body tensed and ready to spring into action.

There were four windows, the first two boarded up just like out front. When we hit the third, my blood ran cold.

This one was boarded too, but a small part of the wooden plank at the edge had rotted away. Behind the wood was a window with safety bars that were useless because the danger was on the inside.

Blue light emanated from the room, a lone light bulb swinging from the ceiling, flickering on and off. The walls were bare, save for two steel rings with chains dangling from them that led to a man curled up in the foetal position on the floor. He was naked, hands clutching his head, with bloody fingers tangled in his matted brown hair.

I didn't need to see his face.

"Jeremy!" I yelled out, banging my fist on the window only for my knuckles to crack as they hid wood that felt more like a rock.

Eve gasped at the sight of him, dropping her grip on my T-shirt as her hands flew to her mouth.

My uncle didn't move, as if some sort of ward blocked sound from reaching him. The barest rise and fall of his chest was the only indication that he was still alive. His pale body was mottled with bruises and covered in deep cuts that were black in places as if charred. My heart hammered, vomit stinging the back of my throat as my stomach threatened to empty at the sight of him.

I grabbed one of the safety bars between my hands, trying to bend the metal that should have given way under my werewolf strength but it refused to yield.

Just as the metal groaned, my uncle flinched, and the door behind him swung open silently. The soundproofing ward must have worked both ways.

Eve snatched my arm, dragging me down with her as she dropped to her knees beneath the window. I peeked up over the ledge through one of the small, exposed gaps in the window. Ryan and Nadine strolled into the room like they were visiting an old friend.

The way my uncle tried to scramble to his feet despite the pain he must have been in told me everything I needed to know. This wasn't their first visit and at least some of those scars were gifted by the duo standing over him without an ounce of pity.

Tears sprang from the corners of my eyes as Jer struggled as Ryan hauled him to his feet, the man's legs thin and his ribs visible from malnourishment. Claws extended from his fingertips, Jer's body convulsing as if trying to change and heal but whether it was a spell or the silver cuffs on his wrists, he simply collapsed from the effort.

If it wasn't for Eve's grip on both of my arms, I'd have tried to launch myself through the window as I watched them drag him away like he was a dead weight. Nadine walked ahead of Ryan, leading the way with a sadistic, hungry smirk.

My uncle's eyes snapped open just before the door closed behind them, the agony in his expression something that would haunt me as he locked eyes with me and mouthed five words.

Tell them I loved them.

CHAPTER 23

EVE

I t didn't feel like Christmas.

I woke alone, my hand closing around air as I reached out to find Luke's side empty, though our bond told me he wasn't far away.

For the five days since we left his uncle behind, he'd been inconsolable. There were at least ten other wolves in the building that night, way too many for us to handle alone. Even Luke knew we didn't stand a chance, though he stayed silent for hours after we made the decision to leave.

Both of us had vowed to go back for Jeremy and save him, despite him seeming to have accepted defeat. It hurt me to watch Luke in pain, though there was nothing I could do to fix it. Maya had no further update on the curse or missing book. Josh tried and failed to talk us through possible ways to crack the flash drive, but it had resulted in two broken laptops. One due to the malware protecting the encrypted drive, the other sat in the trash still with claw-shaped gouges and the screen half hanging off the base half-decapitated.

As if the knife needed twisting, Luke had to relay everything to Tom and the pack. It had broken his heart to describe what we had found, but he had kept his composure during the call. A true alpha in the making even if he was blind to his own strengths. They didn't see his white knuckled grip on my hand, or the way he'd fall apart in my arms after. No wolf left behind, that was the rule, and we intended to honour it.

We just needed a plan.

And I needed to get out of bed because the longer I lay here alone, the more my thoughts turned against me. If we were mates, why had he felt so distant the past few days?

The lock on the door to the other bedroom of our suite clicked open. I rolled over as Luke strolled back into the room with a level of pep in his step that had my eyebrow arching.

"Hey." My lips curved at the sight of his tousled hair and the vampire vibe the red lighting he passed under gave. "You look happy."

He nodded, tossing his phone onto the couch as he passed. "I was on the phone to Dad."

"Oh?" My brow furrowed. Nothing good had come from any of those calls. Though Tom never contributed, Luke had a tendency to lean into the 'not good enough' spiral afterwards since our exile.

"Yeah, just checking up on me again."

"He's checking *in,* there's a difference. He cares." I sat up, and Luke's gaze immediately dropped to my exposed breasts.

Damn, he really was in a much better mood.

Luke shrugged, the mattress dipping as he braced his hands either side of me and leaned down to steal a kiss from my lips. "Plus, we got a response from two alphas of the other London packs. They're willing to meet."

"Good news is nice for once." I smiled against his lips, snaking my arms around his neck to pull him closer.

"You know, with the way you're trying to distract me," Luke murmured, his breath tickling my face as he broke our kiss. "It's making me think you forgot to get me a Christmas present."

"How dare you. Yours is under the tree."

"What tree?" His expression changed from one of

confusion to amusement as he turned to find a Christmas tree in the corner by the fire. It was only three feet tall, as fake as the pot the base sat in, so there was no smell of pine filling the room.

I grinned. "Lawrence and I sorted it during the night. Isn't it cute?"

"It's a fire hazard."

A log splintered in the fire as if to prove his point, but the grate was spelled to not let anything escape.

After too many nights with little to no sleep, Luke had finally caved and taken something to help with the restless nights. I'd snuck around with Lawrence in the early hours of the morning, stealing a tree from one of the hotel seating areas, not because Darius wouldn't foot the bill but because it was very last minute, and we didn't have time to contact our resident vampire Santa Claus.

To say that Christmas in Château Minuit was a strange affair would be an understatement. They went all out. There was an enormous tree in the main foyer of the hotel which stretched to reach the ceiling, adorned with sparkling lights and tasteful ornaments and ribbons. Several others were dotted around the hotel complex, and each hotel room that was occupied had its very own Christmas wreath on the door.

Luke twirled one of the decorations in his hand, a poorly made polar bear that looked more like a wolf that I'd just had to pick up while we were exploring London with Maya. Well, we were stalking my ex-boyfriend and the murderous redhead, but side quests were allowed.

"It's perfect."

His smile only widened at the sight of me tugging on his discarded T-shirt from the night before. He joined me in bed, carrying over a large breakfast tray that must have been dropped off while I was still asleep. I tucked my legs under me, eyeing the plates stacked full of pastries, toast, and anything else you could dream of for breakfast.

"Coffee." I hummed with happiness, nursing the mug in my hands as I took a long sip.

Luke left the food untouched, staring at me, lost deep in thought.

"Penny for your thoughts?" I took a bite of pastry, quickly followed with Nutella-covered toast in an odd combination. I was trying to figure out the best way to sample everything without overfilling my stomach. Though lying around in a food coma for the day didn't sound like a bad option.

Luke shook his head as he snapped back to reality, biting into his muffin with a wry smile. "You know it's after two, right? You're gonna have to fit Christmas dinner in there too."

The curtain was still pulled across the window, but sunlight spilled through a gap at the far end of the room. The kind of golden glow that told me I had slept well past midday, and a small pang of disappointment hit at the thought of missing half of our first Christmas together. Even if we had been up until the early hours of the morning the night before researching, talking, and releasing pent up aggression in the healthiest of ways.

"It'll fit in my dessert belly." I shrugged, patting my stomach.

He stiffened, scratching the back of his neck as he tried to look anywhere but meet my gaze. "Hey, about the other night..."

"And last night, and the night before that?" My eyebrow arched into my hairline, my lips twitching at the way his cool, calm exterior had taken a run and jump out the window as he tried to broach the subject. I knew where he was going, but I was enjoying watching him squirm.

"We didn't use anything. It's my fault, I got caught up in the moment, and the bond..."

I held my hand up to put him out of his misery. "I've been on the pill since we got here. Lawrence hooked me up, just in case. Surprise pregnancy is not on your Christmas wish list, or mine."

There was one other reason, but I didn't need to voice it.

Every time we went to take the Faolchúnna pack on, there was a risk I'd be captured. And if that had to happen, I was quite happy for my hormones to fuck with their experiments until he found me. Because he would, we would always find one another.

"Good." Luke nodded slowly, his shoulders slumping with relief. "Not that I don't want to... I just—"

I pressed my lips to his to silence his ramblings, my heart warming at the point he was trying to make. "I get it. We're both too young and exiled. Besides, I thought you'd look a little more excited at the thought of being able to have your wicked way with me anytime you want without having to worry."

The way his eyes darkened had me regretting my teasing, his arousal a tangible tug on the invisible bond between us.

"I do recall you were the one panicking about being seen in that library." He slid his hand up my leg, trailing a fingertip along the hemline before grabbing my ass and pulling me closer. "Maybe I *do* need to bring you back to Inferno."

My knee bumped against the breakfast tray on his lap, making the ice in his glass of water clink. I could do with being doused with it as my cheeks heated.

He chuckled, and I couldn't help but smile as he threw his arm around my shoulders to pull me closer to him. This wasn't the Christmas that either of us imagined, we both wanted to be back home. I had been looking forwards to my first Christmas as a Crescent wolf.

"What's it like?" Pastry crumbs sprayed all over both of us as I spoke with my mouth full of croissant.

Luke simply shook his head, making no effort to conceal his laughter. "What's what like?"

"Christmas at home with the pack."

His expression softened, his fingers tracing slow patterns on my bare arm and mapping my freckles like he was joining the dots. "We always have Christmas at the pack house in Kildare. Everyone arrives on Christmas Eve and stays over for the holidays. Santa delivers the kid's presents under the tree, Christmas morning is complete and utter chaos, but everyone helps out. Helena cooks a huge breakfast, and everyone pitches in for dinner. She doesn't let us do half as much as she should, and Dad always has to badger her to take a break. Those of us responsible for most of the carnage help clean up after, and we go for a run if it happens to fall during the full moon."

I looked up at him, off in my own little world imagining what our celebrations would be like if everything hadn't gone to shit.

"Are you sure this bond is real?" I finally voiced the worry in my mind that had kept popping up.

"Why, do the floors normally shake when you cum? Have you been holding out on me, sweetheart?"

I rolled my eyes, and he caught my hand as I slapped his arm, linking his fingers with mine. "No, I don't normally blow lightbulbs either."

"I'm not gonna make some cheesy joke about you rocking my world, but I'm fairly certain we both felt the magic in the room that night. Your eyes were silver right up until the full moon retreated, that's not normal for you. The same way being able to communicate through the mind link in human form isn't possible for wolves. Not unless they're mates."

"When did you start suspecting it?"

He shrugged, stroking the back of my hand with his thumb in time with the beat of my heart. "A few days after we got here, but there was so much going on. I didn't think the universe would ever give me a mate, and I didn't want you to feel trapped with me. We were already exiled together; I didn't want you feeling bound by something else too."

"You wanted me to choose you."

He nodded, his expression softening as he gazed down at me with those hazel eyes. "I needed it to be a choice. Even now that we know, it's still a choice."

He had no say in being next in line for the position of alpha, and he'd resented that burden growing up.

"I choose you." I brushed my lips against his, squeezing his hand in promise. "Always."

"I'm not a Pokémon." His grin was contagious as he pulled me closer against him, kissing the top of my head as he murmured. "I love you."

"I love you, too." Despite the circumstances of our stay in London, my heart was full. The weight of his arm wrapped around me as we sat curled up on the bed with the winter raging outside and Christmas lights twinkling in the corner felt more than good, it felt right.

"Has anyone ever rejected the bond?"

He shook his head with a content sigh. "Not that I know of personally, but there are stories. Usually due to one wolf dying or family feuds, it would have to be something pretty serious to make a wolf deny their mate. You're literally made for each other."

I couldn't imagine refusing, not once I'd experienced it. His soul was bound to mine, an invisible string existing between us, surpassing logic or reason, and a love so raw that I knew I'd crawl through hell and back to be with him.

"There was one case I remember Darren mentioning once, where a jealous guy held his ex's mate captive until the next full moon. Because they didn't complete the ritual, the bond refused."

"Of course it was a man," I muttered, my nose wrinkling.

My shoulders tensed at the thought of not being able to complete the bond. Luke had explained what was involved. We had to run together as wolves under the full moon and consummate the pairing. Basically, we had to fuck and there was more biting involved, none of which I had a problem with.

"So it's the next full moon?"

He shook his head with a grin. "I mean, if you want to do it that soon, I'm not going to complain. But we have a full cycle of the moon to decide."

He brushed a kiss to the bridge of my nose, licking his lips as he pulled back. "How you manage to get the chocolate sprinkles from that coffee there I'll never understand."

"Is the bite what triggered it?" Heat crept up the back of my neck.

His gaze dropped to the marks that were now barely visible on my neck. Despite my werewolf healing powers, they had lingered for longer than normal. "As far as I know, it's triggered by sex during a full moon. I did have an overwhelming urge to claim you that night, so I think the bite did have something to do with triggering it. There's a reason the bond has to be completed. Mate bonds are for life, a wolf shouldn't just be forced with it after a one-night stand. So the opportunity is there to refuse."

"I won't be refusing. Do I get to bite you too?"

Luke eyed me up like I was about to be his next meal. "You can bite me anytime, anywhere." His voice dropped lower at the last word, a shudder running down my spine as he leaned in to run his teeth over my collarbone. Breakfast was quickly forgotten, glasses crashing and pastries rolled across the floor as he discarded the tray onto the floor beside us before pouncing on me.

I tried to crawl away, but he caught me by the ankle and pulled me back.

"Run all you want. I'd walk through hellfire to hunt you down."

My mouth popped open, every inch of my body heating at his dirty promise. He pulled on my ankle, and I squealed as I tipped off balance, falling face first onto the bed. His T-shirt rode up as he dragged me backwards, my hands clawing at the bedsheets.

He left a trail of kisses up my spine, pausing between my shoulder blades. "This little scar is one of my favourite things about you."

"My what?" I whined at the loss of contact, lifting my head off the bed.

He stayed straddling my hips and grabbed his phone off the nightstand, the noise of the shutter going off as held it close to my back. I was ready to read him the riot act for taking a picture of my ass, when he slid it in front of me to reveal a small raised, white scar in the shape of a crescent moon.

"I didn't know that was there."

"Well, I doubt you spend long staring at your back in the mirror. It's tiny, but I've explored every inch of your body and committed it to memory."

I shrugged, wiggling my ass beneath him to get us back on track. "Maybe try exploring one more time just in case. Maybe you'll find another cute scar or freckle."

A low growl rumbled from his chest, the sound making me squeeze my thighs together.

"If that fucker has permanently marked you..."

I propped myself up on my elbows, looking over my shoulder to find his staring down at me with a hunger I wanted to satiate. "I'll make you a deal, if it's still there in a few days, you can leave a mark of you own."

"Don't make a deal with the devil unless you mean it." His eyes flashed silver, his hands kneading my ass as he leaned in to nip the point between my shoulder blades where the scar had appeared. He growled his approval as my body shuddered beneath him, wetness pooling in my core. "Or does my mate like the idea of being marked?"

I mumbled my response into the bedsheets, squirming restlessly beneath him as his fingers skimmed along my ribs and the swell of my breasts.

I had no idea what other filth was going to come from that man's lips when a knock came at the door, and we both froze. Luke sat up and cursed, quickly jumping off me and rummaging around for his pants.

"Is that room service? We already had breakfast."

It was Luke's turn to blush this time, the sight of his cheeks colouring an endearing rarity as he pulled his tracksuit bottoms on and tossed me the dress he'd peeled off me the night before. "They're early. It was supposed to be a surprise."

The banging on the door intensified.

I frowned, slipping the dress over my head as he tugged on a T-shirt and ruffled his hair as if we hadn't clearly been tumbling in the sheets.

"Who's early? What surprise?"

A whoop came from outside, and the door clicked. My jaw was on the floor as five familiar figures stumbled into the room. Craig turned to face me with a wide grin, Dylan and Josh right behind him and a sheepish Alice taking up the rear as if she knew what they'd almost walked in and wanted to burn it from her brain.

Luke gestured to his band of musketeers plus one. "Surprise."

I was dreaming. I had to be.

My brain was struggling to play catch up as I sat in the restaurant of Château Minuit surrounded by the friends I called my family. A full-size turkey was carved up on the table in front of us, along with a ham that had my mouth watering and a full spread of Christmas dinner trimmings. It wasn't what I'd imagined for our first Christmas, but it was everything I needed. The place was practically empty besides us, so it was like our own private little Christmas. Any vampires attempting to enjoy a quiet meal quickly vacated.

We'd spent the afternoon bringing everyone up to speed. They knew most of it from being on calls and pack meetings, but Luke hadn't told Tom that we'd contacted the other alphas. Or about the elephant in the room, our mate bond. Alice's face had lit up, her squealing about me being like a sister going a long way to mending something that had long sat broken in my heart. Being orphaned and bouncing between foster homes had left its mark. While my relationship with Alice would never fill the sisterhood I'd lost with Kate, she filled a void that gave me a sense of belonging.

"I still can't believe you're mates," Craig ran his hand

through his hair, the blonde tips now tinged red in honour of his new chance at life. Apparently, he and Alice had destroyed the shower at Tom's house in the process. "It's like something out of a movie."

Despite the circumstances of their visit, my cheeks hurt from smiling so much. "Except vampires don't sparkle, and there's a lot more fucked up shit."

Craig took a long sip of his drink, the scent of blood wafting from his cup. I tried my best not to stare. The blood served in most establishments came from blood banks or donations, nothing sinister. It wasn't his fault he needed it to live.

"When are you meeting the alphas?" Josh fiddled with the paper crown hat from one of the Christmas crackers on his head until it sat just right.

"Two days. It's killing me knowing Jer is spending Christmas being tortured, or worse, but that night is our best chance at getting him out."

Everyone gathered around the table. We were all on the same page, and rescuing Jeremy was top of our list.

I squeezed Luke's knee under the table in silent support as his mood shifted. "Waiting is the right decision."

"I know," he agreed with a sigh, raking his fingers through his hair. His shoulders sagged under the weight of worrying about his uncle. "But that strategy means I'm forced to let one of our own suffer for longer. It feels wrong and I hate it."

Luke had refused to sit at the head of the table, insisting on taking one of the couches so he could sit right beside me. But it was also his subconscious way of showing everyone they were his equal. He couldn't see himself growing into the role of alpha, but from the way every person at the table listened intently to his words, right down Craig, a vampire, everyone else knew it was his destiny.

"At least we know Lila is safe. She and the kids are in Scotland, with the pack near Edinburgh." Alice offered a sliver of hope amidst the darkness.

"Has anyone heard from home?" Dylan stepped up to lighten the mood.

"Dad is going to kill you when he finds out you've snuck off to London." Luke shook his head, dousing his meal in gravy as a reward for having brought everyone up to speed.

Alice shrugged. "I left a note, he knows by now. That's why your phone's off."

"Luke! What if Tom needs us?" I smacked his arm, making his fork catch a Brussels sprout and send it rolling across the table.

Dylan picked up the sprout and tossed it into his mouth like a party act, bowing with a flourish. "Tom's not going to like it, but we sat through one too many meetings with the pack of them doing nothing to help. They were all talk, no action. I know our last plan didn't work out perfectly, but we couldn't sit on our hands for any longer. You can't stay exiled forever, we need you home."

"When did you guys plan all of this?" I placed my hand over my wine glass as a waitress glided past offering more.

"Two days ago." Craig's upper lip curling in warning at the waitress to reveal two pointed shiny fangs. "I took the idea to Jonas, and he agreed to sort everything."

That was going to get some getting used to. Every time I noticed his fangs or the coolness of his skin against mine, it was like a mini shock to the system. But besides his newfound grace and the whole undead part, he was just like old Craig.

My Craig.

"They called me this morning. I promise your *real* gift is upstairs." Luke shot Dylan a pointed look. "At least this one knows how to be on time."

Dylan shrugged with his mouth full. "It's not my fault they decided to run on time for once."

Josh fiddled with the Christmas cracker he'd swiped from Craig, a colourful paper tube stuffed with tiny toys, trinkets, and jokes.

"You need us here, not waiting around back home. I have my full kit. Once I get into the flash drive, we'll hopefully have some proof to show the other alphas. It's one thing ignoring rumours or suspicions, when the truth is slapped in their face and they realise their own have been targeted too, there's no way they'll back Henry the eighth."

He'd already gotten a head-start on hacking the drive before we'd left for dinner. I had no idea what was on it, but information was the key to all of this.

"Unless they're already involved," Luke countered.

"There's no way all of them are. An operation like this demands a certain level of secrecy." Dylan waved a forkful of chicken around as he spoke. "Hopefully, that witch comes back with more info on the curse too."

Josh nodded in agreement. "We need to crack that flash drive, free Jeremy, and then get you back to Ireland."

"That all sounds great, but we're exiled?" I dropped my fork onto my half-finished plate and admitted defeat while the boys continued to dig into their seconds.

"I understand why Darius thought it best that you leave immediately, but given the Faolchúnna pack has followed you over here, it's just as dangerous. Plus, the London alpha sounds like an asshole." Dylan narrowly avoided being stabbed in the hand as he swiped the last roast potato from Luke's plate. "Plus, we got wind that Larissa is on the move as well. So, if she plans on gate crashing, you need backup."

Craig grinned, clearly excited to be involved as he gestured to the gang with his thumb. "We're backup."

"I have a theory on that actually. The curse, that is." All eyes were on Alice as she cleared her throat. "Okay, so we all figured out 'undead' meant vampire and 'hound' is probably werewolf, right?"

Everyone but Dylan nodded.

"Bloodline and moon bound makes me think of the witch's origin story. There was a dagger in that myth too. *Trinity tied by the blade of magic intertwined,'* I think it is talking about the dagger used to kill the lover in the story."

"But it's just a story." Josh's brow furrowed, his tone sceptical.

Where he relied on logic, I'd seen far too much shit to rule anything out at this point.

"I think the trinity piece matters. I don't know how it comes into play, but there were people involved in the original myth. The two sisters, and the lover. One kind sister, one scorned, and one sacrificed..." She trailed off as she looked at me, nervously pushing the remaining food around her plate. "I think Eve is the key. Both Luke and Ryan are in love with her."

Luke stiffened beside me, the muscle in his jaw feathering.

Alice stood firm, meeting her brother's gaze with unwavering determination. "It makes sense. Ryan had his chance to kill Eve more than once. Just because you don't like it, doesn't mean it isn't true."

Never talk about politics or religion at the dinner table unless you want a fight. Or prophecies and myths, apparently.

Luke's mood had plummeted like the temperatures since Alice voiced her theory during dinner. He'd been brooding ever since, draining the life out of festivities. Even when Dylan had spotted snow beginning to fall and screamed like a kid on Christmas morning, Luke barely cracked a smile. So, as we all walked along the streets, I linked arms with him and hung back from the rest. I wasn't having our first Christmas come to an end like this. The universe had thrown far too much shit at me to take this day away. I'd just found out he was my mate, our friends and family had turned up, and for just one day we deserved to celebrate being alive.

Trafalgar square was covered in a blanket of snow, completely transformed from the daytime into a magical image that belonged in a novel. Snow flurries sparkled under the streetlights as they whipped in the wind around us. The fountain that had already frozen over now had a fresh layer of snow, fresh flakes sticking to the icicles of frozen water hanging from the statue. Even the heads of the four lines surrounding Nelson's Column were dusted with snow.

"Luke." I tugged on his arm, spinning him to face me. "We need to talk."

His jaw was set, his hands stuffed in his pockets going no way to hide the fact that they had been balled into fists since dinner. Behind us, the guys were rolling a giant snowball that looked like the beginnings of a snowman, music playing in the distance either from a bar or a busker or braved the cold the soundtrack to their antics.

"What Alice said could be true."

"It could also be a load of shite." His eyes narrowed, his stubborn side winning out in his desperation to deny the possibility.

"*If* it's true, it would explain a lot." I tugged his hands free, forcing him to unfurl his fists so I could link my fingers with his. "But we have no intention of letting Larissa break the curse, so it doesn't matter in the end. Understanding the meaning will only help us stop her."

He shook his head, his hands tightening around mine as he pulled my chest against his. "You don't understand."

"Then tell me."

"You think I haven't noticed them coming after you or the special interest that Larissa had in you?" He leaned down to rest his forehead against mine, the intensity in his hazel eyes made me choke up. "I have no intention of letting them lift any curse, but if you're the key, they're not going to stop coming. We've had so little time together, and so much of it has been drenched in pain. I don't want that to be the life of my mate, I want a future with you. One where we're not looking over our shoulder at every turn. One where I don't spend each day terrified of losing you, because if they take you, I won't recover. I'll lose myself."

I swallowed the lump rising in my throat, leaning up on my tiptoes to nuzzle his nose. "I don't want to live in fear either. We will stop them, this isn't our future."

He released one hand to rummage around in his pocket, producing a rectangular purple box. "Speaking of the present. Before the others interrupted this morning, I wanted to give you this."

A whoop rang out behind us, Dylan tearing up the steps to the National Gallery. He raised an abandoned kid's makeshift toboggan above his head in triumph before throwing down the mishmash of plastic boxes and duct tape and hurdling down the snow-covered steps like a ski slope.

My fingertips melted the snow settling on the silver ribbon binding the box as I loosened it, nerves setting in as I felt Luke's eyes on me. The box snapped open to reveal a silver chain with a perfectly carved pendant in the shape of a crescent moon with the figure of a tiny wolf howling carved on top.

"It's beautiful," I whispered, a smile tugging at the corners of my lips as I traced the curve of the moon with my fingers. "Thank you."

His face lit up, some of the stress morphing into excitement as he nudged the pendant over to reveal an engraving on the back, giddy as he pointed to the inscription. "It's spelled to never harm a wolf so long as you will it. Read it."

"*Anamacha gealaí.*" Tears stung the corners of my eyes, my heart swelling in response to his love coursing down the bond. "You told me it means 'lunar souls'... Did you truly not know we were mates?"

I thought back to that night in the Kildare pack lands where we'd laid beneath the stars, talking and laughing for hours, falling in love. That was the night he'd explained the mind link to me, the first sign of our bond.

"I never dared to dream that I'd ever be lucky enough to find a mate or deserve one. May I?" Luke gestured to the box, and I nodded. He placed the delicate chain around my neck, his fingers brushing against my skin as he fiddled with the clasp. "Beautiful."

A blush warmed my cheeks as he stepped back to admire his gift, the silver pendant cool as it settled against my chest.

"I'd like to take credit for being an extremely talented gift giver, but I got it before the mate thing came to fruition." He cupped my face in his hands as he kissed my tear-stained cheeks, those hazel eyes so full of emotion that I thought the dam might break.

I leaned up on my tiptoes, tasting salt on my lips as I pressed mine to his. He wrapped his arms around me, his large frame dwarfing me as he pulled me close and deepened his kiss.

The music in the distance grew louder, the familiar notes of "Fairytale of New York" calling me home.

"Dance with me?" I murmured against his lips, my smile only widening as he took my hand in his.

Luke stepped back, bowing deeply as he placed a kiss to the back of my hand. His eyes danced with mischief as he looked up at me, and my heart skipped a beat as the realisation that he was my mate hit me all over again.

He rose to his full height, his other hand finding my waist as he pulled me into his hold in a practised move that had me raising my eyebrows.

"I know we danced at that ball but since when can you *really* dance?"

"I was forced to do lessons for Darren's wedding. I'm a fast learner." His thumb stroked the small of my back of we swayed to the music.

"What other skills have you been hiding, Mr. Whelan?"

His lips lifted in a smirk before he spun me out so fast the sculpture of the fountain beside us blurred, and the lions suddenly had two heads. I wobbled as he tugged me back into his hold, my laughter lingering in the winter air as I wrapped my arms around his neck.

"Stick with me, and you'll find out," he whispered in my ear, his smile audible.

We danced around the fountain, snow billowing around us and covering my hair as the wind picked up, carrying the notes of the song to us. The flakes falling in the glow of the streetlights looked like the stars blocked out by the snow clouds covering the sky. I couldn't see the moon, but I could feel her watching. Waiting.

A squeal rang out, Luke turning me in time to the music just in time to see Craig careering down the gallery steps in the toboggan straight towards the snowman Alice was guarding. At the same time, Josh and Dylan raced back and forth pelting everyone with snowballs and doubling over in fits of laughter.

We may not have been in Ireland for Christmas, but home isn't a place, it's your people.

Despite the fact that we were in a public place and plenty of humans were present around the Victoria Palace Theatre, I couldn't shake the feeling that we had walked into the lion's den. I'd forced Henry's hand by contacting the other alphas separately, him choosing the meeting place was a power play. I cared little for pack politics when he had my uncle bound and tortured, he could pick the damn location. It didn't help that the guys and Alice were halfway across the city trying to break Jeremy out, and they were relying on me to keep the London alpha busy.

The air was crisp, the bright lights of the city gave the night sky an eerie glow as we waited in line outside the theatre. The building was the same pale stone as many of the older buildings in the city, with a long line of steps with red carpet rolled out leading up to the front entrance. The marquee illuminated by bright lights displayed the names of current productions, the theatre's name in gold lettering. Even at night the building stood out on the bustling streets, with large columns and arched stained glass windows along with elaborate carvings and sculptures decorating the upper levels.

Eve pulled her coat tight around her, glued to my side as she scanned the area. You would think with all his contacts that the alpha could have gotten us past the queue, but clearly we weren't on his good side.

Once I flashed the tickets at the top of the line, the human working ticketing barely glanced and ushered us straight into the building. The theatre was equally as grand inside as the outside, the spacious foyer exuding charm, velvet drapes framing the doorways leading to the auditorium and ornate chandeliers hanging from the ceiling casting a warm glow across the polished marble floors. A handful of concession stands lined the lobby with kids hanging off their parent's arms begging for either sweets or some overpriced merchandise. The main door led to the floored seating area, a winding staircase with gold decorated banisters that a young usher informed us led to the private bar.

Of course, the London alpha had invited everyone to his box. He owned three, probably compensating for something. I doubted the man ever even watched the plays. According to my sources he spent most of his time propping up the bar and chatting up women who weren't his wife.

Eve handed the attendant her coat before we headed upstairs, nerves bubbling in my stomach as we neared the top. Edmonstone didn't expect me come with any proof. We were going in under prepared. Josh hadn't managed to crack the drive. He got in for all of three seconds before it kicked him out, but we still had the photos Cassandra had given me. They were grainy in quality, all showing different paranormals held captive. We could only hope at least one of them would be recognised by the alphas present tonight. It had to be enough.

I was on high alert as we walked past the booths. Each one was fitted with two or three chairs upholstered in rich velvet, except ours. The private box number marked on our ticket courtesy of the London alpha had velvet and gold couches instead, with an incredible view of the auditorium. The stage curtain was still drawn, the lights dimmed until the musical was due to start. If you were actually here to enjoy the show, it was a pretty good spot. I couldn't ignore the pang of regret that Eve's first time at a musical in London was a business meeting. The only show would be the alpha's reaction, and it was unlikely to be enjoyable.

"So, do we sit and wait to be summoned? Or are you gonna get me a drink?" Eve linked her arm with mine, still a few inches shorter despite the heels she was wearing.

I'd teased her about needing to be able run, but she'd levelled me with a look that should have been illegal. Women could do impressive things in heels, and she was all fired up for tonight. Steely determination shone in her eyes, accentuated by the flowing navy material of her dress that cinched at her waist and skimmed her knees. The plunging neckline had been Alice's idea. I'd argued that all eyes would be on Eve regardless, but Alice had insisted that we leverage every angle we had. Eve wasn't leverage, she was my mate.

She must have noticed the twitch of my jaw, because she reached up to smooth the collar of my shirt and press a kiss to my cheek. "Drink it is."

I scented him as soon as we stepped out of the empty viewing box, Henry Edmonstone met us in the hallway, his stench of cologne wafting in the dead air.

"Ah, Luke. How nice of you to join us." He reached out to shake Eve's hand first, an act of insult. The corners of his eyes creased with a smug smirk as he kissed her knuckles, similar to how I had when we'd danced in the snow. "It's a pleasure to see you again."

Keep your cool. Eve's voice in my mind was a gentle but firm warning.

I smoothed my expression into the cold mask I'd watched my dad perfect over the ears. Despite wanting to break every one of his fingers after removing the nails and feeding them to him, I returned his handshake with a crushing pressure that made him wince. The way he tried to pass it off by brushing something off his suit gave me a small thrill of satisfaction.

"Come, we've been waiting at the bar."

Despite him using plural nouns to describe the party waiting, we walked into a bar devoid of any faces that I recognised. No alphas were present, not unless they'd masked their scent and were hiding behind the bar ready to pop out. Who exactly was *us*? Not only that, but there wasn't a single human in here either, so he was free to cause a scene.

Eve's eyes widened a fraction as she searched the room, her grip on my arm tightening.

I followed her gaze to spot a young blonde at the bar, honey curls cascading down her back accentuating her backless black dress. The glass of wine in front of her was untouched, the glass of bourbon beside it drained. Eve's nails dug into my forearm, the hints of claws extending and catching on the material of my shirt as the girl's side profile became visible in the mirrored shelving of the bar.

Fiona.

Eve started forwards at the sight of her friend from the Faolchúnna pack. Before she could take a step, I slid my arm behind her back and grabbed a fistful of her dress to prevent her from moving.

Don't. Pretend you don't know her. He's going to exploit your feelings for a friend as a weakness, give him nothing.

Eve gave a subtle nod, her throat bobbing as she swallowed and rolled her shoulders to face the alpha with an icy, emotionless stare.

Henry grinned like a Cheshire cat, and I wanted to knock every single pearly-white tooth out. He swaggered over to the bar, motioning for the bartender to pour him another. Fiona's shoulders caved in on herself as he propped himself beside her.

"Fiona, darling. Our guests are here." The alpha botched the pronunciation of her Irish name, glossing over the vowels to say '*f-yuna*' instead of '*fee-own-a*'. His grin grew more sadistic as he watched the recognition on Fiona's face turn to horror as she turned to see her friend. "Eve, Fiona. I hear you're old friends."

"Eve..." Fiona's eyes widened, though there was something off about them. As if they were cloudy, unfocused. Her voice sounded just as unstable as she looked when she tried to get to her feet.

He snatched her arm, pulling her back to sit on the bar stool. "Sit, pet."

It was clear from the way Fiona just slumped there in a daze that she had been drugged. No one in the establishment seemed to care, bile rising in my throat at the thought of this being a regular occurrence. What kind of world did we live in, paranormal or not, if men can commit their shady dealings in public just because they're so wealthy they believe themselves untouchable?

Eve's body was taut as a bowstring as I slid my arm around her, my hand clamped firmly on her waist. I didn't need the bond to know she was screaming internally and dying to rip him to shreds.

"What is this? Where are the other alphas?"

He threw a hundred pound note down on the bar, his roaming eyes lingering on the Fae's ass as she snatched it up and walked away. "What other alphas? I've told you before, I run this city."

"London houses several packs. You may be the figurehead, but I understood the setup to be democracy." I ground my teeth, forcing air in and out of my lungs at a steady pace to stay calm.

The vein in his forehead throbbed at that, his mouth curling into an ugly sneer. "You thought wrong. Maybe if you had more connections, your messages might have reached their intended target. I find ravens are great, but I'm sure pigeons would be suitable for your needs."

Birds. I thought back to the raven that night and realised I'd made a huge mistake. *He's been using ravens to watch us, and we never noticed a fucking thing.*

Eve's brow furrowed a fraction. *How? Since when can wolves control birds?*

They can't. But what if he has some really old, evil vampires on his side?

"Your dad is a great man, but you're not as smart as you think. It's been a disappointment." He took a sip of his drink, running his finger around the rim to elicit a sound that set my teeth on edge. "You came to my city an exile, and you didn't heed my warnings. So, I kept tabs on you, as any good alpha should."

An announcement rang out urging patrons to find their seat, and the bar began to empty, but the alpha staring me down didn't move a muscle.

"Why did you ask us to come here, Henry? I'm not in the mood for games tonight."

"You stole something of mine, and I want it back. So, I invited you here to offer a trade." His eyes narrowed towards Eve, the way he licked his lips making me want to snap his neck then and there. "Give me the flash drive back, and I'll give you your little friend here in one piece."

"And if we refuse?"

He knocked the dredges of his drink back, his jaw twitching in irritation as he rose to his full height to square up to me and still found himself coming up an inch short. "Note that I said one piece. She's been cursed to cut herself into itsy-bitsy pieces if you don't comply."

Eve blanched at that, her knuckles turning white as she gripped my hand.

"I don't have the drive, so there's no point in threatening us or spilling blood in public tonight."

"You came loaded with a few shitty photos as ammunition to discredit me with the other packs, but you were too scared to bring the real proof?" His lips stretched into a sadistic smirk, and he clicked his fingers, holding out his hand. The Fae from the bar reappeared, handing him a knife and walking away without showing any hint of remorse or shock on her face. "As I said, you're not as smart as you think."

It took every ounce of self-control to hold Eve in place while she was howling at me to let her take him, tears brimming in her eyes as she bit her tongue at my order.

I was walking a dangerous line, but I needed to know what game he was playing before I acted.

The noise of music filtered up from the theatre as he trailed the tip of the knife along her jaw, caressing her as if she were a little plaything. "It's a pity, you know? She was rather pretty. We could have had much fun."

Fiona's cloudy eyes pooled black as the magic took hold, reaching up to close her fingers around the handle of the knife that he held inches from her throat.

"Stop." I shot forwards to grab the knife and fire it across the room. It sent several glasses scattering off the shelves and shattering as they crashed to the floor, the knife lodging in the wooden frame of the shelf.

Eve rushed to Fiona's side, clutching the girl's wrists to stop her from reaching for one of the shards of glass to complete the spell.

Henry watched the struggle with a maliciousness I couldn't fathom, his silver bleeding into his irises in warning as he held his hand out to me. "Drive, now. I won't ask a third time."

Each tap of his foot on the ground was another bolt coming loose in my resolve. I pulled the flash drive from my pocket, twirling it between my fingers. "What's on this that has you so scared? How deep in this shit are you that you can't see that you're just a pawn in their game? You don't even know what they're planning."

His cold gaze slid to Eve. "Oh, but I do. Once they're done with her, we'll make sure that werewolves are the surviving race. We'll be stronger than ever, and you and your shitty little pack that have been muddying bloodlines will be eradicated."

The final call for audience members to take their seats echoed through the speakers.

"I warned you, don't push me."

I dropped the drive into his hand, my heart pounding as his fingers closed around it.

"I'd like to say it's been a pleasure." He placed it in the chest pocket of his suit, smoothing the lapels down and readjusting with a victorious smirk.

The air of arrogance around the man made my skin crawl, the wolf in me wanting to assert my dominance. The only thing stopping me was knowing that the drive was a fake replica, with nothing but photoshopped pics of him in compromising positions that Dylan had put together.

A weight lifted off my shoulders as the silver in Fiona's eyes faded, and she blinked rapidly, looking around the room bewildered. "Eve? What am I doing here?"

The alpha wiggled his fingers in a sarcastic wave towards the girl he'd drugged as he strode back in the direction of the main theatre, pausing in the doorway to glance over his shoulder. "Oh, by the way, I did warn you to stay out of my business but appears some members of your pack didn't get the message."

My head snapped up.

He tossed me a flashy tablet which I caught cleanly despite my hands shaking with rage. The large screen displayed a grainy black-and-white CCTV recording. Footage of my three friends and sister struggling to break the chains on Jeremy.

"I didn't want to ruin their fun, so I didn't call security immediately. It's more enjoyable when someone thinks they've won before they lose everything."

My phone buzzed, vibrating in my pocket. A message flashed up on the screen as I unlocked it at the same time a wolf appeared on the security footage.

JOSH

SOS. They're on to us.

I lunged at him, my fingers closing around his throat. A picture frame hanging on the wall rattled and slid to the ground as I pinned him against a wall, slowly increasing my pressure on his windpipe. "I'll fucking kill you."

His face went red, but he choked out a laugh. "You don't have the time. I do hope your friends have said their goodbyes."

CHAPTER 26

LUKE

No way in hell was I losing one of my own tonight.

Complete chaos had broken out by the time we arrived. Dylan and Josh were facing off against a mixture of vamp-like security guards and possessed hybrids similar to those that Ryan had at the club. It seemed like we needed further confirmation that the London alpha was as corrupt as the rest of those power-hungry bastards. I hit the accelerator, speeding straight towards the wolves until they split at the last minute, and I veered right to pull up in front of the townhouse. A loud bang came from the side street, tyres squealing as I pumped the breaks of the car. I'd broken every single traffic law on the way over, not to mention the fact I'd hot-wired a car.

I barely pulled the handbrake before I was out the door, pausing to look back at the girls.

"Stick with the guys, watch each other's backs," I ordered, adding one final part for Eve via the mind link. *And don't fucking get hurt, Love.*

They nodded, fire blazing in their eyes as she jumped out of the car with Fiona. I felt the tug of the bond, almost as if it was resisting as I ran the other way. Bright flashes were visible from gaps in the boarded-up windows of the basement, and I could smell something in the air, fuel maybe. The front door was hanging off the hinges, deep gouges in the wood. Keeping a low profile had gone out the window.

The fancy, souped-up van Darius had loaned us for the mission was sitting idle in the side street, but I peeked in the window to find the driver seat empty. If the guys were out front, Alice and Craig must have still been with Jeremy.

I vaulted over the bonnet of the car, taking the fire escape steps two at a time until I was over the carpark roof. I could hear fighting inside, grabbing the handrail of the stairs and swinging myself over to drop down in the small gap between the buildings. The bars blocking the window to where we'd found Jeremy the first time had been obliterated thanks to a spell and some modern-day ballistics Maya had helped with.

"Get down!" Alice's voice rang out, followed by a crash that had me running headfirst into the fray.

I climbed through the blasted hole in the wall to find the room Jeremy should have been in empty. I really hoped they had crazy ass soundproofing spells or else I was going to get exiled from the entirety of Europe for shit I didn't even start. How long before the humans living above noticed a hole in the building? If the hybrids howling didn't light a fire under my ass, needing to avoid getting wrongly blamed for another evil alpha's misdemeanours did.

The steel rings had been ripped clean off the walls, half the chains discarded on the bloodstained floor. The room looked like it had been under construction but never finished, the bare timber beams still exposed and tarp billowing in the wind coming through the smashed exterior wall. The toilet in the corner stank of faeces, and a small, rusted silver dog bowl was overturned, water seeping into the cement beneath.

It was worse than a prison cell, it was a torture chamber.

Another bang sounded, and I jogged into the hallway littered with chunks of plaster and debris, just in time to have a wolf that wasn't one of my own slam into me. I fell to the ground, landing on my back wrestling with a mass of sharp jaws and limbs. The wolf growled, bloody saliva dripping from its jaw onto my shoulder as I clamped my hands around its neck to keep its snapping muzzle just out of reach of my face.

The colour of their eyes was all wrong, they should have maintained their normal eye colour after shifting, but instead their hybrids had silver eyes. Not the same as a normal werewolf where it was like moonlight dancing in their iris, no. These were glowing silver, their pupils small pinpricks as if the magic had taken over completely, and they had lost all human consciousness.

The small pause was all it needed to twist and clamp its jaw around my wrist. I cursed, curling my legs beneath me and slamming my heels into the wolf's stomach with force. Dust particles hung above us in the air poorly lit by exposed swinging light bulbs above us. Sharp teeth tore through my flesh as I forced it off, scrambling to my feet as the wolf hit the wall with a dull thud.

"I don't want to hurt you." I pleaded with whoever was behind those eyes to see sense.

But whether it was spells, something they'd damaged through experiments, or PTSD from the torture the poor hybrid had endured, their vacant eyes were devoid of emotion.

They leaned back on their haunches, muscles rippling as they tensed and then pounced. This time I was ready, diving on the wolf and clattering to the ground once more. I pinned the beast down, grabbing it in a headlock and twisting hard until their neck snapped. I had to look away as a sickening crack echoed in the hall, guilt washing over me as the wolf's body went limp in my arms.

Before I could apologise to the wolf, a fireball shot right towards us. Plasterboard shattered as I dived out of the way, pain lancing through my back as I landed and watched in horror as the hybrid went up in flames before they even had the chance to revert to their human form in death.

"Luke!" Craig's voice was in my ear, but he moved so fast he was a blur, lifting me into his arms and speeding through the hallway before my brain could catch up with what was going on.

He sped into the room at the base of the hallway, placing me down on my feet. I blinked, and he was crouching by a man on the floor whose hair was matted, his bare body covered by a blanket.

Alice was in the room, her feet planted hip width apart as she faced off with a gaunt vampire that had wild, ruby-red eyes. His black hair was patchy, the movement of his gaunt limbs jagged as he circled her. She only risked glancing up at me for a moment, keeping her attention on the blood starved vampire ready to strike.

"Jer." I rushed to his side, kneeling on the cement floor beside him. My elbow caught the end of the broken chains hanging from his wrist, and I hissed in pain as the silver seared my skin. "Are you okay?"

My uncle struggled to lift his head to look at me, the pain contorting his features making my blood boil. His hair that was usually kept short was matted and unruly, his normal stubble a full-scale beard. Being bound during the full moon must have been agony. I could count the ribs of his exposed chest, his hollow cheeks along with the patchwork of bruises and deep cuts covering his body evidence of the torture he had endured.

But he was alive, there was a focus to his bloodshot eyes despite his battered appearance. They hadn't broken him like the hybrid outside.

He opened his mouth to speak, but only a rasp came out.

I drew the blanket tighter around his shoulders, a lump rising in my throat at how bony his shoulders were. Bile stung my throat at the sight of the strong wolf so weak.

"The cuffs are silver Craig, but they're spelled so they must be removed by a werewolf," Alice explained as Craig's face scrunched up with the effort he was using as he tried to pry the cuffs off Jer's wrists.

There's too many to hold off. We need to get out of here.

Worry laced Eve's words, her fear a tangible essence in my mind.

I looked down at Jer's wrists, the skin blistered and bloody from straining against the cuffs. He'd fought, and his resolve was the only reason there was a shred of the man I knew left behind.

Silver seared the skin of my palms as I gripped the handcuffs, pain jolting through my arms. Craig jumped up to help Alice keep the vampire cornered, one they'd already disposed of slumped lifeless in the corner.

Magic shimmered in the air as my sister shifted, her bones morphing and cracking as her body transformed into that of a wolf. She faced off with the vampire, her ears flattened against her head and spittle flying from her mouth as she snarled.

I didn't need the mind link to know she had my back.

My nerves were alight with pain, the silver burning my flesh. The tug on my magic made my stomach flip as the silver cuffs slowly drained my reserves, the weakness making the room spin around me.

I gritted my teeth and threw everything I had left behind my effort to snap the cuffs. My biceps strained, sweat beading on my brow as the metal slowly began to bend.

The metal finally gave way and snapped, my growl of victory morphing into a hiss of pain as I moved onto one of the cuffs on his ankle. I didn't stop, I couldn't. The combination of silver biting into my skin coupled with the spell clawing at my magic was agony, but I focused on Jeremy. The man who had endured this torture for longer than I could ever imagine.

A loud roar ripped from my throat as I shoved the pain of my melting flash to the back of my mind and channelled every ounce of rage and pain these bastards had caused me. I didn't stop until the last cuff slid from Jeremy's ankle. I growled, shutting my eyes in an attempt to drown out all the pain and threw everything I had behind my efforts to free him.

Craig whooped as the final handcuff clanged on the bare

floor. The moment I released they were silver, my wounds began to heal.

Jeremy's shoulders sagged at the reprieve, silver bleeding into his irises as his freed wolf side rushed to take effect.

An odd crackling noise caught my attention, and I looked to the doorway to find ice rapidly spreading along the door frame, following by a high-pitched cackle to rival a hyena's.

"Threat at nine o'clock," Craig warned, backing away from the door.

A loud crack sounded like a bomb going off, the building around us shaking, dust falling from the ceiling as the beam rattle. The smell of burning started, another bang as something ignited outside.

"What? One element isn't enough?" Red flecked the gold in Craig's molten eyes, the control he was maintaining as a young vampire something I'd have to commend him on once we were out of this mess.

A growl rattled in Alice's throat as she stepped up to flank Craig.

My stomach lurched as I scanned Jeremy's broken body for injuries. "Some of them have multiple."

"Greedy." Craig rolled his eyes, tensing as a piece of rubble cracked under the rival vamp's foot.

"Can we do Witch 101 lessons another time?" I hooked my arms under Jeremy's shoulders and knees, not missing the way the man winced as I hoisted him into my arms. "The guys outside are struggling. We need to go."

The blood-crazed vampire rushed at Craig, and at the same time he surged forwards to grab the vamp by the shoulder and slam him full force into the wall behind. Plaster crumbled at the impact, the vampire screeching in frustration. Its claws left nasty red gashes on Craig's arm as he pinned it against the wall.

Alice's eyes widened as she rushed to help Craig, her paws sending up a cloud of dust as she skidded to a halt in front of the doorway.

Flames licked the baseboards as a witch stepped into view, her blonde curls as wild as her green eyes, pupils blown. She was covered in blood, a murderous, unhinged smile curving her lipstick smudged lips.

The flick of her wrist was our only warning.

"Get down!" I yelled, my instincts howling as I backed up with Jeremy just as she aimed a nasty looking spell right at my sister.

Alice threw herself across the room, ducking and rolling just in time. The spell singed the tips of her coat as it missed its target and blasted into the wall behind, fire and magic flaring as the spell. Rubble and plaster exploded into the air like shrapnel, the witch advancing on us through the cloud of dust.

I passed Jer over to Craig and pointed towards the hole the witch had blasted in the wall, the dull glow of streetlights filtering through. "Get him to safety, Eve is out there."

Craig nodded, an unspoken respect passing between us as I trusted him with my injured uncle. Red tinged the corner of his eyes at the sight of blood leaking all over the blanket from the lacerations on Jer's body, but he pushed it back, his jaw set in determination.

He vanished in a blur through the gap, and I turned to find Alice caught between the witch and blood-starved vampire.

The stench of burning skin and death filled the air, my stomach convulsing as the horrid scents assaulted my senses. The bloodthirsty monster made a keening noise that set my bones on edge and a chill crawling down my spine. The vampire's arm hung limply by its side, a useless mass of charged skin and splintered bone attached by a chunk of muscle still clinging onto its exposed scapula. The monster didn't seem to notice, running its tongue over a sharp set of fangs at the sight of Jer's blood all over Alice.

The witch looked between me and my sister as if deciding who the easier target was, the flames at her fingertips thawing the ice covering her palms.

I took her choice away.

"Incoming," I warned, Alice crouching just in time for me to leap over and charge into the witch shoulder first.

She threw up a shield, but it was a second too late thanks to my enhanced speed. The protection element still struck, magic slamming into my chest stealing the air from my lungs and winding me like a physical force.

I tightened my grip on the witch as we hurtled into a stack of crates in the corner, wood splintering around us. Her back made impact first, and I jumped to my feet, hauling her up with me by the throat, blood dripping from her neck, my claws extended and bit into the skin.

She shrieked, launching her fist at my gut with the added punch of ice coating her knuckles.

My legs buckled, and I used the last of my strength to slam her into the ground, her head cracking off the cement with a sickening crunch. Her body jolted, eyes rolling into the back of her head.

Josh is grabbing the van, Craig is with Jer. We have to go now.

"Out. Now." I struggled to my feet and pointed towards the makeshift exit in the wall as the witch's body convulsed.

She might have been down, but given the half-dead wolves wreaking havoc outside, I didn't trust her to stay there.

Alice twisted in the vamp's grip, lodging her teeth in his shoulder and ripping herself free along with a chunk of flesh. He threw his head back with a furious hiss, the last sinew of muscle snapping and his arm clattering to the floor in a useless pile of broken bones.

Sirens sounded in the distance, our final warning to get the hell out of dodge.

I was hot on Alice's tail, my grip sliding on uneven bricks as I scrambled through the hole in the wall. My feet hit solid ground, coming face to face with another wall. I looked up to follow the light to see black railings above us. That witch had blown a hole in the front of the house, this was going to be a bitch for Edmonstone to clean up.

It was too late to worry about the consequences. Alice jumped and kicked off the surrounding walls to scale the railing. I did the same, landing in a crouch on the sidewalk to find it swarming with hybrids.

Several sets of glowing silver eyes fixed on us.

"Luke!" Eve was at the corner of the side street, covered in blood that my nose confirmed wasn't hers.

I sprinted down the street with Alice by my side, the pack possessed wolves chasing after us. Eve disappeared around the corner just before we caught up to find the van backed up to the edge of the street, the engine revving. She crouched at the rear, holding one of the doors open for us.

Alice dived in first, and I leaped after her, Eve slamming the door in the face of snapping jaws that smelled like rotting flesh.

I hit the floor of the van with a thud, smashing into Dylan's knee. Fiona was helping him prop a barely conscious Jeremy up, Josh and Craig looking over the backs of the front seat. It was like a workman's van except the floor was lined with carbon fibre and several seats with seatbelts that closed around your waist lined the edges in a U-shape.

Eve collapsed between me and Alice, sweaty hair stuck to her face and her chest heaving with exhaustion.

"Hold on tight." Josh slid the van into reverse, accelerating out of the side street. "Whatever you do, don't drop that laptop. I'm so close to cracking that damn drive so guard it with your life."

"Nice to know I come second to a lump of metal." Dylan rolled his eyes with a grin, holding the laptop case firmly against his chest despite his teasing.

One of the hounds yelped, a chorus of snarls and howls accompanied by banging as the wolves fought to claw their way into the van.

Craig shook his head, his red-tipped hair spattered with blood to match. "I know he's our friend, but I'm a little unnerved that Darius has access to military grade shit."

A loud thud made us all jump as a wolf landed on the front of the van, bloody saliva dripping from its jaws as it stared in the tinted window. Josh slammed the handbrake on and tyres screeched as the van drifted on the road, spinning so it faced the wrong way. Metal groaned, the wolf's claws carving into the hood as it was thrown off.

"This isn't *Grand Theft Auto*," Dylan grunted, holding his head and rubbing his temple where he had smacked his head off the side of the van. "Get us the hell outta here."

Eve's laughter became a strangled squeak of surprise as Josh floored the accelerator and whatever jacked up engine Darius had in this thing roared into life. She clutched my hand, almost sliding off her seat and quickly fastened her seatbelt.

Careful. I teased through the bond, relief washing over me at the sight of Jeremy rescued and everyone having returned safely. Especially Eve.

She leaned in to kiss me, her body pitching forwards and her head slamming into my shoulder as the van lurched with a deafening bang. The back of the van caved with the impact as we were rear-ended, the doors buckling as I looked up just in time see us hurtling towards a brick wall through the windscreen. A strangled scream filled the night like a banshee wailing, and then my world went black.

CHAPTER 27

I groaned and covered my ears, trying to drown out the incessant ringing. A painful ache pulsed in my temples and drool slid down my chin, the contents of my stomach threatening to bubble up my sandpaper dry throat. I cringed, curled up in a ball like I could sleep off this hangover from hell.

Something in my brain stirred at the metallic taste on my tongue. Someone was trying to call me, their voice a distant echo.

Eve!

I gave myself into the darkness, but something pulled me back. The memory of Luke holding me against me bracing for impact flitted by, and then it was gone.

Eve!

My head was pounding, as if they were trying to hammer their way through my inner walls. Pain throbbed behind my eyes, a sting starting at my fingertips.

EVE!

Luke infiltrated my mind, his booming voice a tether dragging me back to reality. Time slammed into motion, the searing pain radiating all over my body infiltrating the numbness. My eyes snapped open, and I found myself sprawled on the damp, hard ground between two cars on a strange street. My vision was dotted with stars, blurry images of figures darting and forth across the abandoned street. The sound of glass shattering and something exploding rocked my senses.

I gasped, my lungs working overtime to force air in and pump oxygen to my injuries. When I wiped my mouth, the back of my hand came away red. I wasn't hungover, I was living my own personal nightmare.

Luke.

Memories came flooding back as my vision cleared, a barrage of torment, blood, snapping jaws, and the crash. My chest constricted, my ribs closing in as panic rose at the sight of the van overturned across the street, the front mangled and embedded in and covered in rubble from the wall we'd hit. One of the two rear doors hung open, torn in half by the grill of a huge Jeep that must have rear-ended us. Smoke rose from the hood of Darius' van, the windows smashed, and I could smell blood. The people I cared most about in that world were in that vehicle.

Eve? Luke's voice was air to my lungs. *Where are you?*

My magic could sense him nearby. I had to get to him. Broken glass sliced open my hands and tears stung my eyes as I fought my way to my hands and knees. My left leg gave out, my ankle rolling uselessly as I attempted to stand and my body screaming in protest. I stayed crouched and steadied myself just enough to retch all over the tarmac as the scent of blood, magic, and fuel mixing in the air turned my stomach.

The shadow of a body lying near the van came into view and my stomach flipped all over again, icy tendrils of dread taking hold and rooting me to the spot as my heart rate soared.

Eve! Luke dropped to his knees in front of me, his face covered in dirt and blood as he cupped mine in his hands. He wiped my tears away with his thumb, his voice panicked and his eyes wild as if he'd been searching all over me as he scanned me for injuries. *Are you hurt?*

"S-someone..." The words lodged in my throat, my voice a quiet rasp. "Someone is..."

Shh, use the mind link, Love. He followed my gaze towards the body with no beating heart, shaking his head as he rubbed my shoulders. *It's not one of ours.*

I frowned, the creasing of my brow making the headache behind my eyes throb and colours dance around us. Ours. Our pack. As if what was mine was his.

Before he could explain, Larissa's voice echoed down the street as her heels clicked against the pavement. "Come out, come out wherever you are little wolves," she cooed, her sickly-sweet voice thing of nightmares. "Come out to play."

Is anywhere hurt? Luke's throat bobbed as he swallowed, the only chink in the alpha in chaos armour. *Can you walk?*

I glanced down at my ankle that was twisted at an odd angle with dark purple bruising around the bone, adrenaline coursing through my veins dulling the pain. My tongue was thick in my mouth as Larissa stalked along the street, hunting. *I think I sprained my ankle.*

He eased me up, so I was sitting with my legs straight out. The knee-length dress was shredded, covered in blood and dirt, like the bare soles of my feet. High heels had been the first thing to go when we jumped in to join the rescue mission.

Dylan sprinted past looking over his shoulder as magic struck a light post nearby, metal groaning as it warped and the light above us guttered out. "What the fuck? We've got company."

Go. I urged, my heart hammering as a blur raced past us, Craig's scent lingering in his wake. *They need you.*

Larissa strode down the street, ice-blonde hair whipping around her shoulders and her long black coat billowing in the wind as magic charged the air. "They can't protect you forever, Eve. You're only prolonging the inevitable."

Luke shook his head, his brow furrowed as he examined my ankle. Tension bracketed his mouth as he placed his hand either side of my ankles. *I'm so sorry, Love. This is going to hurt.*

What? My answer was a jolt of white-hot pain as he snapped the ankle back into its normal position. I screamed out, the edges of my vision becoming inky and tears streamed down my face.

Luke was beside me in an instant, kissing the tears on my cheek despite us both being covered in blood. His pain radiated down the bond, guilt shining in his silver eyes. *I'm so sorry.*

A loud bang punctuated his words, his frown only deepening as he looked over his shoulder at the fight ensuing.

Is it healing? The muscles of his shoulders rippled under his shirt as they tensed, his attention switching back and forth between me and our friends.

My magic swelled, seeking the injury out, my healing powers able to flow properly now the ankle was set correctly. *Yes, but next time give me a warning.*

I'm sorry, it would have hurt more if you knew it was coming. His voice wavered as he crushed his lips to mine, a metallic bite to his kiss. *Trust me, I've had to do it before. They have us cornered, but I'm going to figure something out.*

"I can make you scream louder than that, darling," Larissa purred, her shrill cackle sending a shudder down my spine. "You can't hide forever."

One look at my mate's face confirmed she was indeed hunting, and I was the fucking target.

A chorus of howls rang out, followed by the sound of tens of paws thundering against the tarmac.

Shit. Luke's eyes widened as he peered over the bonnet of the car beside us. *Can you stand?*

I nodded, and he helped me to my feet, throwing my arm over his shoulder as he supported most of my body weight. Once I was standing, I could see the full scale of the carnage ensuing.

Magic charged, sparking from Larissa's fingertips, her purple eyes filled with a murderous rage begging to be unleashed. Josh was several feet away guarding an unconscious Jeremy with Fiona, while Dylan and Craig wove between parked cars, dodging the witch's spells. One poor Mini had been completely torched, now a charred chunk of melted metal. Alice had shifted into her wolf form, standing guard with Josh.

A loud howl pierced the night, and I spun to see what looked like a pack of wolves thundering around the corner behind Larissa. While they looked like werewolves, they were shrouded in shadow, their silver eyes glowing orbs. As they drew closer, missing patches of fur and flesh revealed exposed bone, tendrils of shadow acting like a second coat.

I took a step back, my jaw dropping. "Zombie wolves? You've got to be kidding me."

The wolves flanked Larissa, throwing their heads back with piercing screeches that set my teeth on edge, promising pain and bloodshed.

"What the fuck are they?" Dylan crouched on top of the roof of an Audi, his eyes widening.

Luke shook his head, tension rolling through his shoulders. "I've no fucking idea."

Taking on a witch was dicey, but the dozens of silver eyes piercing the shadows guaranteed our execution.

The way Luke's jaw clenched and his hand tightened around me told me he knew it too.

"Bring her to me." Larissa ordered, magic swirling around her hands as she raised them to the sky with a glee. "Kill the rest."

The wolves rushed into action, two groups splitting off to take on our friends while a third stalked straight towards us.

I'm not going down without a fight. She can't have you. Luke turned to me, his irises engulfed by a silver matching the waning moon above us. *You need to run. I'll hold them off as long as I can.*

I shook my hand, ducking out from under his arm and placing my foot down on the ground. Pain shot through the healing bones, but I grit my teeth and set my shoulders. *You're not sacrificing yourself for me.*

Eve, you have t—

"You promised me that I'd always have a choice." I broke away from the mind link to force his hand. "I choose my pack."

He placed our joined hands against my chest, the heart beneath beating in rhythm with his and leaned in to capture my lips in a kiss that was all too brief, but conveyed every ounce of love and devastation. Tears shone in his eyes as he pulled away. "I'll see you on the other side."

The smile curving my lips was short-lived as Larissa slammed her palms together and extended her hands to send a perfectly aimed blast of magic as the blur of Craig moved behind an old telephone box. He cried out, the force of the blow sending him flinging his body into the railing of one of the houses behind.

"Save him," I cried, shoving Luke in that direction as a warlock stepped into view, a shadowy spell forming in her hand that my gut told me was meant for the kill.

Larissa's attention switched to me, her lilac eyes lighting up as she whistled. Three of the hounds darted over to her and surrounded Craig at the flick of her wrist, bloody saliva dripping from their teeth. She had only one command, her voice oozing with excitement. "Kill."

Luke dived into the fray just in time, standing back to back with Craig as the hybrids advanced.

In the distance more howls echoed, and my heart raced as more of the weird zombie wolves began to filter from the shadows. We were in over our heads taking on a witch, never mind a pack of bloodthirsty undead wolves. This really was it.

A streak of red shot in front of me, barrelling into one of the zombie wolves and sending it hurtling into the front door of the nearest building. My jaw dropped. It was Nadine as she sunk a blade into where the wolf's heart should have been, if it was alive. Whatever blade she was using worked, the wolf shrieking before the shadows snuffed out and the half-decomposed corpse collapsed beneath her.

I stared at her for a long moment, my brows knitting together. When she met my gaze, there was no warmth in her expression. If anything, she appeared irritated that she'd had to save my life at all. My theory from back at the club had to be right: Ryan needed me alive.

"Eve!"

I turned to find Ryan standing on the nearest corner. "You need to leave."

"I'm not leaving my pack."

He strode over to me, a vein on his forehead popping. "Come with me, I can get you out of here safely."

"Are you deaf?" I snapped, glancing over my shoulder and flinching as Alice tumbled into a wall with a crack as she fought with one of the shadow wolves. "I'm not deserting my pack. Loyalty might be a foreign concept to you, but I don't have time to play psychiatrist."

Nearby, Josh was defending Luke's uncle, a deep gash marring his bronze chest visible through the shredded material of his blood-soaked T-shirt. Fiona was behind him, Josh facing off with one of the undead wolves to stand between her and certain death.

Ryan held out his hand, as if he was some white knight coming to my rescue. "I can keep you safe."

A shout echoed down the street, followed by a loud growl and a car alarm blaring into life. One of their hounds had Craig pinned against the side of a car, my friend holding its head and roaring for help as he tried to keep the snapping jaws from his neck. Larissa was advancing on him until a wolf sped past, jaws sinking into her outstretched hand and biting a chunk of skin as it sped off into the distance. Luke joined his side, his claws extended as he brought one of the zombie wolves to the ground.

Larissa shrieked, firing a spell that caught the wolf's hind. Blood gushed from her wound, but the witch ran her glowing fingers over the exposed bone, her skin quickly beginning to knit back together. "Mutt. Did Ryan never teach you manners during all that time as a pet?"

Alice bounded behind a car to dodge the next spell sent her

way, at the same time Craig snapped the rabid hybrid's neck and raced after Alice.

"Safe?" I practically shrieked, an unhinged laugh bubbling from my lips. "You couldn't even keep me safe from your own pack. Hell, you only started dating me because I was a target for your pack's twisted experiments. You don't want to keep me safe. You need me, and I don't understand why, but I'm sure as hell not handing myself over to you. I'd rather take my chances with the undead, thanks."

A scowl darkened his expression, his eyes narrowing as he stopped a handful of feet away when I started backing away. "He can't keep you safe. Look at this, look at the state of your life since he came into it."

"Which letter in the word 'no' are you struggling with?" I snapped.

Nadine fought hand to hand with Dylan at the same time as them both trying to hold off the possessed wolves. A glint of silver that wasn't claws told me she was fighting dirty.

"Young love, makes me sick." Larissa strode towards me, a malicious smile stretching her red lips despite her clipped tone. "I didn't know you were joining the fun tonight, Ryan."

He stiffened at her words, his hands clenched into fists by his side. "This wasn't the agreement, Larissa. She's ours."

"I think I've made it abundantly clear that I want nothing to do with you," I corrected, my claws extending as the witch drew closer.

One of the undead wolves walked by her side, following like a pet. Ryan could stand spouting shit about saving me all he wanted, but he was complicit.

"You don't get to call the shots here." Sparks danced on the tips of Larissa's crimson nails, her words dripping with venom. "You hid her from me, and you know I hate lies."

Ryan moved to step in front of me, possibly the only chivalrous act he'd ever attempted, but with one flick of the witch's wrist he was forced to his knees.

Larissa stood between me and the friends I wanted to protect, and my mate who's anger and fear coursed down the bond. An invisible force took a hold of me, magic pulling me to Larissa and pressing the bones of my chest in until I thought my ribs might splinter.

"Love makes men do the most stupid things." The witch reached out to stroke my face with one of her talons, her smile twisting into an ugly sneer as her magic lifted me into the air, suspending me there as it sucked the air from my lungs, and turned her attention to Ryan. "You could have been great, too, you know. I would have offed Damien for you, made you into one of the greatest alphas of all time. But you're just as devious as that bastard father of yours."

She kept one hand raised to maintain the spell on me, while the other lifted Ryan off the ground and flung him like a doll into the building opposite. Behind her the army of undead wolves were closing in on my friends, circling them and pushing back until their backs were against the wall. Luke looked up, his eyes widening in horror as they met mine, and he saw me suspended and clawing at my throat as I fought for air.

A loud horn pierced the chaos, the rev of an engine drowning out the growls as a large Jeep skidded onto the road, its tyres squealing. It sped up, headlights illuminated the possessed wolves as it headed straight for them. I gasped, doing a double take at the woman in the passenger seat. Mary let out a scream, a guttural sound born of years of anger and oppression as the vehicle ploughed into the pack of wolves.

Two more SUVs careered around the corner, loud engines rumbling as they drove full speed down the road. The zombie wolves didn't scatter on instinct, bound by their command, their bodies crushed under the tyres and bouncing off the front grill of the vehicles.

Nadine and Ryan stumbled back, their eyes wide with shock, but it was Larissa's face that twisted into a mask of outrage that promised bloodshed.

"No!" She shrieked, magic thickening in the air as she formed a ball of fire in her hands and blasted it at one of the Jeeps.

I fell to the ground as her spell broke, my knees cracking against the hard pavement. Luke was already racing across the street towards me.

Her fireball didn't connect, an unfamiliar face poking out from one of the truck beds with a grin, her turquoise hair reminding me of Kate. A magic that warred with Larissa's rose in the air as the fire spell seemed to bounce off an invisible shield, ricocheting into a parked car near the two Faolchúnna wolves. The engine exploded with a loud bang as the fire hit the fuel tank, the force sending a fleeing Ryan catapulting through the air. His body hit the windshield of another car with a satisfying crack.

Nadine grabbed him, uncaring for her partner-in-crime's injuries as they retreated from the scene. Larissa backed up too, her mouth contorted as she snarled and fired spells at a Jeep crushing her rabid wolves, bones crunching between the tyres and tarmac.

My knees buckled as they retreated, tears of relief rolling down my face as the ground rose to meet me.

Before I could hit the tarmac, a warm arm wrapped around my waist as Luke caught me. His face was battered and bruised, but his smile told me we were safe. At least safe for now. My body gave out, my eyelids drifting closed as the familiar scent of pine and burnt orange surrounded me.

"It's okay. I've got you."

CHAPTER 28

LUKE

"I said *no*." My voice thundered around the small hotel room all of us had stuffed into, resisting the urge to pick up the lamp beside me and throw it full force at the wall. Anger bubbled up, fuelled by fear like a volcano about to erupt if one more person suggested that my *mate* was the key to a fucking *prophecy*.

"Alice is right, Eve is the key to this. I haven't cracked the prophecy enough to decipher how the spell to lift the Origin Curse would work, but she is at the centre of all of it." Cassandra was perched on the window ledge, her turquoise hair still speckled with blood. Unlike everyone else who had gone to freshen up before meeting, she was seemingly unbothered.

The muscle in my jaw ticked. "Origin Curse? This isn't a thing. Stop giving it a name."

Mary had gotten wind of what we were up to by forcing Jonas to come good on a favour. Her rescue team had consisted of Cassandra and a handful of the main Scottish pack that had helped Lila. Jer had been taken straight to see his wife and kids, but it was too dangerous for me or Eve to go near the rest of pack.

We had driven as far as Edinburgh before holding up in a hotel, all of us stuffing into my room to try figure out a plan.

Most of the Scots had re-joined their pack, bar the Scottish alpha and his younger brother.

"She has a point," Josh piped up from his seat at the ridiculously small desk in the corner where he was trying to revive his laptop that had taken a serious battering during the crash. Shockproof cases didn't extend to car-crash-proof, but he was hopeful he'd be able to fix it. We'd been so close to cracking the flash drive before being forced out of London.

I rolled my eyes, my tone cool. "Prophecies aren't real. Larissa is off her rocker half the time."

"She's been like that forever." Mary murmured in agreement.

"So it's a coincidence that the spell contains a line that the witch said back in Dublin?" Josh swivelled in his seat to look at me, arching an eyebrow. "Or are you being purposefully obtuse?"

I wasn't alpha, I didn't want to be. I viewed my friends as equals. But for some reason the way the Scottish alpha, Russell, snickered at the insult made my hackles raise.

Deep down I knew Larissa had mentioned prophecies during her rant, something had twigged in my mind during one of our discussions with Maya. But I didn't want to believe there was an ounce of truth to Larissa's words. I wanted to be right in my belief that Eve was just an unfortunate victim of Ryan's affections, and that she was targeted just for being a hybrid. I didn't want her to be special, not the type that put her in danger, at least.

I couldn't bear the thought of her being hunted, or the possibility that we might not be able to escape this. The idea that her cruel fate had been written in the stars long before we had the chance to meet beneath them was something I simply couldn't accept.

"One of the symbols in Jer's notes is a triquetra." Josh shrugged when we all wore the same questioning expression. "What? I took a few side classes to spice things up. Coding gets boring."

Dylan snorted. "Alright Indiana Jones. What does that have to do with the prophecy?"

"The second last line says 'Trinity tied'. The triquetra is also known as the Trinity knot. It has as a bunch of different meanings, but it always involves three things all interlinked. The first three lines of the spell mention the undead, a hound, and ancient magic," Josh explained, using air quotes with a pointed look in my direction. "Three things. Whatever Larissa is trying to achieve, it sounds like she's used hybrids in the past and whatever ritual, spell, curse, whatever this is, it hasn't worked. She seems to think it needs to be a hybrid, but what if it needs to be a specific hybrid?"

Eve finally cleared her throat, curled up at the head of the bed beside where I was standing. "Why me though? I'm just like the rest."

"I think it might have something to do with the link. Like Alice said before, you had both Luke and Ryan in love with you." Josh scratched the back of his neck nervously, as if he knew he was about to piss me off with whatever came out of his mouth next. "Except I don't think it's anything to do with Ryan, you have both a werewolf *and* a vampire that love you."

My eyes must have flashed silver because Craig bolted across the room, backing up against the door with his hands held up. "I do love Eve, but not in *that* way."

"See? Eve is the link whether you like it or not." Alice crossed her arms, purple bruises still healing on her pale skin. But my sister's injuries did nothing to deter the determination blazing in her eyes.

Russell finally spoke up, the Scottish alpha's voice a deep rumble that automatically demanded attention. His beard gave him a rugged look, he had light brown hair and eyes to match with a kindness in them despite the authority ringing in his words. "What else did this prophecy say?"

I growled, sending a pillow sliding onto the floor as I plopped down onto the bed since there was no room in the damn room to pace back and forth anyway.

Eve pulled up the notes on her phone. *"Bloodline and moon bound. Trinity tied by the blade of magic intertwined, wielded by the blessed can history unbind."*

"What the hell does 'moon bound' mean?" Russell asked, sharing a confused look with his brother.

His younger brother shrugged. Despite Callum's red hair, he was the image of the Scottish alpha. "All werewolves are bound by the moon. Maybe it's because hybrids aren't?"

I locked eyes with my mate, my throat bobbing as I swallowed hard. My mouth was dry, my head spinning as I thought back to how desperately Larissa had wanted Eve. We knew exactly what 'moon bound' meant, the moon was required for us to complete the bond. The guys knew, too, they just hadn't put two and two together yet.

Don't say it.

Eve's brow furrowed at my request, but she didn't argue. Her trust in me was misplaced, I was selfish. I needed to swim in denial a while longer.

"What's the blade? I mean, that could be *anything*," Dylan clicked the top of the hotel branded pen he was fidgeting with.

Cassandra stared across the room, her eyes narrowed as she studied me. Witches couldn't detect lies, but somehow, she knew I was hiding something.

"I'm not buying the Eve thing. If it's talking about bloodlines, based on how witches normally bake shit into our spells, this prophecy would be talking about a direct descendent of the first werewolf." Cassandra's frown deepened, her fingertips sparking with blue flames as she drummed them on the wall she leaned against. "Going by the myth, the witch Cadhla was technically the first, but she wasn't the only werewolf. All of the men in the tribe were supposedly turned, there's no way to trace bloodlines back that far, neither with genetics nor magic."

"So how the hell would Larissa know?" Eve cut in with a

scowl, throwing her hands in the air in frustration. "There's no way she has some magical sixth sense for genetics. Somehow having a dagger to my throat made her know *I* was the key?"

Dylan cocked his head to one side. "Can she smell it from blood or something?"

"What if it's your scar?" Fiona piped up, perched on the edge of the bed opposite me and my mate.

My spine stiffened, anxiety driving its claws into my vertebrae.

"What scar?" Eve's throat bobbed, her hand seeking mine out.

"The one on your back. It's tiny, but I noticed it one of the nights you stayed at mine in the Faolchúnna manor." Fiona leaned over to tug down the back of the knitted jumper Eve was in, all of us wearing a random assortment of clothes Mary had managed to procure. She pulled the material far enough to expose Eve's back, pointing between her shoulder blades. "See?"

Cassandra got to her feet, moving closer to inspect the mark. The skin of the scar was paler than the rest of her back, a small white crescent moon surrounded by what looked like a constellation of freckles. The blood drained from the witch's face.

"She's moon blessed."

I ground my teeth. "Can we please stop making shit up?"

Cassandra whirled on me, magic blazing at her fingertip as she pointed at the scar. "That is the marking of the moon blessed. It's not some fucking myth, it was what they called the original wolf pack. A lot of stories got lost in translation over the years, but there are records of that mark dating back until the origin of werewolves from multiple sources."

Eve pursed her lips, tears glistening in the corner of her eyes.

"I'm sorry, but Alice is right." Fiona's tone was grave as she reached out to squeeze her friend's knee. "Eve is the key."

"That's no scar, this is no mistake. That mark means you're moon blessed, a direct descendent of Cadhla, the first werewolf.

There's no way that's a coincidence." Cassandra shook her head, sympathy shining in her eyes as she looked between the two of us. "Prophecies can manifest in a number of ways, but I'm afraid Eve is a part of this whether she wants to be or not."

My mate shook her head, pushing her hair back from her face. "No... No. I'm no one."

It was Mary who stepped forwards, crouching so she was level with Eve as if she were speaking to a scared child. "You have never been no one, prophecy or not, dear. But I fear that, while you didn't choose it, the fates have chosen you to be the one to stop this curse from being lifted."

CHAPTER 29

"I don't want to be the chosen one." I'd bolted out of the hotel room and straight through the tiny hotel lobby, not stopping until I was outside. My chest constricted, as if my lungs were struggling to inflate. Scotland was cloaked in darkness and a blanket of unforgiving wind, I took shelter under the overhang at the front of hotel. The smell of smoke hung in the air and a few cigarette butts littered the floor by a steel bin.

I just needed to feel a small sense of freedom, instead of being trapped in a room that had grown smaller and smaller as they spoke about me like I wasn't even there. Prophecies, marks, moons, my fate. My head was ready to explode. I didn't care if I was making a terrible impression on the Scottish alpha or the witch, I desperately needed air.

The witch in question came up behind me.

Her combat boots were light against the pavement as she approached. Cassandra joined me in the little covered smoking area out the front of the hotel where I was taking shelter from the raging winds and rain while having a panic attack.

"I'm sorry, I didn't mean to dump that on you. Prophecies aren't fun, especially when you're born into something you never chose to be a part of." Her sigh hung as a puff of vapour in the cold air, and she shook her head.

There was something in the way she said it, the way she spoke about being chosen made me think she understood all too well the rollercoaster of anger and despair I was riding out.

"I won't just sit here and watch my life be ripped apart all because of something that was decided centuries ago." I scuffed the moss growing between pavement slabs with the toe of my trainers. "I don't want to die."

Her eyes were green one minute and pink the next, as if switching the colour was something she did to stay calm, but the pity in them shone all the same. "Like I said, they don't have to come true. Prophecies usually mean one of two things, you're the key to either breaking the curse, or stopping it from being broken. Sometimes the true outcome isn't what you think. So, don't give up hope just yet. You have a mate in there would fight to the ends of the earth for you."

"How did you know?" My brow furrowed, and I tugged my lip between my teeth.

She tapped her nose with a knowing smile. "I have my ways."

I nodded, staring out at the sheets of rain pelting down. Droplets ricocheted off the pavement, saturating my shoes and the hem of my jeans. The sound was calming. I'd heard people complain about Scottish weather before saying it was gloomy, but I found it atmospheric. I just wished it felt less like a bad omen.

"I'm sorry I have to go, but this has gotten too dangerous for me. I've already drawn too much attention to myself." She shook her head, reaching out to give my shoulder a reassuring squeeze. "My family background is complicated, to say the least. Keep fighting, trust in the bond. And remember, you might be the key to the prophecy, but you don't have to roll over and let it play out the way Larissa wants. Figure out what the rest means, and you might find a way to stop her, witches love a loophole."

With that, she stepped out into the rain and grinned as it almost grew heavier.

"Thank you." I offered the smallest of smiles, waving as the witch stuffed her hands in the pockets of her leather jacket and strode down the street, her dark figure vanishing into the rainy night.

I exhaled a shaky breath, my teeth chattering. Prophecies were real. Of all the pills I'd had to swallow since finding out I was a hybrid, that one was lodging in my throat.

Movement in the shadows across the road caught my attention. A figure stepped under the glow of a streetlamp, bright blue curls peeking out from under her hood and shimmering under the light. My eyes widened, the air leaving my lungs as my body froze, except for my heart which hammered at the sight of the woman across the road.

She turned and dropped her hood to reveal her face, her lips stretching into a wide smile as familiar green eyes lit up at the sight of me.

Kate.

My best friend stood opposite me, in her signature style of figure-hugging jeans, a hoodie, and a black tank top. Despite the rain quickly soaking her hair, blue strands sticking to her exposed shoulders and chest, she didn't seem to feel the cold at all.

This wasn't possible. She was dead. I'd held her body in my arms and sobbed. I'd washed her blood from my hands. I'd watched that casket lower into the ground. I'd seen the tombstone.

Kate was dead.

And yet, she was standing right in front of me.

"Kate!" Her name felt strange on my lips as I called out, my feet finally kicking into gear as I ran straight out into the downpour of rain.

A horn blasted and I skidded to a stop at the edge of the road just as a car sped past, the driver angrily flipping me the finger. I hadn't even noticed the headlights coming, so focused on the presence of my friend across the road.

"Kate? Is that really you?"

She didn't answer, the corners of her eyes creasing as she flashed me a playful grin over her shoulder.

I reached out as I stepped onto her side of the path, my fingers closing around nothing but air as Kate spun on her heel and took off down the street.

"Kate!"

My mind was reeling, trying to process the sight of my blue-haired friend sprinting into the distance.

Luke! I've just seen Kate, she's outside the hotel.

He didn't skip a beat before replying, his worry crystal clear down the bond as he issued one order. *That's impossible. I'm coming, wait right there.*

Rain quickly soaked through my clothes, chilling me to the bone. Kate paused at the top of the street to look over her shoulder at me.

"Wait, Kate. Please wait for me," I pleaded, restlessly shifting my weight as I glanced between my friend and the hotel door for a sign of Luke.

I cursed as Kate disappeared around the corner, my heart pulled in two directions. *Hurry up! We're going to lose her.*

I'm almost there.

Luke's promise was followed by a high-pitched scream that I'd recognise anywhere. My resolve snapped.

I'm sorry, I can't risk losing her.

Rain hammered against the pavement as I sped after my friend, breaking into a jog as a wave of unease tensed my shoulders.

Don't you fucking dare. Get back to the hotel now and we'll track her down together. My mate's voice thundered in my mind and I winced.

I rounded the corner at the top of the street just in time to catch a glimpse of Kate racing across the intersection, her blue hair visible between cars. In the distance, a fork of lightning illuminated the silhouette of Edinburgh Castle.

The soles of my feet burned from running, but I sprinted

across the road between a gap in traffic. Blood pooled in one of the puddles I passed only spurred me on. "Kate!"

She's heading towards the castle.

Luke's response to my directions was string curses followed by another order my wolf side wanted to obey, but my fear for my friend overrode it.

Kate didn't run. In fact, she'd often claimed to be allergic to any form of exercise that didn't end in an orgasm. Yet she kept a good distance between us no matter how much I sped up.

She didn't respond to my calls, damp blue hair my beacon as she led me through the streets of Edinburgh. I didn't have time to admire the architecture or enjoy the cobbled streets and mysterious buildings that made me feel like I was about to step into a dark academia book, when my reality was more like a horror movie. Storm clouds rolled above us, blocking out the glow of the full moon and shrouding us in darkness as Kate took a sharp left turn and disappeared from view.

I skidded to a stop in front of a bar with Christmas designs painted on its windows, covered in snowflakes and colourful festive lights. My sneakers were soaked through as I sloshed through puddles and turned down the same side street as Kate to find a black wrought-iron gate and the dull outline of a chapel visible in the dim lighting.

"Kate?" I called out to her, searching for a pop of blue but she was nowhere to be found.

I pushed my dripping hair out of my face, my head snapping up at the sound of the gate creaking as the wind picked up. Beside the handle a thick metal chain rattled, one of the links near the lock snapped in two, the remainder lying limp on the floor.

How the hell would Kate do that? My mind carried back to the images of Kate fighting alongside my friends. *Was it possible she was a vampire too? Could I have found her while she was transitioning with no heartbeat, and she later turned? What if Ryan has had her all along?*

My head spun with unanswered questions as I pulled the

chain through the lock and dumped the rest of it, the hinges of the old gate groaning in protest as I pulled it open just enough for me to slip through.

I sniffed the air, my nose failing to pick up any trace of her scent. But it was lashing rain, and she would smell different after death, like Craig did.

As I reached out to Luke, our mind link felt weird and fuzzy. I glanced back at the sign and the empty street outside. *I'm at Greyfriars Kirkyard Cemetery. I think Kate's hurt.*

I paced back and forth, waiting for his response, until another scream echoed in the night.

Kate's voice stole my attention, strained with pain. "Eve, please help."

"I'm coming! Where are you?" I called out, moving deeper into what looked like a churchyard.

A tall church with gothic accents stretched into the night sky with its finial piercing the clouds at the apex of the roof. To the right of the chapel small stones dotted the grass and a streak of lightning across the gloomy skies illuminated them to reveal tombstones. I was in a graveyard, which explained the distinct scent of decomposition carrying on the wind.

"Where are you, Kate?" Tendrils of unease wove in my stomach like snakes as I moved deeper into the graveyard, sticking to the puddle-clogged path. My clothes soaked right through to my skin, a chill setting in my bones.

A giggle broke the silence, followed by a clap of thunder that warned the storm was drawing near.

I walked towards the noise, the sound of her laughter a melody I never thought I'd hear again. But as I rounded one of the large trees planted throughout the graveyard, it wasn't my best friend standing in the distance.

Another fork of lightning pierced the sky above to reveal Larissa standing in front of a row of large tombstones. Her black cloak billowed in the gusting wind, glittering like the stars blocked by the storm rolling in, her hand resting on the back of the wolf by her side that stood as tall as her waist. Beneath its shadowy frame bones were visible, flesh peeling away from its ribcage and cords of muscle exposed. Its silver glowing eyes fixed on me, as were its master's.

"Where is she?" I demanded, panic rising in my voice. Tears pricked the corners of my eyes as I looked around, praying to see a hint of blue hair peeking from behind one of the tombstones. "What have you done to her?"

"Eve, sweetheart," Larissa purred, her lips, painted a deep crimson, curving into a smile that promised me a world of pain. "I don't know who you're talking about. Are you feeling alright? I think you need to sit down."

With that, large vines burst from the ground either side of me. Dirt scattered through the air and thorns sliced into my hands as I fought against the veins locking around my legs. They carried me to her, my trainers dragging and kicking up clumps of grass as I fought their grip. But the more I fought, the more sharp thorns dug into my waist and drew blood.

I couldn't reach Luke through our mind link. I could feel the bond, but somehow the witch was blocking our communication.

The vines wound around my wrists, binding them tightly behind my back and forcing my body bend at her will until I was on my knees in front of her. Just like that night back in Dublin, except this time I was alone and at her mercy.

CHAPTER 30

LUKE

Eve was pale as a ghost when she bolted out of the room, ignoring me calling her name both out loud and via the mind link. I had made it as far as the door to chase after her when Mary tapped my arm, her hand paused over my forearm as if she was going to grab me before thinking better of it.

"Can I speak to you outside for a moment?"

My gaze snagged on the scar cutting across her cheek, supposedly given to her by the same alpha who had killed her brother. And yet Mary stayed with the Faolchúnna pack for all those years. "I need to find Eve."

"I know, I'll just be a moment." Her eyebrows drew together, her fingers fidgeting with the hem of her jumper, the edges frayed.

Her normal ballsy attitude, based on the few times we'd interacted, was replaced by a nervousness that did nothing to gain my trust. She'd been there when Eve was hunted like prey by Ryan's pack, and even if she hadn't partaken, she didn't stop it. Helping us infiltrate the hotel that night in Dublin didn't undo all that. One good deed didn't change someone or make them a good person, sometimes it just means they felt guilty. And I didn't know Mary enough to make that distinction.

"I'll go check on her, I've to split anyway." Cassandra grabbed her small leather rucksack off the ground, turning to face everyone with a grin as she saluted them. "I'm sorry I can't stay guys, but I really hope you find a way to stop whatever they're planning."

"Fine." I led the way outside, shutting the door behind me and walking several feet down the hallway because the walls in this damn place were paper thin. Cassandra caught my elbow, pulling me back from Mary for a moment.

"I'm sorry I wasn't more helpful. This is getting too dicey for me, Larissa is going to attract the attention of the Royals if she keeps going... I need to lie low," she explained, tension clear from the lines on her forehead, a crack in her normal, cool-as-a-murderous-cucumber mask. She pulled me into a hug, giving me an extra squeeze for good measure. "I can still give intel, I just don't think showing my face around here right now is wise. I'm gonna head back home for a bit anyway, maybe I'll pop in and visit your parents."

I nodded, swallowing the lump rising in my throat at the fact that I couldn't see them. Having to make do with a phone call on Christmas day, watching Max open his presents over video call, was worse than taking on a possessed hybrid.

"Eve may be moon blessed, but she's your mate. Prophecies can manifest in different ways, don't give up. Fight for her, fight with her. Fight until the very end. I can't lose my drinking buddy, even if I only make an appearance twice a decade."

The corners of my lips twitched, at odds with the tears brimming in my eyes. I didn't even question how she'd figured out we were mates, her powers were a mystery she'd never disclose. "I'll never stop fighting for her."

"Good, then I'll see you at the Dark Night soon to celebrate." Cassandra gave me one last bruising pat on the shoulder before pulling away and waving to Mary. "You too, Mary. You're not too old to try drink me under the table just yet."

With that, she sauntered down the hallway the same way

Eve's scent led, probably out into the foyer. Cassandra never said goodbye. It was her thing, and for once, I understood why.

I turned to Mary who had been awkwardly hovering a few feet away. She didn't need wolf ears to overhear the whole conversation. I'd been uncomfortable with her being a part of our plans, I didn't trust her intentions. Sure, she'd showed up to save our ass. Cassandra seemed to trust her, but she the levels of morally grey she tolerated often walked the line of black.

"I know you don't trust me," she said, stating the obvious. Her chin was raised, her back straight as she met my gaze. "And I understand why, but you don't know the full truth."

"I'm supposed to just take you at your word?"

Claws extended from her fingertips as she held her hand out, slicing a shallow cut in her palm. Blood beaded from the wound. "I'll make a truth pact if that's what you need."

"That won't be necessary." I shook my head, watching as the cut slowly healed. I'd had enough of magic and promises. "I'll hear you out."

"I know you don't believe I could care about Eve or disagree with what Damien and Ryan have been up to, given I'm a member of the Faolchúnna pack. But the only version of my pack you've ever known is the one run by a man desperate for power. It wasn't always this way, our pack was once worth its name." She wrung her hands as her claws slowly withdrew. "I presume your dad told you about the pack splitting all those years ago, and how he became alpha?"

I nodded, choosing my next words carefully so as not to give her too much information. If I was to believe her side, she was going to have to make sure it corroborated with my dad's account. "He told me the pack split when Damien took over, yeah, the same night he became alpha. That the guy who was supposed to be next in line was killed by Damien."

"Damien has more than just my brother's blood on his hands. He worked with Tom's father to kill my parents, the reigning alpha of the Faolchúnna pack." Her upper lip curled in distaste as she spoke of their deaths, an undertone of anger brewing. "My brother, Cormac, was next in line. Damien took his life, too. His rise to alpha was paved on the blood and bones of my family."

My mouth hung open. My dad had mentioned working with the alpha's daughter to try save the pack and her brother. The whole time it was Mary?

"All these years... After what he did to your family, why did you stay?"

Her sigh was loaded with decades of pain. "It's my pack. It was my family's pack and legacy. I couldn't leave and let Damien destroy it. At least by staying I stood a chance at stopping him... Not that it worked. He was born wicked, and that evil was nurtured to the point where I don't think the man feels a shred of emotion. I'd thought there was hope when he had his first child, it seemed to soften him a bit. But when Jake died, that's when he really seemed to snap."

"Jake?"

"Ryan's brother, he was killed by a hybrid." Mary stared off into the distance, as if lost in the memory. "I'll never forget Ryan running into the manor, his legs cut up from the brambles. The kid was barely able to form a word, and by the time we got to the creek, we were too late. His brother was murdered. Ryan was in no fit state to explain what happened, but he kept saying a wolf was there. The only stranger's scent present was that of a hybrid."

The cogs in my brain turned so fast the gears were overheating. "That's why they both despise hybrids so much."

"We never found out why or who committed the murder. Not that Damien was short on enemies, even in the early days."

I'd never thought I could feel sympathy for them, but the small hint that manifested was quickly doused by anger at the thought of Eve walking into a pack that despised her kind so vehemently completely unprepared.

"You let Eve stay there, knowing all of this?" A low growl of warning rumbled in my chest at the thought of her running terrified through the woods as she was hunted and toyed with. "Did you know about the kidnappings? About Alice?"

Mary didn't back down, despite my shoulders spreading as I towered over her. Her jaw was set, unwavering determination in her eyes as she met the fury in mine. "No. If I knew about Alice, I would have told Tom immediately. Your father is an old friend of mine who I value dearly, I'd *never* have let a hybrid or any other paranormal suffer knowingly. I knew he was in bed with Lars and the witch, but he was always careful to keep his plans hidden from me. I did what I could when I could to protect my pack from him as much as possible over the years. I've paid my pound of flesh. I will never forgive myself for letting Eve get hurt or being so close to Alice all those years while your family was hurting."

I studied her for a long moment, but nothing in her body language betrayed her as a liar. Her story lined up with my dad's, and the pain in the waver of her voice was raw and real, honest.

"I believe you."

The smallest hint of a smile showed in the crease of her eyes. "I promise, Damien has never and will never have my loyalty. I don't want to protect anymore, I want to destroy him. Something I should have done a long time ago."

Eve's voice rang in my mind, her words making the hairs on my neck stand on end. *Luke! I've just seen Kate, she's outside the hotel.*

That's impossible. I shook my head, raking my hand through my hair. "Fuck. This can't be happening."

Mary frowned, her eyes narrowing. "What's wrong?"

"Eve thinks she saw Kate."

Craig appeared in the doorway, his pale face a mask of concern. "Kate's dead. I was at her funeral, I saw the body."

I'm coming, wait right there. I sent the order down our mind link, turning to face the others as Dylan and Josh also appeared. "Eve said Kate is outside. It's not possible, unless it's a ghost."

I was already jogging towards the elevator, Mary following

close behind. Josh who had popped his head out to see what the commotion was taking up the rear.

Hurry up! We're going to lose her.

I'm almost there. I promised, unease gnawing at my gut.

Alice sprinted down the corridor to join my side. "Spirits can only travel so far. She has no connection to Edinburgh, does she?"

"No, she doesn't." Craig followed, looking as if he was about to throw up.

The elevator button lit up as I smashed my fist into it, but even two seconds of waiting was too long. I burst through the door to the stairs, the metal hinges groaning. Everyone followed as I took the steps two at a time, cursing the receptionist for assigning us a room on the top floor.

I'm sorry, I can't risk losing her.

My stomach plummeted, dread clawing an icy path up my spine. I cursed out loud, before sending a stream of messages through our link. *Don't you fucking dare. Get back to the hotel now and we'll track her down together.*

"What is it?" Josh sprinted the front, our footsteps echoing in the stairwell.

A low growl rumbled in my chest. "She's gone after Kate. Or her ghost. Or whatever the hell she's seeing."

My mate's scent led us through the foyer and out the front door. Relief washed over me at the sight of her standing outside, her hoodie up to stay warm from the violent Scottish weather as she leaned against the glass exterior of the hotel.

She's heading towards the castle.

I frowned as Eve's voiced filtered into my mind. "How is she tracking Kate from there?"

Craig's confused expression mirrored mine as we shoved through the revolving door.

Eve didn't look up as we approached.

Something was wrong from the moment I grabbed her shoulder. The hooded figure turned to reveal a skeleton skull, empty eye sockets staring into my soul and nothing but bone beneath the hoodie and my hand. The skeleton opened a toothless mouth, its breath stinking of rotten flesh. No words came out, only a deafening screech.

I leaped back at the same time its head snapped back, and the entire skeleton fell apart, crashing to the floor in a pile of clothing and dusty bones.

"What the hell was that?" Josh stepped up beside me, his eyes wide as he stared at the bony remains.

All around us the stench of magic lingered, the kind that made the hairs on the back of my neck and arms stand on end. Magic that had a wicked, dangerous edge to it. Larissa's magic.

My mate's voice rang out in my mind, her words disjointed but her fear was clear. *Graveyard...Hurt.*

Eve? Where are you?

She didn't respond.

"Eve's gone." Saying those words aloud after everything we'd been through broke something in me.

Craig shook his head, raking his fingers through his red-tipped hair. "She can't be. She wouldn't just leave."

"This is a witch's doing. It has to be Larissa." Mary confirmed my suspicions, kicking the heap of bones, sending a radius skittering across the wet pavement into a puddle.

"How do you know it's her? What kind of spell lets you play *Sims* with a fucking skeleton?"

Her expression was solemn as the rest of our group hovered by the exit, just as stunned. "Because Larissa is a necromancer."

CHAPTER 31

"What do you want from me?" I was helpless, trapped on my knees before the psychotic witch who stared at me like I was the answer to all of her prayers and her next plaything to torture all at once. Behind her, rows of large, weathered tombs towered over us and the church in the distance lit up with another flash of lightning like the graveyards very own skyline. The moon had vanished, its glow barely visible behind the storm clouds rolling in, leaving us cloaked in shadows that seemed to feed off and merge with the skeletal body of the undead wolf beside her.

"You know exactly what I want." Larissa's voice was a grating keen, magic flaring to life at her fingertips searing my skin as she lifted my chin. Despite the pouring rain, she was entirely dry as if she had a shield from the weather moulded to the shape of her body so it was almost undetectable. "The same thing that has those two handsome alphas in the making tripping over themselves and starting wars; your heart."

My mouth dried up. Damp grass beneath my knees soaked through the denim of my jeans, the vines sprouting from the ground wrapped around my thighs and calves to keep me bent in a kneeling position at her feet. Thorny tendrils wrapped around my torso, all the way down my arms to bind my wrists at the base of my back so tightly I couldn't even sit up straight. I was completely immobilised, the vines biting into my flesh the only thing stopping me from falling flat on my face.

"Why did you do it? Why did you get in bed with Damien to experiment on hybrids and even witches—your own—all to break a curse?"

Larissa shrugged, leaning against the crumbling wall of the tombstone behind her. "Originally, I believed that there was a way to eradicate hybrids and strengthen my magic in the process. It was a win-win situation, Damien gets his revenge on hybrids and becomes the most powerful alpha, and I'd become an unstoppable force once more. The Royals have all but disowned me, casting me out and limiting my magic. I want the full scale of my powers back. Once I stumbled upon the prophecy during my travels, I realised I could find another way. When I break the curse, the magic used to bind werewolves and vampires to the moon and sun will be all mine."

I had no idea how to get out of this mess, so I did the one thing I could—buy myself more time.

"Why did they bind your magic?" I flinched as a thorn caught in the crease of my thigh and hip on one side as I shifted my weight. "What did you do that was so bad?"

She ran her hands over the granite exterior of the tombstone, small sparks of magic flying from her fingertips. "I fell for the wrong man. I loved him, but he fell for my sister. I warned her, of course, but she always wanted what was mine. I caught them together, the ultimate betrayal. So, I raised a demon to extract my revenge and killed my lover. Needless to say, the Royals have made sure I'd be unable to do so again, and I lost the powers the demon lent me."

"Just like the myth."

Except, instead of calling on Mother Nature, she'd called on a fucking demon.

"It's not a myth, it's the truth. Witches kept it under lock, key, and dragon for centuries before someone found out and blabbed. History is written by those in power, they twisted the narrative, and it was quickly written off as myth, legend, something we retell but don't believe. And when people don't believe in it, when it's just a little bedtime story to scare cubs, they don't ask questions. So the prophecy lay hidden until I unearthed it."

I thought back to the sphinx in the library and her warnings of books falling into the wrong hands. Larissa certainly qualified.

"So yes, I have a soft spot for Béibhinn. Her only crime was to give a man who couldn't be trusted her heart." Her tone grew icy, at odds with the small balls of fire skittering from her hands and floating into the air around us. "As I said, loyalty is *very* important to me."

It was like history repeating itself all over again. She was the evil sister, the scorned lover. And now she planned to lift the curse and take all the magic for herself.

She cocked her head to one side, her lips lifting in amusement as she walked forwards, hips swaying. "I know you've been digging where you shouldn't and found the prophecy. The books have eyes, you know."

Images of the book imbued with the soul and eye of an ancient witch's lover surfaced in my mind. But that one had been out on the other shelves...

"They can have ears too. It was a common trick used by witches back in the day. We were very favourable in the Fae courts for a while thanks to our... creative ways to get information." She flashed her teeth with a hungry grin as she stood over me, dragging her nail along my cheek. "It's very easy to make a human fall for you, especially men. The women are wilier. The key is their loyalty, when you inter your enemy within pages for a lifetime, they tend to hold grudges and refuse to cooperate."

I ground my teeth with a hiss as one of the vines looped around my thigh tightened, another thorn piercing my skin. "I wonder why."

"Ryan did mention you were mouthy." Larissa caught my cheeks between her finger and thumb, her nails slicing into my cheeks. She increased the pressure digging into my jaw until my lips parted, stuffing a small capsule that tasted like herbs in my mouth.

I gagged, but she snapped my jaw shut before I could spit whatever it was out.

"Swallow," the witch ordered, grabbing a fistful of my hair and clamping her hand over my nose and mouth. My lungs burned as I glared at her, begging for air as she pinned me in place. One of the vines whipped across my stomach, the sting of the thorns ripping through my skin making me gasp and gulp for air, swallowing the herbs in the process.

The moment the herbs hit the back of my throat, I knew. The taste of nightshade bloomed in my mouth, making me retch all over again. Nightshade, just like that night in the manor. She was taking away the part of me I needed to survive this, the wolf side that made me strong. Tears sprang to the corners of my eyes as my magic retreated.

"That wasn't so hard, was it?" She released my hair, but I didn't lower my head, glowering at her from my knees. "Good girl."

Those words really didn't hit the same way when they dripped from a murderous witch's lips. I called out to Luke through the mind link, but there was no way it worked at this distance, and as my wolf side slipped deeper into the corners of my mind, I realised I might not be able to use it at all with nightshade in my system.

I was alone.

I'd walked straight into her trap and undone all the good we had fought for. The witch needed me to break the curse, and I'd handed myself to her on a plate.

A low growl rumbled in my chest, causing the undead wolf to step forwards, the exposed muscle of its jaw opening to reveal sharp canines that reeked of death. Tendrils of shadow masking its exposed ribs travelled up Larissa's hand, as if it were tethered to her, its glowing eyes both unseeing but fixed on me at the same time. The small specks of fire she had hovering in the air bloomed as a fork of lightning lit up the sky. The flames grew as they drifted over to rest on two torches either side of the largest tomb behind Larissa. The fire blazed and expanded as the black storm clouds above parted to reveal the full moon in all her glory.

Larissa stepped back, wiping her hands on her leather pants as if she'd touched something dirty. "I apologise for all the mystery and drama, but you have a track record of not coming quietly. Plus, this way your beloved Crescent wolf won't have to witness your death. Who would have thought a worthless little hybrid would have so much importance in how this story would play out?"

I shook my head, regretting the moment as the veins wound their way up my throat. They were like quicksand, the more I moved and shifted from the pain of the thorns biting into my flesh, the tighter they bound me.

"You're a smart girl, Eve. Surely once you read the prophecy, you knew your death was written in the stars?"

The witch caught a drop of blood pooling on my collarbone on her finger and brought it to her lips, closing her eyes as she tasted it. The lilac in her irises swirled like the storm above us when her eyes opened again, and she slid a dagger from her belt. I froze, every muscle in my body begging to run as she ran the dagger down my back. She began to recite the prophecy as if it were a nursery rhyme.

"Life-source of the undead,
The true heart of a hound,
Ancient magic spilled,
Bloodline and moon bound.
Trinity tied by the blade of magic intertwined,
Wielded by the blessed can history unbind."

The ground around us shook and magic sizzled in the air, the flames either side of the tomb flickering as the wind seemed to howl in response and thunder roared above us. She sliced open the kitted jumper to reveal my bare back, circling the tip of the dagger between my shoulder blades. Right over my scar.

"Your friend turning was a mere formality, fated to happen since your inception. Your heart is true, and this mark claims you as one of Cadhla's descendants. The original hybrid bloodline pumps through your veins, one reason every one of my past attempts has failed. This time it won't. Especially now I've found the resting place of the final puzzle piece."

I flinched as the dagger bit into my skin, the movement causing the vines to bite into my ribs. I swear, it was as if my very heartbeat triggered them to tighten, the bite of their thorns a constant reminder of how helpless I was. My only magic was gone, an empty well blocked by the nightshade.

"What's the final piece?"

Her mouth curled into a malicious sneer as she raised her hands, the fire swelling with the movement to illuminate the clearing. The vines tightened, bending and pulling me at her will, the tendrils around my throat forcing my head to turn at a painful ankle. Thorns spiked into my throat as I gasped, we weren't just surrounded by the smaller graves and trees I'd walked past. There were two figures chained to a raised tomb several feet away, but only one heartbeat. The tomb was surrounded by a railing enclosing the large, decorated headstone, and the stone slab on top of the single crypt, the gate at the base hanging open and creaking in the wind. The one nearest was a vampire, his head hanging limply and his wrists cut up from straining against the chains binding him. His face was a stranger's, but from the puncture marks still visible in his neck he was a freshly turned vampire. An innocent.

My stomach plummeted as I twisted to look at the young woman bound to the rusted railings opposite the vampire. For a moment I worried it was Maya, but this girl was taller, with tanned skin and long, soaking wet black hair that clung to her frail body. There was a thick chain around her neck, forcing her to look straight on, her arms hanging loosely by her sides covered in track marks and her pupils dilated much like Fiona's when she had been bewitched. Her heartbeat was sluggish, but it was there.

"Gabi..." My breath caught at the sting of a thorn, the vines whipping my head back round to face the girl. Her face was more gaunt than in the Polaroid and newspaper article Dylan had pulled up, but it was the same witch, Maya's best friend.

She clapped her hands, her giddiness nothing short of disturbing. "Yes, Ryan loaned her to me as an apology for interrupting my fun the other night."

"Ryan's here?"

"No sweetie, Ryan is otherwise engaged until he learns his place." Her mood soured, those cat-eyes narrowing. "As I said before, loyalty is incredibly important to me. Given your pack-hopping tendencies, you clearly have an issue."

"Slut shaming is very 2010," I spat, my temper raging as I wriggled against the vines only for them to tighten further and pitch me forwards.

"Oh honey, I'm not judging. I'd happily bed both of them. Is that what you wanted, little wolf? Were you hoping to let them share you? Having multiple men worship at your feet is a truly incredible experience."

There was a wistfulness in her tone that set me on edge, the vines tensing painfully as I shuddered at the thought of Ryan ever touching me again. I had zero desire to be shared with the man who had caused me so much pain. I had eyes for one man and one man only.

"Ah, but of course. You'd have no interest in bedding the ex now that you've found your fated mate."

My blood chilled and Larissa's smile widened, her expression one of sheer glee. She knew she had me. Knowledge was power, and love was weakness. He was all the leverage she needed.

"I don't have a mate—"

Her palm met my cheek in a stinging slap that made my head

snap sideways, the noise of the impact echoing throughout the graveyard.

"Do not lie to me." She emphasised each venom-laced word. "I'm no fool, darling. I knew he was your mate all the way back in Ireland, long before you even had an inkling."

My brow furrowed, and I shifted my knees to try escape a thorn digging into my kneecap. "How?"

"The way he looked at you gave it away, as if the moon, sun, and stars shone in your eyes." She rolled her eyes, grimacing as if that kind of love made her skin crawl. "I saw your mark, darling. Once I knew you were the one the prophecy spoke of, I knew you had to have a mate. You're moon bound. Or, well you would be if you got to complete the bond. Unfortunately for you, I have almost everything I need to break the curse on hand tonight."

She watched my face, licking her lips as if she could taste my fear.

"Don't be scared, the afterlife has always been your destiny." She sliced the remaining material of the jumper off my body to leave me in nothing but my bra, tracing the dagger over my exposed chest above where my heart hammered. Her smile was a cruel smirk, her cackle carrying on the wind. "Say hello to Mam and Dad for me, it's been a long time since I sent them on their way."

CHAPTER 32

LUKE

I'd always had a temper, but nothing compared to the blazing, rage-fuelled adrenaline pumping through my veins. My mate was missing, and the scent of Larissa's magic had lingered all over the front of the hotel. This was no coincidence, the bond between us felt like a shredded piece of thread and she'd blocked our mind link. Despite it being dulled, I could still feel Eve's fear. She was in danger, and I would burn the city to the ground if that's what it took to get her back. No curse was being lifted tonight.

Either the hotel windows were just as flimsy as their partition walls, or the roar that ripped from my throat once I realised Eve had been taken, shook the street.

Within seconds, Russell and his brother had joined us, along with Fiona. All of them looked at me with wide eyes, I didn't need to look in the window to know my pupils had blown, and my eyes were bright silver. The full moon was shrouded in clouds, but she was calling on my wolf side. I needed every ounce of my magic if I was to save Eve tonight. Not only that, I needed backup. I'd grown enough to know that this wasn't a fight I could win alone.

Mary stepped forwards first, her jaw set in determination. "Lead the way."

They followed me without question as I took off down the street, Eve's scent filling my senses. The wind was cutting, sheets of heavy rain ice cold against my skin as I tracked Eve through the streets of Edinburgh.

The moon watched us, hanging high in the sky as I sprinted full speed up the hilly, winding streets of the city. We barely saw a soul at this hour of the morning, only the odd barman doing late lockups. The others followed close behind me, the sound of their shoes hitting the soaked pavement and sloshing through puddles, along with rolling claps of thunder above us my only company as we hunted for my mate.

Her scent was easy to follow despite the weather. Whether that was the bond or not didn't matter, my only focus was getting to her before Larissa tried to perform the ritual to break this damn curse. My heart beat erratically at thought of Eve's being carved out and sacrificed.

A chill set in my bones as I stopped beside a pub covered in Christmas lights, with cheerful festive drawings all over the windows. Eve's scent took a left turn to lead us onto a cobbled side street with a large, black wrought-iron gate. Behind it, the silhouette of a church stood out against the storm clouds, barely visible on the dull night if it weren't for my enhanced eyesight. I peeked through the gate to spot a handful of gravestones nearby, tufts of grass swamping and moss covering around the unkempt ones. Dread weighed my bones down as I ripped the broken chain hanging off the gate, metal clanging as the metal hit the ground. Nothing good could come of Eve being lured to a graveyard.

No matter how much I hoped this was some kind of shortcut, I knew deep down I was clinging to false hope.

The hinges of the gate groaned, another flash of lightning lighting up the skies above us as I stepped into the graveyard. The uneven gravel beneath my feet was peppered with puddles and mucky, thanks to the deluge of rain, but I didn't need to track footsteps. I could smell her. I could feel her. I could hear her.

Her cry carried to me on the raging winds, like a knife through my heart. I froze, the blood pumping adrenaline through my body feeling like ice. Alice and I shared a look of horror, the same worry etched onto the faces of those following me through the gate.

Another scream had my feet moving on autopilot as I followed the sound of Eve's screams. My wolf side begged me to shift, the magic writhing restlessly within me at the sound of my mate's pain.

I could hear Larissa's voice before I could see the witch, pausing behind the cover of a leafless oak tree. As I peered around the knotted trunk, a flash of lightning lit up the clearing to reveal the witch. The small relief I felt at the sight of her breathing was short-lived.

The moon cast its light upon a single tomb in the centre of this corner of the graveyard as if it was trying to lead me to her. My chest constricted, panic setting in at the image of my mate on her knees before Larissa. Eve was bound to a gravestone, her knees resting on top of the large stone slab covering the crypt while her wrists were tied together above her head. Only when the fire from the torches on either side swelled did I notice that the ropes were actually vines growing out of the earth. They wrapped around her body, writhing and constricting snakes, sharp thorns glinting in the dancing firelight. Blood smeared her arms, her upper body completely exposed but for her bra and the vines pinning her in place. Deep cuts marks marred her arms, and dread pooled like poison in my stomach. They weren't healing anywhere as fast as they should.

Dylan stopped right behind me, reaching out to rest his hand on my shoulder. No matter how much I would love to burn Larissa on a stake, I needed to get Eve out alive.

"What did I tell you about that mouth of yours?" Larissa

hissed, her mouth twisted in an ugly sneer as she traced a dagger in the shape of a heart over Eve's chest.

Eve recoiled, wincing as the vines dug further into her flesh. Blood seeped from her shoulder, angry red bite marks dripping in blood.

Eve? Can you hear me?

No matter how many times I tried to communicate with her through the bond, my calls went unanswered. Her expression didn't change in the slightest, her blue eyes wide with fear, as if she couldn't hear me at all.

The growl of the wolf that stepped back to join Larissa's side was almost lost in another rumble of thunder cracking above us. It was just like the ones from the car crash. A coat of shadows masked chunks of rotting flesh and muscle, making its skeletal form almost invisible in the firelight but for a set of silver glowing eyes. She reached down as if it were her pet, shadows spiralling towards her fingers from the wolf's coat. A very fucked up, decomposing pet. I'd heard of necromancers, but I didn't realise they could raise paranormals in their shifted form.

My heart hurt at the thought that some of the zombie wolves were likely victims of Larissa and the Faolchúnna pack's fucked up plans.

A sheet of lightning illuminating the sky above us revealed two other victims bound to the tomb. A vampire was chained to the railing surrounding the raised tombstone, his arms limp, and his head slumped to one side as if he was unconscious. Craig stiffened beside me at the sight of the fresh bite on the man's neck, a clear sign he was freshly turned and undergoing the transition.

Bile rose in my throat. The witch had turned an innocent human just to be used as a pawn in her plans.

The sound of a low groan had me shuffling around the tree to peer closer. A young woman was tied to the railings on the opposite side. The magic of the spelled manacles blocked her powers, the chains holding her pulled taut so her frail arms were outstretched, and her feet barely skimmed the ground. It was Dylan who gasped, the first of us to recognise the witch held captive.

Gabi's head turned towards us, the movement drowsy as if she had been drugged. Her eyes were barely open slits, her skin coated with blood, and her black hair soaked. The black dress she wore was loose around her shoulders and frayed at the bottom, her sallow skin paler than the photos we'd seen. With her magic cut off by the chains, she was dancing with death if left to the elements for much longer. Her heartbeat was painfully slow and erratic.

I raised my hand and pointed either way in silent signal to the Crescents to move out. Josh nodded, splitting away with Alice towards the right, while Dylan and Fiona went left. They crouched low, still in human form for now.

Larissa hushed the wolf by her side as it pranced impatiently, glowing orbs fixed on Eve as if she were its prize. "Soon. I need the moon to hit its peak. Once we unearth the dagger, you can have your fun."

"Why did you do it?" Eve's voice cracked, her body shaking with the effort to stay still despite the pain she was in.

The witch ran her tongue across her lip, tilting her head to one side with a taunting, thoughtful expression as she paced around the narrow space surrounding the tomb. "I didn't kill your parents because of you. So quit the wounded orphan thing, they were collateral damage a long time before I knew who you were, or of the prophecy."

My jaw dropped. Josh looked to me from his position kneeling behind a moss coated gravestone, a clear question in his eyes. I shook my head, no. I had no idea who Eve's parents were, or what hand Larissa had in their death.

"Your parents were a part of the Faolchúnna pack who fled once they realised you were going to be born a hybrid. Damien was taking over, and while he hadn't decided to dedicate his plans to eradicating hybrids completely, he wasn't fond of them. They knew you wouldn't be safe."

Eve shrieked, the vines tightening around her body as she tried and failed to lunge at the witch. I dug my fingertips into the trunk of the oak tree, my claws extending to sink into the wood.

"I'm not sure what Damien would have done with you, to be honest. But once he heard your father fled the pack just as he became alpha, Damien decided they needed to be dealt with." Larissa shrugged, as if deciding to murder two pack members was a perfectly logical decision. "He needed a job done, and I was happy to do him a favour in order to gain one of my own. So, I hopped on a boat to Scotland."

Eve's parents had been here in Scotland?

She leaned down, brushing a damp strand of hair off Eve's face before placing the point of the dagger in her hand beneath my mate's chin. She forced Eve to meet her malicious gaze, her eyes glinting with pure pleasure at the sight of her pain. "It's fitting, you know. I thought maybe the crash earlier would have brought back memories, but you were only a baby."

The tears streaming down Eve's face along with every single precious drop of her blood that stained her jeans and rolled down her back from those thorns fuelled the anger washing over me. Larissa had a fistful of her hair, Eve's head wrenched back so far I thought her neck might snap.

"I ran them off the road, and then I stabbed them right in the heart." Larissa increased the pressure, the tip of the blade slicing into Eve's flesh. Blood dripped down her throat to match the tears falling down her cheeks. "You weren't supposed to be in the car. Damien had sent his brother along, and Nick insisted that you shouldn't be killed. He was soft. So, you were dumped on the doorstep of this very church."

"No..." Eve sobbed, her chest heaving as the shock set in, triggering the vines to slither around her throat and constrict like a snake. "You're lying."

"If there's one thing I've made very clear, it's that I don't like lies. This is your truth, darling."

She clicked her fingers, two more wolves emerging from the shadows. The way their joints were visible as they moved, bones clicking as they flexed their jaws attached by sinews of exposed, rotting muscle on approach, sent a shudder down my spine.

The wolves fanned out, and I hoped Gabi didn't give us away as she mumbled something incoherent.

"The final piece to this little prophecy requires the original dagger Béibhinn used to kill her lover, one that was passed down through different generations until it was buried with an alpha in the early nineteen hundreds. Right here in this very graveyard."

Larissa's cloak billowed as she shoved the gate open and strode across the clearing to face a large, decorated crypt, the paws of her dead hounds rustling in the grass as they circled the outer walls. The structure was taller than her, the stone whitewashed and well-kept compared to some of the crumbling, moss decorated gravestones and tombs dotted nearby. The front of the crypt was enclosed like a tomb, with a large tombstone at the front. Carved into the stone was the pack crest, featuring two wolves supporting a shield adorned with the image of Edinburgh Castle. Below the crest, there was a listing of the names of every alpha and their immediate family for the last century.

The grave of a wolf was sacrosanct, and I watched in horror as a ball of magic formed between her outstretched hands, a swirling mass of flames and white energy. She slammed the heel of her open palms together, sending the spell slamming straight into the stone slab marking the crypt entrance. The magic blasted a hole straight through the stone slab, sending fissures spreading through the names as the stone cracked from the blast and exploded, sending a shower of rocks and dust into the air.

The stone collapsed, the air clearing to reveal a pile of rubble and a crypt split into three parts. On either side of the crypt mausoleum there was a there was a stack of tombs embedded in the wall with names and dates illegible in the poor light from this distance even with my heightened senses. In the centre, there was a gravestone and a slab of stone marking a tomb embedded in the floor of the crypt.

The moon almost seemed to retreat behind the clouds in disgust.

It looked like another gravestone, but despite craning my neck as much as I could without risking being seen, I couldn't make out the engraving.

Larissa's smile was wild and power-hungry as she readied another blast. I had to grip Russell's, the Scottish alpha's, arm as he stood next to me, his skin hot under my touch. I dug clawed fingers into his biceps to hold him in place. His eyes narrowed in anger, not towards me, but towards the witch destroying his family's resting place. He slipped his phone from his pocket, hitting one button and killing the screen immediately before it could give us away.

The stone slab fractured with a loud bang, rubble and dust flying into the air as the stone slab crumbled. Larissa clapped her hands, throwing her head back with a chilling cackle before gesturing to her zombie-like wolves. "Dig my darlings, find me that dagger."

During her speech, the other Crescents had snuck behind different gravestones, situating themselves to form a semicircle around the witch and her undead wolves. Russell met my gaze and inclined his head, the alpha waiting on my command.

As her wolves raced into the crypt, dirt and broken stones flying in their wake, Larissa turned her attention back to my mate.

"The moon will be in position soon, so we better prepare while the hounds find me that dagger. This one is a poor substitute for now, but it cuts all the same." Larissa spun the dagger, a dark smile curving her ruby-red lips as she tossed the dagger between her hands, eyeing it with disappointment. "I do love full circle moments. Your parent's deaths were quick and painless, I can't promise the same for you."

Eve's eyes widened at the dagger, one of the vines moving to cover her mouth.

"This spell requires a few runes, keep your voice down so we don't wake the locals."

She grabbed Eve by the hair, forcing her head back as she held the dagger like a pen and sank the blade into the top of her breast.

The scream of agony that tore from Eve's lips nearly brought me to my knees.

The moment the blade hit her flesh I stepped out of the shadows and into the light. I raised my hand in signal just as a bolt of lightning forked above us in tandem with Eve's screams, followed by a roll of thunder announcing my presence. At the same time my pack shifted alongside the Faolchúnna and Edinburgh wolves that had followed my command, magic shimmering in the air as they prowled forwards to expose their presence.

No one was taking my mate's life. She was mine, her heart was mine. And I'd kill anyone who dared come between us.

I couldn't see Luke, but I could feel him. As those vines writhed and thorns dug into my flesh, even as my body froze at Larissa's revelations about my parents, his presence was the only thing keeping me from breaking. Pain shot through my nerves as she dug the blade of her dagger into my flesh, a hoarse scream of agony ripping from my throat.

"Get of my mate!"

Even though I'd felt him, the moment Luke stepped out in the clearing, fresh tears rolled down my cheeks at the sound of his voice. Thorns bit into my throat as I turned my head, but I pushed through the pain until my gaze found his silver eyes, pools of the moonlight that bound us. His jaw was clenched, his beautiful face a mask of rage as he strode towards us. Behind him, several wolves advanced, their heads low to the ground and their muscles tensed, all ready to spring into action at his command.

A loud growl rumbled in Luke's chest as he rushed forwards. "Let her go!"

"As you wish," Larissa purred, releasing her grip on my hair so I slumped in the vines and the blade drove deeper into my shoulder.

Luke slammed straight into an invisible wall of magic only

outlined by the raindrops hitting it, the muscle in his jaw feathering, and his eyes narrowed on the witch. I whimpered in pain, tears rolling down my bloodstained face as I grit my teeth against the pain.

Larissa dug the blade deeper, her lips twisting in annoyance as she looked up from her carving in my skin. "I don't have time for interruptions tonight. I'll raise her from the dead after, I promise. Or you can join her?"

A growl rumbled deep in Luke's chest. "Over my dead body."

Irritation clipped her words. "I did offer. Are you volunteering? Your heart's no good to me, but I'm sure I could find other uses for you."

She twisted the blade, and I cried out, my body convulsing as the pain-heightened to unbearable levels. Stars danced in my vision as my nails scratched at the vines binding my wrists. I was so weakened by the nightshade, I couldn't summon my claws.

Luke advanced, his claws extended and the muscles of his chest flexing as if his wolf side was fighting to be set free.

Larissa dragged the blade downwards so quickly that the edges of my vision blurred as I screamed. She didn't seem to enjoy the sound of my pain this time, withdrawing the blade as she clicked her tongue in annoyance. "I thought I'd set up wards, but Ryan must have dismantled them before I sent him to the doghouse."

My body sagged against the tombstone behind me as she removed the knife, warm blood pouring from the wound down my back. Nightshade still blocked the majority of my powers, but the dull remnants worked overtime to stem the blood flow.

I hadn't seen Ryan at all, had he known what she was planning? My brow creased in confusion. Did the spineless git actually try to stop her? Or fuck with her plans to try steal me back as leverage for himself? I didn't care what her version of the proverbial doghouse looked like, but he could rot in hell for all I cared.

Behind us, the full moon neared its peak, casting an eerie

glow across the graveyard. Larissa clicked her tongue, the half-dead wolf by her side gliding to stand at the end of the tomb I was bound to in front of the gate, while the other two stood guard in front of the crypt. Those tasked with guarding the crypt stopped their search for the dagger and raced to the blasted hole of a doorway, shrieking noises of excitement slipping from their mouthless bony muzzles. Luke stood between them, glancing at the sets of glowing eyes focused on him as the zombie wolves pranced, mucky saliva dripping from their teeth.

Larissa's cloak whipped in the wind behind her like a shadow as she whirled on Luke.

"I'll give you one chance." She traced the blade of the dagger down my thigh between the vines pinning me in place. "Stand your dogs down, or I'll make sure my hounds shred them to pieces, and then I'll raise their spirits. I'm not sure you have it in you to kill one of your own."

I swallowed the tears clogging in my throat, my head twisted at a painful angle as I stared at the hellish wolf-like creation nearest me. Chunks of flesh were missing from its skeletal form, nothing of the wolf they once were behind their lifeless eyes. Was one of the souls she tortured was my mam or dad? Tears mingled with blood as I stayed slumped on the floor, silently willing my mate to walk away. I couldn't bear the thought of them ending up like that.

"Those wolves have nothing left of their souls." Luke shook his head in disgust.

"Love really does make you a fool."

I dug my nails into the vines binding my wrists, not even able to summon claws as I looked up at Luke. "Please, take Gabi and go..."

"I'm not leaving you, Eve," Luke promised, the rusted metal of the railing flaking and bending in his grip.

"Ahem." Larissa gestured to the two paranormals she had bound. "You won't be taking anyone, unfortunately you don't qualify as a replacement. If her little friend over there wants to volunteer as the vampire sacrifice or you have a witch in your pocket, then maybe we can talk."

I flinched as I strained to see my friend, my heart constricting at the sight of Craig and his red-tipped hair crouched beside Josh nearby.

"It's pitiful that the only followers you have are those that you have to control. You speak of loyalty, yet you have none. You're just a lonely, powerless, master puppeteer. These wolves may listen to my command, but I guarantee each one wants to rip your throat out for their own reasons. And I'm sure Russell would like to have a word about you desecrating his family's grave."

She sighed, rolling her shoulders as if impatient as she checked the moon's position in the night sky. "Fine, have it your way."

Luke signalled for his wolves to move, the Crescents racing through the grass and leaping over graves as they charged at Larissa. Two wolves I recognised by scent as the Scottish alpha and his brother headed for the crypt with Mary and Fiona as backup. Luke shifted in front of me, his body contorting and limbs snapping into place as his body morphed into the sand-coloured wolf that always came to my rescue.

I pulled on what strength I had left, calling to my magic and centring all of my concentration on forming claws as the fingertips of my hand. If they were going to fight for me, I wasn't going to give up.

Larissa's eyes darkened, her features twisting into a nasty scowl as she sent a blast of magic towards Luke that he narrowly avoided, the neon-blue spell hitting a gravestone behind him and splitting it in two down the middle. She whispered something in Latin I didn't understand and the vines wound tighter, constricting so they were pressing on my ribs to the point my lungs couldn't inflate fully.

She couldn't kill me without the dagger, but that didn't mean she couldn't inflict pain. Torture was her favourite game.

"Don't let them touch her," she ordered, the shadow hound bowing in submission before leaping onto the top of the tomb in front of me. The ground beneath us shook as Larissa raised her hands to the sky, her eyes becoming inky black pools as she murmured a spell so quickly the words blurred, and she threw her head back with a screech. "Rise!"

Magic charged the air in tandem with a sheet of lightning lighting up the graveyard. A mound of soil in front of a grave to my right crumbled, the earth shifting as the ground vibrated. Clumps of grass fractured, dirt flying into the air as something shot out of the grave. My mouth went dry as bony fingers scrambled for purchase, followed by an exposed forearm as the hand clawed its way out of the ground. All around us, bodies in varying stages of decomposition slowly dug their way out of their graves.

I gasped, thorns digging into my side as I jumped in response to a skeleton bursting from the grave nearest the tomb I was bound to. My brain struggled to keep up, but reality smacked me in the face as one of them went straight for Luke.

"Luke!" I jerked against my restraints as a vine slapped over my mouth.

He spun to the side just in time to avoid the skeleton draped in a cloak of shadow similar to the wolves. It was as if her magic fuelled them.

Our wolves were no longer just facing off against the possessed zombie wolves, our superiority in numbers decimated by her raising an army of the dead. They seemed easily to dismantle as Dylan snapped the neck of one, in his jaw, the skeleton's bones falling limp in his mouth. Their numbers were a problem, but the wolves worked in teams to take them down, while the Scots focused on getting access to the crypt.

Larissa sent a nasty looking spell Luke's way, forcing him to duck and roll behind a mound of fresh dirt. Once her path was clear, she sprinted across the uneven ground towards where the two undead wolves faced off with the Scots while Fiona and Mary kept the skeletons at bay.

Luke slammed one of the fresher bodies onto the ground, pinning its body to the damp earth with its paws as he clamped his jaw down on his back. He threw his head back, tearing the possessed man's spine out in one clean movement. He hurled the body at another skeleton stalking in his direction, the undead smashing into a tree behind and disintegrating into a pile of bones.

Luke's silver-ringed gaze was fixed on one thing, and one thing only, as he fought his way towards me. It took all my self-control not to fight against the vines as they crushed my ribs, focusing on sawing the single claw I'd managed to conjure against one of the vines holding me in place. The farther away from me Larissa moved, the looser the vines became.

All around, the sounds of teeth and bones snapping echoed over the raging winds, the rain growing heavier as raindrops bounced angrily off the tombstone.

The hound in front of me stiffened, dropping onto its haunches with a snarl as Luke reached me. I shook my head towards the witch, my warnings muffled by the vine and thorns cutting the corners of my lips. Luke followed my gaze to an unconscious Gabi, and I nodded, the movement making me wince as thorns dug into my throat.

Alice raced over, shifting back into her human side mid-stride as she went straight for the witch I pointed to. Behind her, the Scots advanced on the crypt where Larissa was digging, having disposed of most of the dead bodies mindlessly attacking and one of the zombie wolves.

"I've got her, you get Eve." Alice crouched by the witch to examine the cuffs binding her wrists. She frowned as the vampire opposite groaned, a clear sign he was awake. "Craig! Come help the vamp."

We didn't need another blood-crazed vampire on the run.

Luke stayed in his wolf form, strong cords of muscle moving

under his coat as he prowled around to the open gate, coming face to face with the decaying wolf standing between us.

Craig arrived as a blur, gripping the rusting railings as he skidded to a stop. "I'm on it."

The wolf lowered its head, the shadows coating its body seeming to surge as a guttural snarl rattling in its throat. An ominous clap of thunder rang out, and my heart sank, despair washing over me as more sets of glowing silver eyes appeared in the distance. Wolves draped in shadows emerged from behind headstones and trees, and the leader was heading straight for my mate who thought the only thing standing between us was the single undead wolf.

Larissa screeched in the distance out of view, and her vines loosened enough for me to get the words out. "Behind you!"

CHAPTER 34

LUKE

I turned just in time to see a pack of wolves emerging from the night, as if they were formed within the shadows. They stank of death, decaying muscle, and flesh along with clumps of matted coat clinging and flapping half disconnected from their skeletal forms as they moved. Their unnatural glowing eyes were fixed on us, the leader of the undead wolf pack sprinting straight at me.

I leaped into the air as he reached me, our bodies colliding mid-air in a mass of snapping jaws. The wolf's claws dug into my side as I clamped my jaws around its neck, struggling to get a grip as my teeth ground against bone instead of biting into flesh. The air left my lungs as we hit the ground, the zombie wolf landing on top so I took the brunt of the impact. I braced my paws against its chest, having to lock my claws around ribs to stop my grip from sliding as I fought to keep its snapping jaws away from my jugular.

A chorus of howls pierced the night as I dug my hind paws into the wolf's stomach and bucked it off. The wolf hit the gravestone opposite with a crack, shaking its head and back on its feet within seconds. Behind the other, undead wolves advanced, breaking off in smaller packs to pick off our own. Anxiety knotted my shoulders, panic rising as I counted a two-to-one advantage to them, at minimum. And that didn't even count the witch who seemed to be more interested in blowing the crypt to pieces than fighting us for the moment.

Craig had the vampire freed from the railing, but still bound by chains, the stench of blood and death sending the freshly turned vampire into overdrive. Alice was still working on Gabi's chains, sweat beading her brows as she hacked at the metal links with an axe one of the older skeletons had brought from its grave.

A cry of pain to my left had me twisting to see Fiona struggling under another wolf shrouded in shadow, and Dylan racing over to leap onto the wolf's back and allow her to roll away. These things only seemed to die if you could rip their heart out or snap their neck. Their hearts were a weird mix of shadow and skin that weren't completely corporeal or beating. But I didn't have time to dissect the anatomy of necromancer wolves when they were running straight at me, every time I took one on, another took its place.

I zeroed in on the wolf pacing in circles on the tomb in front of Eve, its shadowy footprints leaving no marks in the rain-soaked surface. We weren't going to hold these wolves off for long, and if I had to watch Eve scream from the pain one more time, I was going to lose control of my wolf side altogether. It was wild with a thirst for revenge, but going after the witch alone was a suicide mission.

The silver-white eyes of the wolf guarding Eve fixed on me as a guttural snarl ripped from my throat. I sprinted towards the tomb, launching myself over Alice who was crouching by the unconscious witch. I leaped straight onto the top of the tomb, my jaw sinking into a hefty chunk of flesh still attached to the wolf's shoulder. The force of my impact knocked the wolf off-balance, sending both of us rolling over the edge and clattering onto the ground.

A rusty, broken spike from the railing dug into my hind at the same time the zombie wolf sank its teeth into the back of my neck. I ripped the lump of flesh from its shoulder with a growl, pain shooting down my spine as I writhed in its grip until I could dig my back legs into its rib cage. I shoved so hard one of the bones splintered as the wolf fell back. The gap between the tomb and railing—to deter grave robbers—was too narrow for two giant wolves to fight, but neither of us backed down. Thick, black blood dripped from my muzzle as I lunged for the wolf again.

We wrestled on the ground, jaws snapping as we took shots at each other until I managed to jam the necromancer possessed wolf's muzzle between two bars of the railing. The wolf snarled, but because of the lack of skin, their mouth was trapped closed as I pinned them there. Their shadows flickered, their touch licking at my magic reserves. I clamped my jaw around the base of their rib cage and pulled until three more ribs popped. The stench of death was overwhelming, and my stomach churned as I shoved my nose into their chest cavity, my teeth closing around their motionless heart. I ripped it free in one swift movement, spitting the lifeless organ out beside the wolf as the shadows faded out and the wolf fell still beneath me.

I pulled the rusting piece of metal from my left hind leg with my teeth, exhaling sharply as the pain hit. I snapped at the vines winding around the back of the tombstone, but they were like chunks of snakeskin and pure muscle. I shifted into my human form, wincing as my leg strained beneath my weight, and rushed over to Eve.

Her weary face lit up at the sight of me, and I fought tears back as I climbed onto the tombstone. My hands shook as I held her face in mine, rage rippling through me at the sight of her body peppered with thorn marks and the deep gashes from Larissa's blade still struggling to heal.

Eve made a muffled sound, wriggling against the vines.

"Shh, Love." I kissed her cheek, struggling to keep calm as I unwound the smaller vine from her mouth. The sight of the cuts all over her lips and blood dripping down her chin was something I'd enjoy avenging. The witch deserved a slow, painful, torturous death. "It's okay, I've got you."

The rain began to ease, the moon illuminating the clearing as the storm clouds thinned and the thunder ceased, replaced by vicious snarling and the shrieking howls of the shadow wolves. A loud bang came from the crypt and the vines around Eve's arms loosened, as if the more the witch focused her magic elsewhere, the weaker her spell controlling the vines grew.

Eve rested her forehead against mine as I slowly uncurled one of the vines around her throat, each flinch she made further igniting the flames of my anger. "Forget me, get the dagger. If we destroy that, the curse can't be lifted."

"I am not leaving you like this."

"You have to, Alice and Craig are here. They'll get me out." Her wide eyes darted towards where Larissa was creating a cloud of dust and rubble as she destroyed the crypt in her search. "Finding the dagger is our way to end this without anyone dying."

I stared at her for a long moment, covered in cuts and blood. How was I supposed to leave anyone I cared about in that state, let alone my mate?

"Go!" Alice urged, one of the chains binding the captive witch now on the ground. "We have her, I promise."

All around me, blood and spittle flew as wolves clashed with the undead. The living were flagging, fighting a losing battle against the bigger undead pack. One of the fire torches had been knocked over during the fighting and rolled beneath one of the large oak trees nearby, its flame slowly following a trail of bones that hadn't surfaced until the rain had eased. Embers sparked to life beneath the canopy of leaves, small flames licking at the base of the tree eating away at the damp wood.

Eve was right, we needed to stop Larissa sooner rather than later, and we needed to stop her for good.

"Don't let those hounds near her and watch your back," I ordered, before brushing my lips against Eve's in the lightest of kisses, terrified I would hurt her. "I'll be right back. I promise."

My instincts screeched in protest as I stepped away from my

mate and launched off the tombstone, shifting in the air. My paws sunk into the muddy grass as I landed on all fours. A plume of dirt spilled from the blasted hole in the crypt. I skidded to a stop at the entrance, dropping my shoulders and sneaking through the dust hazed air. My nose hit an invisible wall, forcing me back, but it didn't smell like Larissa's evil magic.

I frowned, shifting back into my human form on one hell of a hunch. It was a werewolf burial ground, so surely the main thing they'd want to protect against was rival packs?

Sure enough, I was able to step over the threshold of the crypt. It must have been spelled to only allow pack members or humans through to protect their resting place. Pity they never considered power-crazed witches, or soulless, necromancer-controlled wolves.

Larissa threw her head back and shrieked, her cloak covered in dust as she kneeled at the side of the grave she had decimated. Magic sparked from her fingers as she threw a lump of rubble into a sealed tomb on the left. The name engraved on the stone surface cracked, the support beams buckling. I dived across the crypt to dodge a large piece of the ceiling caving in. The stack of coffins collapsed behind the stone exterior, the top one sticking out at an angle. My lip curled as her disrespect, my shoulders tensing as I faced her.

The grave was destroyed, the coffin open to reveal the decayed remains of an old man that must have once been an alpha of the Edinburgh pack. He was nothing but bones now, wisps of white hair stuck to his skull, and his arms crossed over his chest. The bones of his fingers were bent as if he had been buried clasping something between his hands, except there was nothing there. From the murderous look in Larissa's face, the dagger was not where it was supposed to be.

The rage brewing in her eyes matched the storm raging outside, magic flaring from her fingertips as she pointed at me. "Where is the dagger?"

"I didn't even know about the dagger until your little spiel earlier." I backed up with my hands held in defence as I tried to subtly scan the room to see if she'd missed something.

She jumped to her feet, stalking towards me with her hand outstretched. "No one else knew about the prophecy, it was buried with him. Now it's not here. It doesn't take a genius to deduce that you were involved."

My shoulders hit the back of the crypt, and I cursed under my breath. "I swear, I had nothing to do with this. Maybe your little pet Ryan double crossed you."

"Give me the dagger or I'll slit your little mate's throat." She scowled, fire stirring in her palms as she stood between me and the exit.

I cocked my head to one side, catching a glimpse of Alice carefully removing the vines binding Eve. "Except you won't because you need her to break your precious curse."

"When I find that dagger, I'm going to make you watch when I carve her heart out. And then I'll raise her from the dead, just to kill her all over again." Larissa's words dripped with a venom I couldn't fathom, her long nails digging into the side of my throat, and the fire stinging my skin as she pinned me against the wall. "I'll create your personal version of hell."

My hand shot out at the same time, claws slicing into her neck as I copied her grip. I couldn't take on a witch, but I could see Eve finally being freed through the entrance of the crypt. And that was all that I needed.

A series of howls sounded in the distance, rapidly growing closer. As Russell howled in response, I realised the wolf calls ringing out lacked the death rattle of the wolves the necromancer summoned. They were living, breathing members of the Edinburgh wolf pack coming to help us. From the murderous look on Larissa's face, she knew it too.

"Looks like your time is up." I flashed one of those sadistic grins she liked so much.

"Oh darling, I have a lifetime to lift this curse. It's you who is racing against the clock." Larissa's voice dropped to a seductive purr, as if the promise of violence was some sort of sordid turn on.

Magic swelled around us as she placed one palm against the wall behind me and brought it crashing down. Her escape route. She cast one last look at the grave where the dagger should have been before turning her attention back to me, her magic surging as she slammed a needle into my stomach. My blood ran cold as nightshade flooded my system. Behind her, Eve hugged my sister as a pack of wolves filled the clearing and jumped into the fray fighting the undead wolves as the edges of my vision blurred.

She was safe.

Larissa shoved me to the ground, her wicked smile leering over me.

I sent one last message over the mind link, knowing Eve probably couldn't even hear me.

I'm sorry, I love you.

CHAPTER 35

EVE

I felt like a hole had been carved in my chest, and all that remained was broken, jagged edged pieces that would never fit back together. Without him, my heart and soul were broken shards that I could never fix. I would never be complete without him. Though I could still feel Luke's distant presence through the bond, letting me know he was alive, we only had weeks to rescue him or else we'd inadvertently refuse the mate bond.

I'd lose him forever, and I couldn't help but wish that she'd taken me. I was destined to die anyway, at least that way I wouldn't have to attempt to live when my heart had been cleaved in two.

"Stop thinking that." The mattress of the bed sagged as Craig sat beside me. "I don't need a fancy wolf mind link to know exactly where your head is going, and we're not going down that dark road Juliet."

The corners of my lips twitched, a pathetic attempt at a smile.

We were sat in a room on the Edinburgh pack lands, a large house that the alpha owned. It was like the one back home in Kildare, the familiarity another twist of the knife lodged in my chest. The ride here had been a complete blur. I'd stared out the window as the dark, gothic city gave way to rolling hills, but all the while my mind was with him.

"You don't have to make the call. Mary said she's more than willing to do it."

I shook my head, tears brimming in my eyes once more. I was surprised there was any left. "I'm his mate. I want to do it. I *need* to."

Craig squeezed my hand, his cool skin against mine just another reminder of the loss I'd caused everyone around me. Luke was wrong, it was me that death and pain followed.

"You don't have to pretend." Craig handed me a tissue as I sniffed in a pathetic attempt to stop the tears from falling again. "It's okay to show pain. It's safe to be vulnerable around your friends. It doesn't take anything away from your strength."

"I can't. I'm afraid if I let it out, I'll never pull myself back together."

Sympathy swirled in the gold of his irises as he shuffled closer on the bed to wrap his arms around my shoulders. "He's not gone forever. We will get him back, and you will get to complete the bond."

"I don't give a fuck about the bond. I just need him alive. I need him home and safe with his family, I'd sacrifice the bond and my life for that in a heartbeat."

"You don't mean that."

"I do." I exhaled a shaky breath, my voice cracking as a fresh tear rolled down my cheek. "I'm so sick of the pain. I'm sick of hurting and losing people. I just want it to stop."

Craig wrapped both arms around me and cradled me against his chest, rocking back and forth as a sob broke from my lips and the tears began to fall in earnest. I couldn't hold it in any longer. My eyes were bloodshot from exhaustion, but I relished in the sting of my salty tears. The thorns piercing my skin were gone, along with the cuts Larissa had made in my flesh, but the pain was seared in my memory. I called to it, wanting to feel anything but the numbness that had settled over me, as if I was a passenger in this nightmare that my life had become.

Tom's number flashed up on the screen of the phone lying on the bed behind us, and I swallowed hard, forcing air into my lungs.

"I can call Mary…" Craig offered, glancing between the phone and me with a pity that made me want to crawl out of my skin.

I snatched the phone up, my hand shaking as I hit the answer button and lifted the phone to my ear.

"Luke! Darius and Jonas just brought me up to date. Where are you?"

I squeezed my eyes shut, my voice wavering. "It's not Luke. It's Eve."

"Eve? Are you alright? Where's Luke?" Tom paused when I didn't answer, his tone switching from panic to one of resignation that made my heart sink. "It's Luke, isn't it?"

Craig took my hand and laced our fingers, his thumb stroking the back of my hand as tears streamed down my face. "Larissa's taken him. He sacrificed himself for me."

It wasn't the silence, it wasn't Tom's response that pushed me over the edge, it was the sound of Max in the background, Luke's little brother asking if he could speak to his 'big brobro'. He was so excited, so innocent, and I was the reason his brother was in danger.

"No… Not right now, son." Tom's voice cracked on the last word, his exhale on the other end of the line audible. "Go fetch Mam for me."

I buried my face in my hand, swiping at my damp cheeks. "I'm so sorry Tom. I tried to stop him. Larissa was trying to break the curse, she had everything but the dagger. When she realised she couldn't complete it because the dagger was gone, and the Scottish pack arrived as backup, she bolted with Luke. It's my fault we were there, if I hadn't been so stupid…"

"Eve, I need you to breathe for me."

God, he sounded so much like Luke trying to calm me down.

My shoulders slumped as guilt washed over me, I didn't deserve his kindness.

"Where are you right now?"

"We're in Edinburgh with the pack. Alice and Craig, the guys, even Mary and Fiona are here. Jeremy is safe with Lila."

Knowing we had saved his uncle was one of the small mercies I held on to remind myself not to give up all hope. He'd held on for his wife and kids under horrendous torture, I had to cling onto my sanity for Luke.

"Do we know where Luke is being held?"

I glanced at Craig, and he shook his head.

"No, Josh is working on cracking the flash drive and we have other ways to try trace them. But we know she'll reach out?"

"Reach out?"

I took a deep breath, cursing the moon that this was how I had to break the news that should have been a joy. "There's something else. We found out that we're mates, Larissa knows. She's using the fact that Luke is my mate to draw me out before the next full moon, or else we won't be able to complete the bond. I'm sorry, if I'd just—"

"I know what you're about to say, Eve." Tom cut me off, his tone softening. "It's not your fault."

Craig offered the smallest of smiles, easily able to hear the call even without it being on speaker thanks to his vamp hearing.

But it was my fault, Luke had traded himself for me, and there was a slice in my heart that would never heal. I stared at my tear-stained bloody reflection in the window, the storm clouds having cleared to reveal the starry night sky. I could still feel him through the bond, he was out there somewhere. Somewhere under the same stars, that witch held my mate captive, and I wasn't going to stop until I got him back.

EPILOGUE

LUKE

Pain became all I was and all I knew. The cold cement floor beneath me was a small mercy against the searing pain ripping through my veins. I was cut and poked, strange voices speaking over me and discussing my fate as I slipped in and out of consciousness. Eventually, I slipped into a fitful sleep filled with nightmares of fires in ballrooms, my mate's heart stopping, and the sight of her bound and bleeding in that graveyard.

"Is he alive?" A woman's voice pulled me back to the present, but it wasn't Eve's.

"Just about. We've drained the nightshade from his body. He'll survive. He's the first to successfully recover from nightshade, proof that we can work towards exterminating that weakness."

My eyelids fluttered open, and I stared up at a corrugated tin roof. Something sharp dug into my back. I was lying on a bed of straw, the scent of sawdust filling my senses along with that all too familiar scent of the witch, and a strange vampire too. Her head was visible over what looked like a stable door.

"Ah, he's awake. You're dismissed." Larissa unlatched the door, greeting me with a wide smile that was anything but warm as she stepped inside and closed the door behind her. Instead of it being like a horse's stable where the animal could stick their head out, it had been modified so that thick, steel bars blocked lined the gap between the stable door and the ceiling. I could sense the wards and magic on them from where I lay.

I didn't bother lifting my head, my body protesting at the slightest of movements.

She crouched down beside me, her nails digging into my chin as she forced me to meet her lilac eyes. The twitch of her jaw told me she was still furious about the dagger, and that I was going to bear the brunt of that. "Unfortunately, we didn't find the dagger. Your mate has run off with the Scots, just like her cowardly parents. So, you either tell me where the dagger is, or I'll make you."

My groggy brain spun at her comment about Eve's parents, but my head emptied of all thoughts as she slammed the hilt of a hunting knife into the side of my head.

Blood pooled in my mouth, and I gagged, coughing and spluttering blood all over her black leather boots.

"They warned me you wouldn't be fit for games for a few days," Larissa spat, her upper lip curling in disgust. "But I told them a big strong alpha like yourself would be able to handle it."

I didn't have to wonder about what games she was talking about for long.

She grabbed my arm, laughing at my pitiful attempts to push her away as she picked up a set of silver shackles and snapped one onto my right wrist.

My body jolted, the shackle making my skin sizzle as it burned into my flesh. Her smile only grew wider as I cried out, too weak to struggle as she hooked her arms under my shoulders. She dragged me through the straw to where two loops for tying up horses were attached to the wall, except the chains dangling from them were also spelled silver. The touch of the precious metal against my skin was agony. My body convulsed as waves of pain crashed over me, the scent of my own burning flesh filling my nostrils. She snapped the matching cuff into place and my eyes rolled into the back of my head.

"You know, I normally leave the dirty work someone else. But I forgot how much I enjoy this part." Larissa's voice was eerily calm, as if the sight of my pain was soothing to her. "The light leaving your eyes, the realisation that you're trapped. It's glorious."

"They'll come for me," I croaked, my throat dry like sandpaper. I cried out again as she locked the chains in place.

Larissa chuckled, her eyes narrowing as her gaze raked over my naked body. She spent too long admiring certain parts, but I was in too much pain to care. She tightened the chains so my arms were stretched taut, the cuffs constantly digging into the scorched skin of my wrists, and with the nightshade having weakened my body, I was healing slowly.

My chest heaved as I tried to fight the pain and force air into my lungs, but it was unrelenting. The silver was bound to my body, and I couldn't escape.

"I plan on her coming for you. I'll find the dagger, and then I'll need your pretty mate to stop being a little bitch and play her part." There was no warning before she plunged the hunting knife into my thigh, slowly twisting as she continued her little tirade and ignored the roar of pain that burst from my lips. "I realise now the only way to guarantee her cooperation is using you as leverage."

"Love. Such a stupid emotion, a weakness, and the key to breaking the curse." She pulled the knife out before dragging it up my chest, placing the point under my chin. "Do you enjoy being leverage?"

I grit my teeth, and she scowled, slashing the knife in one long arc from my shoulder down to my navel.

"It's not like you'll ever get to complete the bond, your mate is destined for death. I'm sure you'll find each other in the afterlife."

It took all my strength to focus on not blacking out as my

vision blurred, and there were two sadistic witches staring down at me, rapidly morphing back to one.

"I promise, if you cooperate and tell me where the dagger is, I could make this a much more enjoyable form of torture," she purred, walking her fingers along the cut and smearing my blood all over my chest.

I didn't doubt she'd make good on that promise, but I'd never break.

Larissa ran her tongue over her teeth, twisted amusement flickering in her lilac eyes.

"Fine," she huffed, straddling my waist as she retraced the wound, this time with the blade of the knife once more. "Tell me where the dagger is."

"Rot in hell." I drew my head back, summoning all my energy behind the action as I drove my head forwards and slammed my forehead into her nose, mustering up just enough saliva to spit in her face for good measure.

She shrieked, the knife clattering to the ground as she leaped to her feet holding her nose which was pumping blood. I silently swore that wouldn't be the last time I'd make her bleed. Her face was a mask of unbridled rage as she stared down at me. I'd pay for that one, but if I was going to have to endure torture until my pack rescued me, I would.

Magic made the hairs on the back of my neck stand on end, a flash of purple lighting up the stall, but I kept my gaze focused on the inky night sky, counting the stars and holding on tightly to the faint sense of our bond.

I'd endure a lifetime of pain and walk through hellfire to keep Eve safe.

AUTHOR NOTE

Please don't kill me for that cliffhanger. I warned you it was coming! I know you all love Luke, and I promise Larissa won't get to play with him forever. We'll bring him home.

I debated ending Eve and Luke's story at three books, but there was too much to fit in—prophecies, mates, history repeating itself... there's a lot to tie up. I encourage you to read the prequel, *Lone Wolf*, because it links to the main series. For those of you who have read it, I think you know one of the reveals that's coming.

My writing process is chaotic, to say the least, but it means those twists and turns are surprises even for me. It has come to my attention that my brain is a teeny bit dark, so I apologise for the emotional rollercoaster. At least I gave you mates! Still mad at me about that cliffhanger? My bad, it had to happen. It's romance, so I promise you will get your HEA in the end.

I'm an indie author juggling writing with a full-time job. So, if you could spare two minutes to post a review it would mean the world to me.

Hearing from readers is one of my favourite things. Come hang out with me to talk anything books!

Newsletter: www.ciaradelahunt.com/newsletter
PNR Book Club: www.discord.com/invite/dWCFbYGZFz
Reader Group: Ciara's Book Coven

ALSO BY
CIARA DELAHUNT

THE HYBRID WOLF SERIES

Lone Wolf (Prequel)

Wolf Bait

Blood Moon

Truth Bites

Fated Pack

ACKNOWLEDGMENTS

This book sat in my head for far too long and then took several turns even I didn't expect. I'm still getting to grips with the best way to write around life. I feel less like a baby author—I know more—but with that comes new pressures. Juggling everything has been a lot, but I wouldn't trade being an author for anything.

I give my books everything: early starts on the weekends, missing out on plans, and spending my days lost in the worlds I've created. The fire never goes out because writing books is so natural for me. I was always a reader, lost in books growing up. The more I do this author thing, more I know that I want to write forever.

Every message I get from readers goes directly to me, and I read every single one. On the days when this author thing is tough, words of encouragement or hearing how much you love my books keep me going. I'm extremely grateful to have wonderful readers. I'm releasing *Truth Bites* just in time for my first reader signing, the perfect way to celebrate.

This journey wouldn't be possible without a strong support network. First, as always, I'd like to thank my fiancé (I hate that word, but I adore this man) for his endless support. He puts up with early starts, late nights, and a ton of complaining. I'm sorry I wake you early on the weekends when I slip away to write, or stay up until ungodly hours when on tight deadlines. You have not only encouraged me to follow this dream but given me the stability and support to throw myself into this full throttle. Thank you for seeing the parts of me no one else does and reminding me to embrace who I am, and for minding the cats when they're being hyper and I'm a stress-head. I love you to the moon and to Saturn and can't wait to marry you next year.

My author squad has grown over the last year. I have made so many wonderful connections. Thank you, Lasairiona, for editing this book. Your support means the world to me, and I'm extremely proud to call you a friend.. Irene, my ride-or-die lady, I love you so much and I can't wait to build our little nook in the bookish world together. I hate oceans and wish I could hug you more often, but I know you're always there for me no matter what. My relator castle... thank you for embracing my chaos. I'm not sure how or why you ladies put up with me, but I'm so grateful to have yous.

Last but not least, my readers. The *Hybrid Wolf Series* wouldn't be what it is without your support. You cheer me up, check in on me, and keep me motivated. I love getting your messages, especially when they're rants about cliffhangers or real-time reactions. I'm also super excited to meet some of you in the UK this year at signings. You are why I do this! I'm sorry for breaking your hearts a bit with this one, but I promise to make it up to Luke lovers... eventually.

About the Author

Ciara writes paranormal romance with dark twists, spice, and a heavy dose of sarcasm. Her books feature strong women, morally grey love interests, suspense, and found family. She lives in the Irish countryside with her boyfriend and their two cats. When she doesn't have her head stuck in a book, you will find Ciara walking in the parklands nearby, in the gym, passed out on her yoga mat, or screaming at a rugby match.

A book-dragon from birth, her love of reading bled into writing when she was a teenager, and the rest is history. Ciara can't write without music and loves nothing more than to be curled up with her laptop and a mocha in her favourite coffee shop, writing to her heart's content.

amazon.com/author/ciaradelahunt

tiktok.com/@ciaradelahuntbooks

instagram.com/ciaradelahunt

facebook.com/authorciaradelahunt

threads.net/@ciaradelahunt

bsky.app/profile/ciaradelahunt.bsky.social

bookbub.com/authors/ciara-delahunt

goodreads.com/ciaradelahunt